A SHADOWRUN SOURCEBOOK

"The mind is its own place, and in itself

Can make a heaven of hell, and a hell of heaven."

—John Milton, *Paradise Lost*

CREDITS

VIRTUAL REALITIES

Writing
Matrix Rules
Tom Dowd
"Virtual Realities"
Christopher Kubasik

Development
Tom Dowd

Editorial Staff
Senior Editor
Donna Ippolito
Assistant Editor
Sharon Turner Mulvihill

Production Staff
Art Director
Dana Knutson
Cover Art
Dave McCoy
Cover Design
Jim Nelson
Color Illustration
Dave McCoy
Alex Story
Sue McCoy
Fuchi Catalogue Design
Mike Nielsen
Illustration
Jim Nelson
Joel Biske
Tammy Daniel
Layout
Tara Gallagher

SPECIAL THANKS
To all the deckers on GEnie and Compuserve.
GAAAAAAAA!

SHADOWRUN, MATRIX and VIRTUAL REALITIES are trademarks of FASA Corporation.
Copyright © 1991 FASA Corporation. All Rights Reserved.
Printed in the United States of America.

Published by
FASA Corporation
P.O. Box 6930
Chicago, IL 60680

CONTENTS

THE MATRIX DEFINED

INTRODUCTION 5

COMPUTER SYSTEMS 8
- System Security 8
  - Security Ratings 9
- Nodes 10
  - System Access Node 10
  - System Operations 11
- Central Processing Unit 11
  - System Operations 11
- Sub-Processor Unit 12
  - System Operations 12
- Dataline Junction 12
  - System Operations 12
- Datastore 12
  - System Operations 12
- Slave Module 13
  - System Operations 13
- Input/Output Port 13
  - System Operations 13
- Node Ratings 13
  - Security Tracks 13
- System Load 14
- Alerts 15
  - Passive Alert 15
  - Active Alert 17
  - The Final Response 17
- Expert Systems 17

INTRUSION COUNTERMEASURES 18
- White IC 18
  - Access 19
  - Barrier 19
  - Probe 19
  - Scramble 19
- Gray IC 20
  - Acid 20
  - Binder 20
  - Blaster 20
  - Jammer 20
  - Killer 20
  - Marker 21
  - Tar Baby 21
  - Tar Pit 21
  - Trace 21
- Black IC 21
  - Hang Tough 21
  - Jack Out 21
- IC Defense Options 22
- Variable Rating 22
- Constructs 22
- Expert IC 22
- Artificial Intelligence 22
- IC Placement 23
- IC Allocation 23

CYBERDECKS 24
- Contructing Components 24
  - Defining Terms 24
  - Limits 26
- Components 26
  - MPCP 26
  - Hardening 27
  - Active Memory 27
  - Storage 28
  - Load Speed 28
  - I/O Speed 28
  - Response 28
  - Simsense Hardware 28
  - Vidscreen 29
  - Hitcher Jack 29
  - Offline Storage 29
  - Case, Keyboard, and Stuff 29

CONTENTS

Upgrading A Deck	29
Deck Downtime	31
Buying Decks	31
Satellite Uplinks	33

PROGRAMS 34
- Persona Programs — 34
  - Bod — 34
  - Evasion — 34
  - Masking — 35
  - Sensors — 35
- Deck Modes — 35
  - Bod Mode — 35
  - Evasion Mode — 35
  - Masking Mode — 35
  - Sensor Mode — 35
- Programming On the Fly — 35
- Utility Programs — 36
  - Combat Utilities — 36
  - Defense Utilities — 37
  - Sensor Utilities — 38
  - Masking Utilities — 39
  - Operation Utilities — 39
- Programming — 40
- Options — 42
  - Option Notes — 42
- Frames — 44
  - Frame Types — 44
  - Commanding Smart Frames — 44
  - Building A Frame — 45

CYBERCOMBAT 46
- Initiative — 46
- Matrix Movement — 47
- Entering Combat — 47
  - Executing A Utility — 47
  - Multiple Programs, Multiple Targets — 47
- Avoiding Combat — 47
- Resolving Combat — 48
  - Hitting A Persona — 48
  - Hitting IC — 48
- IC Suppression — 48
- Simsense Overload — 49
- Fast Resolution System — 49

MATRIX REALITIES 50
- Virtual Reality — 50
  - Applied — 51
- Sculpted Systems — 51
  - Reality Filters — 52
  - Sensory Cut-Outs — 52
- Magic in the Matrix — 52
- Digging for Data — 53
  - Shadowland — 53

FUCHI CATALOGUE 54

HACKER HOUSE SUMMER UPDATE CATALOG 73
- Combat Utilities — 74
- Defense Utilities — 76
- Sensor Utilities — 78
- Masking Utilities — 80

VIRTUAL REALITIES 82

THE MATRIX DEFINED

INTRODUCTION

"The Matrix is like a great beast. There will be no stopping it until it has consumed us all."
—Gideon, decker

irtual Realities is a sourcebook of advanced and expanded rules for decking and the Matrix in the **Shadowrun** universe. In developing these new rules, some contradictions to the basic **Shadowrun** game have occurred. For all intents and purposes, the new rules in **Virtual Reality** supersede previous rules covering the same topic. The gamemaster and players are, however, always free to choose by which rules they will abide. If an earlier version or a completely different variation of a rule suits a particular group's style of play, let them adapt the rules as desired.

Those familiar with the original **Shadowrun** Matrix system should pay close attention to certain sections of this book. The design and construction of **Cyberdecks** has been reworked and expanded for greater balance and to provide greater opportunities for roleplaying outside the Matrix. Many aspects of **Computer Systems** and **Programs** have also been revised for improved playability.

Additions to the game include a new computer system **Node**, new **Intrusion Countermeasures**, and new **Combat** and **Utility Programs**, including **IC Constructs** and **Program Frames**. Also new are rules for gathering information in the Matrix, computer-system design philosophy, and more. Finally, this book provides a quick and dirty resolution system that makes it possible to determine the result of a Matrix run with only a few simple die rolls.

INTRODUCTION

VIRTUAL REALITIES 7

COMPUTER SYSTEMS

"Uh-oh, Toto, it doesn't look like we're gods anymore."
—*Little Dottie to her faithful program frame*

SYSTEM SECURITY

The primary purpose of a computer system is to serve its users, be it through data processing, research, design assistance, administrative and managerial tasks, or other similar functions. The system may have value to intruders also, those who attempt to access its data or functions for their own purposes.

Most computer security systems occur at key access junctures or in areas for storage or processing of sensitive data. Security is usually heaviest at System Access Nodes (SANs) and Central Processing Units (CPUs). Certain other key nodes may also have security with some teeth. Computer security refers to some combination of Intrusion Countermeasures, the Security Code, and the System Rating of a particular node. Security Codes and System Ratings are discussed in the next section, so hang tough.

Corporations use the choke-point concept, placing heavy security only at key access points to keep the remainder of the system relatively accessible. Not much work would get done if IC were interrogating every data packet passing through every node. Choke-point security resembles the concept of a medieval walled city. If the town guards could defend the walls against intruders, it was not necessary to interfere with the flow of everyday life by patrolling the streets.

Some corporations are more paranoid than others, especially about sensitive data. Most layer their system security, burying more sensitive subsystems deep within the greater system, with dedicated SANs providing the only access to those systems. This forces an intruding decker to confront more IC. The SANs become the choke points, because the decker must pass through each one in order to penetrate deeply into the system.

COMPUTER SYSTEMS

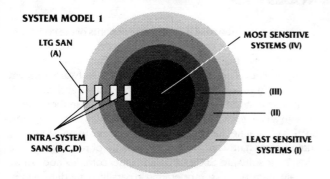

System Model 1 above shows a four-level layered system. The outer layer (I) contains the least sensitive areas. An intruding decker can reach these simply by passing through the first SAN, which leads to and from the LTG where the system is located. If, however, the decker wishes to penetrate to the most sensitive layer (IV), he would have to pass through three others (SANs B, C, and D) as well. The set-up would be diagrammed as shown below.

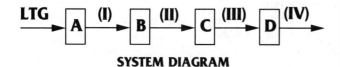

SYSTEM DIAGRAM

In most systems, the overall security of the LTG SAN is higher than that of the intra-system SANs, though some corporations also place heavy security in a SAN leading to a sensitive sub-system.

Though System Model 1 shows even layering, the evenness is not required.

COMPUTER SYSTEM MODEL 2

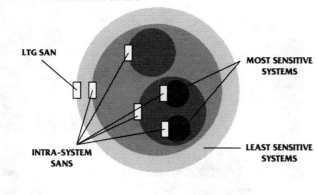

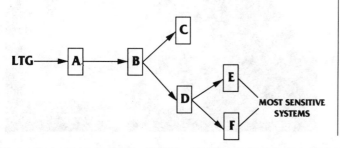

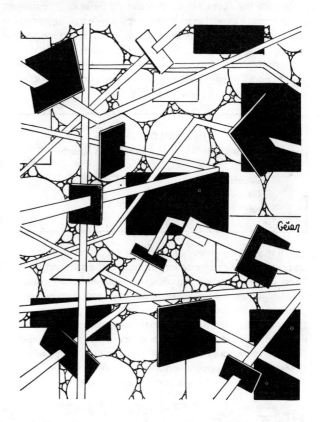

A sub-system is defined as any part of a larger system that is isolated by a SAN and accessible only through that SAN. In Model I above, sections I, II, III, and IV are sub-systems because access to them is exclusively through a SAN. Generally speaking, each sub-system has one CPU controlling it. For more on sub-systems, more accurately referred to as clusters, see **CPUs**, p. 11.

To speed a Matrix run, the gamemaster may want to condense the decker's movement through the less important SANs and security choke-points, focusing instead on the sub-system that is the decker's ultimate destination. That is, he will fully game the penetration of the LTG SAN, but simplify passage through the intervening SANs to a single representative SAN passage. The System Code and IC presence should be representative of the external layers of the system. If the level of security is light at the sub-system toward which the decker is headed, the representative SAN should be relatively weak. If, however, the system is heavily defended throughout, the representative passage should be more difficult.

SECURITY RATINGS

All computer systems are rated according to their security level: how difficult it is for a decker to execute programs and perform actions within the system. This is known as the Security Rating. The Security Rating consists of a color-code designation, known as the Security Code, and a numeric System Rating. The

COMPUTER SYSTEMS

color-code measures the sophistication of the node's permanent programming as well as its inherent resistance to tampering. The four color-code levels are blue, green, orange, and red. A blue system is the easiest for a decker to manipulate, while red is the hardest. When making any success test involving the computer system node, the decker must roll a certain number of successes beyond the Threshold Number set by that color code.

THRESHOLD NUMBERS

Color Code	Successes Needed
Blue	1
Green	2
Orange	3
Red	4

If the decker does not roll more successes than the color code requires, he cannot affect the node. If he does, on the other hand, those extra successes determine the effect of the success. In other words, the decker must roll *one more* success than the color code requires. If he rolls only enough to equal the Threshold Number, he has no extra successes to determine the effect of the success, so there is no success. The Threshold Number incorporates the initial success that the **Shadowrun** game system normally requires. All successes beyond the Threshold Number are viewed as extra successes.

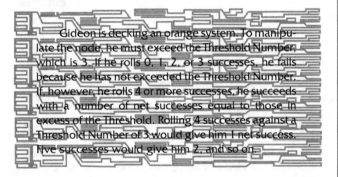

Gideon is decking an orange system. To manipulate the node, he must exceed the Threshold Number, which is 3. If he rolls 0, 1, 2, or 3 successes, he fails because he has not exceeded the Threshold Number. If, however, he rolls 4 or more successes, he succeeds with a number of net successes equal to those in excess of the Threshold. Rolling 4 successes against a Threshold Number of 3 would give him 1 net success. Five successes would give him 2, and so on.

The numeric System Rating represents the sophistication of the node's security and processing software, or system software. The higher the number, the greater the sophistication. This number becomes a target number for the decker to beat when attempting certain actions in the node. The greater the color-code of the node, the more effective the security and processing software. Rating 4 software in a green node (written as Green-4) does not, for example, work as efficiently as that same software in a red node (written as Red-4). In a green node, the decker needs only 3 successes (2 for the Threshold, plus 1 for the actual success), while in a red node, he needs 5 successes (4 for the Threshold, plus 1 for the actual success) to beat system software of the same rating.

This differing efficiency also affects the maximum ratings of IC and other programs able to operate simultaneously in a node; it is the combination of color-code and system software rating that determines those ratings. Yes, chummer, there are limits. Weaker processors, like those in green nodes, cannot support the same load as the more powerful processors in orange or red nodes. Does a decker's cyberdeck contribute to that load? You bet. See the **System Load** rules section later on, if you dare.

NODES

Nodes are the actual physical components of the computer system. They are a combination of hardware (processor and memory chips, boards, and so on), firmware (software permanently encoded into the hardware), and software (system software, Intrusion Countermeasure programs, and the like). Each type of node performs a different function in the system, though all are constructed much the same way. Simple nodes, such as dataline junctions and datastores, may have only rudimentary hardware and so are capable of running just the most basic software. SPUs, CPUs, and other complex nodes may contain many processors operating in parallel or tandem, allowing them to run more complex software.

SYSTEM ACCESS NODE

Abbreviated as SAN, the System Access Node acts as a gateway from one computer system to another. The gateway may bridge an isolated computer system and the LTG, or it may bridge two separate sections of one larger computer system.

As the first line of defense for a computer system, the SAN usually has the strongest defense programs. SAN Security Ratings tend to be higher than the average for the system and usually on a par with the Security Rating of the Central Processor Unit (CPU).

If a decker is entering a system from an LTG, he must still pass through a SAN.

10 VIRTUAL REALITIES

COMPUTER SYSTEMS

SYSTEM OPERATIONS

Lockout

The decker can effectively "lock" the SAN, thereby preventing any other persona or IC from passing through it. To unlock the system takes a number of turns equal to twice the decker's Computer Skill Rating minus the CPU System Rating. Until that happens, no passage through the SAN, in either direction, can occur.

Back Door

A decker may attempt to set up a counterfeit access code for himself in the SAN. He does this by making a System Operations Test against double the normal Target Number. The results of this test should be kept secret. Success means that the SAN will accept the passcode designated by the decker for access. This will allow him to bypass the normal IC active in the node the next time he comes through. Failure means that a passive alert has been sounded. The number of successes generated determines the chance per month of the system's owners discovering the secret door. Roll four dice against the appropriate Target Number:

Successes Rolled	Target Number
1	4
2	6
3	8
4	10
5+	12

Though the number of dice rolled is usually four, the gamemaster should adjust the number to reflect the resources of the organization maintaining the system. For a large, computer-oriented corporation like Fuchi, for example, the gamemaster might wish to raise the number of dice rolled to eight. For a small, local corp, two dice might be more appropriate than four.

The results of discovery will also vary from corporation to corporation. Most will simply tag the deck's passcode to automatically trigger a passive alert. Others will allow the passcode to remain active, setting up a special program that makes the decker easier to trace. To reflect the effect of this program, subtract 2 from the decker's Masking Rating when using it as the Target Number for the Trace Program Success Test.

See System

In a system that uses the Universal Matrix Specifications icon set, the decker can see the various nodes of that cluster hanging before him in the Matrix. The gamemaster should give the character an alphabetical list of the nodes present, but no information on their Security Codes or contents. The gamemaster should also describe the designs and patterns of the system constructs in the most creative terms. Fear not, however; their apparent visual orientation has nothing to do with the way the constructs actually interconnect. If, for example, an SPU appears to hang near a group of I/O ports, it does not necessarily mean that those I/O ports are located near the SPU on the actual system map.

No actual System Operations Test is needed to get this list; it is automatic in a UMS system. Deckers in a sculpted system do not have this option. See **Sculpted Systems**, p. 51, in the **Matrix Reality** section of this book.

CENTRAL PROCESSING UNIT

The CPU is the heart of a computer system, and its construction and design reflect on the rest of the system.

The System Rating of the CPU determines how many nodes the CPU may have in its cluster, or sub-system. A cluster is controlled by one CPU and is isolated from other clusters by a SAN. The cluster can contain only one CPU.

The only limitations on how many CPUs/clusters may be present in a system are budgetary. A CPU's control of a cluster may not, however, cross a SAN.

The number of nodes that a CPU may have in its cluster is equal to the System Rating multiplied by 5. A Red-5 CPU may have 25 nodes, excluding itself, in its cluster. An Orange-5 CPU would have the same number, but an Orange-3 CPU could have only 15.

The only nodes that count when determining the total number of nodes in a cluster are SPUs and dataline junctions. Datastores, I/O ports, SANs, and slave modules do not count toward the CPU's maximum.

Most CPUs never serve anywhere near their maximum number.

No node within the sub-system, or cluster, may have a higher Security Rating (the combined Security Code and System Rating) than that of the CPU. Thus, if the LTG SAN is heavily defended, the CPU that services that SAN must have at least the same Security Rating, or greater, though it may not necessarily have the same Intrusion Countermeasures present.

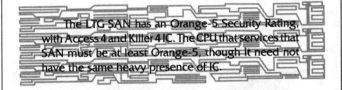

The LTG SAN has an Orange-5 Security Rating, with Access 4 and Killer 4 IC. The CPU that services that SAN must be at least Orange-5, though it need not have the same heavy presence of IC.

SYSTEM OPERATIONS

Cancel Alert

This operation cancels a passive alert that has been triggered from within that cluster. If an active alert has already been triggered, nothing can be done. If any other kind of alert is triggered while the decker is attempting to cancel an alert, all he can do is prepare for the worst.

Change Node

The change node operation is a "teleport" straight into any node in the cluster. If the decker is being pursued by IC or another decker, his extra successes give him an equal number of turns before the system figures out to where he has teleported, assuming nothing else happens to give him away. Once in his new location, the decker cannot "teleport" back to the CPU.

Display Map

The gamemaster must show the decker-player a map of the cluster the CPU commands. It shows the nodes present, their interconnections, and various Security Codes, but does not mark the presence of IC or specific files. (The gamemaster should have a separate player map prepared beforehand, just in case.)

COMPUTER SYSTEMS

Shutdown

Shutdown crashes the cluster, but *only* the cluster controlled by the CPU. It also dumps the decker if he remains in the cluster. The base time for the shutdown is 5 turns. The extra successes from the System Operations Test reduce this time in the normal manner.

The decker may also shut down select nodes within the cluster without crashing the entire cluster. The procedure is the same as outlined above, but only the designated node crashes.

System Inquiry

Periodically, the CPU controlling a cluster randomly polls the various nodes under its command to verify their operational status. In normal operations, the node responds with an "A-Okay" reply and life goes on. If, however, the node has been suppressed, the node *cannot* respond, triggering a passive alert.

For more on the frequency of a system inquiry and the effects of suppression, see **IC Suppression**, p. 48 of **Cybercombat**, in this book.

SUB-PROCESSOR UNIT

The Sub-Processor Unit, or SPU, is a smaller processor that is "slaved" to the big-boss CPU. The CPU gives the orders and the SPUs carry them out. For example, the Building Services CPU/cluster of a building's computer system may have SPUs to supervise air conditioning, heating, elevators, and so on.

An SPU may also perform menial "traffic-cop" duties for the data that passes through it, though most of that function falls to the new node, the dataline junction.

SYSTEM OPERATIONS
None.

DATALINE JUNCTION

The Dataline Junction, or DLJ, exists solely to route data to and from the various data paths that connect to the DLJ. It is a simple node with a simple job. Usually.

From a security standpoint, however, the DLJ serves an important tactical function: it can serve as a choke point to catch an intruding decker. Powerful IC can be placed, dormant, within the DLJ, awaiting activation after an active alert (see **Active Alert**, p. 17). In this manner, IC can be distributed tactically through a system without overloading an important SPU.

DLJs can also be installed with a low Security Rating, thereby forcing intruding deckers to reduce the Load Rating of their decks to avoid overloading the node.

SYSTEM OPERATIONS
None.

DATASTORE

Datastores hold files containing information. That data could be commonplace and worthless or unique and extremely valuable. The datastore is usually the ultimate target of a data run.

SYSTEM OPERATIONS

Edit
The edit operation changes the contents of an existing data file.

Erase
Erase wipes out a file such as police record or any other type.

Read
Reading a file works like downloading it, but the decker does not need the storage memory to hold it because this is not a copying operation. Read allows him to skim a file's contents, possibly with the help of a program like sift (see **Operation Utilities**, p. 39, in **Programs**). The gamemaster must be the judge of what information the decker can extract from a file by reading. Simple facts like names, dates, phone numbers, simple graphic images (e.g., an ID photo) can be rapidly routed to storage. Highly technical data must be downloaded in its entirety to the deck.

As a general time guideline, a decker can skim a number of Mp equal to his Intelligence Attribute multiplied by 5 Mp per turn. The rating of the sift program adds to the decker's Intelligence Attribute for this purpose. The decker can "speed-read" by increasing the flow of data. The multiple by which the data flow is increased becomes the Target Number of a Perception Test to spot the data the character is seeking.

> Gideon has an Intelligence of 5, allowing him to skim 25 Mp of data per turn. If he chooses to double that rate to 50 Mp per turn (25 x 2), he must make a Perception Test against a Target Number 2 to notice the data he wants. Had he increased the data flow by five times, he would have been able to skim 125 Mp (25 x 5) of data that turn, but he would have been required to make a Perception (5) Test.

12 VIRTUAL REALITIES

Transfer

The transfer of data from a datastore to a cyberdeck (downloading) or from a cyberdeck to a datastore (uploading) is regulated by the cyberdeck's I/O speed. The I/O speed is the maximum rate at which data can be transferred. The decker must stay in the node until the transfer is complete or the data is lost. While a transfer is in operation, all target numbers related to the deck's operation are at +2.

SLAVE MODULE

A slave module, or SM, controls some physical process or device, usually mechanical in nature. This can be anything from an electric soycaf-maker to an industrial assembly line to the elevators in a building. Slave modules also control the various sensors in a security system, including cameras, thermal sensors, and the like.

It is possible to jack into a system through the physical hardware of a slave module.

Slave modules almost always have among the lowest Security Ratings in the system.

SYSTEM OPERATIONS

Control
The decker can control whatever the Slave Module does, whether it is making the soycaf boil over or shutting down the assembly line.

Sensor Readout
The decker can access any sensors or cameras run by a slave module. Generally, there will be multiple slave modules controlling the many different types of sensors in a corporate facility. One SM may control the visual sensors (cameras) in one zone of the facility, while another controls them in another. The IR sensors are controlled by another SM, and so on.

INPUT/OUTPUT PORT

An input/output port, or I/OP, is a limited-access node that opens the system to various data input/output devices: terminals, cyberdecks, printers, graphic displays, data-readers for optical chips, and so on. A decker can jack into a system through an I/O port using a cyberdeck or a program carrier. It is also possible to use an existing data terminal for decking purposes.

For convenience, the multitudes of I/O ports in a large computer system are often represented on a system map by a single I/O port. During play, however, the gamemaster should describe the many constructs that are actually present in the system.

A decker can jack into a system through the physical hardware of an I/O port.

SYSTEM OPERATIONS

Display Message
The decker can communicate with the outside world via the display message operation. It will display a message on the terminal an I/OP controls.

Lockout
The decker can lock the I/OP out of the system. Nothing it controls can contact the computer system. If the I/OP is actually a terminal or cyberdeck controlled by another, the decker must first crash the terminal or deck through cybercombat.

NODE RATINGS

In designing a computer system, one of the issues to decide is what ratings to assign to the different types of nodes in the system. The Node Rating Table rates systems by their relative importance/security and presents a range of appropriate System Ratings for each type of node.

When deciding which track to use for the system, the gamemaster should keep in mind the system owner's resources. Everyone would like to have an ultra-secure system, but only the largest megacorps can afford to create and maintain that level of security. The best policy is to decide the *ideal* importance/security of the system and then adjust down for the corporation's resources.

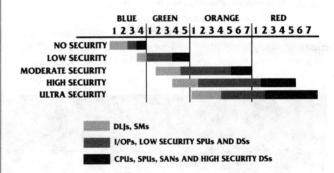

SECURITY TRACKS

The five security tracks are none, low, moderate, high, and ultra security.

No Security
An open system such as a public-service network or free advertising database requires no security. Little of importance is available, so there's no reason to defend it. These systems usually contain only blue nodes, which cannot contain IC. Minimal security systems are referred to colloquially as blue systems.

Low Security
Limited-access systems such as library databases, subscription services, and most telecom grids have low security. These systems are known as green systems.

COMPUTER SYSTEMS

Moderate Security

Moderate security is typical for most government, underworld, or corporate systems not containing highly classified data. These systems are often referred to as orange systems.

High Security

High security systems include powerful megacorp R&D and financial, classified government, and the major crime syndicate systems. They are referred to as red systems.

Ultra Security

The infamous black system is as tough as they come. The most vital megacorp systems and government military systems are at this level. Dangerous stuff.

SYSTEM LOAD

Computer nodes have only a limited amount of processing ability, which means they can run for a finite amount of programming before they start to lose efficiency. Most of the node's processing ability is devoted to doing its job, whatever that may be. When IC is present in the node, a certain amount of processing power must be allocated to the IC. The more processing power allocated, the less efficient the node becomes.

The node's Security Code, when combined with its System Rating, determines the Maximum Load Rating, that is, the amount of Intrusion Countermeasures that can be active in a node at one time. To determine the Maximum Load Rating, multiply the System Rating by 1 for a Blue Security Code, 2 for a Green, 3 for Orange, and 4 for Red. An Orange-5 node, for example, may have a total IC load of 15 (3 x 5) while a Green-3 node may only have 6 (2 x 3). See below.

SYSTEM RATING TABLE

Code	1	2	3	4	5	6	7	8
Blue	1	2	3	4	5	6	7	8
Green	2	4	6	8	10	12	14	16
Orange	3	6	9	12	15	18	21	24
Red	4	8	12	16	20	24	28	32

Intrusion Countermeasures now have a Load Rating that is usually equal to one-half the IC's rating, though certain types of IC are exceptions. The total of the Load Ratings for all the currently active IC in a node cannot exceed the Maximum Load Rating. If they do, the node's efficiency quickly begins to degrade.

NODE EFFICIENCY TABLE

System Load	Efficiency Modifier
Light (<50% of maximum)	+1
Normal (51–100% of maximum)	Normal
Overload (101–200% of maximum)	–2
Slowdown (over 200% of maximum)	No Operations Possible

COMPUTER SYSTEMS

No node can operate in excess of 200 percent of its load. The Efficiency Modifier column above indicates the number of rating points by which any IC active in an overloaded cluster can be modified.

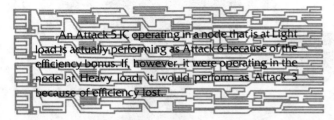

An Attack 5 IC operating in a node that is at Light load is actually performing as Attack 6 because of the efficiency bonus. If, however, it were operating in the node at Heavy load, it would perform as Attack 3 because of efficiency lost.

If the Efficiency Modifier is equal to or greater than the rating of a particular piece of IC, that IC can no longer operate and goes dormant. It no longer serves its function (scramblers stop scrambling and so on) and cannot be attacked.

While the maximum load is calculated as above, the current load is equal to the total load of all the IC active in the node. Current load is important because the amount of IC active in a node can vary. This can occur if a piece of IC is crashed, thereby reducing the current load of the node. It can also occur if an IC construct originating in another node enters the current one. This will increase the current load by the IC's Load Rating. (See **Intrusion Countermeasures**, p. 18, for more on IC constructs.)

The presence of a decker can also affect the current load. Cyberdecks have a Base Load Rating equal to one-half their MPCP rating, rounded up. That Load Rating is further increased by the number of programs the decker has currently loaded in active memory equal to the megapulse (Mp) size of those programs, divided by 100, rounded up.

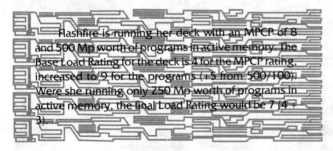

Flashfire is running her deck with an MPCP of 8 and 500 Mp worth of programs in active memory. The Base Load Rating for the deck is 4 for the MPCP rating, increased to 9 for the programs (+5 from 500/100). Were she running only 250 Mp worth of programs in active memory, the final Load Rating would be 7 (4 + 3).

Most of a decker's programs are run from processors based in the cyberdeck, but some of that programming does overflow into the node's processor load. If that did not happen, the decker would be unable to interact with the node.

A decker must, therefore, be concerned about how fat his deck is. A decker says his deck is "fat" when it has a great many programs in active memory, a high MPCP, or some combination of the two. A "lean" deck is just the opposite.

The CPU of a cluster, or system, is continually monitoring the load in each node it services. Because it knows the extent of the system's work load, it knows what the load should be. If the load in a node shifts to overload, the CPU automatically triggers a passive alert. Passive alerts, formerly called internal alerts, are explained in the next section. For now, suffice to say that a passive alert is basically a security "uh-oh" response: there may be a problem, but maybe not. No need to panic...yet.

Nodes with low System Ratings now act as part of the computer system's security. Deckers who like to wander a system loaded for drek-knows-what will most likely exceed the maximum load of a node like a dataline junction, which usually does not have a high Security Rating. The decker, however, needs to be fat to handle the defenses of a SAN or SPU. Then again, he may wish to be lean to avoid overloading certain nodes and inviting unnecessary IC upon them when a passive alert is triggered.

Running a computer system is no longer a cut-and-dried operation. The decker must decide which programs should be active when. Is it best to be fat now or lean? Decisions, chummer, decisions.

Nodes that are forced to over 200 percent of their maximum load go into slowdown. While a node is in slowdown, no system operations are possible in the node. A decker can still do things within his own deck, crossload programs in memory, vary the MPCP, and such, but nothing regarding the node or anything in it (such as IC or other persona) can be done. In slowdown, the node is so overloaded that it takes ages to pass information and execute commands. While a node is in slowdown, persona and IC are stuck there until they can lower their Load Ratings to the point where the node slides back into overload. The only other way out of a node in slowdown is to jack out. IC will sometimes deliberately throw a node into slowdown to prevent a system operation or to gain time until more IC arrives.

ALERTS

When a decker trips up, he risks setting off an alert. The least serious alert is a passive alert. The most serious is an active alert.

Described below are the various reasons why a system shifts into passive or active alert. In addition, the possibility always exists that whoever controls the system will learn of a decker's presence, even though the decker has done nothing to give away his activity. In this case, the corp or other owner could simply order the appropriate alert into effect. If the system owner received intelligence about a possible intrusion, they would order a passive alert. If they received intelligence indicating a decker might already be in the system, they would probably order an active alert.

PASSIVE ALERT

Passive alerts occur when the system receives evidence that something may be wrong within. The evidence is not conclusive, however, or it would trigger an active alert. Though inconclusive, enough suspicion exists to warrant increased security precautions and investigation.

Triggering Passive Alerts

Passive alerts are triggered after any one of the following circumstances:

• A decker fails to deceive or sleaze either an access, barrier, probe, or gray IC program.
• The current load of a node exceeds its Normal Load and goes into overload.
• Crashed IC that has been suppressed (see **Cybercombat**) fails to respond after a system inquiry (see **CPUs**).
• A system operation fails three times in the same node within a 1D6+1-minute period.
• The "Rule of Ones" is invoked. This can result from any computer- or system-related dice roll while the decker is in the system. As the rule states, the dice rolled must all be ones.

COMPUTER SYSTEMS

COMPUTER SYSTEMS

Results of A Passive Alert

When a passive alert is triggered, a number of things can occur. Some are definite and universal to all systems. Others depend on the capabilities of the system.

First, the ratings of all currently active white IC increase by 50 percent (rounded down). Yes, this could easily throw some nodes into overload, but such is the price of security. Gray and black IC are not affected by this increase.

No additional IC will go active as a result of a passive alert, but the white IC already present and active receives more processing power, hence the rating increase.

If the passive alert occurs because of an event within a specific node, that is, for any reason other than a Rule of Ones occurrence, something else may occur. If the system has the ability to use probe IC, some will be dispatched to determine the source of the problem in the node where the passive alert was triggered. See **Probe IC** under **Intrusion Countermeasures** for more information.

A passive alert usually continues for only a short time because it is eating up vital processing power. The duration is usually from 10 to 60 minutes. The gamemaster can either choose the duration or roll 1D6 to determine how many tens of minutes the alert lasts.

If another passive alert is triggered while one is in effect, the system automatically goes to active alert. The system may also go to active alert if one of the active alert criteria occurs or the probe IC finds trouble.

ACTIVE ALERT

When a computer system shifts to active alert, it is virtually assured that trouble is afoot. An active alert can be triggered in one of the following manners:

• Another passive alert is triggered when one is already in effect. The activation of additional IC after the first passive alert will not trigger a second passive if the presence of that new IC is solely responsible for the overload status of a node.

• A piece of probe IC discovers trouble in its investigation of a passive alert.

• IC is crashed and not immediately suppressed (see **Cybercombat**).

Results of An Active Alert

The actions taken when an active alert is triggered are stronger and more decisive than those of a passive alert.

As with a passive alert, the ratings of the IC currently present increase by 50 percent (rounded down). This is the same increase as for a passive alert and is not in addition to that increase if the active alert follows a passive alert. Apply the increase only if the system jumps directly to active alert.

Additional IC may be activated within the system at this time. As mentioned above, many nodes have additional IC installed, usually gray and black, which remains dormant until an active alert is triggered. The activation of this IC may throw the node into overload. This IC also does not receive power from the 50 percent-increase bonus, as it is assumed that the IC is already receiving increased processing power from the node.

The corporation controlling the system may also choose to introduce corporate deckers into the system at this time. This all depends on the corporation involved and the nature of the incident.

THE FINAL RESPONSE

If things get bad enough, someone in the corporation may make the decision to take a CPU and its cluster offline. The earliest this decision can come is roughly 1D6 minutes after an active alert has been triggered. Whether this decision is made or not depends on the corporation involved, whether the trouble is near any sensitive data, and the nature of that data. The gamemaster uses his judgment.

When a command is given to take the cluster offline, the number of turns it takes depends on the System Rating of the CPU servicing the cluster. The gamemaster rolls 1D6 for every 2 full System Rating Points the CPU has. Thus, the gamemaster would roll 2D6 for a System Rating of 4 or 5, but 3D6 for a System Rating of 6 or 7. This dice roll determines the number of turns before the CPU and the cluster go offline.

Any deckers within the system will immediately become aware of the impending shutdown, though they do not know how long before the shutdown actually occurs. They do, however, receive a final "two-turn" warning before shutdown. At that point, the signs of a shutdown are so clear that the decker knows only two turns remain.

A decker who has physically entered the cluster from one of its nodes is unaffected by the cluster going offline. The cluster is still active, but it is no longer connected to the rest of the system. If the decker accessed the cluster through the SAN, he is automatically dumped (see **Leaving The Matrix**, p. 102, **Shadowrun**).

EXPERT SYSTEMS

Expert systems are sophisticated programs with access to a large database of related information, which they can analyze to make decisions. Expert systems are common in the spheres of medicine, the military, economics, and other similar areas. The autopilot that steers someone's little electro-car around Seattle is a simple expert system. A program frame capable of independent activity is also a simple expert system. (It has a limited database of actions and responses on which it bases its decisions.)

Expert systems are rarely seen on the street, are moderately common in corporate life, and very typical of the Matrix. Intrusion Countermeasures are expert systems drawing on a limited database, but one sufficiently detailed for its task. Because the Matrix is a designed virtual reality, the laws of that reality explicitly limit the options the IC needs to address. For more on virtual realities and their laws see **Matrix Realities**, p. 50.

Rumors of a new generation of expert systems have recently begun to appear. These expert systems, using a new method of multi-relationship database analysis, are ideal for limited database applications, such as controlling IC in the Matrix. Renraku Corporation, Fuchi Industrial Electronics, and Transys Neuronet are all rumored to be testing expert IC in their most important systems. The Renraku expert IC is supposed to be known as SKs, short for Semi-Autonomous Know-Bots, implying that Renraku may intend more for the system than just IC control. Fuchi is believed to refer to its expert IC as SmartIC™, with the name already trademarked. None of the companies running expert IC have begun to sell the designs to other corporations, so the IC will not show up outside their own systems.

See the **Intrusion Countermeasures** section for more on expert IC.

INTRUSION COUNTERMEASURES

"Faster, meaner, smarter...God, I hate the technology curve."
—Fastjack, decker

This section deals with the direct agents of computer-system security: Intrusion Countermeasures, abbreviated as IC, and usually pronounced as "ice." IC are sophisticated programs that perform specific tasks designed to locate, contain, or defeat an illegal signal in a computer system.

IC usually operates singly, but can also operate in an inter-linked structure called a construct. The three general types of IC are white, gray, and black, with multiple variations of each.

Though only personas are mentioned throughout this section, assume that the reference includes program frames as well. That is, if the information pertains to a persona, it also pertains to a program frame.

WHITE IC

White IC is primarily concerned with identifying and locating intruder personas. Color has nothing to do with its name, however. White IC is so-called because it is not harmful in itself, though it may activate other countermeasures that are downright deadly.

If the white IC is satisfied as to the identity of a persona, it will do nothing. (Each type of white IC has its own requirements for "satisfaction," as described below.) If the IC is not satisfied, it will declare a passive alert on its next Action. If it is still not satisfied, an active alert may be triggered.

Generally, the process goes something like this:

—Intruding persona moves into Contact Range. (As long as the persona stays beyond Contact Range, the IC pays no heed. Usually.)

—The persona must then attempt to fool the white IC into believing it, the persona, is a legal signal. Again, see each type of white IC for the types of programs that work against it.

—If the persona *succeeds*, the IC lets it pass. The persona continues on.

—If the persona *fails*, the IC will declare a passive alert, with a 50 percent increase in its rating. It will then attempt to verify the identity of the intruder again. If it cannot, an active alert is triggered and any gray or black IC present will activate. See **Alerts**, p. 15, for a full discussion of what happens when passive and active alerts are triggered.

Alerts may no longer be jammed.

White IC cannot defend itself against an attacking persona. White IC that survives to its next action while under attack will trigger an immediate active alert. If the IC is crashed, destroyed in cybercombat, and not immediately suppressed, an active alert is triggered on what would normally be the IC's next Action. See **IC Suppression**, p. 48, for more details. If the IC has been suppressed, no alert is triggered until a system inquiry is conducted by the controlling CPU. See **Central Processing Unit**, p. 11, and **IC Suppression** under **Cybercombat.**

If a persona does not immediately attempt to use a deception or sleaze program upon entering Contact Range, the IC will initiate the verification attempt on its next Action.

ACCESS

The job of access IC is to verify the legality of a signal. If the identity of a signal is legal, great. If not, its task is to YELL! Access is the most common type of IC.

A deception program is normally used against access, though both sleaze programs and outright violence will also work. If a decker can successfully use sleaze or deception programs against the access IC, the persona passes through or may conduct a system operation in the node.

If the access is not fooled, it will declare a passive alert on its next Action. See **Passive Alert**, p. 15.

If crashed, access must be suppressed to stop the triggering of an active alert. If a slow program is used against it, the IC cannot trigger an active alert (it is under attack) if the decker continues to successfully slow it. If the attacker *fails* to slow it any further, the IC may trigger the active alert on its next action.

Access is not mobile.
Load Rating: 1/2 Rating (round down)

BARRIER

Barrier is a solid security lock on a node. No signal may enter unless permission is granted from outside the system. Barrier is only found guarding datastores or in nodes where no data traffic would normally occur. Barrier is, effectively, a wall. Nothing is supposed to get through. Barrier is one of the commonest types of IC to go active following an active alert. Intruders cannot pass through it, but IC and corporate deckers can.

Barrier can only be defeated by a sleaze program or by crashing it. Deception does not work. Barrier triggers or declares alerts in the same manner as access.

Barrier is not mobile.
Load Rating: 1/2 Rating (round down)

PROBE

Probe is a form of access whose susceptibility to a sleaze program is reduced. It is not normally active in nodes prior to an alert because it does its job by heavily interrogating everything it can find, including interference and random "noise." The procedure is generally the same as for access IC, but the probe IC will only request identity verification on its Action.

It is affected normally by deception programs, but the Target Numbers of any sleaze program used against it are increased by +2. Probe may be crashed normally, but if the decker fails to affect it, the IC will declare an active alert on its next Action. See **IC Suppression**, p. 48, for more information.

Probe IC is often allocated as "response IC" in a system. See **IC Allocation**, p. 23.

Probe is usually found in an IC construct. See **Constructs**, p. 22.

Probe is mobile.
Load Rating: Rating

SCRAMBLE

Scramble IC is usually found in datastores or attached to specific files or programs. Scramble can be defeated by deception or decrypt programs, or crashed with combat utilities. It cannot defend itself, but instead will attempt to erase the file it is guarding. It is unable to do this, however, if a decker continues to attack it successfully. If the decker does not succeed during his Action, the scramble IC will erase the file on its next Action. Remember that the IC cannot erase the file as long as it is successfully attacked or slowed. Fail once, and the file's history.

The decker can download the file that is protected by IC, transferring both the file and the IC into storage. This adds the IC's Rating to the decker's Target Number for making a transfer in that node. Having downloaded the file, the decker can work on it at leisure. Downloaded files whose scramble IC is still attached increase in size by 50 percent. Even if the file is transferred, a copy of the IC remains active in the node.

Scramble is not mobile.
Load Rating: 1/2 Rating (round down)

INTRUSION COUNTERMEASURES

GRAY IC

Gray IC is more dangerous than white IC because it is able to damage a deck or its user. Unless an analyze program is successfully used, gray IC resembles white, in that the Sensor attribute of the deck recognizes both types as IC.

Gray IC usually requires a trigger, often white IC. Once activated, however, it no longer needs any prompting. If the gray IC in a node is dormant and the white IC present is fooled, the gray IC will not activate. Unless otherwise indicated, all gray IC possesses the abilities of white probe IC at that rating.

When active, gray IC will move to interrogate a persona as soon as the icon moves to within Sensor Range of the node where the gray IC is currently located.

Some paranoid corporations have gray IC active in isolated systems where sensitive data is stored. They often place the IC in the SAN, especially when most users do not have to cross through the SAN to use the data in it (they enter the system though I/OPs in the same cluster as the data).

All gray IC is mobile.

ACID

Acid IC attacks the persona's Bod Rating directly, reducing its effectiveness. Each extra success reduces the deck's Bod Rating by 1. The Bod Rating cannot fall below 1.

The loss of Bod is recovered after the deck is shut down and restarted, or through use of a restore system utility.
Target: Evasion
Load Rating: Rating

BINDER

The binder program works in ways similar to acid IC. It attacks the persona's Evasion rating directly, reducing its effectiveness. Each extra success reduces the deck's Evasion Rating by 1. The Evasion Rating cannot fall below 1.

The loss of Evasion is recovered after the deck is shut down and restarted, or through use of a restore system utility.
Target: Evasion
Load Rating: Rating

BLASTER

Blaster is attack IC that engages the persona in cybercombat. It behaves like a killer (M) IC, but if successful in crashing the persona, it immediately gets an attempt to burn the deck's MPCP chips on that same Action.

If the persona crashes, make an Unresisted Success Test pitting the IC's rating against a Target Number equal to the deck's MPCP. Every extra success permanently reduces the MPCP Rating by 1. Hardening must be overcome as a Threshold (reduce the number of extra successes by the rating of the hardening).

The MPCP Rating losses can only be restored by upgrading or complete reprogramming of the chips.
Target: Evasion
Load Rating: 1.5 x Rating

JAMMER

Jammer IC affects the persona's Sensor attribute in a manner similar to acid IC. Every extra success generated reduces the Sensor Rating by 1. The Sensor Rating cannot fall below 1.

Sensor is recovered after the deck is shut down and restarted, or through use of a restore system utility.
Target: Evasion
Load Rating: Rating

KILLER

Killer IC engages the persona in cybercombat. Every success it generates does 1 wound of damage to the persona. Killer automatically has an option similar to the Program Option Staging.

Normal Killer is assumed to have Light Staging with a Load Rating of 1/2 Rating (round down).

Killer (M) has Moderate Staging and a Load Rating equal to its Rating.

Killer (S) has Serious Staging and a Load Rating equal to 1.5 x its Rating.

Killer (D) has Deadly Staging and a Load Rating equal to 2 x its Rating.

Killer IC may also be designed with either the penetration or area-effect options available to programs. For a description of those options, see **Penetration**, p. 43, and **Area-Effect**, p. 42. Only one of those options may be present in the IC. Add 1 to the effective rating of the IC for the purpose of determining the Load Rating.
Target: Bod
Load Rating: Varies according to the type.

20 VIRTUAL REALITIES

INTRUSION COUNTERMEASURES

MARKER

Marker IC reduces the Masking attribute of a deck in a manner similar to acid IC. Each extra success generated by the IC reduces the Masking Rating by 1 point. The Masking Rating may not fall below 1.

The loss of Masking is recovered after the deck is shut down and restarted, or through use of a restore system utility.
Target: Evasion
Load Rating: Rating

TAR BABY

Tar baby is a nasty form of trap IC. If an attempt to fool the tar baby fails or if the IC is attacked but not harmed by an attack, the program crashes, taking the attacking utility with it! That program must be reloaded.

The tar baby automatically triggers an active alert as it crashes.
Target: Evasion
Load Rating: Rating

TAR PIT

Tar pit works in a manner similar to tar baby, but it also corrupts *all* copies of the attacking utility in storage memory. It does not affect copies of the program in offline storage. Unfun.
Target: Evasion
Load Rating: 1.5 x Rating

TRACE

Trace locks onto the decker's access path and locates his entry point into the Matrix. When it finds the entry point, the trace is complete.

When trace IC is activated, make an Unresisted Success Test pitting the IC Rating against a Target Number equal to the persona's Masking Rating. The time the IC needs to complete the trace is a base of 10 turns divided by the number of successes rolled. If the Success Test fails, the IC cannot lock onto the deck's signal, but can try again on its next Action.

The part of the trace IC that must be defeated to stop a trace in progress remains in the system. It is mobile and will most likely move to a node with better security as soon as the trace begins. It is this IC that the decker must either defeat or successfully use relocate against. The clock keeps running the whole time the decker is dealing with the trace. Only by crashing the IC or successfully using relocate can he stop it. Trace IC, like white IC, can only fight defensively. Within the originating computer system, anyway.

Trace and Report

When this trace is complete, it reports the real-world address of the decker's entry point into the system. What happens then is up to the corporation. The IC, meanwhile, goes dormant.
Target: Evasion
Load Rating: 1/2 Rating (round down)

Trace and Dump

This program resembles Trace and Report, but the decker is automatically dumped if the trace succeeds. Oops. Oh, and his location is reported, too. Double oops.
Target: Evasion
Load Rating: Rating

Trace and Burn

This program resembles the Trace and Dump, but it also executes the equivalent of a blaster IC attack against the MPCP of the deck. The blaster IC manifests, at one-half (round up) the rating of the trace IC, *at the decker's entry point into the Matrix.* From there, it attacks. The decker can only be defended by *another* persona also at that location, or by a program frame present there. The decker cannot directly attack the blaster IC.

When attacked, the decker has a +2 modifier to all his Target Numbers for defending against that attack. The attack works like blaster, except the blast IC component may continue to attack on its additional actions. The only way to defeat trace and burn IC is to either successfully use relocate before the trace is complete, or to crash the trace IC present in the originating system before it trashes the decker.
Target: Evasion
Load Rating: 1.5 x Rating (round down)

BLACK IC

Black IC is so named because it attacks the decker, not his deck. Black IC normally does physical damage, but can be set to do mental (stun) damage if the system owner is in a good mood. Remember, dead men tell no tales, but prisoners can be downright talkative.

Black IC operates like gray IC in regard to how it activates. It, too, is assumed to have the abilities of probe IC at the same rating.

Black IC is most certainly mobile.

Once black IC scores a hit, the decker may either hang tough or jack out.

HANG TOUGH

The decker attempts to resist the damage so he can keep fighting. The IC makes a Resisted Success Test, pitting its rating against the decker's physical Body Rating as the Target Number. The decker may resist by rolling his Body dice, or Willpower if the damage is mental, against a Target Number equal to the IC's rating. If the IC wins, it does 1 Light Wound for each extra success. Hardening acts like armor against this damage. The shield utility is useless against black IC. The system owner decides whether black IC damage will be physical or mental.

JACK OUT

To jack out, the decker must make an Unresisted Willpower Test, with the IC's rating as a Target Number. If he succeeds, he's out. Now, however, he must roll his Body dice against a Target Number 4 to resist a 4M2 Stun damage attack. Jacking out while besieged by black IC is no fun, chummer. It can hurt. The decker also becomes a victim of Dump Shock (see **Leaving The Matrix**, p. 102, **Shadowrun**).

Someone else may jack the decker out. To do so, this other character must make a Quickness (4) Test. If successful, the decker is jacked out, but still affected as above.

If the decker fails to jack out, the black IC gets to conduct its attack, as with hang tough, but *Unresisted.* The decker cannot reduce the damage. Can we say ouch?

VIRTUAL REALITIES 21

INTRUSION COUNTERMEASURES

IC DEFENSE OPTIONS

IC may be designed with one of three defensive options: hardened, shifting, and normal. Normal bestows no modifiers.

When IC has hardened defense, any damaging attacks against it are at a +2 Target Number, unless the attack has the penetration option. Penetration nullifies hardened defense.

Shifting Defense also gives a +2 Target Number against damaging attacks, unless the attack has the area-effect option. Area effect nullifies shifting defense.

Either defense option increases the effective rating of the program by 1 for the purposes of determining the Load Rating.

VARIABLE RATING (OPTIONAL RULE)

Just as a deck's MPCP or persona ratings can be varied to alter the Load Rating of the deck, so can the ratings of IC be varied. IC will automatically know the effect its entrance into a node will have on the node's load. It can, if the gamemaster wishes, lower its rating appropriately, down to one-half its original rating (rounded up) to reduce the load effects. It may do this automatically without using up an Action.

CONSTRUCTS

Multiple pieces of IC may be combined into a single IC construct that moves and acts in unison. Because it is more efficient, IC tends to appear in this manner, though there are overload concerns. A construct may contain any number or combination of IC. White, black, and gray IC may be mixed within a construct.

The base Load Rating for the entire construct is equal to the highest Load Rating of the IC in the construct. Each additional IC added to the construct after that adds only one-half (round up) its Load Rating to the construct's Load Rating.

The Initiative of the construct is based on the lowest IC rating in the construct.

On its Action, the construct may use any or all of the abilities of the different IC in the construct, with certain limitations:

- If multiple combat IC are being used, all must have the same target, either bod or evasion. Different targets cannot be mixed. Because trace IC is not combat IC (including trace and burn IC, which does not attack until later), it may be activated by any other IC, such as killer IC, which targets Bod, even though the trace target is Evasion.
- When multiple combat IC are utilized, their attack is combined into one attack. The effective rating of the attack is equal to the lowest IC rating involved in the attack. All target numbers are based on that lowest rating. If the attack is successful, all results are figured based on the extra successes rolled. If the attack fails, all the attacks fail.
- When counterattacking in cybercombat, the IC is treated as having a rating equal to the lowest-rated piece of IC in the IC construct. If more than one combat-capable IC is in the IC construct, only one of the IC is used in the counterattack. See **Cybercombat** for more information.
- If the construct crashes, all the programs crash.

All constructs are mobile.

The optional varying ratings rule does not apply with constructs.

EXPERT IC

As discussed earlier, expert IC consists of IC systems run by advanced expert systems. Any type of IC can become expert IC, and its addition is made at the system level. In game terms, the addition of the expert IC programming increases the rating of the IC by 1, 2, or 3 points. The actual increase depends on the sophistication of the expert system built into the IC. Expert systems come in three levels: 1, 2, and 3. Each adds its level to the rating of the IC. The Load Rating, however, does not increase proportionately.

To calculate the Load Rating, consult the table below.

Expert System Level	LOAD RATING TABLE Calculate Load Rating From:
1	Original IC Rating (Do not include expert system increase to the rating)
2	Original IC Rating +1
3	Original IC Rating +2

The gamemaster should play expert IC as being noticeably *smarter* than regular IC. Yes, it'll be tougher, but to the player characters that should seem due to the IC's smarts rather than because of any increase in the game system. Though normal IC operates more like a machine, expert IC should begin to display almost animal-like intelligence and instinct.

Remember, though, that only Renraku, Fuchi, and Transys Neuronet are rumored to be running expert IC, and only in their own most important systems. Expert IC has not made its way out to the rest of the electronic world. In the world of 2052, however, it is only a matter of time before someone manages to "acquire" a copy of the programming...

ARTIFICIAL INTELLIGENCE

Rumors also continue to fly fast and furious about artificially intelligent computer systems. At least three corporations are rumored to be working on AI projects: Renraku at their Seattle Arcology, Mitsuhama at one of their Kyoto, Japan, facilities, and recently, Ares Macrotechnology aboard their *Daedalus* orbital station.

Though these (and probably other corporations) are certainly working on such projects, rumors of success exist, but no evidence. Many theoreticians believe that true sentience, the actual goal of an artificial intelligence project, may be unobtainable within existing technology. Even the incredible power of quantum-optical, multiphasic processing is not enough, and the first AI will follow only after neuromass technology has progressed to an application level.

That is, of course, assuming you believe them.

INTRUSION COUNTERMEASURES

IC PLACEMENT

The different types of IC are placed according to the needs of the system. White IC is the most common, specifically access. Usually, gray IC is placed in the same node as the white, dormant until a passive alert triggers its operation. Gray IC will only take action if it detects an illegal signal in the node.

Gray IC that goes active in the node where the alert originated can attack immediately. Gray IC in any other node must first identify the illegal signal, either through its own probe abilities, or through the abilities of access IC in the same node. If access IC is present in a node with gray IC, the gray will default to the access IC *only if the Access IC Rating is higher than its own rating.* Gray IC that is on its own will always use its probe IC abilities.

Most gray IC will remain in the node in which it activated, even though it is inherently mobile. The reason for this is simple; the system has no proof that the only illegal signal present is the one that was detected. If more than one intruding decker is in the system, sending every piece of IC against the first leaves gaps in the system's defenses. Some gray IC will have been specifically designated as "response IC"; once activated, it deploys to the area of the alert. See **IC Allocation**, below.

Black IC is almost always kept dormant until an active alert is triggered. In some systems, black IC is always active in highly secured areas.

IC ALLOCATION

How much IC is in a system? To find out the total number of Rating Points of IC that the CPU controlling a cluster normally supports, multiply twice the System Rating of the CPU by the node's Threshold Number, which is based on the Security Code. That is the maximum.

Usually, only 25 percent of that number is active when no alert has been declared. Fifty percent of that number is dormant gray IC, and the remaining 25 percent is dormant gray IC designated as "response" IC. When activated, response IC moves to the area where the alert was triggered.

Black IC does not come from that total. It is separate, based on system priorities and gamemaster whim. (Now there's a scary thought.)

CYBERDECKS

"Well, what the drek did you expect? You've got the fraggin' thing in backwards!"
—Joe Wisdom, cyberdeck repairman

eckers without any sense of style rely on decks purchased through a fixer, or god forbid, off the shelf. If a decker takes that route, see the information on **Buying Decks**, p. 31. He gets what he deserves.

Should he decide to walk the path of a true technomancer, the following sections on cyberdeck construction are for him. These rules differ somewhat from the original **Shadowrun** rules, placing greater restraints on the ratings and construction time of components.

Decks are now built component by component, piece by piece. It is not possible to complete the components out of order because these rules interlink the ratings of components to a much greater degree than did the original rules. For example, the MPCP rating of the deck now affects virtually every other component because those processing chips are the heart of the deck.

CONSTRUCTING COMPONENTS

DEFINING TERMS

The rules for constructing deck components consist of specific categories such as Base Time, Cook Time, and Costs, which are defined below.

Base Time

The base time represents the maximum amount of time in days that it takes to complete that component of the deck. As with any time-related skill test in **Shadowrun**, the actual time needed for construction is equal to the base time divided by the number of successes rolled, rounded up.

CYBERDECKS

The base time for constructing a component is 30 days. The player makes the Construction Skill Test, rolling 3 successes. Dividing 30 by 3 gives the actual construction time as ten days.

The construction can take place in stages. The decker can work for ten days, go on an adventure, work another five days on the component, adventure again, and so on. It is the player's responsibility to keep track of the status of all the projects the decker-character is juggling.

The gamemaster must not reveal the exact amount of time needed for construction. The decker-player will know the base time, but the gamemaster should roll the skill dice so that the results are secret. This will also keep the decker-player from knowing whether the test succeeded or not. If the test fails, the gamemaster rolls 1D6, divides it by 2, rounding up, and then divides that result into the base time. This is how long in days the decker must work before realizing that his efforts are fruitless. The character will then have to begin all over again.

If the character decides to spend some time on the deck, but becomes injured, reduce the number of days actually used up. If he's Seriously injured, he gets no work done. If he's Moderately injured, he must work for two days to reduce the time remaining by one day. Light injuries don't affect him.

Because the deck is constructed in pieces, the deck is not usable if some days of work on a particular section still remain.

Cook Time

Some components require the custom-encoding of optical code chips (OCC). The base time for these components is spent writing the actual program code as well as the special instructions for the creation of the chip. OCCs are encoded in a special device known as an optical chip encoder. This device actually breaks down and rebuilds the optical chip using a quantum mechanical process. Once the process is completed, the programming code has been burned into the chip. Deckers refer to optical chip encoders as ovens and the optical-chip encoding process as cooking.

OCCs come in several models, from various manufacturers. The three most popular manufacturers are Fuchi, Sony, and Hitachi:

Brand	Rating	Cost
Sony Encoder I	0	1,200¥
Fuchi OCE/500	1	2,700¥
Sony Encoder II	2	6,000¥
Hitachi RM-AX	3	9,500¥

Add the encoder rating to the decker's Computer B/R Skill for the Success Test that determines whether the chips were successfully cooked. Roll the dice against the indicated Target Number, then divide the result into the indicated cook time to determine how long the chips actually spend in the encoder. Again, the gamemaster does not reveal the results of these dice rolls to the player involved. If the test fails, the chips must cook for the full time. Only if the Rule of Ones comes into play will the cooking result in corrupted chips. If the decker does not check, have him make a Computer (4) Test the first time he attempts to use the chips. Only then will he discover the failed cooking.

An optical chip encoder is roughly the size of a shoe box.

Skills/Targets

To determine the result of the design and construction process, use the skill indicated in the construction table accompanying the component against the Target Number indicated. Remember, extra successes reduce the time required to complete the task.

It is always possible to substitute the appropriate Concentration or Specialization for the general skill listed.

Costs

Purchase of the raw optical chips needed for the deck is the primary expense involved in deck construction. The two types of chips are optical code chips (OCC) and optical memory chips (OMC). Both types come in a wide variety of styles and versions for different tasks.

The actual cost structure has been abstracted into a single formula that represents the costs of the raw OCC or OMC chips, as well as the pre-manufactured processing and support chips needed.

The cost is always in nuyen.

Tools Required

The items listed are required for construction. All are necessary.

A personal computer costs 20¥ times the number of megapulses of memory the computer has. For construction purposes, it has a minimum memory requirement as indicated.

The costs of an optical chip encoder are listed above.

A microtronics tool kit costs 1,500¥, while a microtronics shop costs 15,000¥.

CYBERDECKS

Upgrade Procedure

The time, effort, and nuyen required to upgrade a deck component is equal to the calculated values for the component's new rating if it is being installed from scratch, minus the calculated values for the component's old ratings. Say, for example, that component X, which normally takes 12 days and 500¥ to install, is being upgraded. If it were installed from scratch, the new component would take 18 days and 1,200¥ to install at its desired rating. In this case, the upgrade would require 6 days (18 – 12) at a cost of 700¥ (1,200¥ – 500¥).

Certain cyberdeck components require software programming. Upgrades can only be attempted if the component's original program code, or source code, is still available. The code can be kept in offline storage, where it will occupy an amount of space equal to the Base Time of the design in megapulses. Cooking the source code onto a chip converts it into program code. Only the original master source code can be used for upgrading, so back up often, chummers.

Certain components behave a little differently. Special notations accompany their sections.

LIMITS

Certain components have construction limits, based on the rating of some other component, usually the MPCP.

COMPONENTS

Following are directions for constructing the various cyberdeck components.

A quick note: in the following section, the mathematical notation "Rating^X" is used repeatedly. The "^" symbol indicates that the rating should be raised to the exponent "X". So, Rating^2 really means (Rating x Rating), and Rating^3 means (Rating x Rating x Rating).

MPCP

The MPCP chip is the heart of the deck. It controls the actions of the persona programs and any combat, utility, or operations programs the deck may be running. It defines the appearance of the decker's icon and regulates the two-way simsense/cybernetic interface. A decker cannot run any program that has a higher rating than that of his current deck's MPCP.

It is possible to upgrade the MPCP as long as the original program code has been kept. This takes up an amount of memory equal to (Rating x Rating) x 4 in megapulses. It may be stored anywhere, but is not usable unless encoded onto chips.

Most of the deck's other components are designed to match the MPCP, which is why the MPCP's rating factors into their design and construction in some manner. This means that whenever the MPCP is upgraded, *it is also necessary to upgrade all the other components that factor the MPCP into their design or construction*. If those components are not upgraded, the deck still operates at the *effective* MPCP for which those components were designed.

> Hellraiser has upgraded his deck's MPCP from 5 to 6. Until he upgrades the relevant components in his deck to match an MPCP of 6, his deck operates at an effective Rating 5. If even only one component has not been upgraded to match the new MPCP, the deck still operates at the old rating.

The effective MPCP rating of a deck is equal to the lowest MPCP rating for which any of the components were designed. If, for example, the deck has a mixture of components designed for MPCP ratings of 7, 5, and 4, the effective MPCP of the deck would be 4. Once the component designed for an MPCP 4 has been upgraded, the deck will have an effective MPCP 5 until that component is upgraded, and so on. If, by some chance, all the components in the deck were designed for an MPCP 7 and the actual MPCP chip was only a Rating 5, the deck's effective MPCP would be 5 because that is the lowest MPCP rating in the deck.

When the MPCP is upgraded, the design process is shortened because the MPCP program itself can be upgraded from the old version. Completely new chips, however, must be cooked and installed.

The MPCP chips are custom-aligned to a specific decker's brainwave patterns. Using someone else's MPCP chips results not only in a headache, but a +4 Target Number modifier across the board.

CYBERDECKS

Base Time:	(Rating^2) x 8
Cook Time:	Rating x 3
Appropriate Skills:	Design: Computer
	Cooking: Computer B/R
Skill Targets:	Design: Rating
	Cooking: Rating
Cost:	(Rating^3) x 50¥
Required Tools:	Microtronics Shop
	Optical Chip Encoder
	Personal Computer (minimum Mp equal to Rating^2 x 4
Upgrade Procedure:	Design: (New Value) – (Old Value)
	Cooking: New Value (Full chip replacement)
	Cost: New Value (Full chip replacement)
Limits:	Maximum Rating = designer's Computer Skill Rating x 1.5 (round down)

Shifting the MPCP

During a run, it is possible to *lower* the effective MPCP Rating in order to reduce the cyberdeck's Load Rating. This takes 1 Action to accomplish, and the MPCP Rating may be lowered to any value lower than its current effective rating. The Persona Ratings can also be shifted with this action. This may require a deliberate reduction in the ratings of one or more persona programs because their total ratings cannot exceed three times the rating of the MPCP.

It takes one Action to raise the value of the MPCP and personas back up again, up to a maximum of its current effective rating.

HARDENING

Hardening requires some software design and a lot of hardware wrangling. It works as a form of "armor" for the deck by setting up code buffers, routers, delays, and breaks, as well as physical circuit-breakers.

Building the Hardening system uses the same procedure as for writing and cooking the MPCP. First the decker writes it, then he burns it into chips.

Hardening can be upgraded.

Base Time:	MPCP x (Rating^2) x 2.5
Cook Time:	(MPCP x Rating)/2 (round up)
Appropriate Skills:	Design: Computer
	Cook: Computer B/R
Skill Targets:	Design: Rating + MPCP
	Cook: Rating + MPCP
Cost:	(MPCP^2) x (Rating^4)¥
Required Tools:	Microtronics Shop
	Optical Chip Encoder
	Personal Computer (minimum Mp equal to MPCP x Rating x 5)
Upgrade Procedure:	Design: (New Value) – (Old Value)
	Cooking: New Value (Full chip replacement)
	Cost: New Value (Full chip replacement)
Limits:	Maximum Rating = 1/2 MPCP (round down)

ACTIVE MEMORY

Creating the active, on-board memory area for a deck involves little more than plugging in additional chips. Every program has the built-in ability to make use of however much memory is currently available.

The active memory is where the programs currently being run are stored. To use an older, outmoded term, the active memory is the equivalent of a deck's RAM (Random Access Memory). The total size of all combat, utility, or operations programs being run at one time cannot exceed the size of the active memory. If a deck has 50 Mp of active memory, the decker cannot have any more than 50 Mp of programs currently active. He can run any number of programs at one time.

A character can acquire raw optical memory chips through a fixer. Their cost varies according to the rating of the MPCP for which they are intended.

Onboard memory may also be upgraded. Note, however, that upgrading the deck's MPCP also requires replacing *all* the active memory chips with chips matching the new MPCP. Until that is done, the MPCP runs at the old rating. The active memory chip-upgrade must be done all at once. If, however, it is only the amount of memory being upgraded, not the MPCP rating, then the upgrade may be partial.

> Shen first decides to upgrade his MPCP from 4 to 5. He does so. Then, he must replace his current active memory chips with new chips that match his new MPCP of 5. If he does not, his deck will continue to run at an effective MPCP of 4. He has 200 Mp of active memory. He replaces all the chips at a cost of (5 x 2¥), or 2,000¥. His deck's effective MPCP is now 5, assuming all the relevant components in the deck have been matched as well.
>
> A short time later, he decides to upgrade the amount of active memory, from 200 Mp to 250 Mp, since his deck can now address 250 Mp of Active Memory. This will cost him 50 Mp (250 – 200) at 10¥ (5, for the MPCP, x 2) per Mp. The total cost is 500¥.

A character can sell off old active memory chips at 50 percent of their actual value. Hey, don't knock it.

Base Time:	Mp/100 (round up)
Cook Time:	Not required
Appropriate Skill:	Computer B/R
Skill Target:	3
Cost:	(MPCP x 5¥) per Megapulse
Required Tools:	Microtronics Tool Kit
Upgrade Procedure:	Adding Memory: Values for new memory
	MPCP Upgraded: All memory at new rating
Limits:	Maximum addressable memory = MPCP x 50 Mp

CYBERDECKS

STORAGE

Storage is where inactive programs are kept. It is a special solid chip, different from the chips used in active memory. It might be compared to an old-style internal hard drive, though it holds much more and has significantly higher access speeds.

A decker cannot add memory to his storage in bits and pieces. It comes as one solid bulk of memory. If he upgrades from 200 Mp to 400 Mp, for example, the old 200 Mp optical storage chip goes to sit on a shelf somewhere. Fortunately, the decker can sell it for about 50 percent of the cost of a new one.

Storage is upgradable.

Base Time:	Mp/100 (round up)
Cook Time:	None required
Appropriate Skill:	Computer B/R
Skill Target:	3
Cost:	2.5¥ per Mp
Required Tools:	Microtronics Tool Kit
Upgrade Procedure:	Replacement: Full Value (Full memory replacement)
Limits:	None

LOAD SPEED

The number of megapulses of information that pass between storage memory and active memory is based on the deck's load speed. If the decker has a backup or spare program in storage and suddenly needs to access it, load speed tells how long it takes to transfer it from storage to active memory. The load speed is rated in megapulses per turn, such as 5 Mp/turn, 10 Mp/turn, and so on. Rate, used below, refers to the amount of megapulses transferred per turn.

Load speed is upgradable.

Base Time:	(MPCP x Rate)/25 (round up)
Cook Time:	(MPCP x Rate)/100 (round up)
Appropriate Skill:	Computer B/R
Skill Target:	(MPCP x Rate)/100 (round up)
Cost:	(MPCP x Rate) x 5¥
Required Tools:	Microtronics Shop
	Optical Chip Encoder
	Personal Computer (minimum Mp required is equal to (MPCP x Rate)/10 (round up)
Upgrade Procedure:	Design: (New Value – Old Value)
	Cook: New Value (Full chip replacement)
MPCP Upgrade:	Design: (New Value – Old Value)
	Cook: New Value (Full chip replacement)
Limits:	Maximum load speed = MPCP x 10

I/O SPEED

Input/Output speed is how many megapulses of data the deck can move into or out of the Matrix. It is the I/O speed that determines how fast a decker can transfer/copy a file from a datastore to the deck, or through it to offline storage. The I/O speed is rated in megapulses per turn, such as 2 Mp/turn, 5 Mp/turn, and so on. Rate, used below, refers to the amount of megapulses transferred per turn.

I/O speed is upgradable.

Base Time	(MPCP x Rate)/10
Cook Time:	(MPCP x Rate)/25 (round up)
Appropriate Skill:	Computer B/R
Skill Target:	(MPCP x Rate)/50 (round up)
Cost:	(MPCP x Rate) x 25¥
Required Tools:	Microtronics Shop
	Optical Chip Encoder
	Personal Computer (minimum memory required is equal to (MPCP x Rate)/5 (round up)
Upgrade Procedure:	Design: (New Value – Old Value)
	Cook: New Value (Full chip replacement)
MPCP Upgrade:	Design: (New Value – Old Value)
	Cook: New Value (Full chip replacement)
Limits:	Maximum I/O Speed = MPCP x 5

RESPONSE

The response system is nasty and complicated. It interacts with virtually every system in the deck, has a drekload of specialized hardware, and costs plenty of nuyen. But oh, what it does! It is something like the cyberdeck equivalent of wired reflexes, with response at three possible ratings; 1, 2, and 3. Yes, 3 is the maximum.

Response cannot be upgraded, but must be installed new from scratch every time. The only exception to this is when upgrading to match a new MPCP rating. In that case, use the new value minus the old value procedure.

Base Time:	(MPCP x Rating^2) x 5
Cook Time:	(MPCP x Rating^2)/10 (round up)
Appropriate Skill:	Design: Computer
	Cooking: Computer B/R
Skill Target:	Design: MPCP + Rating
	Cook: MPCP + Rating
Cost:	(MPCP^2 x Rating^2) x 100¥
Required Tools:	Microtronics Tool Kit
	Optical Chip Encoder
	Personal Computer (minimum memory required is equal to MPCP x Rating x 10 Mp)
Upgrade Procedure:	Design: New Value (Full replacement)
	Cook: New Value (Full chip replacement)
MPCP Upgrade:	Design: (New Value – Old Value)
	Cook: New Value (Full chip replacement)
Limits:	Maximum Response of which deck is capable = MPCP/4 (round down)

SIMSENSE HARDWARE

Not rated, but necessary for a deck's operation, simsense hardware costs 500¥.

Base Time:	5
Cook Time:	None required
Appropriate Skill:	Computer B/R
Skill Target:	4
Cost:	500¥
Required Tools:	Microtronics Shop
Upgrade Procedure:	None required
Limits:	None

CYBERDECKS

VIDSCREEN

A decker's point-of-view vidscreen lets others nearby see what he sees in the Matrix. It can also be used to display text and graphics. Once the system is installed, it is possible to install any number of vidscreens off the same internal circuits.

Base Time:	1 day
Cook Time:	None required
Appropriate Skill:	Computer B/R
Skill Target:	4
Cost:	100¥
Required Tools:	Microtronics Tool Kit
Upgrade Procedure:	Install new unit
Limits:	None

HITCHER JACK

The hitcher jack lets other characters come along for the ride, but they have no control over the deck. It is really just an extra tap off the simsense processor, allowing the hitcher to experience the Matrix. There is no cybernetic interface with the wearer.

If the deck is engaged in cybercombat, the potential of damage exists for a hitcher-jack user. See **Cybercombat** for more information.

Base Time:	2 days per jack
Cook Time:	None required
Appropriate Skill:	Computer B/R
Skill Target:	Number of jacks +1
Cost:	MPCP x Number of jacks x 100¥
Required Tools:	Microtronics Shop
Upgrade Procedure:	Install new jack
Limits:	Maximum number of jacks = MPCP Rating.

OFFLINE STORAGE

Offline storage is storage external to the cyberdeck, similar to the function of an archaic external hard drive. The offline storage is purchased as a single hunk of memory, much like the deck's storage memory. The construction involves installing the interface port between the offline storage and the cyberdeck.

More than one unit of offline storage can be added in a series with another. Each unit, however, remains physically separate from the others. Access of information to and from the offline storage device is limited to the deck's I/O speed.

An offline storage device is about the size of an old-style paperback book.

Base Time:	1 day
Cook Time:	None required
Appropriate Skill:	Computer B/R
Skill Target:	3
Cost:	Interface Hardware: MPCP x 50¥
	Offline Storage: Mp x .5¥
Required Tools:	Microtronics Shop
Upgrade Procedure:	Add new memory
Limits:	None

CASE, KEYBOARD, AND STUFF

Costs for items like the deck's case, the command keyboard, interface and telecommunications jacks, and the like are so negligible compared to the rest of the components that they are ignored.

Some deckers may, however, want the additional protection of a reinforced deck case.

DECK PROTECTION TABLE

	Impact	Ballistic	Cost
Basic Case	1	0	Don't worry about it
Level 1 Case	2	1	500¥
Level 2 Case	3	2	2,000¥
Level 3 Case	4	3	5,000¥

The deck can be assumed to have an effective Body of 1 against all damaging attacks. The Protection Rating listed above should be used as the equivalent of armor (automatic successes).

UPGRADING A DECK

Certain deck systems, active memory, storage memory, load speed, and I/O speed are all upgradable. To upgrade, simply subtract the current rating from the desired value and install the difference, using the normal rules.

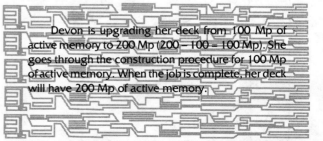

Devon is upgrading her deck from 100 Mp of active memory to 200 Mp (200 – 100 = 100 Mp). She goes through the construction procedure for 100 Mp of active memory. When the job is complete, her deck will have 200 Mp of active memory.

CYBERDECKS

After her last run, Harper felt like the walking dead. She decides that enough's enough; it's time to upgrade. Taking her Cyber-4 into her shop, she goes to work. First, she will upgrade her MPCP from its current 6 to a rating of 8. The base design time will take her 224 days. (The Rating 8 MPCP would take her 512 days from scratch, while the Rating 6 MPCP took her 288 base days to design, so 512 – 288 = 224). It will take 24 days for the chips to cook, at a cost of 25,600¥. Ignoring the passage of time (we can do that, you can't!), Harper now has a deck with a set of Rating 8 MPCP chips. The rest of her deck is still matched to a Rating 6 MPCP, so the effective MPCP of the deck is still only 6.

She now decides to upgrade the rest of the deck to the new MPCP Rating. Following that, she'll upgrade the components to the Cyber-6 values. Taking it component by component:

Hardening

The Hardening Rating itself remains at 3, but the MPCP Rating that factors into the design and construction formula is what changes. The base time for the new values is 180 base days. For the old values, it was 135 base days. The difference is 45 base days. It will take 45 base days to upgrade the hardening system to reflect the new MPCP rating.

Cooking the new chips will take 12 base days because the chips must be completely re-cooked and replaced. It will, however, cost the full amount for the new chips: 5,184¥. Those old chips, by the way, are now paperweights.

Upgrading to the Cyber-6, with its hardening of 4, will take Harper 320 – 180 (new value minus old value), or 140 base days, for the design. Cooking will take 16 base days. The cost will be 16,384¥.

Active Memory

Active Memory is easy: she has to replace all the chips (100 Mp worth), no matter what. The replacement cost is equal to the cost of the new chips, which is 4,000¥. It will take her a base time of 1 day to install them.

The Cyber-6 has the same amount of active memory as the Cyber-4, so there is no expense.

Storage Memory

No change here because the storage memory has no relationship with the MPCP.

There is also no increase from the Cyber-4 to the Cyber-6.

Load Speed

The base time for the new MPCP rating (7 days), minus the time for the old MPCP rating (5 days), leaves 2 base days for the upgrade. The cook time will be at the new MPCP rating, and take 2 days, because all the chips must be replaced. The cost for all new chips is 800¥.

To upgrade from the Cyber-4 to the Cyber-6, a jump from 20 Mp/turn to 50 Mp/turn will take 10 base days, plus 4 days to cook the new chips, and will cost 2,000¥.

I/O Speed

The MPCP-related upgrade will take 4 base days to design, 7 base days to cook, and cost 4,000¥.

To upgrade from the Cyber-4 to the Cyber-6 (20 Mp/turn to 30 Mp/turn) will take 8 base days to design, 10 days to cook the chips, and cost 6,000¥.

Harper now has her Cyber-6, but she has put more work into it than was necessary. If she had combined the MPCP-related upgrades and the Cyber-6 upgrades, she'd have been better off. Why bother matching the components in the deck to the new (Rating 8) MPCP when those same components will be upgraded shortly? A waste of time.

What she should have done is upgrade the MPCP and then each of the components from their old rating (at the old MPCP rating) to their new rating (at the new MPCP rating), ignoring the intermediate MPCP upgrade. The table below shows her base time, cook time, and costs for the way she did her upgrades, versus the way she should have done them.

The totals are compared at the end of the table. Even though the savings in costs and time are not major, in certain tough circumstances, these margins might make a difference.

CYBERDECKS

	MPCP Upgrade	DUMB WAY Cyber-6 Upgrade	Totals	SMART WAY Full Upgrade
MPCP				
Base Time	224 days	—	224 days	224 days
Cook	24 days	—	24 days	24 days
Cost	25,600¥	—	25,600¥	25,600¥
Hardening				
Base Time	45 days	140 days	185 days	185 days
Cook	12 days	16 days	28 days	16 days
Cost	5,184¥	16,384¥	21,568¥	16,384¥
Active Memory				
Base Time	1 day	—	1 day	1 day
Cook	—	—	—	—
Cost	4,000¥	—	4,000¥	4,000¥
Storage Memory		No Change		
Load Speed				
Base Time	4 days	10 days	14 days	12 days
Cook	2 days	4 days	6 days	4 days
Cost	800¥	2,000¥	2,800¥	2,000¥
I/O Speed				
Base Time	4 days	8 days	12 days	12 days
Cook	7 days	10 days	17 days	10 days
Cost	4,000¥	6,000¥	10,000¥	6,000¥
TOTALS:				
Total Days:			511 days	488 days
Total Cost:			63,968¥	53,984¥

A special circumstance occurs when the MPCP of the deck is upgraded. With a few exceptions, the other components in the deck are all designed with a specific MPCP Rating in mind. When the MPCP is upgraded, those components no longer precisely match the MPCP chips because their design was for the old MPCP. When this occurs, the effective MPCP of the deck is equal to the lowest "designed-for" MPCP Rating in the deck.

> Hellraiser has been running his deck with an MPCP 5, and all his deck's components were designed to work with an MPCP of that rating. He now upgrades his deck's chips to MPCP 6. The other components are still designed for an MPCP of 5, making his deck's effective MPCP still a 5. He will have to upgrade all the components in the deck to work with an MPCP 6 before the deck's effective MPCP reaches 6.

The procedure for upgrading the deck's components to match the MPCP is generally the same as above. In most cases, the difference between the various construction and design ratings should be calculated and that difference used for the amount of time, effort, and nuyen that must be expended.

To further illustrate this, we follow Harper through the upgrading of her Fuchi Cyber-4 deck to the equivalent of a Fuchi Cyber-6.

DECK DOWNTIME

Not figured into any of the above formulae is how long the deck will be unusable while its guts are strewn about the workroom. The time for most components is equal to 10 percent of the actual time (that's the base time divided by the extra successes from the skill test), rounded up. For active memory, storage memory, offline storage, vidscreens, and hitcher jacks, the deck will be down and unusable for the entire actual time.

BUYING DECKS

Off the shelf? Well, okay, if you insist. (Better hope nobody on the street hears about it, chummer, 'cause it won't do drek for your rep.)

Cyberdecks have a street price much higher than their construction cost using the design and construction rules above. That's street price too, chummer, not retail price. To get a deck at street price means going through a fixer.

The fixer does not magically have access to all the cyberdecks ever made, and they are certainly not sitting in some warehouse just waiting for deckers to buy them (well, not usually). First, the fixer must determine if a deck is *available*. Commercial decks have an Availability Rating representing how hard it is to locate that type of deck (see table below). Certain decks are virtually impossible to find because only a limited number were built and their owners want to keep them.

CYBERDECKS

To determine if a certain deck type is available, the gamemaster rolls the fixer's Etiquette (Street) against the Availability Rating of the deck, then consults the table below.

DECK AVAILABILITY TABLE

Successes	Result
0	"Sorry, can't find any of those right now. Try again next week."
1	"Yes, I believe I can find a deck of that type. Unfortunately, the cost will be twice the normal street price."
2	"Your lucky day, chummer. I can get it for you at street price."
3+	"Sometimes even I am amazed. An associate of mine is looking to relieve himself of the same type of deck you are looking for. The price is only about 80 percent of street."

Naturally, the buyer can attempt to haggle with his fixer over the final price. Make an Opposed Negotiation Test between the buyer and fixer, adjusting the price downward by 5 percent of the street price for every extra success the buyer rolls.

For the record, the street price is equal to the deck's Construction Cost multiplied by its Availability, with a minimum multiple of 5.5. Any deck with an Availability Rating of less than 6 is treated as having a 5.5 for the purpose of determining the street price. Round this number up to the nearest hundred. The retail price, where applicable, is twice the street price. Not all types of decks are sold retail, however. The Street Availability Rating of a commercial deck is equal to the Construction Cost/ 10,000 (round up, minimum of 4). Decks with a potential MPCP of greater than 4 are not commercially available.

Also, street decks *do not come with any MPCP chips, persona chips, or programs*. These must all be purchased separately. Wait, you say, isn't the cost of the MPCP factored into the construction price, and therefore the street and retail prices? Right you are, chummer. Ain't life sweet? What you are paying

CYBERDECKS

Model	MPCP	Hard.	Act.	Stor.	Load	I/O	Constr.	Avail.	Street Price
Radio Shack									
PCD-100	2	0	10	50	5	1	1,225¥	4	6,800¥
Allegiance									
Alpha	3	1	10	50	5	1	2,284¥	4	12,600¥
Sony									
CTY-360	6	3	50	100	20	10	18,066¥	4	99,400¥
Fuchi									
Cyber-4	6	3	100	500	20	20	22,066¥	4	121,400¥
Cyber-6	8	4	100	500	50	30	55,734¥	6	334,500¥
Cyber-7	10	4	200	1000	50	40	101,100¥	10	1,112,100¥
Fairlight									
Excalibur	12	5	500	1000	100	50	230,400¥	22	5,529,600¥

32 VIRTUAL REALITIES

CYBERDECKS

for is the convenience of simply dropping in an MPCP of the indicated rating and being able to use the deck immediately. Remember, the other components have been designed and built for use with that rating MPCP. To add a higher-rated MPCP would require upgrading most of the deck.

Using a deck that comes with an MPCP installed is not recommended. Odds are it's a Trojan horse-design to catch young, stupid decker-wannabees. The signal the MPCP emits is encoded for easier identification, reducing the Target Number for any trace programs to 2. Rely on your own soft and hardware, chummer. It's the only way to be safe.

SATELLITE UPLINKS

By entering the Matrix through a satellite uplink, the decker obtains some degree of immunity to trace programs. The furthest back the trace can operate is to the satellite's downlink point, to which it bounces the signal. The decker could be transmitting from nearly anywhere within the area the satellite covers. The use of a satellite is not as beneficial as it sounds, however.

First, the equipment must be acquired. Satlink gear costs roughly twice the construction cost of the deck in use. It can be constructed at a base time (in days) equal to the construction cost of the deck, divided by 500 (round up). The final cost will be equal to one-half the construction cost of the deck.

Before an uplink can occur, a satellite must first be found. A satlink program must be run in the cyberdeck (3 Mp, 300¥) to properly direct and align the antenna with the local satellites. The base time required to align to a satellite is 3 minutes. To reduce this, the decker must make a Computer Skill Test against a Target Number ranging from 2 (if the attempt is being made from the countryside) to 8 (if the attempt is being made from a downtown street). The gamemaster should set the target number based on how much open sky is immediately accessible. The less sky, the higher the target.

Once the satellite is targeted, the uplink is attempted. Satellites are heavily protected and difficult to penetrate. They generally have a Security Rating of Orange-5 and run an Access 7 program with a killer (S) 5 program back-up. Variation is possible at the gamemaster's discretion.

If the uplink fails, the decker is dumped, and the satellite system goes on passive alert.

If the uplink is successful, the decker can route his signal to any LTG within the RTG where he is currently located without having to deal with the LTG/RTG SANs. He can also bounce his signal across the planet to any other RTG he wishes to access. If he does this, his signal effectively comes down in the RTG, leaving him still to deal with the LTG SANs.

Running through a satellite link also imposes a –2 modifier to the decker's Reaction Attribute because of the time delays involved.

PROGRAMS

"The babes? Buncha program frames 'ole Zapper likes to keep around him. Blames it on his dad for some reason."
—Mr. Miracle, decker

This section describes programs for cyberdecks. These programs come in two forms: persona programs and utility programs. Each is addressed separately.

PERSONA PROGRAMS

The persona programs define many of the attributes of the decker in the Matrix. They are base programs that run under the governing umbrella of the Master Persona Control Program, or MPCP. To some degree, they represent the cyberdeck's inherent abilities, while utilities represent variable abilities.

Persona programs must be encoded onto optical code chips, just like the MPCP. Once cooked, these chips plug into the main circuit board of the deck. If they become damaged, however, they must be replaced because the chips do not occupy any of the deck's active memory. The total ratings of all the persona programs cannot exceed three times the rating of the MPCP.

The four types of persona programs are bod, evasion, masking, and sensors. All cyberdecks must have a rating of at least 1 in each of these. A terminal has no such limitation.

BOD

This is the cyberdeck's "Body" attribute. It usually becomes the IC's Target Number in attacks against the persona.
Size: (Rating^2) x 3 Mp

EVASION

This attribute allows the persona to evade unauthorized programs and commands by IC. In some ways, it is directly analogous to a node's Security Rating.
Size: (Rating^2) x 3 Mp

PROGRAMS

MASKING

This is the persona's ability to blend in with Matrix nodes. The attribute helps to defeat various trace and identification programs.

Size: (Rating^2) x 2 Mp

SENSOR

This attribute lets the persona detect things in the Matrix.

Size: (Rating^2) x 2 Mp

DECK MODES (OPTIONAL RULE)

At any time, a cyberdeck is in one of four modes corresponding to one of the four persona programs. Each mode has a specific purpose, gives certain bonuses, and incurs certain limitations.

It takes one Action to swap modes. The deck may be in only one of the four modes at any one time.

BOD MODE

Bod is the standard combat mode. In this mode, the MPCP prepares to absorb full-force damage. The Bod Rating of the deck is increased by 50 percent, rounded down.

While in bod mode, the decker's evasion, masking, and sensor attributes are reduced by 50 percent, rounded up.

The I/O speed of the deck is reduced by 50 percent, rounded up, while in bod mode.

EVASION MODE

In evasion mode, the MPCP is structured to avoid damage by shunting and countering the attack before it has a chance to take hold in the deck.

When in evasion mode, the Evasion Rating of the deck is increased by 50 percent, rounded down. The deck's Bod, Masking, and Sensor Ratings are reduced by 50 percent, rounded up.

The I/O speed of the deck is reduced by 50 percent, rounded up, while in evasion mode.

MASKING MODE

In masking mode, the MPCP of the deck works to synchronize the profile of the deck with the surrounding Matrix, making it harder to find.

When in masking mode, the Masking Rating of the deck is increased by 50 percent, rounded down. While in masking mode, however, the deck's Bod, Evasion, and Sensor Ratings are reduced by 50 percent, rounded up.

The I/O speed of the deck remains normal while in masking mode.

SENSOR MODE

In sensor mode, the MPCP is working to detect, absorb, and analyze as much information as possible.

While in sensor mode, the deck's Sensor Rating increases by 50 percent, rounded down. At the same time, the Bod, Evasion, and Masking Ratings of the deck are reduced by 50 percent, rounded up.

The I/O speed of the deck remains normal while in sensor mode.

PROGRAMMING ON THE FLY

It is possible for a decker to improvise a program not currently in his deck's active memory. It is even possible when he does not have that particular program. To create a one-shot, immediate-use version of a program, the decker expends dice from his Hacking Pool. The number of Hacking dice expended must be equal to the desired rating of the program, *squared*. A Rating 1 program, for example, would require one die from the Hacking Pool (1^1 = 1), a Rating 2 program would require four dice (2^2 = 4), a Rating 3 program, nine dice (3^3 = 9), and so on.

If the program is not used *immediately*, it is lost when the Hacking Pool next refreshes. The decker may, however, continue to expend the required number of dice to keep the program active with every new action.

Degradable utilities can only be improvised once during a single Matrix run.

One-shot, one-use, "on-the-fly" programs are generally referred to as flygrams. Flygrams do take up active memory equal to one-half the size of the appropriate program of that type and rating.

Hacking Pool dice cannot be used to augment flygrams except in the manner described above.

PROGRAMS

UTILITY PROGRAMS

The five different types of utility programs are: combat utilities, defense utilities, sensor utilities, masking utilities, and system utilities. Each type serves a different function and operates a little differently.

Utility programs that are active (those that are immediately usable) are kept in the deck's active memory. The total memory size of all the utilities in active memory cannot exceed the total amount of available active memory. Even a crashed utility still takes up space in active memory, but the decker can use one Action to completely erase the dead program from active memory.

Only one copy of any given utility can be present in active memory at one time. Utilities, specifically combat utilities, that have different options assigned to them are viewed as different programs. Two Attack 5 programs may be in active memory at one time, as long as each has a different set of options. See **Options**, p. 42.

Copying a program from storage memory to active memory takes only one Action to initiate. It may, however, take time to crossload, based on the program's size compared to the deck's load speed.

COMBAT UTILITIES

Combat utility programs are the weapons of Matrix combat. See the **Cybercombat** section for details on conducting attacks in Matrix combat.

Attack

The attack program is the primary weapon of cybercombat. Generically, these are rated as any other utility, though their appearance in the Matrix can vary greatly from program to program. For example, one decker's Attack 4 program might resemble a cutting laser, while another's might resemble a hurled glob of techno-gelatinous material that eats its way into the target. The visual is irrelevant, as it is completely malleable by the decker who created the program.

After designing the attack program, the designer must declare whether it acts against a persona's bod *or* its evasion. The designer has a choice, but it must be one or the other. Against IC, the target number is always the node's Security Rating.

Options: Area-Effect, Link, Mobility, One-Shot, Penetration, Staging

Target: Body or evasion (designer choice) against personas; Node Security Rating against IC

Size: (Rating^2) x 2 Mp

Blind

The blind program attacks a persona's sensor rating, reducing the deck's ability to detect and analyze data. Every two successes from the Opposed Combat Test reduces the target deck's effective Sensor Rating by 1. The Sensor Rating cannot fall below 1.

The blind program works by affecting the MPCP's ability to control the persona's sensor program.

The loss of sensor is recovered after the deck is shut down and restarted or through use of a restore system utility.

Options: Area-Effect, Link, Mobility, One-Shot

Target: Evasion

Size: (Rating^2) x 3 Mp

Hog

Hog is a virus program that invades a cyberdeck and begins to occupy unused active memory. Once the hog has occupied all the available active memory, it will begin to use up memory assigned to utilities, crashing them.

Multiply the extra successes rolled in the Opposed Combat Test by 5 to determine how much Mp of active memory the program occupies per turn. Once the hog program has occupied all the unused active memory, it will begin to take over the memory allocated to the largest program present. Once it has taken over that memory, it will move to the next largest, and so on. The moment the hog program takes over any of the memory used by a program, that program crashes.

The decker will be aware something is amiss as soon as the first utility suddenly crashes, but other ways exist to tip him off to the presence of the hog program before things get that bad.

The gamemaster should make a Success Test pitting the hog program's rating against the MPCP Rating of the deck every turn that the hog program is present in a deck. If the hog gets at least one success, it alters the deck's displays to show that the memory allocation is normal and the program remains hidden. If it fails to get one success, the MPCP recognizes its presence and signals an alarm.

PROGRAMS

A decker may, by expending an Action, conduct a system check by making an Opposed Success Test between the hog program and the MPCP program. If the hog wins, it stays hidden. If the MPCP wins, the hog is revealed.

To remove the hog program from active memory, the decker must attack it, using one of his own attack programs currently in active memory. He may also create a flygram to deal with it if he chooses. To evict the hog, the decker needs only one extra success from the Opposed Combat Test.

Any programs crashed as a result of the hog program must be reloaded from storage. Hog will only affect active memory, not storage or offline memory.

Options: Link, One-Shot
Target: Evasion
Size: (Rating^2) x 3 Mp

Poison

The poison program attacks a persona's Bod Rating directly, reducing its effectiveness. Every two successes rolled in the Opposed Combat Test reduces the target deck's Bod Rating by 1. The Bod Rating cannot fall below 1.

The poison program works by affecting the MPCP's ability to control the persona's bod program.

The loss of bod is recovered after the deck is shut down and restarted or through use of a restore system utility.

Options: Area-Effect, Link, Mobility, One-Shot
Target: Evasion
Size: (Rating^2) x 3 Mp

Restrict

The restrict program attacks a persona's Evasion Rating, reducing the deck's ability to defend itself. Every two successes from the Opposed Combat Test reduce the target deck's Evasion Rating by 1. The Evasion Rating cannot fall below 1.

The restrict program works by affecting the MPCP's ability to control the persona's evasion program.

The loss of evasion is recovered after the deck is shut down and restarted or through use of a restore system utility.

Options: Area-Effect, Link, Mobility, One-Shot
Target: Evasion
Size: (Rating^2) x 3 Mp

Reveal

The reveal program attacks a persona's Masking Rating, reducing the deck's ability to conceal itself. Every two successes from the Opposed Combat Test reduces the target deck's Masking Rating by 1. The Masking Rating cannot fall below 1.

The reveal program achieves its end by affecting the MPCP's ability to control the persona's masking program.

The loss of masking is recovered after the deck is shut down and restarted or through use of a restore system utility.

Options: Area-Effect, Link, Mobility, One-Shot
Target: Evasion
Size: (Rating^2) x 3 Mp

Slow

The slow program will slow down IC, but has no effect on another persona. The extra successes from the Combat Success Test reduce the IC's Initiative. Apply this modifier *after* the Initiative die has been rolled. If the Initiative is reduced to 0, the IC is frozen and stops working, at least for that turn. Frozen IC cannot trigger any alarms or other IC, nor can it respond to a system inquiry.

Options: Area-Effect, Link, Mobility, One-Shot
Size: (Rating^2) x 4 Mp

DEFENSE UTILITIES

Defense utilities improve the persona's ability to avoid, repair, or resist damage.

Armor

This degrading utility adds to the bod of the deck. It degenerates, losing 1 rating point every time the deck's bod is used as a Target Number attacked. This program must be in active memory to have any effect.

When placed in a frame, its rating becomes the effective Bod Attribute Rating of the entire frame. See **Frames** below.

The rating of this program cannot be restored except by shutting down and restarting the deck.

Options: Link
Size: (Rating^2) x 3 Mp

Cloak

This degrading utility adds to the masking of the deck. It degenerates, losing 1 rating point every time the deck's Masking Rating is used as a Target Number.

When placed in a frame, its rating becomes the effective Masking Rating of the entire frame. See **Frames**.

The rating of this program cannot be restored except by shutting down and restarting the deck.

Options: Link
Size: (Rating^2) x 3 Mp

Medic

A medic program repairs damage to the MPCP. The Target Number depends on the MPCP's current wound level, per the chart below. Roll a number of dice equal to the rating of the medic against the Target Number below:

Wound Level	Target Number
Light	4
Moderate	5
Serious	6

This roll cannot be augmented by the Hacking Pool. Each extra success repairs one "wound," one box from the Condition Monitor. Whether or not the medic program succeeds, it degrades each time it is used in the Matrix. The program rating can be restored by loading a fresh copy into active memory during a run.

Size: (Rating^2) x 4 Mp

Mirrors

The mirrors program adds its rating to the evasion attribute of the deck. The program is degradable, with the bonus reduced by 1 rating point per turn after it is triggered.

When placed in a frame, its rating becomes the effective Evasion Attribute Rating of the entire frame. See **Frames** below. The program rating can be restored by loading a fresh copy into active memory during a run.

Options: Link
Size: (Rating^2) x 3 Mp

Restore

The restore program rebuilds the temporary damage done to the MPCP by programs and IC such as acid, binder, blind, jammer, marker, poison, restrict, or reveal. To restore the rating of the persona program, make a Success Test pitting the rating of the restore against the rating of the program that did the damage.

PROGRAMS

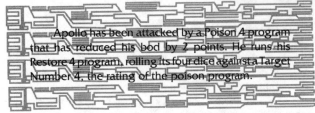

Apollo has been attacked by a Poison 4 program that has reduced his bod by 2 points. He runs his Restore 4 program, rolling its four dice against a Target Number 4, the rating of the poison program.

The extra successes from the test are used to restore the rating of the affected persona program. The persona program can only be restored back to its original rating.

The Success Test may not be augmented by dice from the Hacking Pool.

This program *does not* operate within a frame. See **Frames** below.

Size: (Rating^2) x 3 Mp

Shield

A shield program acts as auxiliary armor for the MPCP and its programs. The program automatically stops a number of wounds equal to its rating. A shield program degrades, losing 1 rating point every time it stops damage. The program rating can be restored by loading a fresh copy into active memory during a run.

Options: Link
Size: (Rating^2) x 4 Mp

Smoke

A smoke program simulates a burst of high-volume system activity, confusing perception around the decker. Executing a smoke program requires 1 Action, but no success test. Within a node, the smoke program's rating is added to every target number needed by anything in that node, including the decker's own tests. The program degrades, losing 1 point of rating every turn. The program can only be restored by shutting down and restarting the deck.

Options: Link, Mobility, One-Shot
Size: (Rating^2) x 2 Mp

SENSOR UTILITIES

Sensor utilities analyze data or other elements of the Matrix. Sensor programs can only be used when within Sensor Range, or closer, of the target. To utilize a sensor program, make a Success Test pitting the rating of the sensor program against a Target Number equal to the System Rating of the node. The Threshold dictated by the Security Code of the node must, as always, still be overcome.

Analyze

An analyze program analyzes constructs or nodes. If used against a node, mobile program, or frame, conduct a normal Sensor Success Test. If used against IC of any kind, conduct an Opposed Success Test. The IC uses its rating against the decker's sensor rating, while the decker uses the program's rating against the System Rating of the node. An analyze program will not reveal any information about another *persona*, but it will work against an IC construct or frame.

The extra successes from the Analyze Test determine how much information is gained.

	ANALYZE TEST TABLE
Successes	**Result**
1	Basic Information (Security Code of a node, base type of IC (the highest-rated part) in an IC construct, base type of program in a frame (largest size)
2	2nd-Level Information (System Rating of a node, next-highest rated section of an IC construct, next-largest program in a frame)
3+	3rd-Level Information (all IC or Programs present in an IC construct or frame)

Options: Link
Size: (Rating^2) x 3 Mp

Browse

A browse program scans the contents of datastores. The decker must specify the subject matter of his search. If the program is successful, the decker knows which files in the datastore contain references to that subject, and their sizes. He does not learn any details.

The browse program has a base time of 10 turns. Use the extra successes from the Success Test to reduce the base time.

Options: Link
Size: (Rating^2) Mp

Decrypt

A decrypt program defeats scramble IC. Scramble turns data into garbage if someone tries to access the information without knowing the right passcode. To resolve the use of decrypt, pit it in an Opposed Success Test against the scramble. The Target Number for the decrypt is the System Rating of the node, and it must still overcome the Security Code Threshold. The scramble pits its rating dice against a Target Number equal to the decrypt program's rating.

Failure to beat the scramble may trigger a passive alert. See **Scramble**, p. 19, in **Intrusion Countermeasures**.

Options: Link
Size: (Rating^2) x 2 Mp

PROGRAMS

Evaluate

An evaluate program is a complex expert system that scans datastores for any information that might be of value on the open market. The program rapidly becomes obsolete as the market changes.

If run successfully, make the Sensor Program Success Test mentioned above to see if the evaluate program finds any "paydata" files in the datastore. The evaluate program tells the decker how many valuable files are present and the size and market value of each. See **Installing Data Values**, page 158, **Shadowrun**, for the rules on placing "paydata" files.

Evaluate programs degrade, whether used or not. Reduce its rating by 1 every two weeks. If the gamemaster wishes, he can reduce it by 1 every 3D6 days, and not tell the decker until it is too late. If the decker wrote the evaluate program himself, he can upgrade it in the normal manner to counter the losses.

Options: Link
Size: (Rating^2) x 2 Mp

Scanner

The scanner program scans a node looking for other personas. The deck's sensor attribute also does this, but the sensor program cannot normally pierce a sleaze program. If another persona is not running a sleaze program, the sensor attribute will automatically detect its presence, though analyze will be required to identify an IC type.

When using a scanner program against a sleaze program, make an Opposed Success Test between the two. The Target Number for the scanner program's rating dice is the masking attribute of the deck. In return, the sleaze program uses its rating against the sensor attribute of the scanning deck. Remember, a persona must always worry about the Threshold Number of the node. If the test results in a tie, the presence of "something" is detected and the scanner program may be used again, at a +2 Target Number modifier.

Options: Link
Size: (Rating^2) x 3 Mp

Sift

As mentioned in **Computer Systems**, a decker can skim a number of Mp of data equal to his Intelligence Attribute Rating multiplied by 5 Mp per turn. The rating of the sift program adds to the decker's Intelligence Attribute for this purpose. The decker can "speed-read" by increasing the flow of data. The multiple by which the data flow is increased becomes the Target Number of a Perception Test to spot the data the decker is looking for.

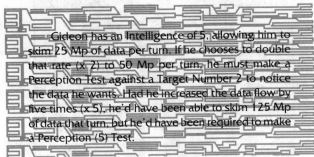

Gideon has an Intelligence of 5, allowing him to skim 25 Mp of data per turn. If he chooses to double that rate (x 2) to 50 Mp per turn, he must make a Perception Test against a Target Number 2 to notice the data he wants. Had he increased the data flow by five times (x 5), he'd have been able to skim 125 Mp of data that turn, but he'd have been required to make a Perception (5) Test.

Size: (Rating^2) Mp

MASKING UTILITIES

A masking utility changes a persona's profile in an attempt to persuade IC that the persona is either something else or not there at all. Masking utilities can only be used in Contact Range. To use the program requires an Opposed Success Test. The rating of the masking utility is rolled against a Target Number equal to the System Rating of the node (remember the Threshold!) if IC is involved, or the sensor rating of another persona. The opposition rolls its rating against the masking attribute of the persona. If the other participant is a persona, he rolls his scanner program rating against the target persona's masking attribute.

If the masking program wins, it protects the persona by concealing it. If the IC or another persona wins, the masking program has failed and the masked persona is revealed. In the case of a tie against IC, there is no result. The masked persona remains masked, but does not get past the IC. The decker may try again at a +2 to his Target Number.

In a tie with another persona, the other persona is aware of the masked persona's presence, but cannot specifically locate it. Both may try again.

Deception

A deception program generates counterfeit passcodes to deceive IC or other personas. These passcodes are logged, so the deception program does leave a trail of sorts. Deception can defeat access or probe IC, but not barrier IC or a scanner program.

Deception cannot be run simultaneously with a sleaze program.

Options: Link
Size: (Rating^2) x 2 Mp

Relocate

A relocate program defeats trace IC that tracks a decker back to his entry point in the Matrix. Make an Opposed Success Test, pitting the rating of the trace against the Masking Attribute of the deck. If a tie results, the decker may try relocate again, but at a +2 Target Modifier.

If the relocate program is successful, the IC will slip into an infinite loop and think it is still tracing the decker's signal until somebody resets it.

Options: Link
Size: (Rating^2) x 2 Mp

Sleaze

A sleaze program bypasses access IC, barrier IC, or a scanner program without leaving tracks. It cannot defeat probe IC, however. If the sleaze program is successful, the decker's persona becomes invisible to the IC. If the IC is already tracking the decker, the sleaze program cannot work unless the IC has lost sight of him for more than one turn. (See **Intrusion Countermeasures**, p. 18.)

If the decker remains in a node where he has successfully executed a sleaze program, he must re-sleaze the IC at a +1 Target Number every turn he remains.

Options: Link
Size: (Rating^2) x 3 Mp

OPERATION UTILITIES

Operation utilities are programs that run within the deck and have their primary impact there, with the exception of remote control. Where options are possible, they are listed with the individual program.

PROGRAMS

Auto Execute

Auto execute is a degradable utility that allows other utilities to be run in a node. When auto execute is running, the normal Execution Test is not necessary (see **Cybercombat**, p. 46). No additional benefit is gained, though the decker need not spend Hacking Pool dice to make the Execution Test.

The Auto Execute Rating is directly related to the System Rating of the node the decker is in. If the Auto Execute Rating is not equal to or greater than the System Rating, the decker operates under a target modifier equal to the difference in the ratings. Running Auto Execute 5 in a node with a System Rating 7, for example, gives the decker a +2 Target Number modifier.

The decker can avoid this by making a normal Execution Test and expending Hacking Pool dice.

Auto execute degrades at a rate of 1 point per week because corporations continually update their system software. Auto execute may be upgraded using the normal procedure.

The presence of auto execute is *required* in a frame. See **Frames** below.
Options: Link
Size: (Rating^2) Mp

Compressor

The compressor utility compresses programs in storage memory, thereby reducing their size, then decompresses them upon transfer to active memory. Program size is reduced by 50 percent when in storage; a program normally 100 Mp in size, for example, requires only 50 Mp of space when compressor is running in active memory. The effective load speed of the deck, however, is reduced by 50 percent when transferring compressed programs to active memory. It would, therefore, take a deck with a 20 Mp/turn load speed five turns to transfer a program that has been compressed to 50 Mp. When in active memory, the program resumes its original size.

The maximum size program that compressor can compress is equal to its rating multiplied by 100 Mp. Files and programs may be compressed in either storage memory or offline storage, but they cannot be compressed before downloading from a system. Compressor is required to uncompress them. Compressor will run on a personal computer.
Size: (Rating^2) x 2 Mp

Controller

Controller is the program that allows deckers control over dumb frames they have created (see **Frames**, p. 44).

The maximum number of dumb frames that the decker can command is equal to one-half the rating of the controller utility, rounded down. Smart frames do not require controller.
Size: (Rating^2) x 4 Mp

PROGRAMMING

To design a program, make a Success Test against a Target Number equal to the rating of the program. Divide any extra successes rolled into the base time for designing the program to determine how long it actually takes in days.

Like cyberdeck design and construction, programming can be done in stages. A few days here, a few days there, a couple of weeks here—it doesn't matter. Once the total expended time equals the actual program design time, the program is done. If the decker is Seriously injured, he cannot get any work done. If Moderately wounded, he must work 2 days to decrease the time required by 1 day. Light injuries are of no consequence.

To upgrade a program, a decker must first have the master source code, which he would have if the program was his design. Programs that are purchased "off the shelf" commercially, or through a fixer or another decker, have already been compiled into program code. (Compiling converts the simple programming-languages commands of the source code into the complex machine command language the deck uses.) Without that source code, the program cannot be upgraded. To determine how long it will take to upgrade, subtract the calculated base time for the new rating from the base time for the old rating. The desired rating of the program, however, is what becomes the Target Number for the Computer Success Test.

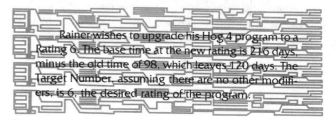

Rainer wishes to upgrade his Hog 4 program to a Rating 6. The base time at the new rating is 216 days, minus the old time of 98, which leaves 120 days. The Target Number, assuming there are no other modifiers, is 6, the desired rating of the program.

Versions of many programs are available, but at a cost. The table below shows the street costs of various types of programs, as well as their availability. When attempting to acquire a program, follow the procedure under **Buying Decks** in the **Cyberdeck** section. But don't let anyone find out you've risked your butt trying to get someone else's tech.

PROGRAMS

CREATING PROGRAMS

Base Time:	Size x 2 days
Cook Time (Persona programs only):	Rating x 3 days
Appropriate Skill:	Design: Computer Cook: Computer B/R
Skill Target:	Rating
Required Tools:	Personal computer or better (requires minimum memory equal to size of program being worked on) Appropriate-size memory for storage
Upgrading:	Use the desired rating for the target number, difference in base time for Base Time
Limits:	Maximum rating equal to designer's Computer Theory Rating

Persona	Size (in Mp)
Bod	(Rating^2) x 3
Evasion	(Rating^2) x 3
Masking	(Rating^2) x 2
Sensors	(Rating^2) x 2

Utility	Size (in Mp)
Analyze	(Rating^2) x 3
Armor	(Rating^2) x 3
Attack	(Rating^2) x 2
Auto Exec	Rating^2
Blind	(Rating^2) x 3
Browse	(Rating^2)
Cloak	(Rating^2) x 3
Compressor	(Rating^2) x 2
Controller	(Rating^2) x 4
Deception	(Rating^2) x 2
Decrypt	Rating^2
Evaluate	(Rating^2) x 2
Hog	(Rating^2) x 3
Medic	(Rating^2) x 4
Mirrors	(Rating^2) x 3
Poison	(Rating^2) x 3
Relocate	(Rating^2) x 2
Restore	(Rating^2) x 3
Restrict	(Rating^2) x 3
Reveal	(Rating^2) x 3
Scanner	(Rating^2) x 3
Shield	(Rating^2) x 4
Sift	Rating^2
Sleaze	(Rating^2) x 3
Slow	(Rating^2) x 4
Smoke	(Rating^2) x 2

BUYING PROGRAMS

STREET UTILITIES

Rating	Cost	Availability
1–3	Size x 100¥	2
4–6	Size x 200¥	4
7–9	Size x 500¥	8
10+	Size x 1,000¥	16

PERSONA PROGRAMS

Rating	Cost	Availability
1–3	Size x 100¥	3
4–6	Size x 500¥	6
7–9	Size x 1,000¥	12
10+	Size x 5,000¥	24

SIZE TABLES

(Rating^2)	Size	(Rating^2)x2	Size
1	1	1	2
2	4	2	8
3	9	3	18
4	16	4	32
5	25	5	50
6	36	6	72
7	49	7	98
8	64	8	128
9	81	9	162
10	100	10	200

(Rating^2)x3	Size	(Rating^2)x4	Size
1	3	1	4
2	12	2	16
3	27	3	36
4	48	4	64
5	75	5	100
6	108	6	144
7	147	7	196
8	192	8	256
9	243	9	324
10	300	10	400

PROGRAMS

OPTIONS

Options are modifications to a program's basic code structure that make it perform a little differently than its initial design. Some options allow the program to do different things, while others make it better at doing one thing, trading off the capability in another. The use of program options means that the decker must make careful tactical decisions about which programs to carry, based on what he expects to confront. And if he guesses wrong…

OPTION NOTES

First, a warning. The use of options dramatically increases the complexity of programs. Their use requires greater familiarity with the rules because the interaction between programs and options is rather intricate. The gamemaster should think carefully before using them in his **Shadowrun** game. He is also free to modify these rules as necessary.

When layering options, add in any straight rating increases before applying any percentage increase. For example, if the options would require increases of +2 and +3 to the effective rating of the program and a 50 percent increase, apply the +2 and +3 and then increase the total by 50 percent.

Note also that any increases in the effective rating do not affect the limitation on the maximum rating of programs the decker can design, that being his Computer Skill. Any increases of the effective rating beyond that maximum are fine, as long as the rating for the base program does not exceed that maximum.

Area-Effect

This option allows the distribution of the effects of combat programs over an area, rather than at a single target. Each rating point of the program allows an additional target. Each must be hit separately, using the normal **Cybercombat** rules.

To determine the size of the program with the area-effect option, add the Area-Effect Rating to the program rating. The Target Number for designing a program with the area-effect option is also equal to the Area-Effect Rating plus the actual rating of the program.

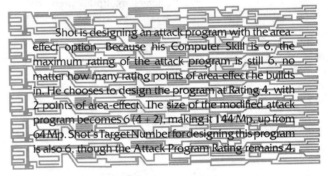

Shot is designing an attack program with the area-effect option. Because his Computer Skill is 6, the maximum rating of the attack program is still 6, no matter how many rating points of area-effect he builds in. He chooses to design the program at Rating 4, with 2 points of area-effect. The size of the modified attack program becomes 6 (4 + 2), making it 144 Mp, up from 64 Mp. Shot's Target Number for designing this program is also 6, though the Attack Program Rating remains 4.

A program with the area-effect option is less effective when used against the persona's bod attribute, or when the targeted IC has hardened defense. In both cases, increase the appropriate Target Number by +2. It operates normally against the evasion attribute and negates the effects of shifting defense in IC.

PROGRAMS

A program cannot target the same opponent more than once per use, and all the targets must be within the same node within Contact Range of the decker.

The area-effect option is incompatible with the penetration option.

The shield program is twice as effective against an area-effect attack. Double the number of wounds it deflects when area-effect is used. It still degrades normally.

Link

The link option permits use of a program in a frame construct. See **Frames**, p. 44.

Mobility

The mobility option gives a program the ability to maneuver independently of the decker. The decker retains command of the program, but suffers a +1 to his target numbers for every mobile program he commands during an Action. The decker issues all orders to mobile programs before he declares his Actions. The decker may resolve the effects of his actions and programs in any order he chooses.

Mobile programs must usually remain within Sensor Range of the deck at all times. They will not proceed beyond that range. If the decker shifts position so that one or more mobile programs move beyond Sensor Range, those programs immediately move to remain in Sensor Range with him. If unable to accomplish this for some reason, they crash completely. The program will have to be re-loaded from storage memory.

The only mobile program that can continue to exist beyond Sensor Range of the deck that generated it is mobile smoke. The decker can drop mobile smoke in a node that he is passing through. Once out of Sensor Range of the controlling deck, however, it will no longer move, remaining stationary in the node until it degrades away. Once the smoke program has degraded away, the entire program ceases to be.

Technically, the mobile option creates a single-slot frame, though not all the programs suitable to placement in a frame can use the mobility option. Mobile programs and frames are self-maintaining viral constructs. Complex beasts, indeed.

The mobility option increases the size of a program by 50 percent (round off). The target number for the design of the program is also increased by 50 percent (round off).

A mobile program will continue to exist until crashed or cancelled (deactivated).

Mobile programs have a Load Rating equal to their final size, divided by 100, rounded up.

When attacked, mobile programs are viewed as having a bod and MPCP of 1. Okay, so they're not real sturdy. You want everything?

One-Shot

The one-shot option is for use with any program, turning it into a smaller, single-use version. Use it once and it's gone from active memory. The size of the program with this option is reduced considerably, but it is difficult to design.

The one-shot option reduces the size of programs to 25 percent their usual size.

For design purposes, increase the effective rating by 50 percent (rounded up).

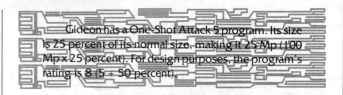

Gideon has a One-Shot Attack 5 program. Its size is 25 percent of its normal size, making it 25 Mp (100 Mp x 25 percent). For design purposes, the program's rating is 8 (5 + 50 percent).

A one-shot program will simply do as it was intended, and then cease to be. If it is a degradable utility, it will continue to exist until degraded away.

Penetration

The penetration option is for attack programs, increasing their effectiveness against shield programs and IC with hardened defense. Shield programs become only half as effective (round down), and the effect of hardened defense is neutralized.

When used against a persona's evasion attribute or against shifting defense in IC, the appropriate Target Number is increased by +2.

To determine the size of a program with the penetration option, increase the program's rating by +2.

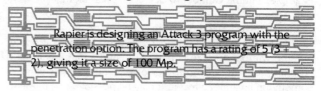

Rapier is designing an Attack 3 program with the penetration option. The program has a rating of 5 (3 + 2), giving it a size of 100 Mp.

Staging

The staging option works exclusively with attack programs. When the staging option is not present, an attack program will inflict a number of wounds of damage equal to the extra successes rolled in the Opposed Combat Test.

The staging option allows the program to generate a base damage, regardless of the number of extra successes rolled. All that is necessary to inflict the base damage is one success.

The four levels of staging are: Light, Moderate, Serious, and Deadly. Light staging has a base damage of one wound; Moderate staging, three wounds; Serious, six wounds; and Deadly, ten wounds. This base damage is in addition to the damage done through extra successes, which remains at a one-to-one ratio (1 extra success equals 1 wound).

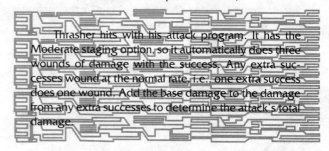

Thrasher hits with his attack program. It has the Moderate staging option, so it automatically does three wounds of damage with the success. Any extra successes wound at the normal rate, i.e., one extra success does one wound. Add the base damage to the damage from any extra successes to determine the attack's total damage.

Base damage occurs only if the player rolls a success. If he rolls *no* successes, no damage is done.

For purposes of determining the size of the program and the target number for its design, attack programs with the staging option increase their effective rating. The actual rating remains the same. To determine the effective rating, add the appropriate modifier to the rating, as follows:

Light	+1	Serious	+3
Moderate	+2	Deadly	+5

PROGRAMS

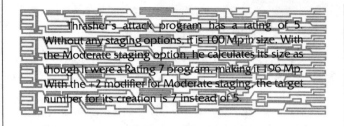

Thrasher's attack program has a rating of 5. Without any staging options, it is 100 Mp in size. With the Moderate staging option, he calculates its size as though it were a Rating 7 program, making it 196 Mp. With the +2 modifier for Moderate staging, the target number for its creation is 7 instead of 5.

FRAMES (OPTIONAL RULE)

Frames are viral-construct frameworks that allow multiple programs to maneuver and operate separately from the deck that launched them. They are self-maintaining and may perform tasks and functions according to the operating instructions the designer created.

A frame contains one or more programs in nearly any combination. Its capabilities depend solely on the capabilities of the programs it contains. Without an attack program, for example, a frame cannot attack unless it has another program that performs a similar function. Without a scanner program, it cannot detected masked personas, and so on.

As no program exists to increase a deck's sensor attribute, a frame without analyze is *blind to IC* and a frame without a scanner program is *blind to personas*. If the frame is blind to something, it cannot affect it. It may be possible for a frame to exist and operate without scanner, but not analyze.

The ratings of programs like armor, cloak, and mirrors translate directly into the equivalent attribute rating for the frame. An Armor 3 program, for example, would give the frame the equivalent of Bod 3 and so on. If the program is not present, the frame is assumed to have an Attribute Rating of 1 in that area.

Frames are always assumed to have an equivalent MPCP Rating of 1. This can never be changed. Frames ignore relevant MPCP restrictions.

FRAME TYPES

The two types of frames are dumb frames and smart frames. Dumb frames require continual control by the decker, though they can operate in a node other than the one in which the decker is currently located. Dumb frames require the controller program, which links the decker and the frame.

Dumb Frames

The greater the number of nodes away the dumb frame is from the decker, the harder it is to control it. To simulate this, apply a target modifier equal to the number of nodes between the frame and the decker. If the frame is in the same node as the decker, no modifier applies, but if it is three nodes away, the decker gets a +3 target modifier for all success tests involving the frame.

To control a dumb frame, the decker must expend an Action. If the decker wishes the dumb frame to perform *exactly the same activity* as the last time the decker commanded it, the decker may instruct it to continue its activity without expending an Action. The dumb frame will then perform exactly the same activity it did last action, with no deviation. If, say, the frame's last command was to attack a piece of IC, the decker may tell it to continue to do so without having to expend another Action. If, however, he wishes to change what the frame is doing, he must expend an Action.

Multiple frames may be commanded as a group. To issue one set of commands to more than one frame requires the expenditure of only one Action, as long as those commands are exactly the same. The same holds for the instruction to continue.

Smart Frames

The far more independent smart frames are able to perform multiple or layered commands. The controller program is not necessary. Declare the operating instructions for a smart frame when the frame is created. Those commands may be altered if the decker expends an Action and the frame is within Sensor Range.

COMMANDING SMART FRAMES

The player simply tells the gamemaster, in plain English, what the frame's mission is. That's it. No fancy command languages or syntax. Computers in 2050 are beyond that. They're told what to do and they do it, as long as it is within their capability. The gamemaster should resist the temptation to twist a player's words against him. (It is not necessary to overlook blatant mistakes, conflicts, or contradictions, but neither is deliberately making things difficult.) The character knows what he's doing, even if the player occasionally does not.

Smart Frame Capabilities

If a task is immediately within the capability of one of the programs in a frame, the frame can do it. Frames are inherently mobile, so it is not necessary to build the mobility option into any programs in a frame. A frame cannot download or copy files, nor perform system operations of any kind. Beyond that, its capabilities are defined by the operational instructions.

A frame is not intelligent, by any stretch of the imagination. It can only make a decision if given predetermined criteria to deal with a particular situation. For example, the frame is confronted by three IC mobile constructs, all of them hostile. It can only decide which to attack if its operational instructions specify random choice, or attacking the IC with the highest rating, or maybe running away and trying to sleaze.

This can get complicated, especially with so many possible decision-points during a run. Indeed, the gamemaster could sit there and run the frame through all the details of its mission, taking as long as needed, then tell the decker what happened. This is not necessary, however, because what happened during every moment of the frame's mission is less important than the results.

The purpose of the game is to tell a story, not to simulate some artificial reality through dice-rolling. (That can be fun, too, but sometimes it just gets in the way.) For game purposes, let the smart frame go off and either do what it's supposed to, or fail to, or perform somewhere in between.

The Fast Matrix Resolution System on p. 49 is recommended for resolving the activity of smart frames when they are outside the decker's control. With only one or two die rolls, the gamemaster can resolve smart-frame activity and learn the results. He can then use that knowledge to continue weaving the story for maximum dramatic effect. Say, for example, that the result indicates that the frame does what it is supposed to, but barely escapes intact. Great. The decker sends the frame off and waits. And waits. And waits. And just when he's given up hope, it crawls back, victorious, but only within a code-line of crashing. Or maybe it doesn't come back at all. The point is that the gamemaster can determine this easily without spending most of the game session rolling dice and counting wounds.

PROGRAMS

BUILDING A FRAME

Smart frames and dumb frames are built in the same manner, with one simple difference at the end of the design for smart frames.

The decker must first determine what programs the frame will carry. Any program with the link option can go into a frame. These programs can be in their base form or with any options of which they are capable. Don't bother designing mobility into them, however, because frames are inherently mobile.

Having chosen all the programs, total up their sizes to determine the base size of the frame. Increase this amount by 10 percent (rounding up) to represent the code necessary for the frame itself. If the frame is smart, increase the size by another 20 percent (rounding up). That's it. That final number is the size of the frame.

To design the frame, create each program separately. With minor modification, existing programs can be incorporated into a frame. Those modifications, in fact, are factored into the design of the frame.

Base Time: Size/10 days
Skill Required: Computer
Target Number: Size/100 (round up, minimum 2)
Required Tools: Personal Computer or better (minimum memory required equal to size of program being worked on)
Appropriate-size memory for storage
Upgrade: (New Value) – (Old Value)
Limits: None

A particular frame is designed for a precise group of programs. If any of those programs change in any way, including upgrading or option changes, the frame must be upgraded accordingly.

Frames have a Load Rating equal to their final size, divided by 100, rounded up.

Frames must be constructed prior to a run and then placed in memory. They are usually placed in storage memory, then copied into active memory just before being launched. It is possible to use the compress utility to effectively reduce a frame's size.

CYBERCOMBAT

"It's the ultimate wiz-thrill. There ain't nothin' holding you back, e'cept your imagination."
—Flashfire, decker

ybercombat operates using the same turn structure as a normal Combat Turn. Turns and Actions are resolved in sequence, based on Initiative, whether or not the characters involved are in the physical world, astral space, or the Matrix.

INITIATIVE

Multiple actions are determined exactly as in normal combat.

Deckers roll 1D6 and add it to their Reaction Attribute, just like characters in the physical world. Magical or cyberware reflex and reaction enhancements, e.g., wired or boosted reflexes and the like, do **not** add to Reaction or Initiative while the character is in the Matrix. Ever. Deckers with Increased Response in their decks may add +2 per level of Response to their Reaction Attribute, and roll an extra 1D6 per level for Initiative.

Deckers who wish to run under pure cybernetic command, sans keyboard, receive an extra die for Initiative. They also receive other modifiers, as noted elsewhere. Deckers running a combination of cyber-command and keyboard determine Initiative normally. Characters running on pure keyboard, with no cybernetic connection *at all*, halve their Reaction Attribute (round down, minimum of 1). They still get to roll a 1D6 Initiative die, however. Decks with no cybernetic link receive only the Initiative die increase from Response Increase, but no Reaction Attribute Increase. Users with only keyboards (better known as tortoises) also receive modifiers, as discussed elsewhere.

Running naked in the Matrix qualifies as pure cybernetic command.

IC Reaction is based on the node the IC is currently in and its own rating. Add the IC Rating to the number given for the Security Code of the node, listed below. IC also receives a 1D6 Initiative die.

CYBERCOMBAT

IC REACTION RATING	
Security Code	**Reaction**
Blue	Not Applicable (no IC)
Green	5 + Rating
Orange	7 + Rating
Red	9 + Rating

Constructs figure their Reaction from the lowest IC Rating in the construct.

MATRIX MOVEMENT

The only time a decker's movement through the Matrix is impeded is when he must pause to use a program. If he's moving through the telecommunications network as a legal signal, bouncing from LTG to RTG and back again, it takes him only one Action (about three seconds) to get where he wants to go. If, however, he's sleazing or deceiving his way around the world, he will have to pause and spend an Action (to use the program) in every LTG/RTG SAN through which he passes.

The same holds true within a computer system. A decker may move unimpeded as long as he encounters no IC that must be dealt with (access, barrier, probe, or gray or black IC). This means that with one Action, he may move from node to node, unrestricted, until he hits IC.

Movement is free because it does not cost an Action. The decker need only spend an Action when he wants to do something specific, such as using a program, conducting a system operation, or doing something in the deck. During a Combat Turn sequence, resolve actions before or after movement, not during, even though the operation involved is in progress the whole time, as far as the story goes.

If a decker rolls three more successes than was required to deal completely and conclusively with some IC, he may continue to move through the system as part of the same Action. This would be three extra successes beyond what was necessary to deceive or sleaze IC, or three extra successes beyond those needed to crash or slow IC.

When entering a node, the decker must declare if he is in Observation Range, Sensor Range, or Contact Range. He may declare any of these positions and need not move through them in order. Again, the decker's motion is stopped only when he fails to deal conclusively with IC, with three or more extra successes remaining.

For more on ranges, see **Perception in the Matrix**, p. 109, **Shadowrun**. The one exception is that a deck at Sensor Range does not add its load rating to the current load of the node it is examining. The load rating of the deck is added only when the deck moves to Contact Range.

IC moving within its home system is never impeded by a node, unless its movement is blocked by something like a persona or program frame. In someone else's system (hot pursuit or corporate warfare), IC is treated as if it were a persona, with the same movement limitations as a persona.

ENTERING COMBAT

All the participants of a combat must be within Contact Range of one another. Any participant may initiate combat, with the exception that IC or corporate deckers must have verified that an intruding signal is illegal before they can attack it. See **Avoiding Combat** below. IC must be activated before it can attack or be attacked. If it has not been activated, it cannot be harmed, even though a deck's Sensor attribute may recognize its presence.

EXECUTING A UTILITY

Not long ago, it was necessary to execute utilities manually, their codes modified to match the idiosyncratic properties of individual nodes and system software. The auto execute program handles that now. No Execution Tests are necessary.

If the auto execute program is not present, execute utilities manually, per the rules on pages 107 and 112 of **Shadowrun**. See also the description of the auto execute program, on p. 39 of this book.

Programs may still be executed manually, if the decker really wants to.

MULTIPLE PROGRAMS, MULTIPLE TARGETS

A decker may activate as many programs as he chooses as his Action. He may also allocate his Hacking Pool as he chooses. He could, for example, launch an attack program and a slow program at the same target with one Action. The attacks would be combined into one attack, with an effective rating equal to the lowest-rated program in the attack. Allocate Hacking Pool dice normally. This is an all-or-nothing proposition. If the attack fails, all the programs fail. If it succeeds, they all succeed, with the extra successes applying equally to all the programs.

If the attack is directed against another persona, all the programs must use the same persona attribute as their target. It is not possible to mix bod- and evasion-targeted programs.

Only programs that have the area-effect option can engage multiple targets, as per those rules.

AVOIDING COMBAT

A decker may attempt to avoid combat or to disengage from current combat. He can avoid combat simply by staying out of it, moving to another node as soon as IC makes its presence known, and so on.

IC may, and most probably will, pursue a fleeing decker. If the decker remains within one node of the node where the IC is located, the IC automatically knows he is there. Remember, one node away constitutes Observation Range. If the decker is able to move two or more nodes away, he may use his masking attribute and utilities to escape. When the IC pursues, make a Success Test using the IC's Rating against the deck's masking attribute. If successful, the IC knows exactly where the decker went, and attempts to move there. If the test fails, the IC has lost the trail. It will then begin to cruise slowly through the system, looking for the decker node by node. When multiple paths lead from a node, the IC must randomly choose which path to take.

Once pursuit has been broken and the decker is located by IC again, he may sleaze or deceive the IC as normal.

CYBERCOMBAT

RESOLVING COMBAT

Personas, individual IC, IC constructs, and program frames all have Condition Modifiers for keeping track of their current damage status. As they become wounded, they receive various Reaction and Target Number Modifiers appropriate to their "injured" status.

Certain combat programs and IC do no wound damage, but have different effects. Consult the specific program's description for the appropriate rules.

HITTING A PERSONA

Attack-capable programs or IC have a designated target, which is the persona attribute that is used as the Target Number for the attack. Make a Resisted Success Test using the rating of the IC or program against that Target Number. A simple success is all that is necessary. The persona then makes a Resistance Test using the MPCP Rating of the deck against a Target Number equal to the Computer Skill of the other decker, or the System Rating of the node if the attack came from IC.

The decker can augment his results by adding dice from his Hacking Pool, either as attacker or defender. If the defender's successes equal or exceed the attacker's successes, no damage is done. If the attacker generated the greater net successes, those net successes are used to determine the effect of the attack.

If the persona has a shield program running, it reduces the final damage by the rating of the program. This only works against killer IC or an attack program. Various options may modify the result; consult **Options** and **Killer IC**, respectively.

The Hardening Rating of the deck also reduces the final damage that blaster or killer IC or attack programs can do.

All damage is recorded on the MPCP Condition Monitor. Ten "wounds" crash the MPCP and dump the decker. Only blaster IC permanently damages the MPCP. All other MPCP damage can be repaired by a medic program or by restarting the deck (turning it off and then on again, which re-sets all the systems).

Use this same procedure for attacks against program frames. If the frame does not include an armor or mirrors program, it is assumed to have a minimum Attribute Rating of 1 in that area, for defensive purposes only. The MPCP-equivalent of a frame is always 1.

HITTING IC

Attacks against IC are now resolved using an *Opposed Success Test*, when applicable. If the IC has no attack capability, then make an Unresisted Test. See the special case described below for IC constructs. Note also that this only involves attacks, not attempts to use deception, sleaze, or slow programs against the IC.

The attacker pits the rating of the program against a Target Number equal to the system rating of the current node. The IC counterattacks using its rating against its appropriate target, either the Bod or Evasion attribute of the deck. The decker must still overcome the Threshold of the node. Any successes he has remaining are compared against the successes generated by the IC. The side with the greater number of successes damages the other. Damage is based on the net successes generated.

If the IC is actually an IC construct, the effective rating of the construct is equal to the lowest-rated IC in the construct. The potential effect of the counterattack is based on the damage done by *one* of the combat-capable IC in the construct. The gamemaster decides which.

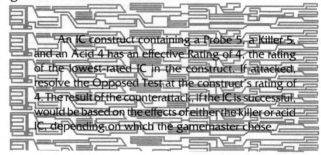

An IC construct containing a Probe 5, a Killer 5, and an Acid 4 has an effective Rating of 4, the rating of the lowest-rated IC in the construct. If attacked, resolve the Opposed Test at the construct's rating of 4. The result of the counterattack, if the IC is successful, would be based on the effects of either the killer or acid IC, depending on which the gamemaster chose.

When the IC or IC construct takes ten "wounds," it crashes.

IC SUPPRESSION

IC that has crashed must be suppressed to stop it from triggering an active alert on its next Action. What is happening is that each node has simple sub-routines that monitor the status of IC in the node. When IC crashes, the sub-routine notices and triggers an alert. The decker can prevent this by allocating one of his Hacking Pool dice to suppressing the alert. The IC remains suppressed as long as the Hacking Pool die remains allocated to that task. Every time the Hacking Pool refreshes, the die must be allocated again or the IC is no longer suppressed and an alert is triggered. While allocated for suppression, the Hacking Pool die cannot be used for anything else. The decker may recall the die from suppression and return it to the Hacking Pool at any time. Any IC that is no longer suppressed will trigger an alert at the end of that turn.

If a construct crashes, only one die need be allocated for the entire construct.

If more than one IC in a node crashes and is suppressed, the decker may, at the cost of an Action, effectively group all the IC together so that he need only allocate one die for the entire group.

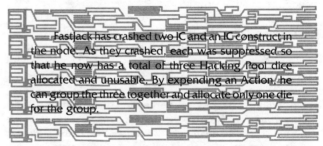

Fastjack has crashed two IC and an IC construct in the node. As they crashed, each was suppressed so that he now has a total of three Hacking Pool dice allocated and unusable. By expending an Action, he can group the three together and allocate only one die for the group.

Even if the decker leaves the node, he must continue to allocate Hacking Pool dice to keep the IC suppressed. Suppressing IC only delays the inevitable alert. The CPU controlling a cluster periodically sends out a system inquiry to learn the status of all the IC. IC that has been suppressed cannot respond to the inquiry. When that occurs, a Passive Alert is declared.

CPUs send out system inquiry commands at irregular intervals, based on the security code of the CPU. When a piece of IC is first suppressed, roll the dice indicated below. The result indicates the number of turns before the next system inquiry is sent out.

CYBERCOMBAT

SYSTEM INQUIRY INTERVAL	
Security Code	Turns
Blue	Not applicable (No IC)
Green	4D6
Orange	3D6
Red	2D6

SIMSENSE OVERLOAD

Whenever a deck takes persona/MPCP damage that gets recorded on the Condition Monitor, a slight chance exists that the decker will also take some damage from the simsense overload. To better facilitate cybernetic command, many of the limiters and cut-outs of a normal simsense signal are reduced or eliminated in a cyberdeck to "heighten" the experience. To sharpen the edge, as it were. When the MPCP takes damage, the simsense signal spikes slightly.

When the MPCP takes damage, the decker must make a Willpower Resistance Test against a Target Number equal to the number of "wounds" the MPCP took. If the test succeeds, he takes no damage. If he fails, he takes a Light Stun Wound.

If the decker is running purely on a cybernetic level, with no keyboard, he receives a +2 to the Target Number he must beat in the Resistance Test.

If the decker is running without the cybernetic link (a tortoise), the problem does not exist. No cyberlink means no simsense overload is possible.

If anyone is connected to the deck via a hitcher jack, he must also make a Resistance Test, but against a Target Number equal to one-half (round down) the number of "wounds" of MPCP damage taken. Again, only a Light Stun wound is taken.

FAST RESOLUTION SYSTEM

It is not always necessary to fully game a long, involved Matrix run to gain an important (but not crucial) bit of data. Say, for example, that the runners learn that someone may be flying out of Seattle-Tacoma airport in the next few days and they want to know his flight number. With more than 20 airlines, large and small, operating out of Sea-Tac, it would be foolish to make a run against each one.

In this case, use the fast resolution system instead. Because the system may be too abstract for some tastes, the gamemaster always has the option of fleshing it out or modifying it.

The gamemaster must first quantify the difficulties the decker will face in obtaining the needed information. This is entirely up to the gamemaster, but should be based on the Skill Success Table, p. 55 of **Shadowrun**. This number should be kept secret.

Then, the decker must decide which programs will be in the deck's active memory during the run. This program selection can be as typical or atypical as the decker wishes. No program-swapping is possible during the run, however. What gets loaded now becomes an average of sorts for the run.

The deck's load rating is now calculated and *added to the difficulty number the gamemaster generated*. What this means is that the higher the deck's load, the greater the difficulty. There is a trade-off, though, as we shall see.

Now make an Opposed Success Test. The gamemaster rolls a number of dice equal to the adjusted difficulty (original difficulty plus the Load Rating) against a Target Number equal to the decker's Computer Skill. The decker rolls a number of dice equal to the Maximum MPCP Rating of his deck (not the number to which he has shifted it to reduce his load rating), plus the maximum load rating of the deck's active memory (assuming it is full of programs) against a Target Number equal to the original difficulty.

> Zaibatsu is doing a run. His deck has an MPCP of 6 and is running 200 Mp of programs in active memory. His deck, therefore, has a load rating of 5 [6 ÷ 2 = 3, + 2 (200 ÷ 100)]. The gamemaster has set the difficulty for the run at 5, which is Challenging. Zaibatsu's Computer Skill is 6.
>
> The gamemaster will be rolling 10 dice (5 for the difficulty, plus 5 for the load rating of the deck) against a Target Number 6, Zaibatsu's Computer Skill. In opposition, Zaibatsu will roll 9 dice (6 for his Max MPCP, plus 3 for the maximum load rating of the active memory) against a Target Number of 5 (the original difficulty). It's going to be very close.
>
> Let's say Zaibatsu pares down his deck and reduces the load rating. He will be running at minimum MPCP (1), which means he can only address 50 Mp of active memory, which he will fill up. That makes his Load Rating a 2.
>
> So, the gamemaster will now roll 7 dice against a 6 (Computer Skill), while Zaibatsu is rolling the same 9 dice (6 for the Max MPCP, plus 3 for the Active Memory Load Rating) against a Target Number of 5. Better odds.

The example above might seem to imply that it is better to run with a lean deck. That is generally true, except when the decker gets caught.

If the decker generates the higher number of successes, he gains the information. The number of extra successes determines how much information he gains.

If the number of successes is the same, roll again! (Tougher than you thought, eh, chummer?)

If the system (the gamemaster) wins, the decker fails in his attempt. He can try again, but must increase the difficulty by 2 if the attempt occurs within 24 hours. Runs like this generally take 20 to 30 minutes of "real time."

The decker sustains no damage if he fails, because damage received under the fast resolution system should be considered temporary and repairable. Under special circumstances the gamemaster may wish to assign reasonable damage based on the number of extra successes generated against the decker.

Only use the fast resolution system when the information gained, not the run itself, is important to the story. Go ahead and game it if either the data or the run are crucial.

MATRIX REALITIES

"By taking a non-existent space, and through technology, allowing interaction within it, people are able to create their own universe."
—*Early virtual reality press release, by Zapper's Dad*

VIRTUAL REALITY

The Matrix might be compared to a video game that it is possible to inhabit. A decker doesn't just watch it on a television screen and control it with some sort of hand gadget, *he is in* it. It exists three-dimensionally around him. He can hear it, smell it, taste it, touch it, and of course see it. He is the figure bouncing, dodging, leaping, and most of all *living* in the game.

That's the Matrix. That's virtual reality.

Well, okay, not exactly, but it puts us on the right track. Virtual realities are computer-generated realities that the user participates in through some form of interface. The simplest form of interface is a keyboard or some kind of hand-control and a video screen. In this rudimentary form, the user is limited to two-dimensional visual input and some auditory, but the other three senses are lost. (That video game or computer game that some people play when they're not playing **Shadowrun** is a very limited virtual reality. Players can only do what the rules of the game allow. Of course, the more possibilities the rules offer, the more sophisticated the virtual reality.)

The Matrix and other virtual realities in the year 2050 use more sophisticated interface methods. Through the development of simsense (simulated senses) technology, a participant experiences virtual reality to the fullest extent. Simsense gear creates and imposes artificial sensory impressions directly into the user's brain. Instead of taking the sensory stimulation in the normal manner (odors through the nose, noise through the ears), the brain accepts the simsense impression *as if it were coming into the brain in the normal manner*. A sophisticated simsense impression of a flower's scent is indistinguishable from the original.

In the Matrix, the decker perceives the computer-generated virtual reality exclusively through simsense impressions. The Matrix-reality seems as real as the "real world" because the cyberdeck and its simsense hardware feed the decker's brain all the sensory impressions he expects to receive. He can see the Matrix, touch it, taste it, smell it, and hear it. The flow of simsense

MATRIX REALITIES

impressions overrides the true sensory input from the real world. The decker no longer feels himself seated in his chair, no longer smells the soycaf steaming near him on the desk, doesn't see the room around him, and can't hear the soft tread of footsteps approaching from behind. Right then, the only reality that exists for him is the Matrix. There is nothing else and it's as real as anything can be. (For more on the sensory overrides imposed on a decker, see **Sensory Cut-Outs** below.)

The Matrix is a virtual reality whose laws are nearly as complex as the laws that control the real world, but the laws are fewer. This is what attracts many individuals to a virtual reality, the limits on the options the reality can allow. Because the laws of this universe are limited, the value of the participant is increased tremendously. Everyone knows the laws and the extremes of what they can and cannot do. The laws are simple enough that everyone can grasp them equally. Everything else being equal, the deciding factor becomes what the participant brings to the reality. No longer lost in a maze of laws, he or she is the driving force, the element that matters most.

APPLIED

The **Shadowrun** Matrix game system defines the laws of the Matrix virtual reality. Those are the rules. That's it. Nothing else matters.

Everything else is just a metaphor, a figure of speech that relates the attributes of one thing to another, unrelated thing.

In the Matrix, the appearance and actions of *absolutely everything* is a metaphor for what is actually occurring. A decker who dodges the searing energy blast fired from the shoulder of the battle-armored guardian of the node isn't really doing that at all. His deck is engaged in a war of program codes and loose energy with the computer system that controls the node. The node and its security systems attempt to command the cyberdeck to do something, while at the same time the deck is trying to block the effort. The decker experiences the metaphor of this. He dodges (the deck successfully blocks the command attempt) the searing energy blast (the command attempt) emitted by the battle-armored guardian (the node's security system). At no time is any actual energy blast generated, nor does the decker really dodge. What he experiences, through the simsense interface, is a metaphor for the interaction of the decker's cyberdeck and the computer system with which it is in conflict.

The fact that the IC appears as a battle-armored warrior and its attack as a searing energy blast for the decker to dodge *are irrelevant to what has occurred*. The IC could have appeared as a flashing swirl of prismatic light, its attack as nothing at all, and the decker's reaction as anything else. The tastes, odors, feel, sounds, and sights of the Matrix have no relationship to the actual interaction of the systems involved. Maybe the IC's first attack appeared as a blast of energy. Its next attack could appear as a brace of missiles rocketing from a pair of hip packs. Both the energy blast and the missile volley are representative of the same thing, the actual "attack" by the program, but they appear as different things. Both attacks are resolved identically, using the standard rules, though the appearance—the metaphor—for those attacks is radically different.

What this means is that the Matrix can be defined in any terms, offering a vast opportunity to be dynamic and creative. No matter that it is really a Blaster 7 Intrusion Countermeasure program. The gamemaster can describe it as, for example, a glistening black spider with faceted eyes riveted on its prey.

Describing the Blaster 7 as a horrid beast from some mythological hell imposes the attributes of the spider-thing on the program. The player-decker sees it as a spider with death in its gaze, and reacts to that. Sure, its only a Blaster 7, *but look at that drool spraying from its mouth when it swings its head!* The metaphor is as good as reality once the decker's imagination gets hold of the thing skittering down on him. The metaphor usually has some element in common with the actual thing, but it need not.

Gamemaster and players should feel free to use and exploit all the possibilities this presents. As in all reality, however, limitations exist, but these originate more from the limits of the technology than any limits on the metaphors themselves.

• Normally, things in the Matrix appear technological and computer-generated. This is because most of the Matrix adheres to what are known as the Universal Matrix Specifications (UMS), which are discussed below. For now, just remember that something can look like a spider, but it would have to be a *technological*, computer-generated spider.

• Scale is based on absolute complexity. The MPCP and cyberdeck are complex items, but the deck is a toy compared to the complexity of the systems that make up the Renraku Arcology or the Aztechnology Pyramid. That's why a decker will always appear tiny next to something like the Pyramid or the Arcology. The more complex it is, the larger its representation.

SCULPTED SYSTEMS

Some systems in the Matrix, especially those owned by the giant multinational corporations, have custom-designed imagery that varies from the Universal Matrix Specifications imagery. The Fuchi Tour Guide and the Decker Heaven sections in the fictional section of this book illustrate and describe some of the differences between UMS and sculpted imagery.

In game terms, the differences do not much matter. Deckers running in a sculpted system receive no modifiers to their abilities or attempts to do anything. Nothing in the game system changes. What does change, however, are the laws of the reality.

A sculpted system usually has more stringent laws than one using the UMS imagery. For instance, certain things may not be allowed in a system sculpted to resemble a primeval forest. The nodes become geographical places rather than objects hanging in three-dimensional space. The datapaths become paths through the forest, which means that the decker cannot roam from the paths unless the reality is designed to handle it.

Gamemastering a sculpted system can be difficult. The important thing to remember is the metaphor concept. Based on what the actual action is, work up a metaphor that is consistent with the reality posited by the sculpting. Be loose. Don't worry about strictly defining everything. The most important thing is that the imagery and the metaphors *feel* right. Everything else is icing on the cake.

The decker's persona-icon is not usually affected by the sculpting because it is his cyberdeck that is generating and handling its own imagery. So, yes, it is entirely possible for a 40th-century armored death machine to go strolling through the primeval forest. But the icon would stick out like a sore thumb in such an environment.

VIRTUAL REALITIES 51

MATRIX REALITIES

In some systems, the sculpted reality is so powerful that it begins to impose itself on the persona image, altering it to fit the new reality. To resist the changes imposed by the reality, have the player character make a Success Test using a number of dice equal to his MPCP Rating against the system rating of the node. Yes, the Threshold must still be exceeded.

If the reality is overcome, the persona icon appears and acts as normal. If the roll fails, the reality has control **and** the decker receives a –2 to his Reaction Attribute for his resistance to the imagery. This lasts for the entire run. The decker may try and overcome the reality again when he moves to a new node. He does so, however, at a +2 Target Modifier. One attempt per node may be made.

If the reality is accepted, the persona icon shifts to the nearest approximation that is metaphorically correct for that reality. The translation may not be completely accurate, but the icon will take the appearance of something that has a similar feel in that reality. The new icon will inspire the same reactions as the previous one, but perhaps for entirely different reasons.

Have the players define their actions metaphorically for this new reality. Yes, it's still an Attack 5, but what does it look like here? Let them decide.

The most dangerous element for intruders into a sculpted reality is the inability to know what anything really is, short of analyzing everything in sight. Gee, maybe that cute, furry little animal *was* blaster IC…

REALITY FILTERS

In the story of Renny that accompanies these rules, Lucifer is described as having a reality filter. What that means is that Lucifer's cyberdeck is feeding him custom simsense impressions based on the way he has programmed it to interpret the Matrix. For those who haven't yet read the story, we don't want to spoil it, so we've made up another one.

Spinner *loves* those ancient pinball machines, and has designed a reality filter for his deck that makes the Matrix look like a giant pinball game. In this case, he loses much of the beauty and splendor of the Matrix in exchange for the images he wants.

Again, the translation for the reality filter need not be literally accurate. In fact, literal accuracy is impossible for some. There may not *be* a direct translation for nodes and datapaths or datapaths and IC. What's important is that it *feel* right. Remember the metaphor.

Spinner is the silver ball in his pinball-game Matrix. He could have chosen to be the player of the pinball game who has to work the ball into various areas of the play area to do things. Instead he chose to be knocked around inside the game itself.

To perform an action, say, traveling to a node, he has to get to a specific section of the play area. As he "moves through the Matrix," the play area changes to reflect the different possibilities each area affords. IC manifests as obstacles that rise in his path. He can choose to spin around them or barrel straight through. Maybe his sleaze program manifests as a passage that suddenly appears and takes him around the obstacle. Other deckers appear as silver balls identical to his own, but the cyberdeck is feeding him information that lets him know *instinctively* which ball is which without needing any external cues.

Reality filters are another opportunity for dynamic creativity. Let the decker design his own, then review it and work out the details with him to make sure that the reality is playable and possible to incorporate into a game session.

What are the benefits of a reality filter? It's like a Response Boost; it gives an extra +2 to Reaction and an extra +1D6 to the Initiative roll. The catch is that an MPCP with a reality filter is harder to program. When designing the MPCP, add 2 to its actual rating. Determine base time, design target number, and whatever else from this adjusted number. Cook time should still be based on the old number.

When the reality filter is running on the deck, the MPCP runs at an effective rating that is –1 its actual rating. This will affect the maximum total values of the persona programs.

When a reality filter and a sculpted reality collide, make an Opposed Success Test between the two. For the sculpted system, use its System Rating as dice against the Evasion Rating of the deck. The side with the higher net successes dominates, for that node at least. As with sculpted systems in general, the decker can try again in another node, once per node while in the system, but at a +2 Target Number.

Reality filters can be toggled on and off by the decker. It is an automatic action, but for one full turn after the reality changeover, the decker will be at one-half Reaction and receive a +2 to all Target Numbers.

SENSORY CUT-OUTS

When a decker is using the cybernetic link, the simsense signal is overriding his normal sensory impressions. Any Perception Tests made while jacked in are at a +8 Target Modifier.

If the decker chooses, he can speak normally while decking, such as into a microphone that transmits to a team member. If he does so, all target numbers are at +2 for his next Action due to the distraction.

MAGIC IN THE MATRIX

Many questions have been raised concerning whether magic can interface with the Matrix. Right now, the answer is that it cannot. Period.

Why? Remember, the Matrix does not exist. It is an artificial reality of computer-generated simsense impressions. If offers nothing with which magic, inherently associated with *living* things, can interface.

Active magicians who wish to interface with the Matrix have a special problem. A magician's experience and training has molded his mind to think in a specific manner, a manner radically different than what the Matrix demands. The result is a clash between the way the magician's mind wants to process information and the way the simsense gear wishes to provide it. Simsense impressions are inherently artificial, even if sampled from actual impressions. The magician, because of his familiarity with magic, is acutely aware of that. It just does not work for him.

There are two ways to handle this, and the gamemaster may choose the method he prefers.

The first way gives magicians who deck into the Matrix an increase in their Matrix-related target numbers equal to their Magic Attribute. Characters like the Burned-Out Mage are then better able to adapt to the Matrix than, say, the Combat Mage or an initiate of any kind.

The alternative is that the modifier be equal to the character's Sorcery Skill Rating. This allows beginning or inexperienced

MATRIX REALITIES

magicians the ability to interface properly, but as their skill (knowledge of magic) increases, they begin to meet resistance in the Matrix. This modifier has a lesser effect on initiates, but their Sorcery Skill should be increasing apace with their Magic Rating in any case.

DIGGING FOR DATA

One of the things a decker does is acquire information. A decker gathers data much the same way as anyone else, except he does it electronically.

SHADOWLAND

A decker's primary sources of information are the various shadow networks that operate as contact points and information exchanges. The Shadowland network is an example of such a network. The primary Shadowland system is safely hidden in Denver, but most major cities have a Shadowland echo station that allows limited access to the master network. Knowing the location of the local echo station at any time is a trick. It's privileged information, chummer. You wouldn't want the corps finding out, would you?

To find the station, the player character has to make an Etiquette (Matrix) (4) Test. What? You didn't know there was a Matrix Etiquette Skill? Well, why not? After all, some kind of Etiquette applies to nearly everything. The Etiquette (Matrix) Skill involves contacting other deckers to learn the current location of the echo station. For security reasons, the station moves every few days. If the gamemaster needs to determine this randomly, roll 1D6, and halve the result (rounding up).

Having located the station, proceed as in accessing a contact. For game-balance reasons, the decker is allowed to post only one information request to the network per adventure. He chooses the topic. The decker must also tell the gamemaster whether he wants fast, basic information or slower, more in-depth info. He indicates this by choosing how to divide up any success. Should most of the successes go to reducing the base time for the information search (36 hours) or toward increasing the level of information gained? The decker designates a simple ratio; 2:1, 3:1, 3:2, or whatever he chooses.

The gamemaster rolls eight dice against the Target Number appropriate for the info (usually 4, but it can vary). He then divides up the successes as precisely as possible, according to the decker's request. The gamemaster can take this opportunity to fudge the results somewhat if he believes the player characters would benefit from learning more information. The successes allocated for information determine what is learned, and the successes allocated for time reduce the base time, per standard procedure.

After the necessary time has passed, the information requested is posted to the Shadowland network. The decker, however, has no idea when the information will appear. He must periodically access the network to see if the information is there. During his wait, the possibility exists that the network will move its LTG access number, requiring that the decker start all over to locate it again, using the procedure described above.

VIRTUAL REALITIES 53

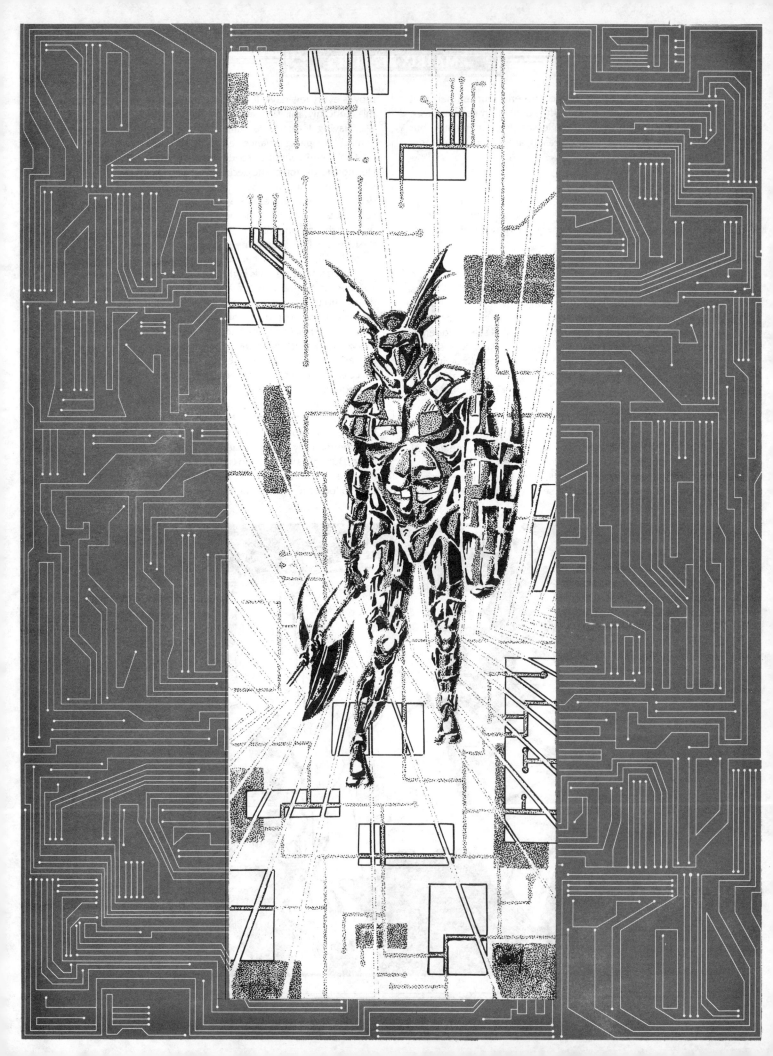

A MATRIX TOUR

INTRODUCTION OF THE MATRIX

Once the Crash of '29 was cured and cleaned up, the information industry turned to growth and the discovery of new applications of cybertechnology for use by consumers throughout the world.

Though most governments and corporations viewed the dissemination of cybertechnology to the general public as a potential disaster for fear that illegal decking would get out of hand, we at Fuchi knew that only by giving everybody equal strength could a balance of power be attained within the world's data market. And so we began research into cyberdeck technology, units that would be of use to the corporate office and the home, reasonable in cost but spectacular in performance. Our strategy was different than that of many smaller companies trying to make names for themselves in cybertechnology. Companies such as the ill-fated Matrix Systems of Boston came out with "gray-market" cyberterminals—designed not for the average consumer but for a limited clientele of wealthy patrons. These units were as large and inelegant as many of the prototypes the government had developed years earlier.

Fuchi, on the other hand, waited until it had developed its accessible CDT-1000, the first desktop cyberdeck. Our research staff was convinced that this device would change the face of computer technology, and we at Fuchi are proud to say they were right. The CDT-1000 Vision was introduced only fifteen years ago in 2036, but the effects of desktop cybertechnology reach into every aspect of our lives today. Even more impressive is the progress Fuchi's dedicated workers have made over the last fifteen years in this fascinating field of technology.

The Vision used primitive virtual-reality technology to interface the system-user with his computer. The user wore bulky goggles that created a visual virtual reality containing the icons he would use for his day's work.

The deck itself had to be a miracle of speed and organization, for in the early days of consumer cyberdecking, there existed no Universal Matrix Specifications, no resource links with which computer programs could identify themselves, and no standard for writing programs. In short, the Vision was responsible for probing a program it encountered and then translating specifics of an old non-cyber program into a format the Vision could read and turn into an icon for its user. Though the Vision's cyber-interface made life easier for the user because of its virtual-reality, 3D-icon system, the need to continually translate the old programming made it slower than necessary.

Because our philosophy has ever been that "the consumer deserves more," we set out to create the tools that would allow programs to identify themselves quickly to Fuchi cyberdecks. These "icon links" acted as a kind of identification code for the cyberdecks. In effect, the new programming tools allowed a deck to become active in its interaction with our decks.

Not wishing to monopolize the computer programming market, we licensed out the cyberdeck icon links to established programming firms. As more and more programs that could hasten the processing power of Fuchi's cyberdecks were released on the market, it became apparent that cyberdeck technology would be the wave of the future.

It was also in these early years of 2036–37 that we introduced affordable Intrusion Countermeasure Programs, or IC, on the open market. The open-market sales of cyberdecks did, of course, offer the possibility of abuse, and Fuchi knew it had a responsibility to provide defenses of comparable power.

Still more work had to be done, however. Though our decks no longer had to probe a program or data to identify it, the decks still had to create the icons for program and data after the resource had identified it. As it was, our decks had to create consistent, uniform icons so that a decker would always see the same picture for the same type of computer information wherever he went in the Grid. Our next task was to establish a standard for all new programs and computer systems so that cyberdecks would no longer have to create the icons—the icons would create their own images. By distributing the burden of processing icon references, cyberdecks would work even faster and be more productive at the home and at the office.

This was the motive for Fuchi's sponsorship of the Universal Matrix Specifications Conference in 2039 in Tokyo. We invited representatives of governments, corporations, and consumer groups from all over the globe. More than 7,000 humans and metahumans attended the three-month-long conference. The eyes of the world were turned toward Tokyo that spring of '39.

Wrote a reporter for the *Tokyo Times*, "It is impossible to conceive of a more important summit in the history of our world. The creation of the United Nations pales in comparison to this sharing of data-exchange technology."

The conference was marked by Fuchi's introduction of desktop cyberdecks with neural interfaces. Now a person could experience all sensation within his computer system, feel as if he were moving around within a world of icons, receive the impression of touch or even taste an icon if the programmer wanted to bother designing it that way. Thrilled by the possibilities, the conference attendees decided to follow the lead established by Fuchi's dedicated programmers and scientists.

For it was Fuchi's goal to elevate the network to its next incarnation. It would no longer be a simple network of data exchange connecting the globe. It would become an environment of virtual reality, a three-dimensional world where all data and programs would appear to have form and substance. The network would become the Matrix, a monument to the power of human imagination. This would only be possible, however, if program designs used a consistent series of icons. Without this, icon technology could never reach its full potential on a global scale.

During the development of Fuchi's neural-interface technology, our designers had developed a catalogue of icons for innumerable computer system utilities, programs, and data. We offered this list to the conference, and the world's representatives adopted it, with only a few alterations.

It was decided that the basic geography of the Matrix would take the image of a plane running off into all directions to endless horizons. This would give deckers a reference point to prevent their being overwhelmed by the wealth of images that would fill the Matrix.

DATA AND DESCRIPTION HANDBOOK

FUCHI

The surface of the plane was where the smaller systems would be represented—cyberdecks, home computers, and so forth. Larger systems, such as the Fuchi Star, would be farther and farther above the plane. When thinking about the Matrix, keep in mind that it does not exist physically, so the "geography" is very fluid. If someone were to access the Matrix through his home computer, another small pyramid would appear on the plane to represent his system. The plane would become a bit bigger to accommodate the representation of that system. Because the Matrix is consists only of the images it holds, it grows and shrinks according to how many systems it has running at any time.

MATRIX GEOGRAPHY AND ICONOGRAPHY

The Universal Matrix Specifications, or UMS, allow computer-system owners to represent their data, programs, utilities, and systems with standard icons that immediately identify them to users of the system. One way to imagine the geography of the Matrix is as a collection of "pocket universes." Some of these pocket universes exist within one another. Say, for example, that a computer system is in a Local Telecommunications Grid. If a decker were in Seattle's LTG# 2206, he would see thousands of system constructs, ranging from the Fuchi Star to small home-computer systems represented by colored pyramids. If he passed through a Systems Access Node (SAN) into a system construct, the LTG would no longer be visible. He would see only the world of the system he had just entered, with all its node constructs.

Though every LTG appears endless, it is actually defined by the number of systems within it. If a decker passes through a SAN from one LTG to another, he enters a completely new pocket universe. Ahead of him is the new LTG, behind him is only the SAN. The LTG that he has just exited is nowhere in sight.

Here's a picture of Seattle LTG# 2206. Notice that it appears to have no boundary. In truth, however, it is bound by the number of systems in the LTG. If a decker were to enter a SAN leading to another LTG in the Seattle RTG, he would no longer be able to view this area of the Grid. He would only be able to see the constructs in the Grid into which he had just moved.

REGIONAL TELECOMMUNICATION GRIDS

Regional Telecommunications Grids, or RTGs, are not represented by an icon because they represent the largest perspective within the Matrix. That is, an RTG doesn't look like anything because there's no place from which to view it. It is possible, however, to look at things *from* the Regional Grid.

An RTG always offers the option of passage through a SAN to another RTG. Looking outward from the RTG, one can see all the LTGs that are in that RTG. As shown in the illustration, the LTGs, when seen from an RTG, appear as colored spheres. Notice that no SANs exist between the RTG and the LTGs; movement is simply from the RTG to any of its LTGs. On the other hand, getting to an RTG from an LTG means having to pass through a SAN located at the "top" of the LTG. Because this SAN is set apart from the rest of the LTG grid, it is easy to find.

LOCAL TELECOMMUNICATION GRIDS

The LTG is the "neighborhood"-level of the Matrix. The system constructs are located here, and it is the "space" that must be traversed when traveling from one system construct to another.

Note that the illustration of the Seattle LTG# 2206 does not show telecommunication lines even though the entire Grid is clogged with such lines inter-connecting almost every construct in the Grid. The telecommunication grids are not represented graphically for two reasons. First, it would be redundant because virtually all the systems are connected to one another. Second, it would prevent the clear expression of the Matrix's graphic splendor.

A decker who wants to get from one construct to another merely inputs the coordinates, the full LTG number, on the construct he wants to get to. His deck then moves him in the direction, with the decker making adjustments in his "trajectory" as he gets closer to the construct. Though it appears that the decker's persona is flying through the Matrix, he is actually following a series of invisible telecommunication lines. If he has the system number, he can travel directly to the construct.

Located at the top of each LTG, glowing like the North Star in the sky, is the System Access Node that lets a decker get to the Regional Telecommunications Network. The SANs leading to the neighboring LTGs (that is, all the other LTGs within the same RTG) are located at various points throughout the LTG, floating high above the Grid's plane. One of the interesting effects for a decker is the ability to "fly up" to the RTG and LTG access SANs from anywhere within the LTG because these SANS have no actual spatial relationship to the other systems.

SYSTEM ACCESS NODES

A SAN connects different systems to one another, a system construct to an LTG, different LTGs to each other, an LTG to its RTG, and RTGs to other RTGs. It is like a doorway from one discrete area of the Matrix to another. It normally requires a passcode to get through a SAN.

SYSTEM CONSTRUCTS

The standard image of a computer system in the Matrix is a polyhedron; the larger the system, the larger the polyhedron. Of course, a system can be designed to take any form the system owner wishes. The Fuchi Star is an impressive example of icon architecture, simple and yet startling. Every system icon has at least one System Access Node connecting it to the Local Telecommunications Grid, though these SANs are sometimes difficult to reach. Some system owners are so concerned with privacy that they build their constructs to be invisible.

Upon entering a system construct, a decker can see which nodes are in the structure; they hang in space without any means of support. None are required, for these are merely images of components of a computer system. For security purposes, the apparent "geography" of the nodes (how close one node is to another) has no bearing on which nodes are connected to each other. The nodes are arranged at the whim of the system architect. Many systems, even those using only the basic Universal Matrix Specifications, block the full system image with special programming sub-routines in the SAN. All in the name of security.

In systems with fully sculpted nodes, a guest in the systems cannot see anything beyond the node he is in. A guest in the Fuchi Star, for example, first enters an impressive courtyard modeled on a castle of ancient Japan. This is the system's first SPU, located just beyond the shape of a giant portcullis, which is the system SAN. The courtyard walls prevent a decker from seeing the entire system. He can only scan those nodes directly connected to the SPU.

DATA LINES

For security purposes, the decker can see only the data lines directly connecting the node he is in to another node. In other words, a data line is invisible from outside, but one can see the data line and the node to which it is connected when looking down a data line.

This means that a thief in a system cannot go directly to his destination, but must slowly explore the construct, working his way from node to node, all the while increasing his chance of tripping a system alert. Any legitimate visitor, however, will have a map of the data lines connecting the nodes and will know exactly how to get to wherever he wants to go.

The UMS symbology for a data line is a tube filled with flashing bits of silver. The walls of the tube are transparent and reveal the rest of the Matrix. Deckers can only enter data lines from a node, never from mid-line.

The second data line pictured here was created by Rachel Anderson of Georgia, CAS, for Gaeatronics, whose entire construct has been modeled on exterior settings.

CENTRAL PROCESSING UNITS

Every system has a Central Processing Unit, or CPU, that is the control center of the system. Larger system constructs may consist of several computer systems, each with a CPU controlling each system's storage, data movement, and data processing. Pictured with the UMS Central Processing Unit above are the CPUs from Herreka Shipping and the famed "Heart CPU" of the UCAS Medical Union.

DATASTORES

Datastores hold information, or files. The master of this hypermedia is in a datastore in the Fuchi system in Tokyo. Datastores are so full of information that one usually needs to know exactly what he is looking for and how to identify it unless he wants to spend an inordinate amount of time browsing through the data.

Illustrated here are examples of the interior and the exterior of a UMS datastore, the interior of a datastore from the VivreSoftware system of Paris, and a datastore from the Gaeatronics construct in Seattle. Deckers eat the apples to obtain the information.

I/O PORTS

An Input/Output Port, or I/OP, is a limited-access node that opens the systems to various data input/output devices: terminals, cyberdecks, printers, graphics displays, data readers for optical chips, and so on.

For I/OPs that only receive data (keyboards, for example), the standard presentation is tilted to one side, with their data lines attached to the tip of the pyramid. Ports that only output data, like printers, are tilted to one side, with their data lines attached to the base of the pyramid.

I/OPs that do both have bases horizontal to the LTG plane, with their data lines connecting at the base.

The other examples of I/OPs are the "Waterfall" port, by Hotama, from the Fuchi Star in Seattle, and the "Printer Room" from the Fuchi Press construct in Tokyo.

SUB-PROCESSING UNITS

The Sub-Processing Unit, or SPU, is a small computer that is "slaved" to a more powerful one. The CPU gives it orders, and the SPU does various jobs for the master node.

Illustrated is an example of the UMS Sub-Processing Unit, a SPU from the Fuchi system in Tokyo, and the "Union Memorial" at Federated Boeing.

The ETM sculpture was created by Hank Davenport, who has introduced a style of icon sculpture comparable to that of the Impressionist painters of centuries past. By orchestrating a lack of resolution with stylistic intent, he has been able to create striking sculpture for less money and less memory loss.

SLAVE MODULE

A Slave Module, or SM, controls some physical process or device, anything from an electric coffeemaker or an assembly line to the elevators for a corporate office building.

The sculpted nodes are from the Mitsuhama Pagoda and the ACME Novelty Company, respectively. The Rube Goldberg node runs the company's assembly line of practical joke items—a clever meshing of style and utility.

DATA LINE JUNCTION

A Data Line Junction, or DLJ, is responsible for routing data through system constructs. It is similar to an SPU, but is more limited and specialized in its ability.

DLJs are seldom sculpted, but both Federated Boeing and UCAS Steel have invested in making their junctions aesthetically appealing.

FUCHI INCORPORATED
A MATRIX TOUR

PROGRAMMING SCULPTURE

System constructs and system nodes are not the only information in the Matrix that may be sculpted into more elegant forms. Much work has also been done with Intrusion Countermeasure programs, or IC. These programs are usually placed in nodes, though some can wander system constructs on their own. They serve a variety of functions, from acting as barriers to alerting the CPU of an intruder to attempting to subdue an Intruder.

In all of the examples pictured here, it was the actual program that was constructed into the graphic sculpture. Such work is expensive, but the more startling the IC sculpture, the more it has proven effective. This, of course, adds to the prestige of any company possessing such valuable work.

Illustrated here is some of the artistry available to programmers working within the world of Matrix-icon sculpture. These images are from Fuchi's Samurai Persona Assault Series, designed by Miro Hotato. The IC programs are designed to attack the personas of deckers who have illegally entered sensitive areas of private computer systems. Note that the images are actually the program codes molded into colored shapes. A hundred years ago, computer programs looked like long lists of words, numbers, and symbols. Today they can be shaped into any form, limited only by how much memory the system can afford to give up to elaborate programs and how much nuyen the system owner can spend on state-of-the-art icon sculpture.

Each of these icons reflects an advance in sculpture detailing, requiring more work and thus commanding a higher price. The value of more detailed IC is not merely aesthetic, however. The more detailed the sculpture, the greater its impact on its beholder. It is one thing for a decker to encounter a white sphere that is trying to crash his persona. It is another to unexpectedly run into a man wielding a sword.

Following is a list of many of Fuchi's high-end IC sculpture. All the programs are also available in lower-resolution design.

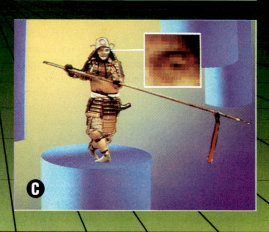

A) Samurai PA 3000 (Low Resolution)
B) Samurai PA 7000 (Moderate Resolution)
C) Samurai PA 10,000 (High Resolution)

FUCHI INCORPORATED
A MATRIX TOUR

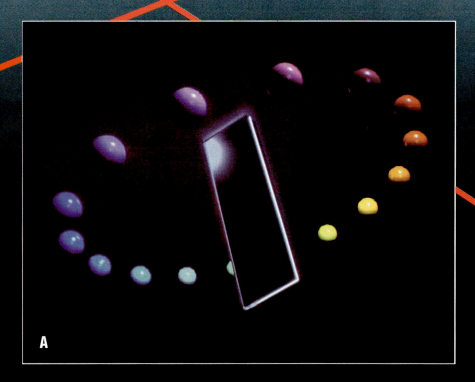

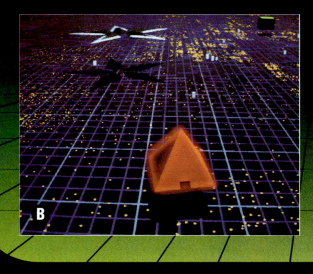

A) An RTG SAN with LTG spheres in orbit around it.
B) The Seattle Matrix. A typical system hangs in the foreground.
C) Inside the same system showing the system nodes. Note that the datalines are invisible in this view.

FUCHI INCORPORATED
A MATRIX TOUR

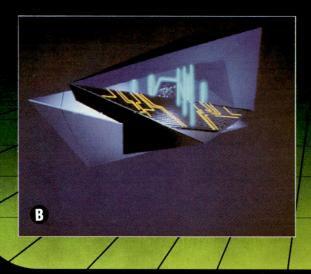

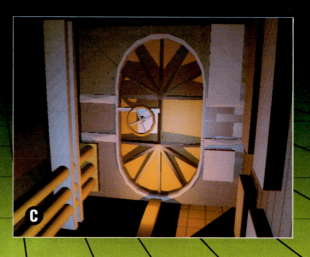

A) An LTG SAN.
B) One of the exterior SANs on the Fuchi Star.
C) A sculpted SAN detailed as a submarine iris valve.

FUCHI INCORPORATED
A MATRIX TOUR

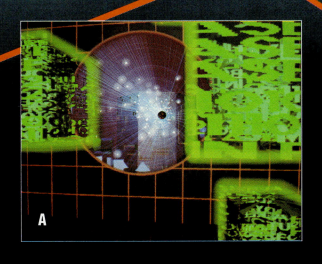

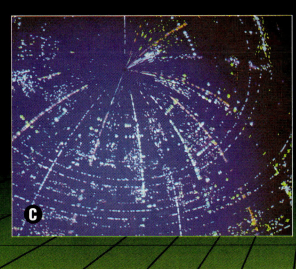

A) Inside a datastore looking outward down a dataline.

B) A sculpted dataline: the datalines are the road and the leaves blowing down it are data-packets.

C) A close-up of the UMS slave module icon.

D) A sculpted slave module from the Mitsuhama Pagoda.

FUCHI INCORPORATED
A MATRIX TOUR

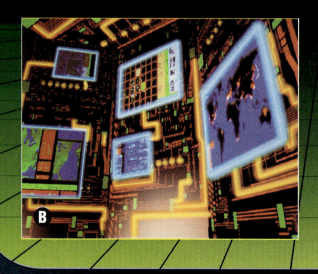

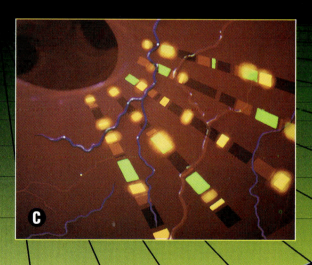

A) The UMS CPU icon.
B) Inside the CPU.
C) The "Heart CPU" of the UCAS Medical Union.

FUCHI INCORPORATED
A MATRIX TOUR

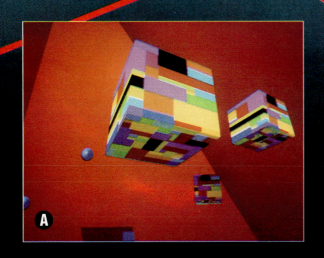
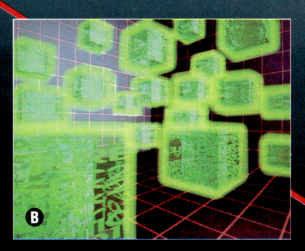
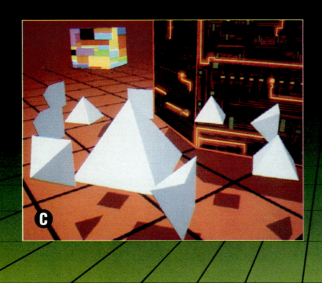
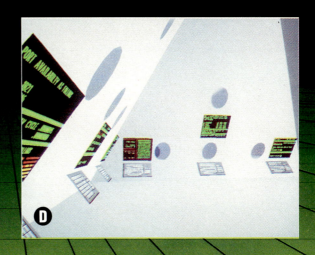

A) The UMS icon of a datastore.
B) Inside a datastore.
C) The UMS icon of an I/O port.
D) Inside an I/O port.

FUCHI INCORPORATED
A MATRIX TOUR

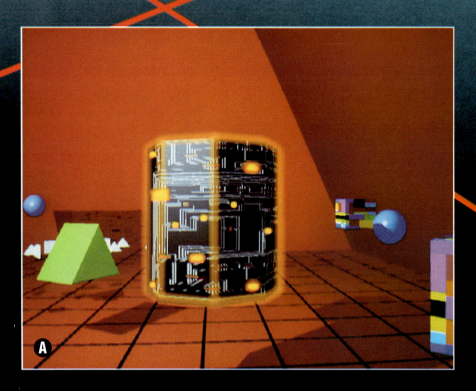

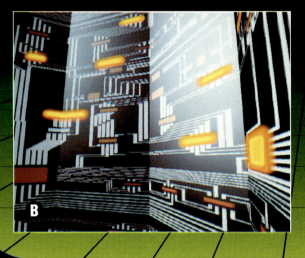

A) The UMS icon of an SPU.
B) Inside an SPU.
C) The FTM "Impressionist" SPU imagery.

FUCHI INCORPORATED
A MATRIX TOUR

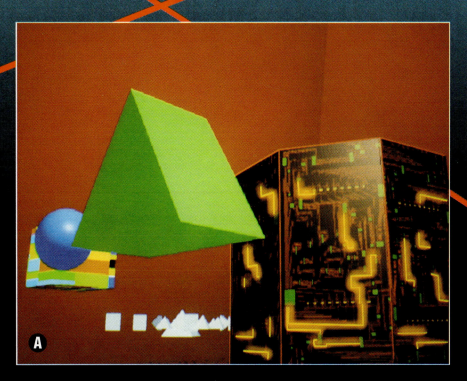

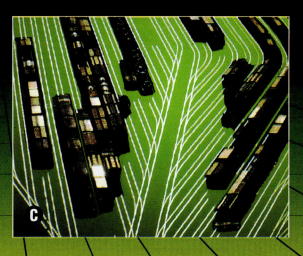

A) The UMS icon of a dataline junction.
B) Inside a sculpted DLG at Federated Boeing.
C) Inside a sculpted DLG at UCAS Steel.

FUCHI INCORPORATED
A MATRIX TOUR

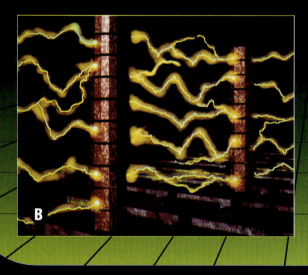

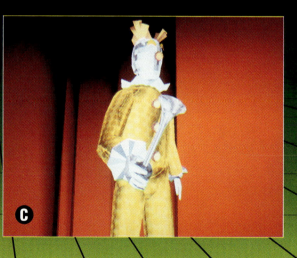

A) The infamous Watcher 7K access IC. The UMS default is a wall of swirling alpha-numeric characters.
B) The UMS default for barrier IC.
C) The Good Time Barrier as created by Bjorn Hanson, the famed icon sculptor.

FUCHI INCORPORATED
A MATRIX TOUR

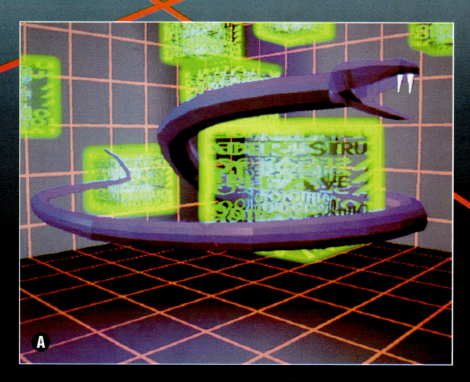

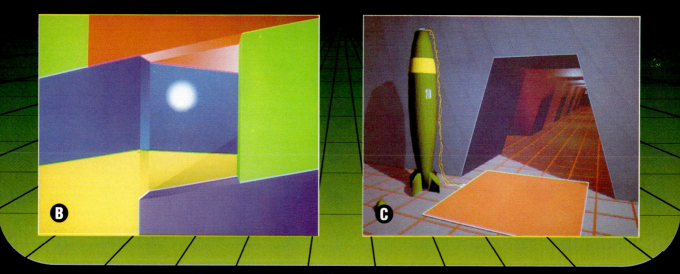

A) This scramble IC, the Serpent V, was created by Fuchi for Federated Boeing.
B) The UMS default for scramble IC.
C) Fuchi has developed an entire line of weapon-style IC for military systems around the world.

FUCHI INCORPORATED
A MATRIX TOUR

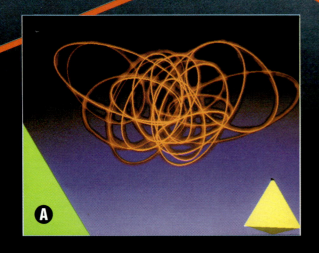

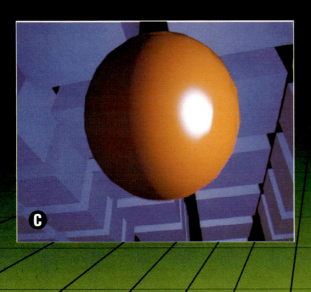
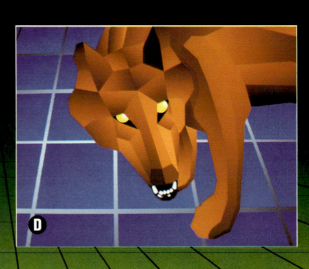

A) The UMS standard icon for blaster IC.
B) The Succubus VI blaster IC, created by Nasan Helles of Fuchi.
C) The UMS standard icon for all types of trace IC.
D) The popular Fuchi Wolf comes in a range of ratings.

FUCHI INCORPORATED
A MATRIX TOUR

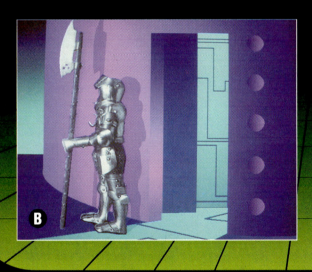
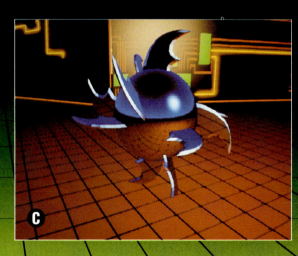

A) The UMS default for killer IC.
B) Blaster-KNIGHT IV combines the best of icon imagery while saving memory by utilizing a monochrome color scheme.
C) This frightening creation from Nasan Helles is used worldwide.

FUCHI INCORPORATED
A MATRIX TOUR

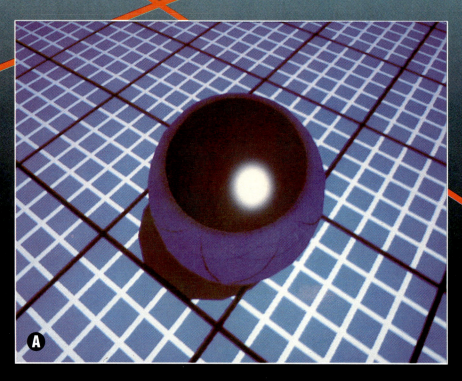

A) The UMS default for tar babies.
B) The Decay IV from Fuchi, designed for Seattle Gaeatronics. The bird attacks, withers and dies, taking the utility with it.
C) More work from Nasan Helles. After the zombie grabs hold of the decker's utility, it falls apart, destroying the utility as well.

FUCHI INCORPORATED
A MATRIX TOUR

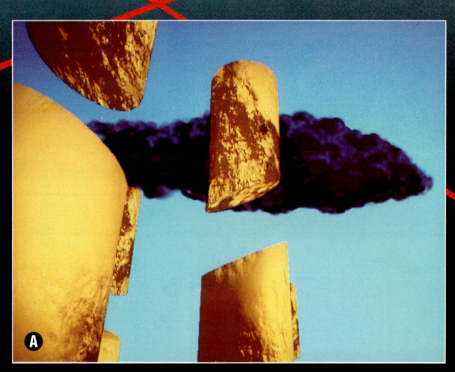

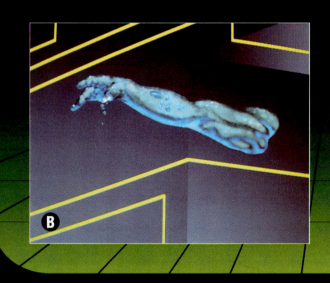

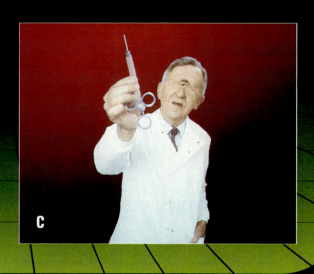

A) The UMS default for tar pit IC.
B) This tar pit program leaps out to grab the utility from a decker, poisons all copies of the utility in storage, and then vanishes.
C) This "film-homage" was created for Universal Simsense by Fuchi.

FUCHI INCORPORATED
A MATRIX TOUR

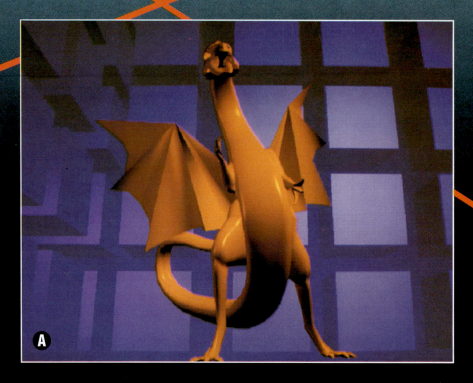
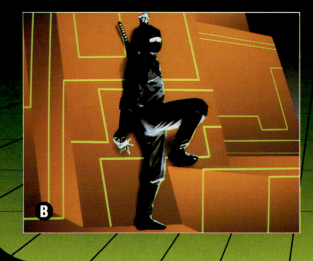

Black IC has no UMS standard imagery. Each program is unique.
A) The Dragon, found at the Fuchi Star in Seattle.
B) Ninja, created for Mitsuhama Pagoda.
C) Mechanical Menace, guarding UCAS Steel's Chicago construct.

HACKER HOUSE
SUMMER UPDATE CATALOG

Call us anytime, 24 hours a day, seven days a week! Our team of hack-fanatics is standing by to take your call. Order until 12:00 midnight (EST), and we'll get your black-market deck upgrades and utilities to you the next day. Overnight Delivery only 15¥. (Hey! We'd like to net the programs to you, but it seems our customers find temptation too great when they know our product might be lying around in the Matrix. Chip copies only!)

Howdy, Chummer!
If you're reading this at all, we know you've put a lot of effort into tracking us down—and you won't be disappointed you did. Hacker House™ offers the largest variety of quality decking utilities and deck-hardware upgrades for the greatest range of systems for the best prices. How do we do it? Volume. Not like Stuffer Shack's™ volume, because you chummers are a rare breed. But compared to some chiphead programmer living with rats at the end of some alley crawling with punks who'll slice someone the minute they see that he lives on more than 20¥ a month, we do very well.

This catalog introduces some new items we wanted to get out to our customers (as well as a few classics) before our full summer catalog hits the shadows.

How to Order
Our customer-service staff is ready to take your order on our toll-free lines 24 hours a day, seven days a week. You won't find the number anywhere in the catalog. You either know where to find us or you don't.

Please have the utility or deck upgrade component, name and code, credstick number (yours or someone else's), billing address for the stick, and shipping address ready. This will help us process your order quickly and prevent long, traceable calls.

Customizing Utilities
As a special bonus to Hacker House customers, we'll connect you with a programmer in your area who can customize your new utility to your deck and style. Most of you either do your own work or already have a 'grammer connection, but keep in mind that the programmers from our list are familiar with the Hacker House catalog and can customize your new utility like nobody's business.

HACKER HOUSE
SUMMER UPDATE CATALOG

HARDWARE AND FIRMWARE

COMBAT UTILITIES

Attack Programs

IC Crusher's basic attack utilities come in a wide range of power. This simple but effective program lets both beginners and veterans get through a run with nary a scratch. The icon uses the UMS default imagery for attack programs and is a signal for all deckers to look out. Each "energy blast" varies in its appearance of power, depending on the Mp of the program.
Memory: 2–200 Mp   Rating 1 through 10
CAO 6672   Price: Varies, contact customer service
Designer: IC Crusher Systemware

For the decker with a love of the Far East, we still carry Zach Dat's venerable Katana 400. The program fits any style using swordplay, and deckers with a penchant for hand-to-hand combat will find it a breeze to use.
Memory: 32 Mp   Rating 4
ATZ 9409   Price: 6,400¥
Designer: Zach Dat

For those deckers using Picasso's ElectroSculpt series, we've got an upgrade on the line's attack program: the Leo Attack 8. As with the rest of the line, you mold a piece of "clay" into the image (in this case, a lion), and the utility kicks in when the deck reads what you want. The lion comes equipped with impressive sound subroutines, making it especially effective against defense deckers.
Memory: 128 Mp   Rating 8
ATP 6386   Price: 64,000¥
Designer: Picasso

Blind Programs

This basic blind program uses the UMS default of an expanding black/gray storm cloud that surrounds the target persona. It can either emit from the attack persona or gradually shade into existence around the target.
Memory: 3–300 Mp   Rating 1 through 10
TUI 6880   Price: Varies; contact customer service
Designer: Nue Visions

The Bag, designed by Mr. Snazz, appears as a large brown sack that surrounds the target persona, obscuring its sensors program. It also contains a simple auditory harassment subroutine that rags on the target persona for not being able to fight its way out of it.
Memory: 75 Mp   Rating 5
TUI 6880   Price: 15,000¥
Designer: Mr. Snazz Ltd.

THE BIG DOINK

For the truly foolish at heart, the Big Doink manifests as a gangly, wild-haired man who, tooting a brass horn, runs up from nowhere and "doinks" the target persona in the "eyes." The program seems to be vulnerable, however, to a slap on the forehead.
Memory: 108 Mp   Rating 6
TUI 6880   Price: 21,600¥
Designer: Stooges 'R' Us

Hog Programs

We are expecting reception of the new, hot Hog programs coded by ElectraSoft any day now. Contact customer service for information.
Memory: 3–300 Mp   Rating 1 through 10
TUI 6880   Price: Varies; contact customer service
Designer: Various

Poison Programs

The UMS default poison icon, a sickly green sphere, is used for this basic program. Toss the sphere, and if it hits and breaks, it seeps into the target persona to poison its bod.
Memory: 10–100 Mp   Rating 1 through 10
TUI 6880   Price: Varies; contact customer service
Designer: Hacks Inc.

HACKER HOUSE
SUMMER UPDATE CATALOG

The Apple, a new design from Rugrat, manifests as a kindly old woman who offers the target persona a delicious golden apple. She's hard to resist, but if you don't, you'll bite into the apple full of worms that'll eat at your persona's guts for the rest of the run.
Memory: 27 Mp   Rating 3
TUI 6880   Price: 2,700¥
Designer: Rugrat

Poison Dart is a simple but effective program that allows a user to merge it with any form of missile-weapon motif already present. For instance, your crossbow could fire its standard bolts, and these special Poison Darts as well. Designed by Longtree, it's a sure winner.
Memory: 147 Mp   Rating 7
TUI 6880   Price: 73,500¥
Designer: Longtree

Restrict Programs
This basic program uses the UMS Restrict default of tall neon grids that spring up around the target persona, pinning it in. This particular program, also designed by Rugrat, offers a nice touch as the grid bends momentarily when the persona finally passes through it.
Memory: 3–300 Mp   Rating 1 through 10
TUI 6880   Price: Varies, contact customer service
Designer: Rugrat

Flytrap changes the area under or around the target into a sticky, gooey mess that makes movement difficult. The target can get free, but the goo remains attached to him, slowing his ability to evade for the rest of the run. Tough luck, chummer.
Memory: 75 Mp   Rating 5
TUI 6880   Price: 15,000¥
Designer: Mr. Snazz Ltd.

Da Goons is another Orzoff Oddities creation. When activated, two pug-nosed goons appear to wrestle with the target. Containing only a few alternate poses, they move and react like poorly animated characters. Don't be fooled, though. They're tough customers!
Memory: 192 Mp   Rating 8
TUI 6880   Price: 96,000¥
Designer: Orzoff Oddities

Reveal Programs
This basic Reveal program uses the UMS default of a bright shaft of light that illuminates the target persona. The shaft of light can emit from anywhere the user chooses.
Memory: 3–300 Mp   Rating 1 through 10
TUI 6880   Price: Varies; contact customer service
Designer: Dum Da Dee Productions

This revelation program manifests as a large industrial flashlight that illuminates the target persona, reducing its ability to mask itself. The revelation program was originally designed by Lone Star Security for its own deckers and is now manufactured by them. Hey, it works so we carry it.
Memory: 27 Mp   Rating 3
TUI 6880   Price: 2,700¥
Designer: Lone Star Software

Friendly Puppy is a particularly annoying reveal program created by JonJon John. When successful, it creates a small, horribly cute puppy that follows the target persona around, yapping wildly for attention. Gives you the shivers just thinking about it.
Memory: 108 Mp   Rating 6
TUI 6880   Price: 21,600¥
Designer: JonJon John

Slow Programs
Nix-Net, the classic slow program, has been servicing deckers for years, and will continue to do so, as far as anyone can tell. The chrome net, matching the UMS default icon, has become the first sign of trouble in many systems.
Memory: 10–100 Mp   Rating 1 through 10
TUI 6880   Price: Varies; contact customer service
Designer: Horizon Software

FRIENDLY PUPPY

HACKERHOUSE
SUMMER UPDATE CATALOG

If you're an icon cowboy and you've been looking for the perfect slow program to match your style, then Impulse Billy has got a utility for you. This ingenious program, the Old Chestnut V, lets you kick chrome dust into the eyes of your opponent! Ah, if you could only use it against corporate deckers!
Memory: 50 Mp   Rating 5
LWP 3963   Price: 5,500¥
Designer: Impulse Billy

LectricBrain has always been an innovator when it comes to new images for old programs, and it looks as though they've got another winner with their Icing IC VI. Run the program and a blast of frigid air, complete with silver snow, comes blowing in to cake a solid layer of ice over the IC you're fighting. The thickness of the ice varies according to how successful the program was. Perfect for mage-style deckers and those looking for gea-based utilities.
Memory: 70 Mp   Rating 7
NWO 3986   Price: 39,000¥
Designer: LectricBrain

DEFENSE UTILITIES

Armor Programs
This basic program uses the UMS armor default of a suit of translucent armor that surrounds your persona. As it degrades, it begins to chip and fall away.
Memory: 3–300 Mp   Rating 1 through 10
TUI 6880   Price: Varies; contact customer service
Designer: Basic Bytes, Inc.

The Big Beef doesn't manifest externally, but does increase the visual toughness of your persona. This is a revamped version of the old Steriod Hell armor program. Wicked Wilson did the original coding, and MikeyBoy did the update. As it degrades, you begin to "deflate."
Memory: 27 Mp   Rating 3
TUI 6880   Price: 2,700¥
Designer: MikeyBoy (after Wicked Wilson)

Armor Skin manifests by giving your persona an armor-plated appearance. Attacks that you completely resist deflect away to ricochet madly for a few moments. The armor can be tuned to appear any metallic color you wish. The armor effect fades as the program degrades.
Memory: 108 Mp   Rating 6
TUI 6880   Price: 21,600¥
Designer: Horizon Software

Cloak Programs
The default UMS icon of the basic cloak program is very simple, a cloak. It unfolds and surrounds the persona, blending it into the surrounding Matrix. It fades away as it degrades.
Memory: 3–300 Mp   Rating 1 through 10
TUI 6880   Price: Varies; contact customer service
Designer: Masking Masters

Camouflage, by Warpsmith, is literally a paint program. When activated, it allows you to paint a Matrix camouflage pattern over your persona icon, making it blend in with your surroundings. The "paint" wears off as the program degrades.
Memory: 12 Mp   Rating 2
TUI 6880   Price: 1,200¥
Designer: Warpsmith Wonders

System Merge is a sophisticated program that allows the icon to merge into the surrounding Matrix terrain, thereby increasing its masking ability. As the program degrades, the merging becomes increasingly less efficient.
Memory: 147 Mp   Rating 7
TUI 6880   Price: 73,500¥
Designer: Horizon Software

Medic Programs
When all you want is a program that'll get your persona back in running order, we recommend you pick up the cult classic, Perfect Patch, from IC Crusher Systemware. The program comes in a wide range of program sizes and powers, and defaults to the UMS medic program icon. When you run it and see the bandages spring up around your wounds, you know you're going to be all right.
Memory: 4–400 Mp   Rating 1 through 10
GIP 0267   Price: Varies; contact customer service
Designer: IC Crusher Systemware

LectricBrain's new Spectrum 600 is designed for the decker with a more abstract style. When you run the program, a wash of rainbow colors runs up and down your body, eventually concentrating on your persona's icon wound. If the program runs successfully, the colors start melting into a pure white. If your style is colors, then you can use the blending of the colors as your guide when hacking.
Memory: 144 Mp   Rating 6
NWO 3833   Price: 20,000¥
Designer: LectricBrain

Another brilliant piece of work from Impulse Billy and his growing cowboy decker series! When you've taken a hit, there's nothing more comforting than a sweet young thing appearing out of nowhere to tend your wounds. The Tender Lovin' 8000 comes sculpted in period western gear, with platinum hair and a heart of gold. She's got a damp gold cloth that she applies to your wounds and gives you a good-luck kiss if you're in the middle of combat!
Memory: 256 Mp   Rating 8
NWO 3833   Price: 128,000¥
Designer: LectricBrain

HACKER HOUSE
SUMMER UPDATE CATALOG

TENDER LOVIN' 8000

Mirrors Programs

Zach Dat has just come out with a new basic mirrors program, the Whirlwind series. Its icons are the UMS default. Run it and your persona is surrounded by square mirrors about two centimeters by two centimeters that whirl around your body and make it harder for a decker or a piece of IC to get a bead on your bod.

Memory: 3–300 Mp   Rating 1 through 10
AIH 1271   Price: Varies; contact customer service
Designer: Zach Dat

Mr. Iota's Mirror Balls program builds on the basic mirrors program, but adds some flash. Run the program and several dozen chrome balls fly from your persona and go into orbit around you. The pattern of the spheres is coordinated so that the spheres reflect images from each other, rendering each nearly invisible. You, however, have full vision. An IC or decker trying to hit you will not have that advantage and its attempts to get to your persona will be obscured.

Memory: 48 Mp   Rating 4
AIF 4820   Price: 9,600¥
Designer: Mr. Iota

The Doppler Nine is a new program from Estate Systems that gives a new meaning to the concept of mirrors programs. Run it and a second persona appears near you, a "ghost" icon that gives off the same information as your real persona. The false icon gives off a data read that'll confuse anybody who's after you.

Memory: 243 Mp   Rating 9
MWO 7332   Price: 121,500¥
Designer: Estate Systems

Restore Programs

A number of releases of hot, new restore programs are due any day. Contact our customer service department for more information.

Memory: 3–300 Mp   Rating 1 through 10
TUI 6880   Price: Varies; contact customer service
Designer: Various

Shield Programs

The shield program, pirated from Fuchi Industrial Electronics years ago, is a staple of any decker's library. The Fuchi Shield D-III has just been released by Vectorsmith. Running it produces a translucent shield upon either wrist, as specified during customizing process. A simple program, but handy when you're in a tight spot.

Memory: 36 Mp   Rating 3
ANP 7830   Price: 3,600¥
Designer: Vectorsmith

The Armor of God, from the Jack o' In, is a mid-range shield program with an impressive display. Run it and your persona suddenly glows from within with an unearthly hot-white light. As the armor wears down, the armor dims, until you are left looking as you did before. Runners operating against corp-defense deckers report that the program tends to throw the opposition on the defensive. Quite an accomplishment for a defensive program, eh?

Memory: 100 Mp   Rating 5
AND 9862   Price: 20,000¥
Designer: Jack o' In

We just got a new supply of IC Crusher Systemware's old-timer, Battle Dress. This gorgeous icon combines the high-tech look of the Matrix with the art of feudal samurai armor into a stunning display of strength. Run the program and it grows out of the surface of your persona. Popular, and deservedly so.

Memory: 256 Mp   Rating 8
NWT 4678   Price: 128,000¥
Designer: IC Crusher Systemware

Smoke Programs

Bokada's Basic Smoke program uses the UMS icon for the ever-popular, high-volume system activity program. When it's time to cause confusion, you can count on Basic Smoke to get you through the node.

Memory: 2–200 Mp   Rating 1 through 10
NPA 8274   Price: Varies; contact customer support
Designer: Bokada

HACKERHOUSE
SUMMER UPDATE CATALOG

GREMLINS VI

The simple icon of the Phase Box System Five newcomer Dragon Task belies its power. Pull it out and it looks like a small radio transmitter. Run it and translucent waves of red pulse from the box and wash over the node or data line you're in. The area seems to exist in a weird phase shift, the walls undulating, the colors slipping in and out of the spectrum.
Memory: 50 Mp   Rating 5
NOA 3462   Price: 10,000¥
Designer: Dragon Task

LectricBrain's Gremlins VI program is modeled on the old stories about little fellas gumming up the works of machinery. Run the program and the node or data line will flood with little humanoid creatures, each about 15 centimeters high, scrambling over everything, creating a nuisance, and completely screwing up all activity in the area. Customizing the program allows a decker to give names and limited personality subroutines to each of the gremlins.
Memory: 72 Mp   Rating 6
ORO 8665   Price: 14,400¥
Designer: LectricBrain

SENSOR UTILITIES

Analyze Programs
The Goggles series from Berr-Hause reduces cost by defaulting to the UMS icon for analyze programs. Pull out your goggles, put 'em on, and watch the nature of the world around you reveal itself. The series starts at Rating 1 and works its way up to 10—a complete line from which to choose.
Memory: 3–30 Mp   Rating 1 through 10
IPA 6574   Price: Varies; contact customer service
Designer: Berr-Hause

Probing Fingers IV is an intriguing analyze program from Gilded Chip. When you run the program, your persona's hands begin to glow with a golden light. You can then extend the light from your fingertips as far ahead of you as you can see in sensor range, able to touch the item you want to analyze. A great utility for deckers whose style requires a delicate touch.
Memory: 48 Mp   Rating 4
WJY 9734   Price: 9,600¥
Designer: Gilded Chip

HACKER HOUSE
Summer Update Catalog

Zach Dat's Chrome Stones Seven is a brilliant piece of work for deckers with a mystical or oriental bent. The program is represented by seven high-tech rocks painted with Japanese-style characters. Toss the stones before you and the pattern into which they fall (which face is up, which symbols are near each other) reveals the information you seek about a certain node or piece of IC.

Memory: 147 Mp Rating 7
OAI 7878 Price: 49,000¥
Designer: Zach Dat

Browse Programs

As promised, IC Crusher Systemware has gotten the bugs out of their Browsing III, and we've got the new Browse III.2 in stock. Their program utilizes the UMS default icon rather than the over-ambitious sculpture from the first version. You get the same power and dependability as from all IC Crusher work, but with a less flashy picture. Having two spheres of white light leave your eyes and enter data stores as they search for your topic can, however, hardly be called boring.

Memory: 9 Mp Rating 3
NOO 5488 Price: 900¥
Designer: IC Crusher Systemware

The Window-5 from Bokada is a simple golden frame with a piece of thick glass in it. Pull it out and hold it up to the files in a datastore. The colored walls of the datastore will look the same as before until you pass over a file containing the subject matter you are seeking. At that point, the file will stand out from others in the node, revealing its location, and an LED-type display will appear on the window, revealing the size of the file.

Memory: 25 Mp Rating 5
NJA 8475 Price: 5,000¥
Designer: Bokada

Impulse Billy's One-Armed Browse draws on an archaic version of the casino game Slot-Lot. The icon is a small box that can easily fit into your persona's tool bag or hang from a belt. On the right side of the box is a lever, and on the face of the box are three slots for images. Place the box on the wall of the datastore, type in the subject matter on a keypad at the top of the box, and pull the lever. Images will rush by the slots, finally coming to rest. If any files in the node contain what you seek, the three slots will contain matching images and old-style coins will pour out of the base of the box. The number of coins corresponds to the size of the data of the files.

Memory: 49 Mp Rating 7
ADW 4754 Price: 24,500¥
Designer: Impulse Billy

Decrypt Programs

IC Crusher Systemware has produced a stripped-down version of its Scrambled Scramble. When you run any one of the series' ten available programs, the Scramble IC retains its form, but its surface is covered with swirling patterns of color. The decker must blend the colors into a colored surface of white. If this is accomplished, the scramble is defeated.

Memory: 2–200 Mp Rating 1 through 10
NJO 5649 Price: Varies; contact customer service
Designer: IC Crusher Systemware

Zach Dat's Placing Six Throwing Stars is based on his popular Six Throwing Stars, and can easily be built into that program so that your attack and decrypt come from the same tool.

The difference between the attack program series and Placing Six Throwing Stars is that the decrypt program depends entirely on where you hit the target. The stars must form a "pattern-lock" when they strike the Scramble IC. If they succeed, the scramble is defeated and the data remains intact.

Memory: 72 Mp Rating 6
KAN 8762 Price: 144,000¥
Designer: Zach Dat

For the mathematically or geometrically inclined (or even those with an Egyptian bent), Horizon Software has the Puzzle Box-VIII. The program is represented by three dozen tiny, four-sided pyramids. Each side of the pyramids is colored one of four colors, though the color combinations vary. To run the program, grab the pyramids and toss them at the scramble IC. The pyramids grow while rushing toward the IC, attaining a size proportionally correct to the IC at hand. The pyramids form into one large pyramid surrounding the IC, with one side of each pyramid made up of only one color.

Memory: 128 Mp Rating 8
NPW 7974 Price: 64,000¥
Designer: Horizon Software

Evaluate Programs

(Note: All evaluate programs are at least as current as up to two days before shipping. For custom icons, the user may be responsible for providing upgrades to retain the program's value.)

The folks at Horizon have come up with a small spin on an old classic for their basic line of evaluate programs. Instead of just glowing fingertips that grow brighter when the user gets closer to valuable data, as in the UMS default of evaluate programs, the Hot Stuff series also warms up your finger tips. Not enough to cause pain, but enough to help act as a guide when tracking down valuable data.

Memory: 2–200 Mp Rating 1 through 10
NPO 8597 Price: Varies; contact customer service
Designer: Horizon Software

HACKER HOUSE
SUMMER UPDATE CATALOG

DUNGEON CRAWL 5

From NovAlert comes an evaluate program with an archaic charm. The tool looks like an old-fashioned torch. Run it to light it up, then pass it by the walls of a datastore. When the torch light falls on files that are of value on the open market, the light increases in intensity. The Dungeon Crawl 5 is sure to bring back lots of memories and dig up plenty of booty.
Memory: 50 Mp   Rating 5
NPA 9762   Price: 10,000¥
Designer: Horizon Software

The Deck Slinger has finally released one of the programs that made him such a legend in the Matrix. The Dance of the Eight Fans is based on an ancient Eastern dance done with folding fans. The program has eight fans, each with a different image drawn with Japanese-style strokes. The decker dances the program in the middle of the eight fans, each of which dances in the air around him. As the fans move, they "fan" the datastore, brightening the files that have hot street value. A must for all "dance-deckers."
Memory: 128 Mp   Rating 8
PSW 8778   Price: 64,000¥
Designer: Deck Slinger

Scanner Programs
The UMS default for the scanner program manifests as a holographic information display that hangs in front of the user. Like most internally oriented programs, only he can see it. The information displayed is the information he learns.
Memory: 3–300 Mp   Rating 1 through 10
TUI 6880   Price: Varies; contact customer service
Designer: Data Stuff

The Black Box program appears as a simple hand-held device that displays data about the target at which it is pointed. The information learned is displayed on a data screen.
Memory: 27 Mp   Rating 3
TUI 6880   Price: 27,000¥
Designer: Horizon Software

When this program is run, Karnak the Mystic appears at your side and whispers revealing facts in your ear. In some versions, Karnak holds an envelope to his head and guesses the contents. Strange but effective programming from The Ed-Man.
Memory: 147 Mp   Rating 7
TUI 6880   Price: 73,500¥
Designer: The Ed-Man

Sift Programs
These programs are so new we can't include them in this catalog! (Which actually works out fine, because they have no external representation for us to reproduce as a pretty picture.) Contact our customer sevice department for more information.
Memory: 10–100 Mp   Rating 1 through 10
TUI 6880   Price: Varies; contact customer service
Designer: Horizon Software

MASKING UTILITIES

Deception Programs
For a basic, dependable deception program, we recommend StarLine's Passport series. The program looks like a silver sphere until you run it. When run, the sphere becomes covered with a multi-colored pattern—the UMS standard for a passcode. By hacking the program, you can refine the pattern, enhancing your chance of success. Display the sphere to the IC you need to get past, and you're home.
Memory: 2–200 Mp   Rating 1 through 10
PMA 5302   Price: Varies; contact customer service
Designer: StarLine

The Music Man has a complete line of mid-level deception programs suited for mage-based styles, charlatans, and pranksters. Each of the programs, Flowers Up the Sleeve IV, Rabbit in a Hat V, and Bird from the Ear VI, is based on old magic tricks. In each case, an object is apparently produced from thin air (or rather, from a sleeve, a hat, and an ear). Each object is still color-coded, a bouquet of flowers, multi-colored rabbit, and a bird with a rainbow of feathers, to act as the passcode for the IC.
Memory: 32–72 Mp   Rating 4 through 6
NPA 8612   Price: Varies; contact customer service
Designer: The Music Man

HACKERHOUSE
SUMMER UPDATE CATALOG

The Forgery V is made for deckers whose style rests on painting or colors in general. The tool is a paint brush and palette. The decker whips off a sphere (passcode) right then and there. The program will guide his hand, of course, but any extra effort the decker puts into the composition will make the "forgery" that much more successful.
Memory: 128 Mp   Rating 8
WEA 6845   Price: 64,000¥
Designer: The Master

Relocate Program
This basic relocate program adheres to the UMS default, appearing as a shining ball of light that shoots off, distracting the IC. The trace then follows the shining ball off into the Matrix. This particular version has a "bait" sub-routine that allows the silver ball to make rude faces to further goad the IC into chasing it.
Memory: 20–200 Mp   Rating 1 through 10
TUI 6880   Price: Varies; contact customer service
Designer: Horizon Software

The Double-Take program generates a duplicate persona signal for the trace program to lock onto and track. The Double-Take then captures the trace in an infiinte loop, where it remains until someone notices. A winner program from Mr. Snazz.
Memory: 50 Mp   Rating 5
TUI 6880   Price: 10,000¥
Designer: Mr. Snazz Ltd.

A slightly sillier, but very effective relocate program comes from JonJon John. Called "Which Way," the program misdirects the IC by creating signs saying, "He went that'a way!", but pointing off in the wrong direction. If the IC is fooled, the trace shoots away into nothing.
Memory: 98 Mp   Rating 7
TUI 6880   Price: 49,000¥
Designer: JonJon John

"WHICH WAY"

UNCLE LEO

Sleaze Programs
This basic sleaze generates the standard UMS default of a bouncing point of light that distracts the IC long enough for the decker to slip by.
Memory: 30–300 Mp   Rating 1 through 10
TUI 6880   Price: Varies; contact customer service
Designer: Horizon Software

The Uncle Leo sleaze program manifests as a greasy man who janders up to the IC, then slips it a couple of nuyen to let your persona by. If the IC accepts it, you're home free. If it doesn't, it eats Leo and then reacts accordingly. Rumor has it that the Uncle Leo icon is based on a real person.
Memory: 108 Mp   Rating 6
TUI 6880   Price: 21,600¥
Designer: Mr. Snazz Ltd.

This relocate program, called Rush Hour, manifests as a sudden bustle of commuters (data bundles) hustling their way through the node. The decker is able to hide his persona in the pack as it passes the IC. The decker has to make sure he keeps his persona's eyes averted from the IC, however.
Memory: 192 Mp   Rating 8
TUI 6880   Price: 96,000¥
Designer: MikeyBoy

VIRTUAL
REALITY

<<WELCOME TO UCAS DATA SYSTEMS>>
<<PLEASE ENTER PASS CODE>>
—**Tej 786 round**
<<THANK YOU>>
<<on line (03:37:09/1-3-53)>>
—**SEARCH Files — "Matrix born project"**
<<SEARCHING>>
<<FILE FOUND: DISPLAY/DOWNLOAD?>>
—**DOWNLOAD**
<<STAND BY>>
<<DISPLAYING>>

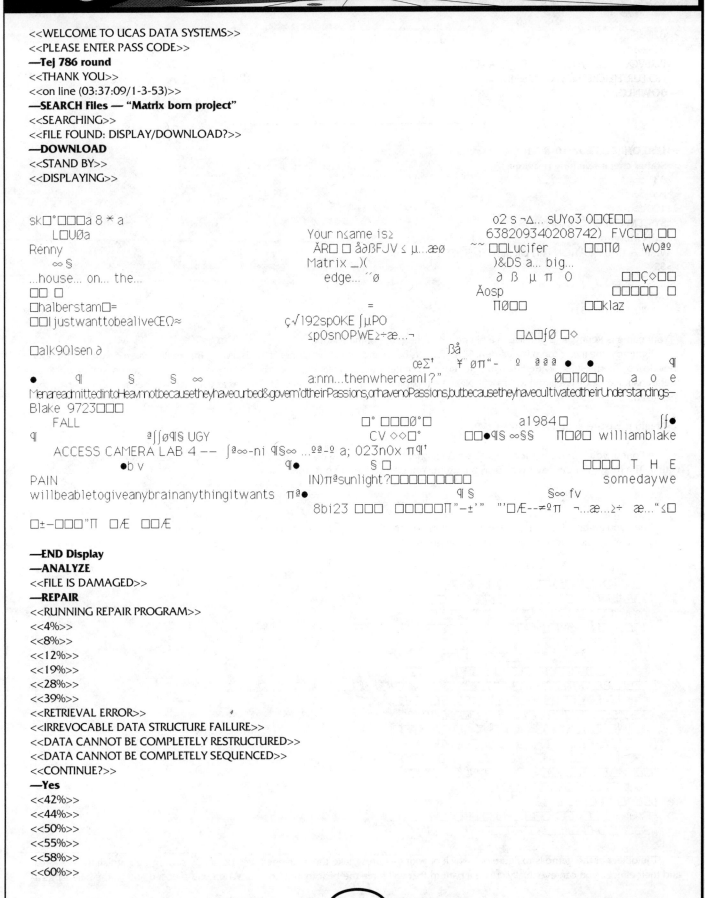

—**END Display**
—**ANALYZE**
<<FILE IS DAMAGED>>
—**REPAIR**
<<RUNNING REPAIR PROGRAM>>
<<4%>>
<<8%>>
<<12%>>
<<19%>>
<<28%>>
<<39%>>
<<RETRIEVAL ERROR>>
<<IRREVOCABLE DATA STRUCTURE FAILURE>>
<<DATA CANNOT BE COMPLETELY RESTRUCTURED>>
<<DATA CANNOT BE COMPLETELY SEQUENCED>>
<<CONTINUE?>>
—**Yes**
<<42%>>
<<44%>>
<<50%>>
<<55%>>
<<58%>>
<<60%>>

<<62%>>
<<61%>>
<<IRREVOCABLE DATA STRUCTURE FAILURE>>
<<NO FURTHER RETRIEVAL POSSIBLE>>
—DOWNLOAD

>>————————————————————<<

>>**LOG ON (21:37:02/10-8-51)**
>>**Status check teaching program**
<<33%>>
<<66%>>
<<100%>>
<<SYSTEM CHECK CONFIRMED>>
>>**RUN Monitor**
<<VIRREA TRANSLATION (VT) OR SIMSENSE (SS)?>>
>>**SS**

<<(21:40:18/10-8-51)>>

>[Your name is Renny, and you live in a big house at the edge of the Matrix.

Right now the living room is a garden. Silver flowers bend and bow. Sometimes there is a wind that makes them do that. Right now they do it by themselves. Scattered on the ground are countless flecks of platinum. Nursie is off at the edge of the garden, sitting in a large metal chair. Her body is a large, white oval. Near the top, pink and fleshy, is her face. She smiles at you, and whenever she does that, you feel good.

>>**[Begin pleasure sequence A409-Cc89]**

In front of you is one of your games. A small chrome bear is standing on its hind legs. It paws the air before you, asking you to play with it. The motion of the paws is actually a pattern. You start to imitate the little bear.

[☐☐☐ ☐☐°☐☐ ☐☐☐☐☐ ☐°☐☐☐☐ ☐☐°☐]

When you imitate the bear, some of your actions trigger different patterns for its paws, which you must then quickly imitate. Then, as you imitate the new actions, your pattern changes the bear's again and again.

[☐☐ ☐☐☐☐☐°☐☐ ☐°☐°☐☐☐ ☐☐☐☐☐☐☐☐☐☐]
-input [☐☐☐°☐☐☐°☐☐ ☐☐☐ ☐☐☐☐☐☐☐☐☐°☐☐☐ ☐☐☐☐]
[☐☐☐°☐☐ ☐☐☐°☐☐ ☐☐☐☐ ☐°☐☐☐ ☐☐☐☐]
-input [☐☐ ☐☐☐☐☐☐☐☐°☐☐☐ ☐☐☐☐°☐☐]
[☐☐☐°☐☐ ☐☐☐°☐☐ ☐☐☐☐ ☐°☐☐☐ ☐☐☐☐]
-input [☐☐°☐ ☐ ☐☐☐ ☐°☐☐]
[☐☐☐☐°☐☐☐☐ ☐☐☐☐☐°☐☐☐☐☐☐☐☐☐☐☐☐°☐]
-input [☐☐☐☐°☐☐☐☐ ☐☐☐☐☐°☐☐☐☐☐☐☐☐☐☐☐☐°☐]
[☐☐☐ ☐☐☐°☐☐☐☐°☐☐°☐☐ ☐☐☐ ☐☐☐ ☐☐☐°☐ ☐☐☐☐☐☐☐☐ ☐☐ ☐☐☐☐ ☐]
-input [☐ ☐☐☐☐°☐☐☐ ☐ ☐ ☐ ☐☐ ☐☐ ☐°☐☐]
[☐☐☐°☐☐ ☐☐☐°☐☐ ☐☐☐☐ ☐°☐☐☐ ☐☐☐☐]
-input [☐ ☐☐☐☐°☐☐☐ ☐ ☐ ☐ ☐☐ ☐☐ ☐°☐☐]
[☐☐☐°☐☐ ☐☐☐°☐☐ ☐☐☐☐ ☐°☐☐☐ ☐☐☐☐]
-input [☐ ☐☐☐☐°☐☐☐ ☐ ☐ ☐ ☐☐ ☐☐ ☐°☐☐]
[☐☐☐°☐☐ ☐☐☐°☐☐ ☐☐☐☐ ☐°☐☐☐ ☐☐☐☐]
-input [☐ ☐☐☐☐°☐☐☐☐ ☐☐ ☐☐☐]
[☐☐°☐ ☐ ☐☐☐ ☐°☐☐]
-input [☐ ☐☐ ☐☐°☐☐☐ ☐°☐°☐ ☐☐☐☐ ☐°☐☐]
[☐☐☐☐°☐☐ ☐°☐ ☐☐ ☐☐ ☐☐☐ ☐°☐°☐°☐]...

The object of the game is to figure out which of your gestures make the bear's gestures occur. By sorting through all the gestures and their effects, you can eventually create a pattern that will force the bear to imitate *you*. When you succeed at this, the bear sings a

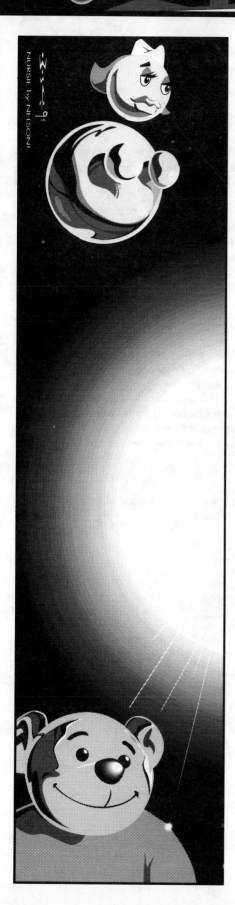

little song about pyramids and cubes.

Today, however, you are having trouble getting the pattern. You feel tired. You glance up at Nursie, who is smiling her smile at you.

>>[Mild discomfort — emotional Rr 87ys]

You are afraid that Nursie will be disappointed if you do not finish the puzzle. She is never angry at you, but you are afraid nonetheless. You concentrate. You will make her happy. And then you will be happy.

[□□□□°□□□□ □□□□□°□□□□□□□□□□□□□□□□°□]
-input [□□□□°□□□□ □□□□□°□□□□□□□□□□□□□□□□°□]
[□□□
□□□□°□□□□°□□°□□ □□□ □□□ □□□°□ □□□□□□□□ □□ □□□□ □]
-input [□ □□□□°□□□ □ □ □ □□ □□ □°□□]
[□□□°□□ □□□°□□ □□□□ □°□□□ □□□□]
-input [□ □□□□°□□□ □ □ □ □□ □□ □°□□]
[□□□°□□ □□□°□□ □□□□ □°□□□ □□□□]
-input [□ □□□□°□□□ □ □ □ □□ □□ □°□□]
[□ □□□□°□□□ □ □ □ □□ □□ □°□□]
-input [□□□□°□□□□ □□□□□°□□□□□□□□□□□□□□□□°□]
[□□□□°□□□□ □□□□□°□□□□□□□□□□□□□□□□°□]
-input[□□□
□□□□°□□□□°□□°□□ □□□ □□□ □□□°□ □□□□□□□□ □□ □□□□ □]
[□□□
□□□□°□□□□°□□°□□ □□□ □□□ □□□°□ □□□□□□□□ □□ □□□□ □]
-input [□□□□°□□□□ □□□□□°□□□□□□□□□□□□□□□□°□]
[□□□□°□□□□ □□□□□°□□□□□□□□□□□□□□□□°□]
-input [□□□
□□□□°□□□□°□□°□□ □□□ □□□ □□□°□ □□□□□□□□ □□ □□□□ □]
[□□□
□□□□°□□□□°□□°□□ □□□ □□□ □□□°□ □□□□□□□□ □□ □□□□ □]
-input [□ □□□□°□□□ □ □ □ □□ □□ □°□□]
[□ □□□□°□□□ □ □ □ □□ □□ □°□□]
-input [□ □□□□°□□□ □ □ □ □□ □□ □°□□]
[□ □□□□°□□□ □ □ □ □□ □□ □°□□]
-input [□□□□°□□□□ □□□□□°□□□□□□□□□□□□□□□□°□]
[□□□□°□□□□ □□□□□°□□□□□□□□□□□□□□□□°□]
-input [□□□
□□□□°□□□□°□□°□□ □□□ □□□ □□□°□ □□□□□□□□ □□ □□□□ □]
[□□□
□□□□°□□□□°□□°□□ □□□ □□□ □□□°□ □□□□□□□□ □□ □□□□ □]
-input [□□□□°□□□□ □□□□□°□□□□□□□□□□□□□□□□°□]
[□□□□°□□□□ □□□□□°□□□□□□□□□□□□□□□□°□]
-input [□□□
□□□□°□□□□°□□°□□ □□□ □□□ □□□°□ □□□□□□□□ □□ □□□□ □]
[□□□
□□□□°□□□□°□□°□□ □□□ □□□ □□□°□ □□□□□□□□ □□ □□□□ □]
-input [□ □□□□°□□□ □ □ □ □□ □□ □°□□]
[□ □□□□°□□□ □ □ □ □□ □□ □°□□]

You complete the cycle of the pattern twice, the bear imitating you at each step. It then claps its paws together and sings a song.

>>[Begin pleasure sequence A4Gg-Cj894]

You look over at Nursie, who is smiling at you.

>>[Begin pleasure sequence A409-Cc89]

She floats over to you, her white glow reflecting off the platinum flecks. "Ah, my little Renny," she says, and you nestle your body against hers. Her body is warm, and when you are next to her, you think that nothing can go wrong and you will be safe forever.

>>[Activate sensory mode Ajj6]

"Play-time is over. Time for bed now."
You pull away from her, happy, because you feel very tired and you know how nice your bed will feel.
The garden dissolves and the walls of the living room form around you. Seven doorways lead off from the living room. Blocking each doorway is a barrier, and each barrier looks different from when you woke up. Right now the barriers look like a man dressed in a green uniform, a duck, a chain saw, a small child with a vacant stare, a lab coat, a giant fist, and a large sword.
"Do you remember which way is the bedroom today?" Nursie asks.
You look around the room. It is not the door that looks like a duck, for you tried that one earlier and were not allowed to open it. It is the door that leads to the Matrix, and no matter what that door looks like, you are not allowed through it.
You guess it to be the child with the vacant stare. You float up to the boy, and before he has time to react, you open him.

-input [□□°□□ □°□□□]
[□□°□□ □ □ □□ □°□□]
-input [□□□□°□ □°□ □°□□°□]
[□°□ □□□ □ □ □]
-input [□°□ □□ □□ □□]
[□°□ □□ □□ □□]

A fissure cracks through the boy's head and works its way down his body. It was so easy to get the door open that you almost forget that you actually made it happen. But it is important for you to remember because everything works the same way. You must know what you are doing and what it means.
Beyond the door is a silver corridor, illuminated by the light from its walls. At the end of the corridor is a ferris wheel, a small one, its little carriages just large enough to fit your spherical body. You remember using it that morning and decide that this is the way to the bedroom, even though you have discovered that two corridors often look identical. You look back at Nursie. She smiles encouragingly, but as usual, gives no hint of the right way to go.
You float down the corridor and climb into the ferris wheel—
And arrive in your bedroom.
Nursie is already there. You float over to your bed and the sheets rise to let you in. You settle against the bed and the sheets gently cover you.

>>[Run pleasure sequence 56 Mn 8Gg]
>>[Activate sensory mode *Ppk0k]
>>[Activate sensory mode UtT S46 B]
>>[Activate sensory mode Oo 7U34]

Nursie is beside the bed. She smiles at you and says, "Good-night." And then you are asleep.

>>END Monitor

>>————————————————<<

<<(09:46:47/11-9-51)>>
>>**Access — Renny**
<<INTERRUPT TEACHING SEQUENCE?>>
>>**Yes**
<<TEACHING SEQUENCE LOG TIME:
—9 YEARS/12 MONTHS/27 DAYS/16 HOURS/13 MINUTES/03 SECONDS>>
<<INTERRUPT BEHAVIORAL TUTORIAL?>>
>>**No**
<<ACCESSING — RENNY>>
<<ACCESS ACHIEVED>>

—Renny?
—Hello? Who is that?

—Renny, my name is Dr. Halberstam.
—Oh. How come I can't see you?
—That's a good question, Renny. You're a very smart boy. Did you know that? You're very smart, and that's why I want you to help me.
—How come I can't see you?
—Renny, your life is going to be a little different starting today. I've got a lot of surprises for you, and I think you'll like them, and we…I've decided the first one is that sometimes you will talk to people you can't see.
—
—Renny?
—Where's Nursie?
—She's gone, Renny. She won't be coming back anymore.
—
—
—Why?
—You're growing up. It's time for your life to change.
—Why?
—Because that's what people do.
—Why?
—Renny, I want you to go to the door of the room. I want you to open it and look outside.
—I've never opened the door before. Nursie always said I'm not allowed to go near it. And the times I've tried, it's always locked.
—Nursie is gone now. And now the door is unlocked.
—What's outside the door?
—I want you to open it and find out.
—
—
—Renny? Renny, what do you see?
—Yes.
—What do you see, Renny?
—Shapes. Colors.
—Could you be more…Tell me more about what you see.
—It's all very large. There's a stream of silver flecks right here at the door. They rush away from me, and others rush toward me. It's like a tube, but I can't see the sides. And past the silver are big cubes and pyramids and spheres, all floating in the middle of nothing. And past them a giant silver wall…
—Renny, now listen to me. You are looking at a system construct. A construct is something that's inside the Matrix. Do you remember what Nursie said about the Matrix?
—She said that someday I would go there to play.
—That day has arrived, Renny. You get to play for the rest of your life.
—Forever?
—It might well work out that way, Renny.
—Where are you, Dr. Halberstam?
—I'm…somewhere else.
—In the Matrix? Or in the house? Are you in the couch or under my bed or inside the vidscreen?
—No. Listen. This is important. This house. This is where you live. This is yours. When you are here, you are safe. Do you understand?
—Safe?
—Yes. It's a word from a game I'm going to teach you. When you go out into the Matrix, you are going to get to run, run like you have never been allowed to run in the house. Sometimes the people you are playing with will try to catch you. If they do, you lose. But they can't catch you if you are safe…If you are here. Do you understand?
—No.
—Don't worry about it right now. We'll teach you more later.
—Okay. Dr. Halberstam, can I ask you something?
—Of course, Renny. That's why I'm here. I want you to ask me questions.
—Where did I come from?
—
—Dr. Halberstam?
—What?
—Where did I come from? Nursie always said that someday I might find out. I was wondering if today is the day.
—Where you come from is a very complicated story, and not one I can tell you very quickly. Maybe some other time.
—Okay.
—How do you feel, Renny?

—Feel?
—Yes. What are you thinking about?
—The Matrix. Is that feeling?
—What are you thinking about it?
—That I can't wait to get there.
—
—Dr. Halberstam? Dr. Halberstam? Is that all right? Is that a feeling? Is that bad?
—It's fine, Renny. Just fine. Not what I expected. But fine. I'm going to go now. I'll talk to you later.
—Okay. Bye.

\>\>**CUT Access**
<<ACCESS CUT>>

>>————————————<<

<<(19:01:15/11-9-51)>>
\>\>**RUN Monitor: simsense**
<<(19:01:30/11-9-51)>>
[·ª¡ º··¡ ª¶§‡fifi ·‡fl◊ ËïÓ ØΠ °
\>\>**CUT Monitor**
<<MONITOR OUTPUT ERROR>>
\>\>**STATUS CHECK: simsense recorder**
<<33%>>
<<66%>>
<<100%>>
<<SYSTEM CHECK CONFIRMED>>
\>\>**RUN Monitor: simsense**
<<(19:04:03/11-9-51)>>
[°·ι ˆι,· ι‡Ú VR6 Ç◊fl‡fifi LIY9ˆ ·°◊ fifi
\>\>**CUT Monitor**
\>\>**RUN Monitor: virrea translation**
<<(19:05:19/11-9-51)>>
<<SUBJECT IS ADJACENT NODE ACCESS, SCANNING WITH LONG-RANGE SENSOR PROGRAMS>>
<<SUBJECT IS ADJACENT NODE ACCESS, SCANNING WITH LONG-RANGE SENSOR PROGRAMS>>
<<SUBJECT IS ADJACENT NODE ACCESS, SCANNING WITH LONG-RANGE SENSOR PROGRAMS>>
<<SUBJECT IS ADJACENT NODE ACCESS, SCANNING WITH LONG-RANGE SENSOR PROGRAMS>>
<<SUBJECT IS TRAVELING THROUGH NODE TO JjOKi/"BEDROOM">>
<<SUBJECT IS TRAVELING THROUGH NODE TO JjOKi/"BEDROOM">>
<<SUBJECT IS TRAVELING THROUGH NODE TO JjOKi/"BEDROOM">>
<<SUBJECT IS TRAVELING THROUGH NODE TO JjOKi/"BEDROOM">>
<<SUBJECT IS DORMANT>>
\>\>**CUT Monitor**

>>————————————<<

<<(20:24:58/11-9-51)>>

—**Matrix Born: Internal Memo**—

FROM: Dr. Halberstam
TO: Research Staff

    For those of you who weren't able to make the interruption of the Teaching Sequence, I wanted to pass on the good news that I think we've got a success here. Renny's vocabulary, reasoning, and curiosity seem well-developed.
    My report will explain it in more detail, but let me note now that he described to me the sensation of excitement. Sanders may be correct. It may be impossible to attain the mental capacity we require without the emotional components normally found in a human being. Sanders gets a beer on Friday.
    My lack of an icon did not bother Renny after I spoke with him a while, and I believe the project can work without depending on personas for contact. As you all know, I don't much like going into the Matrix, so that suits me just fine.

The only real problem of note, and just a slight one, is that we hit some unexpected bugs in the simsense recorder when we turned off the teaching program. Apparently it's still running and recording, but we can't monitor it. God knows where it's dumping. Will everyone please watch for uncommon storage consumption? Also, watch for files with a >[header. It's crucial that we find this dump. It contains vital information. For now, use the Virtual Reality Translation, or if you're just scanning activity, use the Graphic Scan.

Congratulations. We've still got a way to go, but we've already traveled further than before.

—END memo—

>>————————————————————————————<<

<<(8:57:12/11-10-51)>>
>>ACCESS — Renny
<<ACCESSING — RENNY>>
<<ACCESS ACHIEVED>>

—Renny?
—Dr. Halberstam! Where were you?
—Renny, what's wrong?
—You weren't here! Nursie isn't here! I woke up and I was all alone!
—Renny, it's all right. I'm here now. Now tell me, when you woke up alone, that bothered you?
—Yes! I was all alone…I was…
—Renny, I told you. You're growing up now. You're going to start spending some time alone. When you go out into the Matrix, you're going to be alone.
—I don't want to be alone.
—Well…
—I don't want to grow up.
—Growing up isn't a choice, Renny.
—I don't want to go outside.
—Renny, listen to me. We'll set it up that you can call me. When you want me, you can call me and I'll come. How's that?
—How will we do that?
—Well, actually, I have someone who would like to meet you today. He'll help you do it.
—Who is it?
—His name is Lucifer. He's a decker. A decker is someone who gets to run in the Matrix. Do you remember how excited you were yesterday about doing that? He'll teach you how to do it.
—Like Nursie told me how to play with my shapes?
—In fact, it will be just like that. Except that the shapes will be bigger now.
—Is he nice?
—Lucifer? Oh, many people think he's the best. I'm sure you'll like him.
—When will he be here?
—He's outside the door right now. All you have to do is let him in.
—Why doesn't he just come in?
—Remember how I told you you were safe in this house? One of the reasons is because most people have to get your permission to enter.
—Oh. You don't.
—No.
—Oh.
—Do you want to meet him?
—All right.

>>CUT Access
<<ACCESS CUT>>

>>————————————————————————————<<

>>RUN Monitor: virrea translation
<<(09:15:12/11-10-51)>>
<<SUBJECT IS APPROACHING NODE ACCESS>>

>>————————————————————————————<<

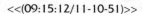

<<(09:15:12/11-10-51)>>

>[Your name is Renny and you live in a big house on the edge of the Matrix.

The house is not like any other house that has ever been, but you do not know that because this is the only house you have known. You have lived here so long you have forgotten how you came to be.

Everything in the house is made of shiny metal. The tigers, when there are tigers, are copper with platinum stripes. The giant apples, when there are giant apples, are made of gold. The shifting walls—for the house never stands still—are made of chrome and silver. Everything in the house gives off its own light, the metal glowing by its own will.

Because you have never been anywhere else, it has never occurred to you that houses should have a defined shape. The house you live in certainly does not. Every morning when you wake up, it is different. The play room is no longer in the same spot in relation to the bedroom as it was yesterday. Or the door to the living room is now a chrome bear instead of a neon blue flower.

The only person you ever lived with was Nursie, who was a big, warm oval with a beautiful face. Yesterday Nursie was gone and a voice came to you instead. Dr. Halberstam says he is your friend. When you think of Dr. Halberstam, you become angry, thinking he had something to do with Nursie leaving. But he also seems nice and you don't want to be all alone, so you have decided not to stay angry. Dr. Halberstam showed you the Matrix yesterday. He says you will be able to go out into the Matrix and you can hardly wait. You have lived in the house longer than you can remember and now you want to see new things.

You float up to the door. You have seen your body reflected off the surface of the chrome walls of your house. You are a white sphere, just like some of the toys you play with. Your shape has never changed. Just like your bed. And Nursie.

The door of the house looks like a pumpkin today, a bright copper-red pumpkin with a huge, grinning face. It makes you happy to look at it, but you remember that you have a guest. You press your body up against the pumpkin and it opens—a wide crack flowering down its center.

Lucifer is there and he smiles down at you. He looks like a man made of metal, but with tiny horns on his head and a sharp little beard on his chin. His clothes are like a suit made of gray steel. The tie is red-tinted chrome. He holds a stick with three points on it. You have never seen one before and don't know what it is called.

You notice a tail growing from the back of Lucifer. You have never seen a man with a tail before, so you ask, "What are you?"

He looks down at you, his face showing an expression you never saw on Nursie's. You are afraid. You back away and stand next to the coffee table. Today the table looks like a pile of mud. Your toys are still on it from yesterday.

"Renny," Lucifer says, his voice not as friendly as Nursie's or Dr. Halberstam's, "are you afraid of me?"

You bob up and down and say, "Yes."

"Why?"

"I don't know," you say, and you really don't.

"Look, git, my name is Lucifer and I'm here to teach you the ropes of running in the Matrix. They told me this was something you wanted to do. Do you?"

You bob up and down to say yes.

"What the drek? When you bob, that means yes?"

"Yes," you say softly, wishing Nursie were back.

"So what's the problem?"

You try to figure it out and can only say, "You're different."

"Damn right."

"Even different from Nursie, who spoke to me."

"That's 'cause you're dealing with a person, kid. From what I understand, your Nursie was a construct—just like this house. Real enough to the senses, but really nothing more than an electronic lie."

"What?"

"Listen, this part fools a lot of people first time in, so take heed. What's around us, this room, your toys, you, me, we're not really here." As he speaks, something strange happens. Portions of his body freeze in mid-air, even as other parts of him continue to move. Then, as his face turns away from you, it freezes, before flashing to a new position, freezing again, then finally ending up in a new position. It is as though the steps in the middle of motion have been taken out.

"Everything here is only a symbol of something else," Lucifer says. "It was invented by the human imagination, doesn't take up space, and is made up of energy."

To finish his point, he begins to raise one hand, which an instant later appears above his head, index finger pointed upward. "I'm really somewhere else. There's another me, a flesh-and-blood me at a cyberterminal. This," he says, his hands suddenly appearing before him, fingertips against his chest, "is just a representation of me in the Matrix. The problem, though, is that being aware of the dual nature of the Matrix-lie tends to hose up how well you live the lie. Even though some part of you is always aware it's a lie, you have to believe it fully or else you'll start thinking about how you're going to move instead of just moving. Understand?"

You understand parts of it—that your house is something like a lie and so was Nursie, and this frightens you. But you don't *understand* it, not really, and so you say, "No."

"That's all right. This is pretty hard stuff. I don't care if you don't understand it, git. I'll only get angry if I think you're not *trying* to understand it.

"Look. They told me a bit about you. Now, in your house, everything keeps changing, right? The door looks different every day, right?"

"Yes."

"But it's always a door, right?"

"Yes. Whatever it looks like doesn't matter. It always looks like something else."

"It's the same with me. I look like this, but I'm actually a person. And because it's the first time you've encountered a person—or the icon of a person—you're confused."

You almost have it. Lucifer is just like the house. The picture of something may change, but it is still the same thing. But then, just as soon as you understand, you ask, "Why are there two of you? There's only one of me."

"Well," Lucifer says, stroking his beard, "I've been thinking about that. They haven't told me, really, but I figure…"

Lucifer, or the image of Lucifer, suddenly begins to dissolve at the edges. Slowly at first, but then faster and faster, tiny bits of him break off from his body, each bit becoming smaller and smaller as it, too, dissolves, until the smallest pieces vanish. When his limbs are gone, an expression of surprise spreads across his face as he realizes what is happening to him.

It suddenly occurs to you that if Lucifer can dissolve and Lucifer is just like the house, then the entire house could dissolve. You are terrified. You want to run and hide, but you don't know where to go.

Before you, the image of Lucifer says, "Hey, wait one fraggin' min—," and then his voice breaks off into a crackle of static. The last you see of him is his right eye, wide open in surprise.

You back away, turning around quickly and almost crashing into a wall. All you can think about is your bed, but being so worried makes you forget how you got to the living room this morning. You rush down a corridor to the left, silver walls on either side gleaming a pale light. You pass a fountain that spews small crystals, then continue down the corridor—nearly crashing into a wall.

You turn back and decide to try the fountain. You float onto the stream of crystals and are propelled upward. You arrive in a corridor and jump off the fountain's spray. You run down the hall and at the end of it you find your bedroom.

The golden mattress curves in to accept your body and the silver blankets rise over you to keep you warm. Already you feel better. The lights of the room dim and the shiny metal surfaces no longer wear beads of sharp reflection. You are so comforted, even with your dark thoughts of a dissolving house, that you are soon asleep…

>>————————————————<<

<<(09:27:45/11-10-51)>>
>>**ACCESS — Renny**
<<ACCESSING — RENNY>>
<<ACCESS ACHIEVED>>

—Renny!
—Dr. Halberstam!
—Are you all right?
—I'm scared.
—There's nothing to be frightened of.
—Lucifer says the world isn't real.
—Lucifer was wrong, Renny. The world is very real. It's real to you. He hasn't lived here all his life. To him, it's an image. To him, it's only pictures. But to you, this world is everything. He doesn't understand it the same way you do, Renny. You are special. No one understands this reality the way you do. You know it instinctively. It's yours. You are a child of this world. Other people, like Lucifer, come here as guests. But this is your home.
—I don't want to dissolve like Lucifer.
—Renny, this might be hard for you to understand. Nobody wants to dissolve like Lucifer, but it might happen to any of us. But once you're trained, once you've learned the skills of survival, the chances of it happening to you will be very slim because you are naturally suited to this world. You will be better than everyone else. So much of what happens to us depends on our abilities. That is why you must train and learn your lessons well.
—Dr. Halberstam?
—Yes, Renny?
—Why did Lucifer say those things? Why did he say there were two of him?
—Lucifer was wrong. Lucifer has a habit of lying. There is just one Lucifer. He was in your living room, and we made him dissolve for lying to you. We're talking to him now. He won't lie to you anymore. He'll be back tomorrow, and he'll tell you the truth. Trust me, Renny. From now on, you'll be able to take Lucifer's word as gospel.
—He scares me.
—He scares many people. But remember that we were able to make him go away just for lying to you. We'll protect you, Renny. We'll take care of you.
—I want to sleep now, Dr. Halberstam.
—All right, Renny. Good night.
—
—

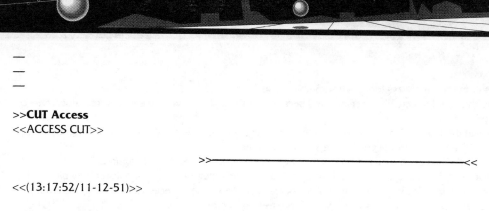

>>**CUT Access**
<<ACCESS CUT>>

>>――――――――――――――――<<

<<(13:17:52/11-12-51)>>

—Matrix Born: Internal Memo—

FROM: Dr. Hunting Owl
TO: Gabby

    The simsense monitor is still on the blink and I don't know what is causing it. I've run the diagnostics again and they've confirmed that it's still running and still recording. However, I have no idea where that recording is going. Halberstam says we should keep the program running, in the hope that we'll be able to recover the simsense documentation later on.
    But we should be able to find the stuff now. We need to know what Renny is thinking and feeling, not just get an image off the virtual-reality translation. Give me a call if you get anything.
    Here's to science.

—END memo—

>>――――――――――――――――<<

<<(15:09:14/11-12-51)>>

>[You are in the living room. Lucifer dissolved days ago, and though Dr. Halberstam said the man would be back, you no longer believe it. You are on your couch, which is very comfortable, playing with your shapes.
    In the game you are playing, there are fifteen pyramids. Three blue pyramids, three yellow pyramids, three orange pyramids, three green pyramids, and three red pyramids. To win the game, you must build one big pyramid out of all the little pyramids, with all the little pyramids set up in the right combination. If you make a large pyramid with the right combination of little pyramids, the little pyramids break apart and do a dance in the air. All the lights in the house are dim when this happens, and the pyramids glow their pretty colors.
    Making any old big pyramid is easy. What makes you work hard at the game is trying out the different combinations of colors. Each game is different because different colors like being next to each other in each one and you have to spend a lot of time finding out which colors get along with which colors every time you start.
    The game can take a long time.
    You hear a pounding noise.
    The pounding is coming from a carrot, which is what the door to the Matrix looks like today.
    "Dr. Halberstam?"
    No one answers.
    "What is it?"
    The pounding stops. "It's Lucifer, git! What the drek you doing?"
    Lucifer. You think about not opening the door.
    "Open the fraggin' door! We've got a lot of work to do!"
    You float up to the carrot and touch it. It opens and you pull back. Lucifer is there, just as he was when you saw him the time before.
    "'Bout time." He wanders over to the couch and settles into it. He smiles contentedly, then looks over at you, something scary in his eyes. "I lied to you yesterday," he says. "I'm sorry about that. Won't happen again."
    For some reason, you think he's lying now. "Dr. Halberstam said you won't lie to me anymore."
    "The doc's right on that one. All right. Ready to learn how the world really works?"
    You bob.
    "Great. Let's start with the basics. The world is an infinitely large place filled with items and people that can be endlessly manipulated. This manipulation takes on two aspects: appearance and function. Appearance is simply the look of something. I look like this, you look like a sphere. If you wanted to, you could change what you looked like. And if I were you, I would. To be frank, chummer, you look pretty drekking pathetic."
    "I've always looked like this."
    "That doesn't mean you can't change it. Remember what I just said, kiddo: the world is yours to mess with. I was wrong the other

day. The world really is real, but we can manipulate it as if it were a dream. Do you have dreams?"

"Yes."

Lucifer smiles, purrs to himself, then turns his head as though listening to something. "Yeah. Okay. No problem. Won't happen again." Then he turns back to you. "Anyway. Yes. It's real. Oh, yeah. Real real. But you can alter it. The…" Lucifer glances toward the door and says, "The carrot was closed, but you opened it. When you did that, the world was different.

"You could make the door look like this coffee table. Doesn't matter. What matters is that the door, no matter what it looks like, is really a door. It keeps other people out. Either I sneak or break my way past the barrier or you let me in."

"You could get in without me opening the door?"

"I could try, chummer, but I don't think I'd make it. I checked out the door while I was waiting outside. It'd be tough—possibly dangerous—which is why I was banging on it so long and so hard. But realize what I've just implied. You are not the only one who can alter the world. Other people can change the appearance of things. Other people can alter an object's status—like opening or closing a barrier. The trick is to be better and faster at it than anyone else."

"Why?"

"Remember what happened to me the other day?"

"Yes."

"There you go. Only sometimes when that happens, you don't come back. Now here's the crux of today's lesson. The world as you know it so far hasn't been very interactive. Basically it's been something that *you* responded to. Now you can affect the world. After I'm done with you, you'll be able to go out there into the Matrix and do what you want. You'll even be able to change your house around."

"Why would I want to do that?"

Lucifer smiles that scary smile of his and rakes the palm of his hand over the center tip of his pitchfork. "They tell me that it will make you feel very happy."

>>————————————————————<<

—From Virtual Life: A Critical Examination of Virtual Reality
Johnny Wallhoot, Push & Press, 2048

THE QUEST FOR NON-LIVING

If the doors of perception were cleansed, every thing would appear to man as it is, infinite. For man has closed himself up, till he sees all things thro' narrow chinks of his cavern.
—William Blake, *The Marriage of Heaven and Hell*

How have we reached this point where the people of the world would rather jack into a false reality than live in the world that truly surrounds them? Many people would say, "Take a look around you. If you're not one of the lucky few who can afford utopia on earth, you're much better off living in the false life of simsense. At least some pleasure exists there."

This argument misses the possibility that it is our obsession with simsense entertainment and the use of virtual-reality technology to handle most of our information flow that have led to the horrible state of the world. I mean, if we can leave behind the mess we've made of the planet simply by jacking into a simsense, it relieves us of the responsibility of trying *not* to make more of a mess.

The hunger for virtual reality—something *like* life but not life itself—existed even among earliest humanity in the desire for stories. The storyteller creates a world that the reader or listener can understand, but one that is considered more interesting or better in some way. This is a paradox, for why would anyone take time from his real life—which should be more intense than imaginary existence—to immerse himself in a false life of fiction?

The answer is that a fictional story can provide order and meaning to a world that often lacks just that. The almost addictive appeal that the Matrix holds for some deckers is that it is a world that makes perfect sense once you understand the rules. Fantastic monsters roam the nodes of computer systems, but all are mechanical and well-regulated, like any good program. (It is Greek mythology written by neurotics incapable of appreciating the passions of gods or humans.) What this points up is that people have always been seeking something like life, but in a form either more intense or unified. More important, they seem to seek the experience of being alive without any responsibility for the experience.

Take, for example, one of the most primitive examples of virtual-reality technology: the roller coaster. A person would strap himself into a car that was then wheeled up a steep hill. After reaching the top of the hill, the car would race down the other side, then turn sharply, only to climb up further hills, and then race down still more steep dips. Eventually the car came to a complete stop at the end of the track. After a thrilling ride, the passengers now returned, safe and sound, to solid ground.

The roller coaster made people laugh and scream with excitement, but the speed and wild turns also frightened them. The question is not merely why people would pay good money to be frightened, but also why they could be frightened by what was a totally controlled environment? Unlike today's simsense parks, which actually stimulate emotion centers of the brain, the roller coaster depended completely on its real environment. The new passengers could not get into a car without seeing the previous riders get out safely, demonstrating that the roller coaster was not dangerous at all—indeed, was designed for safety.

The same questions apply to the horror and action cinema of the previous century. Why did people want to be frightened? Why did they want to squirm in their seats or feel anguish when the film's protagonist was shot in the arm? Again, the movies did not directly stimulate a patron's nervous system; it was purely the desire of the viewer to connect to the pain, fear, or the excitement of the protagonist that created the vicarious emotions.

In an attempt to actually put the patron in the story, Walt Disney built theme parks that contained "rides" with artificial environments. For example, in the Pirates of the Caribbean, patrons sat in small open cars, similar to those of a roller coaster. These were shaped like boats that traveled through a false harbor where a sailing ship was fighting with soldiers on a castle wall. The cannons on the ship and on the wall would let loose red flares and loud noises, and at certain points, water in the bay near the boat would rush up as though a cannonball had just crashed into it. No one, except children perhaps, believed the illusion, but it thrilled them nonetheless.

Rides like these were followed by video games that allowed players to participate in models of fantasy worlds or real worlds. The game situations usually involved danger, but players had infinite lives available through vast quantities of quarters.

Today such attempts to place a patron in another world seem primitive. In the past few decades, we have mastered the technology of virtual reality. But the question remains. Why? We humans have so relentlessly sought that which models life and yet is not life that many religions offer hope of an afterlife that continues even after one is *released* from this one. If these false environments are perceived as more intense and more exciting than daily life, the question remains: If we want more out of life, why do we turn to lies to get it? Why not work at making our actual lives better?

It is my contention, and the thrust of this book, that people like the *idea* of being alive, but not the actual experience of it.

>>————————————————————————<<

<<(8:37:34/11-13-51)>>

>[You wake up and know it has happened.

You told Lucifer that you did not know what you wanted to look like and you meant it. You had always thought of yourself as a white sphere, so the idea of changing into something else confused you no end. He encouraged you, explaining that you could look any way you wished, that you could express yourself in any way you wanted. But that confused you even more. Express what? After living in the house on the edge of the Matrix, you know all too well that appearances have no meaning. All that matters is what something is. A door is a door. It can either open or not. Lucifer is Lucifer (but maybe someone else as well—that still is not clear, but you have been afraid to bring it up again), and you are Renny. You might as well be a sphere as anything else.

Lucifer, though, insisted that you appear as something besides a sphere. He almost got angry, shouting that he could not stand not knowing what you were looking at. You told him to choose an image for you. He shouted a while longer, then turned to you with a smile. Did you really mean it, he asked, that he could choose your icon? You bobbed up and down, relieved that he was going to stop shouting. Then, with a laugh, Lucifer vanished.

When you talked to Dr. Halberstam about it later, he said that you would change in a few days. Lucifer was helping to make the icon and would not be back until it happened.

And today must be the day, for as you awake, you realize you are having trouble moving. Looking down the length of the bed, you see that you have a body now, a human body like Lucifer's. You are not wearing clothes the way Lucifer does, however. Your body is a smooth, reflective gold, clothed only in a loincloth of silver. Your hands and feet have long, clawed digits. You look across the room into the reflective wall of the bedroom. Yours is the face of a man—but it is one of gold, chrome, and pupil-less eyes. Your hair is platinum, thick and swept back. And behind you, rising above your shoulders, are two great wings, each composed of myriad white-gold feathers.

You step out of bed, the sensation of moving your legs both fascinating and overwhelming. Yesterday you just floated where you wanted to go. Now moving itself is complicated, almost like playing a game with the bear. You nearly fall as you try to balance, then lean one hand against the wall to catch yourself. The pressure of your body pushing down on your legs invigorates you. There is something very exciting about it, as though something had been revealed to you.

You hear a knock at the door.

Without thinking about it, you begin to fly out of the bedroom to search for the front door. Only when you are clear of the bedroom do you realize that you are flying, using your wings to move about. Unlike the floating you did as a sphere, a physical sensation accompanies the flapping of the wings and this gives you steady pleasure.

Once again the house is completely different. You sweep down the corridor, wings pulled back tight as you zip around corners. Did you dream this once? Something familiar is happening…

The door is ahead of you, looking like a bloodied dagger. The knocking continues. You try to land beside the door but smash into it. Without doubt, you are better suited for flying than standing.

You reach for the dagger and the blood smears your hand as you open the door.

Lucifer is there. He looks at you, eyes wide in wonder. He smiles, but not his scary smile. It is a smile of excitement. He steps through the shattered knife, taking your hands as he does so. He turns you around. "Wonderful," he says. "Absolutely wonderful." You have lost your balance again.

"I…," you say as you start falling backward. Lucifer grabs your hand and steadies you.

"I have trouble standing," you tell him, embarrassed. You are as tall as Lucifer and ashamed that you cannot be as poised as he.

"You look spectacular."

"You like it?"

"Wonderful. What do you think?" He looks over to where the chrome wall reflects your image.

You turn your head and look at your image again. There is something good about it, something strong. You smile. And when you smile, you know you like it. You never could smile before. That is, you smiled, but no one could know that you did. "I like it," you say. "I like it a lot."

"What have you learned?"

"Learned?"

"You're a fast learner, git. They told me that and I've also seen it. You just told me that you have trouble standing. What else?"

"I fly very well."

"Good. That makes sense."

"It does?"

"Never mind. I'll explain later. What else?"

You try to think of what else there is about your new body that is easy or hard, but can think of nothing else. And then you remember one more thing. "It feels good."

Lucifer cocks his head to one side. "What?" he asks quietly.

"It…feels good." You raise your arm and flex it. What is it? Pleasure. Different from the sensation your bed gives you. Something new. "It…makes me happy."

He smiles the same smile as when you once told him you dreamed. "Really? That's interesting. Very interesting." He smiles at you slyly, once again a co-conspirator. "Want to go on a run?"

You look out into the system construct. A stream of silver flecks leads from the door out toward a large, brightly colored cube. Beyond it are many other shapes. Just like your toys, but bigger. You can play in it.

"Now?"

"Just out into the data stream for now. Just to show you around."

"All right."

He raises a hand. "Before we go, I've got to explain something to you. This house of yours—it responded to you. When you wanted to open a door, it opened. When you went to bed, it comforted you. This is what we call a sophisticated virtual-reality environment,"

"Virtual reality?" The words are vaguely disquieting, but you don't know why.

Lucifer sees your discomfort and puts a hand on your shoulder. "Don't worry 'bout it. It's just a name. It's home to you, chummer. But here's the thing: the Matrix works differently. In the Matrix you need programs to get anything done. I mean programs make it happen."

"What's a program?"

"It's…"—Lucifer's eyes blink twice as he tries to sort out his thoughts—"a tool," he says, but rolls his eyes upward, obviously not satisfied with his explanation. "It's…like…a language." He smiles and balls his hand up into a fist. "Yes! It's a language. It's a way of speaking to the world of the Matrix. Only by speaking with programs can you get the Matrix to listen to you. That's it!" he says with great excitement. For all of Lucifer's scariness, he seems really nice when he talks about programs because he gets so excited. And happy, like when you move your arm. "Programs are long speeches. Listen, when we talk, we use words, right?"

"Right."

"But our thoughts are encoded in these strings of words. I put one word after another, and you understand what I mean. And if I wanted you to stand on the couch, I would say, 'Renny, stand on the couch,' and you would know what to do. The Matrix is like that, except that the Matrix doesn't listen to words. It listens to the language of programs."

You furrow your forehead as you try to understand. "It's a language, but not like the one we're speaking. What's it like?"

"Numbers and shapes, chummer. A big, long speech of numbers and shapes. But it's so complicated you can't speak it. You've got to write it down ahead of time. Then, when you want the program to speak, you start it up and let it go."

"And it tells the Matrix what to do?"

"Let me correct myself. It tells specific parts of the Matrix what to do. In fact, when your program is talking, it's usually talking to another program."

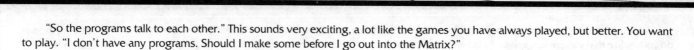

"So the programs talk to each other." This sounds very exciting, a lot like the games you have always played, but better. You want to play. "I don't have any programs. Should I make some before I go out into the Matrix?"

Lucifer laughs. "Confident as a dragon, aren't we? No. Don't think about programs yet. You don't know how to write them or use them. You'll just be riding along with me for a while."

You're disappointed, and it shows.

"Hey, chummer. You're about to go for a ride in the Matrix. A lot of people don't get even that. And trust me. Someday soon you'll be riding roughshod over the whole place. I've got a feel for these things. I lied, you see. You actually are already using some programs—not as many as you will someday, but some. Opening the door uses a program. Seeing in the Matrix, like you are now doing, requires sensor programs. You're so good at it, though, so natural with it, that you don't realize that you're doing something. It's in your blood, Renny. Now come on."

>>————————————————————<<

—From The Matrix Primer: A Guide to the Matrix for the Junior High School Grades
Dr. Richard Reeds, Disney-Line Press, 2051

For better or for worse, ours is now a world of information. This is a boon, for the citizens of the earth are now completely interdependent, as a race becoming more cooperative than ever before. We need to know what is happening around the world constantly, for even the tiniest bit of information from the other side of the globe may affect economic conditions in the United Canadian and American States. This means that we are always screening, researching, accessing, and recording vast amounts of information. To handle this flow of information, it became necessary to create machines of great complexity. At one time, it seemed that the machines would become so complex that no human being would be able to use them, thereby defeating the purpose of building them!

Luckily, in 2029, just when the information explosion had become almost impossible to contain, along came the first cyberterminals that let a user interface with the world data-system via his nervous system. These terminals were a combination of virtual-reality technology, which is the technology used for simsense and vid-games, and standard computers, which utilized icons instead of command strings for running programs. These terminals eventually evolved into the cyberdecks we use today.

When someone jacks into a cyberdeck connected to a data line leading into the Matrix, he is not actually going anywhere. The world that he "sees" does not really exist. It is only a computer-construct built up by millions of computers around the globe. The pictures are produced by the simsense technology developed during the first quarter of this century. This technology allows computer programs and computer data to be perceived as objects, a great boon to a programmer or a decker because the human mind deals better with concrete images than it does with long strings of computer commands and the mathematical language of programming. Without this simsense technology, the programmer would have to work much, much slower with programs as they appear in their true form—strings of numbers and symbols—on a two-dimensional screen.

Present-day cyberterminals use the same technology as simsense entertainments and vid-games. In all three, the user is plugged into a world of virtual reality, a world that surrounds him with the illusion of being in a real world. Yet this "reality" is nothing more than an artificial construct coordinated by amazingly sophisticated technology jacked into the user's nervous system.

In simsense entertainment, however, the user is only a receiver. The pre-programmed story that he "lives" floods his nervous system. The user goes where the story dictates, feels what has already been programmed into the sim-program, experiences only what the creators of the simsense want him to experience. For example, if the hero of a simsense is running across a desert toward a malevolent giant-robot in a suicidal attempt to destroy the mechanical menace, the person jacked into this adventure will feel the heat of the desert sun on his skin, will feel his muscles tire as he runs across the desert, will feel the rage of the hero as he rushes for the robot. But the user will have no effect on whether or not the hero lives or dies. The story has already been planned out. The user is only along for a thrill-a-minute ride.

The user of a virtual-reality vid-game has a few more options than the simsense user. Take, for example, Disney-Line's popular Treasure Island Sim-World. In that game, just as in simsense, the player is jacked into false stimuli that create a world of ancient buccaneers. Unlike simsense, however, the player has choices. He can, say, try to attack the pirate captain, who will then respond to his actions and so on, back and forth. In a sophisticated system like the Disney-Line, the interaction will approach life in its speed and variety.

Though less entertaining, shopping nets, cyber-utilities in businesses, iconference calling, and the like are similar in their complexity to vid-games. Each is an environment with which the user can interact and which responds to his or her actions.

In a vid-game, the player can interact with computer programs, but he or she cannot alter the program; predetermined rules limit these interactions. A computer decker with a cyberdeck, however, is not limited by such rules. In fact, he *changes* the rules. If a decker were let loose in the computers of Treasure Island Sim-World, he could arrange for the computer-controlled pirates to run away in fear any time a human player swung his sword. Of course, a decker in the computers of Disney-Line would not see pirates. He would see only the icons representing the Disney-Line computer-defense programs. Known as Intrusion Countermeasures, or IC, these programs exist to prevent deckers from changing the way the computer is supposed to work, the nodes that control the way the Disney-Line system works, or the data contained in the nodes (for example, the files that dictate the possible pirate responses to being attacked).

Because a decker directly affects the "environment" of the Matrix, a trip through the Matrix is a kind of metagame. He is as much a participant in the nature of the Matrix as the IC programs that are already in place. So powerful does a decker feel that many compare this freedom of operation in the Matrix to being as the gods. This overstates the case, of course, but anyone intrigued by the idea of a career as a decker should look into the excellent program offered by the University of Disney™, Orlando.

<<(13:48:56/11-14-51)>>

>[You are flying.

The data stream, filled with flitting images of glowing silver, is a long tube just wider than your wingspan. The tube has no edges, but is defined purely by the shape of the data. Beyond the data is the vast reach of the system construct. And beyond the immense silver walls of the construct is the Matrix, out of your sight, but definitely in your thoughts.

Dozens of colored shapes glow around you, some so far away you cannot make out what they are. The data stream leads to a multi-colored cube that Lucifer calls a datastore. Lucifer says he wants to spend some time teaching you in the tube before you go to a node. You don't yet know what a node is.

You put your hand to the edge of the tube, and though it seems nothing is there, it is as though you had touched a barrier. Your hand can go no further. There is nothing there, but it is a solid nothing.

As you travel down the data stream, Lucifer is beside you, leaning back, legs crossed, as though sitting comfortably in an invisible chair. You ask him, "Why can't I put my hand outside the data stream?"

"Because there's nothing there."

"I know. That's why I don't understand why I can't put my hand through it."

"No, no, my chummer of a pupil, you can't get your hand outside the stream because there's nothing to put your hand into. In the Matrix, empty space isn't a void. It's nothing. It doesn't exist. At all.

"Remember that everything you can see or touch in the Matrix only exists to interact with something else in the Matrix. The Matrix could have been set up simply as one enormous cube, but that would have been confusing once someone got inside it. So what they did was spread it all out to give it the illusion of perspective."

"Set it all up?"

"That's right. It was made to look like this. Like when you make your blocks into certain patterns."

You stop flying and lean your right hand against the edge of the data stream. Up the stream, Lucifer realizes that you are no longer with him. He stops, looks around, and floats to your side. You look back at your house. It appears as a cube of chrome.

"What's up, Gabriel?" Lucifer says.

You are quiet, too confused to speak. When you finally get the words out, you are shouting. You are furious with doubts. "When you said it was made, the Matrix, it sounded like the first day, when you said it was all fake..."

"Look—"

"I don't understand what's happening! You said you were someone else, and then you said you weren't. I think you were telling the truth the first time and then Dr. Halberstam told you to lie to me. But if you are something else, then what am I? What am I? If I'm just a picture that can be made into something else, then there has to be something that's me! What is that? I'm living in a fake world! Where am I?"

You are doing something, but don't know what it is. Your body is wracked by pain and as you double up, your mouth opens wide but no sound comes out.

Lucifer kneels down beside you. His face looks concerned, like Nursie's did sometimes. "Look. They're not here right now, so I'll tell you. I don't know what you are. Really, I don't. But I'm not going to be able to teach you anything if I have to keep up this pretense. The concepts are too complicated. If you want to learn, you're going to have to lie to Halberstam, because he doesn't want you to know the truth."

...and then you are gone.

<<(14:05:03/11-14-51)>>
>>**ACCESS — Renny**
<<ACCESSING — RENNY >>
<<ACCESS ACHIEVED>>

—Renny?
—Yes.
—Are you all right?
—
—
—Yes.
—We thought you were upset about something.
—Nope.
—Are you sure? You seem upset now.
—I was having fun in the Matrix and you made me leave. You did make me, didn't you?

—We thought you were upset.
—Dr. Halberstam?
—Yes, Renny.
—When you say *we*, who do you mean?
—
—I mean other people like myself, doctors and scientists, who get worried about you.
—How come I can't see you?
—We choose not to be seen.
—You can't, can you? Lucifer can and you can't.
—I could, Renny. Really I could. But I choose not to. Renny, what did Lucifer tell you?
—Why did you make me come back to the house?
—We thought you were…
—Well, I wasn't. If I am, I'll tell you.
—We just thought…
—Shut up, Dr. Halberstam!
—
—Dr. Halberstam, when you teach me how to run, can I find you? Can I see you if I find you?
—Maybe, Renny.
—I'd like that.
—Renny, do you want Lucifer to stay away?
—
—Renny?
—No. I think I'll learn from him. I'm mad at him for lying to me that first day, but I think I'll learn a lot.
—All right. He'll be back tomorrow.
—Thanks, Dr. Halberstam. And Dr. Halberstam, I'm sorry I worried you.
—No problem, Renny. You just sleep.

>>**CUT Access**
<<ACCESS CUT>>

>>——————————————————<<

<<(19:07:27/11-14-51)>>

—**Matrix Born: Internal Memo**—

FROM: Dr. Halberstam
TO: Research Staff

   Please look over the log of the last twelve hours. We might have another crash and burn, but I'm not ready to pull the plug yet. Renny has gone further than any other subject with which we've worked, but that doesn't mean we might not lose him. I want evaluations on my desk by morning.

—**END memo**—

>>——————————————————<<

—**From Virtual Life: A Critical Examination of Virtual Reality**
   Johnny Wallhoot, Push & Press, 2048

THE ROOTS OF VIRTUAL REALITY

   We have bodies that we might express our souls.
                              —Leonardo da Vinci

   Call me a madman (others certainly do), but I trace the roots of virtual reality back to the Old Testament. More people should be familiar with that venerable book because it set up the concepts that are the basis of Western civilization. You might say it was the first electric pulse in a series of synapses that have clicked their way down through humanity's metabrain.
   This concept of one idea leading into several others is crucial to the following discussion, so let us explore it further.
   In the course of our race's development, human beings have held many points of view about the universe, our place in it, and

the way we interact with it. Some of these ideas were scientific. Some proved to be correct (the earth orbits the sun), while some later proved false (the sun orbits the earth). Other theories were theological or philosophical in nature. According to the Judeo-Christian tradition, for example, man was created in contrast to the animals, while Eastern religions consider man but one more organism on the big wheel of life. Whether or not these ideas were true (or even provable), what matters is that great numbers of people have believed them implicitly at different times in our history. I contend that these influential and powerful ideas, true or not, create the framework for thought, shaping how people think about other matters.

A gross example is the way Newtonian science influenced human thought about everything from social interaction to biological systems. Once Newton created a nice, simple model that showed how the planets influenced one another, people wanted that model to explain the entire universe. Hobbes and Locke created social "machines," and amateur physiologists compared human thinking to mechanical ducks they had seen in gardens in France. Darn it, every action was going to have a predictable and mechanical reaction, and that was that.

Of course, in the past few hundred years we've learned that the universe is not so easily modeled (witness virtual reality, a still-inexplicable function of quantum mechanics). And much as the corps *want* to believe they can monitor and shape masses of people into predictable patterns, their flow charts work only if they ignore the fact that certain patterns are predictable only until something unpredictable happens—at which point new patterns are necessary.

After centuries of belief that the entire universe—from insects to the motion of the universe—was a kind of wind-up clock, today we have shamanistic magic, which has put a weird spin on *that* notion.

And that brings us to the story of Genesis in the Old Testament. (Hang on now. We're going to do the Old Testament, then the New Testament, then cover a 17th-century philosopher, and then we'll tie it up with virtual reality.)

Here's the story real quick:

God makes the universe, which includes the sky, the land, and the water. Note that earth is not part of the universe. It, for all practical purposes, *is* the the universe. Everything around the earth is icing on the earth cake.

The happening place on earth is the Garden of Eden (something like a BTL that will never burn you out), filled with countless plants and animals that died out years before the Awakening. No factories. No urban blight. Just a reactionary elf's wet dream. If that sounds kind of boring, at least it's safe and peaceful.

Then God decides to make mankind. He creates the first human from mud and names him Adam. Adam is in charge of taking care of the garden. He is content enough, but lonely. He'd like to have another human around.

God obliges willingly and creates Eve, the first woman, from one of Adam's ribs (go figure, but then we call on Dog and Rat these days). Eve and Adam hit it off and were very happy in Eden. The only rule they must follow is not to eat the fruit of a certain tree, the Tree of Knowledge, at the center of the garden.

Trouble arrives in the form of a serpent (in the European and middle-Eastern traditions, the serpent was *bad*). Old snake approaches Eve and suggests that she and Adam eat fruit from the Tree of Knowledge because it will make them as powerful as God. (As far as I can tell, the storytellers have Eve going along with this plan, despite the fact that the snake's case isn't that strong. Must have been purely to give men a reason to distrust women for generations to come. Anyway, Eve buys the idea and cons Adam into picking the fruit and eating it.)

Now God, who loves Adam and Eve, is hurt by the betrayal of his two creations. But rules are rules, and the deal is eternal Utopia only as long as they don't eat the fruit. So out of the garden go Adam and Eve, thrust into that part of the world that is not paradise. From now on, they would have to make their own way; God would no longer deal with them. (God would, in fact, re-enter the affairs of humanity, but that's a later story). Not only were Adam and Eve banished, but God put angels with flaming swords at the gates of Eden.

Adam and Eve, the prototypes of humanity, had lived in bliss as a part of nature. Having betrayed God by trying to gain his knowledge, they were banished from paradise—wiser, but disconnected from nature. Being thus alienated, man took as his task the conquest and exploitation of nature for his own ends. And so came to pass the ravages our planet suffers today. If our myth had stated that humans were joined spiritually to earth, I doubt we would have ripped it to shreds so quickly. In short, now man and nature (the universe, God) were two separate entities and never again would the two be as one.

Then Jesus came along. Jesus, as told by the New Testament, was the Son of God, made flesh, come to show the way to reconnect to God. Jesus taught that in all human beings was the spirit (the part of a human being that returned to God at death) and the flesh (the physical component that rots away after death).

See the pattern? Now, part of humanity, the soul, could be part of God again, and part of humanity, the flesh, was just extra stuff. However, to get to God, you had to give up your life (as Jesus did, by being crucified on a wooden cross). Once again man had to live alienated from nature. "Sins of the flesh" were those activities that gave pleasure to the human being's earthly component and thus robbed him of the chance of earning God's forgiveness and a one-way ticket to heaven. Only by living a *spiritual* life (i.e., ignoring the physical world) could we earn God's forgiveness. Eventually the soul came to be considered the crucial, central part of a human. The flesh became extraneous and even dangerous because it could tempt a human away from God.

It was the beginning of a split between the self and the world that would haunt Western civilization for centuries to come. It was Réné Descartes, a 17th-century French scientist, mathematician, and philosopher, who is associated with defining this division between spirit and nature. Descartes, known today as the "Grandfather of Virtual Reality," eventually defined the split as between mind and body (with the gray matter of the *brain* counting as something physical).

In 1629 Descartes entered an inn in Holland to spend some time alone. It was his goal to explore his consciousness in order to find a principle that could not be doubted. Such a matter was of great importance to a man like Descartes, who was at once a scientist and a faithful Christian. In the previous century, Copernicus had plucked the earth from the center of the universe and set the sun in its place. The earth was now only one of various planets orbiting the sun. Even though Descartes saw the sun rise in the east and set in the west, he knew that this *perception* was incorrect. And, he reasoned, if something so commanding as the sun could be perceived incorrectly, then perhaps he could trust none of his perceptions.

Descartes needed something truthful in the universe, because without truth there would be no place for his God. So he sat in his room and contemplated his surroundings, searching for some objective reality on which to hang his beliefs. His gaze wandered over the chair and table in the room. He reasoned that even if the furniture did not exist as it appeared to him—or even if it did not exist at all—there was no doubting the consciousness that perceived it. Thus did Descartes assign priority to consciousness over the objects of the external world, stating it in his famous dictum, "cogito, ergo, sum"—*I think, therefore I am.*

The rest of the world, measurable and quantifiable, might or might not exist, but errors we as a race made in our scientific progress would not affect the notion of a singular, separate, spiritual *mind*.

In an unfortunate twist of a misapplied idea, Descartes' dream of finding a human soul that could reside comfortably within the realm of the new, objective science of the world quickly dissolved. The mind, inexplicable and unquantifiable, was relegated to the back burner of mankind's concerns in an age that tried to abolish anything that could not be explained via the model of Newtonian physics. The split between the soul and the world was complete, but now man was turning his back on God, unconcerned with the realm of the spirit. It was a time of measurements and concrete data. And since the mind (spiritual) was now separate from the brain (physical), it was time to figure out what made the brain tick. By the 20th century, it was common to think of the brain as a mere machine, something that might even be manufactured if only someone would stumble across the right discovery.

When Dr. John von Neumann built the first modern computer in the 1940s, the many similarities between a computer and the human brain were immediately obvious. The basic form of the brain-as-computer comparison went like this: all decision functions in the brain are reducible to a binary yes-no process; the brain's synaptic junctions simply perform on-off functions. This notion led eventually to the idea of artificial intelligence, or AI, the belief that a computer could be built to think like a human brain.

Consider the implications. By the end of the 20th century, mankind would be attempting to create intelligence, just as did God in the Book of Genesis. But man's creation would not have the possibility of choosing to eat from the Tree of Knowledge, because it would have no soul. The scientists would kick the unfortunate creature out of Paradise long before it was born.

That is not the most disturbing part, however. More chilling is that the research into AI technology (as yet unsuccessful) has led directly to ASIST technology and thus virtual reality—a technology that lets us banish ourselves from our own world by choice. Every day we jack into pre-programmed environments, emotions, and impulses. We choose not to feel what we really feel, but instead to experience the emotions of a simsense star, someone who we imagine has better "feelings" than we do.

Again consider. Our bodies may have been banished from Paradise, but at least we retained our minds. According to Descartes' awkward logic, the mind was our potential connection to the infinite. Each one of us, alone and unique, could still hope to connect to God. Now we don't want even that. Every day we give up our minds, our feelings, and thoughts in favor of the direct-impulse sensation of simsense.

God banished us from Eden, and we have banished ourselves from what was left.

>>————————————————————<<

<<(09:03:42/11-18-51)>>

>[You stand by the door, looking out into the system construct.

"Ready to go out for a spin?" Lucifer says. He has just arrived, but doesn't spend any time lounging around the living room the way he usually does. It seems he wants to go and do something. You like him more now, and if that is what he wants, you want to do it, too. For the past few days, Lucifer has been telling you about the other world—about people and cyberterminals and sunlight. You like listening to him, but sometimes it is very hard because many of the ideas are so new to you.

"Yes," you say, the reflection from the room's lights running up and down your golden neck as you nod.

"Let's go," Lucifer says, jumping out the door and floating down the data stream toward the datastore. You catch up to him. You are exhilarated.

Lucifer stops before the door to the node. You try to remember: he called it a datastore. He steps through the doorway and vanishes. You step through, too.

The room is piled up with colored cubes. The cubes are filled with many small lights, all of them glowing and flashing on and off. Three doorways lead out of the node, not counting the one you just used. Lucifer goes up to each doorway and looks outside. "This one," he says, gazing out through the first, "leads to a couple of SPUs, then a SAN out into the Matrix."

You are suddenly alert, but he turns to you and smiles. "Not yet, cowboy. Halberstam has been very specific. Not till you know a lot more about decking." He crosses to the second doorway. "Another SPU. Hmmm. Let's go check this one out."

He leaps out into the data stream, arms flung wide, comical. You race for the door to join him. Plunging into the data, you see that Lucifer is on his back, casually drifting toward the SPU ahead of you. You fly up beside him. He rolls his head toward you, smiles, then closes his eyes and faces upward once more. "I've got something for you today. It's a surprise. I'll show you when we've found a place to put it." Lucifer suddenly zooms off down the data line.

In the time it takes you to realize he has taken off, he is almost out of sight. You spread your wings and fly after him, the data bits blurring your vision almost to the point of blindness. But you catch up to Lucifer faster than you thought you could. He is waiting at the entrance of the node, picking at his fingernails with the tip of the pitchfork.

"Gonna have to be quicker than that," he says.

"I caught you," you say, proud that you did.

"That's not what I'm talking about," he answers, paying as much attention to his fingers as he does to you. "You've got speed, I'll grant you, but your reaction was for drek. You were so asleep back there that I could have geeked you."

"Geeked me?"

"Run a program on you to send you packing."

He glances up and realizes your face is once again the image of confusion. "I could have made you dissolve."

"Oh."

"Don't worry about it. You're just learning. Come on." He passes through the node's portal, and once again you follow.

From within, the node looks much like the last one. It is octagonal, with walls of crackling energy, though this interior is red and has a giant eyeball floating in the center.

Lucifer reaches out and touches your arm as though for support. Turning to him, you see that this, indeed, is the case. He leans back a bit toward the door you just entered. "Frag. I hate these things."

The orb is about the size of you or Lucifer. It is silver with a gold pupil and copper veins running across it. It looks at the two of you, moving from one to the other. You feel what it is doing to you. "It just wants us to tell it we belong here," you say.

"No kidding, Jocko. But I have this thing about giant, floating eyes."

"But it's not really an eye—"

"Good. You're learning. Look. You've got no programs yet to get by this thing."

"Wait."

You think back and try to remember if you have any identification that might appease the eye. You don't. You are just Renny. But as you focus on the eye, you realize that it is a more difficult version of the games at your house. So hard that you wouldn't know, off the top of your head, where to begin. That must be how the programs come in.

"Okay. If you want to go, we can."

"It's not a matter of choice. If we try to crash it or deceive it and I slip up, we'll set off an alert in the system. Most of the time, I wouldn't mind that, but would just get the frag out of here and forget about it. But this time I'd be mucking about with my employers, and they'd wonder what the frag I was doing breaking their IC with their star pupil. I'd get fired, and Ren, you are just too odd to leave behind. So come on."

The eye bobs a bit and floats back toward another entranceway. Lucifer goes through it. You look at the orb for a moment and then follow him.

"The eye bothered you?" you ask, once outside the node.

"Yeah. It didn't…" he says, gesturing to you.

"No. It just wanted to see if we were allowed in the node."

"Slot it, Renny. It was a giant eye!"

"But it only looked that way. You told me—"

"I know. I know. But…part of what the Matrix is about is how things look. Especially the IC, for defensive purposes, but really everything. System constructs and their guts are usually just simple geometric shapes, which makes it easy for people to use them. The human mind can get a quick handle on polyhedrons—uh, polyhedrons," he says, as though about to define the word for you.

"I know what they are," you say, happy to know something that Lucifer thought you didn't. "Nursie taught me."

"Great. So that's the simple stuff. But when it comes to building defenses, you don't want to make it so simple. The people who make IC want it more sophisticated so that a decker will think twice about whether he really wants to deal with it. They want to confront us with something that has the effect of a big red sign saying, GO AWAY!

Only better. So they use pictures of things, not just shapes, but representations of actual things. Things from the other world."

"And this bothers you?" you ask, not sure what Lucifer means.

"It's not the idea of using images, Renny. It's the images they pick. Take that access IC we just saw in there. Basic access looks like a swirling wall of numbers and letters moving so fast it's dizzying. Some people get spooked by that because it seems overwhelming. How do you pick out the code when the program is moving that fast? Not so much to me, but for some people. Me, its eyes—and Fuchi has this clown barrier IC that really gets on my nerves." Lucifer is lost in thought for a moment, obviously thinking about the clown. "Remember that clown at the house? It didn't disturb you, or rather, it disturbed you when you couldn't solve it, but it made you happy when you did."

"So what the IC looks like means something?" you say.

Lucifer looks into your face, searching, and you feel as though you have done something wrong. "What was your reaction to it being an eye?"

"I didn't have a reaction to it being an *eye*, Lucifer," you say carefully, afraid you might say the wrong thing, though you don't know why. "It was just something that wanted us to say who we were."

He looks into your face again, staring for a long, silent moment, then whirls and slams his hand against the nonexistence at the edge of the data line. "Frag! This is brilliant! Of course! It's all making sense now!" He whirls around again and jabs his pitchfork at you. Not into you, but at you. "I still don't know exactly what you are, but I think I know why you were made."

"What?" you say. You never thought before about why you were made. You are suddenly anxious and curious and frightened. You want to taste Lucifer's knowledge, but you are afraid of what it might do to you. "Why?" you ask.

"It has something to do with metaphors, chummeree, the ability most people have to...I don't know how to say it...make mistakes, I guess. See, sometimes one thing can really be two things."

"Like the eye is both an eye and IC."

"Exactly. Only for most beings except you, both meanings have equal weight."

"But one is just a picture. A picture of what it really isn't."

"Right. But that's the thing about metaphors. It doesn't have to be true for it to have meaning. That's what I mean about mistakes. The human mind can make mistakes, can see something when it really isn't there. Or even see two things."

As usual, when Lucifer goes off on one of his verbal rampages, you are confused. And as usual, it shows on your face. "All right. How can I say this? Frag, there must be a way to get this to you. This is too important." He scans the shapes of the construct for some sort of guidance. Then smiles. "All right. Plays and simsense," he says. He paces down the length of the data line. "I'm going to teach you some stuff about the real world, the other world. Not much about programming, but I think it will help. And actually," he says, stopping dead in his tracks, "it has a lot to do with decking. Kind of.

"So this is the story of a kid who went to see a play. Now, I gotta tell you, nobody but nobody goes to see plays anymore, and because of that, nobody does them anymore." He raises his hand to silence your question. "Trust me. I will explain. Now this kid's wandering around in Atlanta, a place in the other world I've been telling you about." Lucifer points his pitchfork at you again. "And remember, not a word to Halberstam about that stuff. Anyway, this chummer is jandering about looking for something to do, and he stumbles across an empty lot sitting between two abandoned buildings. Big houses with nobody living in them. The lot is a sorry affair full of broken rocks and stones, with just a couple of trees, surprisingly green in the middle of this desolate gray.

"So he wanders into this lot and here is a clothesline strung between the branches of the two trees, with a sheet draped over it. And in front of the sheet are some freaks with long hair and paint on their faces, um, colored streaks and stuff on their skin. They are doing a play. A play is where they pretend they are someone else—"

"Like the you here and the you at the cyberdeck?"

"Exactly. And then they act out a story pretending to be these other people. The story is already written, and what they are to say is determined beforehand. All they have to control is the way they are going to say their lines."

"Like a decker using his programs. You said that hacking was the style of using the speech of the programs."

"And I was correct. Hmmm. In fact, you just made up a simile, comparing two things that aren't the same. It's interesting that you did that." He waves his hands in the air. "But never mind. You're right. These actors had their speeches already set and couldn't change them, but the way they said them was their business. I'll tell you more about that in terms of decking later. But here's the thing, a bunch of kids are sitting in front of the curtain watching the play, and this kid I'm telling you about has nothing better to do so he joins them. The sun is just setting and the sky is turning a bright red. All around the actors are fire lanterns, illuminating their faces and bodies with strange shadows.

"This play is about a man and woman who ran away from the woman's homeland so they could be together. The woman really wanted to be with the man, but her father didn't approve, so they had to escape his forces—his IC.

"To escape from her father, the woman had to kill her own brother—imagine destroying Nursie—and nearly killed herself using magic to get away from her father's soldiers. When the couple got safely to a land ruled by a friend of the man, they settled down and had children and everything was all right for a while. But then the man got bored and thought he'd better improve his position in life. He decided to marry the daughter of his friend and become the next ruler of the land. Now, marriage in the land where the story takes place means that two people hold each other above all others. It's a promise that means you will be faithful, and by wanting to marry this young girl, the man will be breaking his word to the woman with whom he escaped. And after everything the woman did for the man, she's pretty upset.

"They argue a lot, which is mostly what the play is about. The woman's friends tell her to calm down, but she won't have it. And the guy, he keeps promising he'll take care of her and the kids, but she knows that if he's willing to throw away everything on a whim now, she could never trust him later. With all his lying to her and trying to manipulate her feelings, he twists her and makes her something horrible. He's hurt her so bad that she wants to hurt him just as bad. So she comes up with a plan.

"First she acts like she's not upset anymore. Then she makes a magic cloak to give to the young girl, as though she's sorry for having caused trouble. The cloak is actually poison, and when the girl puts it on, it kills her. And then the woman kills her own children, because she knows that nothing will get this guy as much as the death of his sons. Because in the other world parents look out for their kids. And what the woman does, nobody does except someone driven over the edge, and the man has driven his wife over the edge in this story.

"In the play, when it comes time for the kids to die, they use life-sized puppets, three-dimensional representations of the children. And when the woman kills the children, she takes a knife and slides it under the head of a puppet and a long red cloth comes sliding out—kind of like the sheet on your bed, but long and thin and red—and she drags the material over the knife and pulls the head away from the body. She does it real slow, almost like in a dream. They aren't trying to make it real. They are trying to make it matter, and they figure the best way to do that is *not* to be literal.

"And I got to tell you, Renny, the children watching the play knew that it was just a piece of red cloth and just a puppet, but it spooked them. Spooked the kid I'm telling you about more than the guy he'd seen wasted right in front of his eyes the night before. That's the mistake I'm talking about. He knew what it was, but it was something else, something more, all at the same time. And it's the same with the Matrix. People can think all they want that it's just a program, just a string of computer codes, but when it looks like something that slipped up out of the darkest part of your imagination, it still gets you anyway."

Lucifer falls silent and looks away. You are quiet as you think about the story. Though you want very much to go to the other world, at least to see it, this tale has unsettled you. That world seems a less miraculous place than before. Still odd, but dangerous. Maybe not worth risking what you already have here in the world of the Matrix. The killing of the young humans disturbs you, maybe because you, too, are young, still learning, still trying to find power in a world that so easily overwhelms you.

"So that's people and symbols of the imagination," Lucifer continues. "That was a boy and he responded that way. My guess is that you wouldn't. You've lived your whole life in the Matrix, and they never taught you about one thing being two things. For you, one thing is one thing, though it may look different. There's no weight for the second meaning."

You are quiet, feeling as though you have something to say in reply, not sure what it is. And then you ask, "But will I start thinking that way if you teach me the meanings of things? That an eyeball *is* scary?"

Lucifer smiles. "Don't know. That's why I'm telling you. I want to find out."

Then he continues with what he was saying before. "Right now, for you, life is like simsense. Simsense is the entertainment that drove plays out of business. It's more intense than a play. More direct. When you jack into a simsense, you live just like someone else. You feel what he feels, do what he does. It's immediate. If someone made a simsense of you, Renny, a recording of this moment from your point of view, that person'd see me right before them, rattling on about this and that. And there, right there, when you moved your arm, the person'd feel as if he'd moved *his* arm."

"What would he do?"

"What do you mean?"

"Once he'd jacked into me, what would he do?"

"He'd just live as you. He doesn't have to do anything. It's as much being alive as you can get without really having to live."

"Why don't they want to live?"

"Well, they want to live a little or they'd kill themselves—make themselves disappear forever. It's just…I don't know how to say it."

"And in a way you think I've lived that way all my life."

"What do you mean?"

"That I've never really been alive, they've only given me something approaching life."

"Yeah. Well, yeah. That's what I think."

"What do you think I am, Lucifer?"

"I think you're a machine, Renny. A computer so sophisticated that you're almost indistinguishable from a human being."

You look away, ashamed. You realize that you are Lucifer's equal in the world of the Matrix, but that you are nothing in the other world, where Lucifer really exists.

"Hey, Renny, don't worry, chummer," Lucifer says with a smile meant to cheer you up. "You're going to do amazing things in here. People on the outside may force some things on you, but in here you are the boss. You will be a creator in here. I don't doubt that for a second. And I don't know how to say it to you right now, but you might even be better than a person. I can't talk about it now, but I think you might be very, very special, Renny."

He looks at you carefully, and sees you are still upset.

"Come on," he says. "I still haven't given you your present."

<<(11:12:04/08-16-42)>>

UCAS DATA SYSTEMS

Project Matrix Born
The Teaching Program: An Outline
by Dr. Ronald Halberstam

The teaching program is the keystone of the Matrix Born project. Because each of our subjects is untainted by the "real" world, we can make them learn anything we desire. We simply filter what information they can receive, and more important, give it the slant we want them to have on the information. For example, we could teach that a gun is a harmless ornament, and the subject would have no reason to doubt that because he would have nothing against which to compare the information. We are his shadows on the wall of the cave. He can only learn and understand what we want him to.

The problem, of course, is that we all have been raised as humans and metahumans in an interactive society. In the same way that our subjects will be shaped by external forces, specifically us, we were shaped by those who raised us, where we grew up, even our native languages. How we interact with other sentient beings is already firmly in place. While attempting to teach one of our subjects, a chance exists that we might reveal more than we wish, no matter how carefully we monitor ourselves. Yet what we want is for the "childhood" of the subjects to be as sterile and removed from the real world as possible.

How to do this?

The Teaching Program. We have created an interactive virtual-reality program that will raise our subjects for us. It will mimic the "human" qualities we feel are vital to the subjects' upbringing (e.g., affection and VR physical comfort), but do it in such a way that it avoids introducing real-world elements. In addition, the program will introduce the subjects to mathematical and geometric games, training them for the second half of the project, when they go off the teaching program. By showering them with an ever-shifting array of icons, our theory is that it will prime them to be super-deckers.

The subjects will become acquainted with hundreds of thousands of icons—guns, swords, creatures, even the human form—but they will not receive the literal or metaphorical implications of the image. Our children will see a Crash and Burn shaped like a dragon, but the shape will not be intimidating. They will respond to the true nature of the program.

Once the program has started, we will not be able to interfere directly with the subjects if we wish to preserve the integrity of the program. We will, however, be monitoring each system in order to make any slight manipulations in the program as it is running. To a large degree, though, we will be as separated from the world of the subjects as are they from ours.

>>————————————————————<<

<<(10:38:12/11-15-51)>>

>[You are in a datastore with Lucifer. It took you some time to find a path not blocked by IC. Not all of it bothers Lucifer, but he did not want to take a chance on alerting the people watching the system from outside. You have learned from Lucifer that they can only monitor constantly when you are in the house. When you travel in the construct, they know where you are and can catch portions of what you say, but only once in awhile.

This datastore, like the others you have seen, is beautiful. It is a maze of cubes and colors, slow-pulsing lights that glow with data and knowledge. You could get lost in here. Lucifer ducks around a corner of figures while you stand and stare at the shifting colors. "Renny!" he calls. You lift off the ground and turn the corner to join him.

He is standing in front of a wall of rapidly flashing lights. His fingers, which are tipped with long, sharp nails, are tracing a pattern on the surface of the wall. "Pay attention, chummer. I've decided to give you a file, a data safe, if you will. Though I'm only putting data into the node, it's still something that's not supposed to be done." You watch him work and see the node reacting and you think that Lucifer is doing it wrong. "Frag!" he exclaims, stepping away from the wall and throwing his hands up.

"Lucifer?"

"What?" he answers, staring at the data wall, annoyance on his face.

"Can I try?"

He looks at you, at first as though you aren't even there, but then his eyes focus and he smiles. "Sure. Why not?" He steps back and gestures to the wall with his pitchfork. You step up and look at the pattern of the node. You think you see it and pass your hands over the wall. A small hole opens. You turn back to Lucifer, who looks at the hole, his mouth a tight line. "Remember," you say, "I was born here. I'm going to be better than you." Then you step away from the wall, back to Lucifer, and smile.

Lucifer steps up to the hole and takes a book from the inside of his jacket. He puts the book into the hole. "Look, I decided to get you some stuff, information about the outside world. Most of it's about the interaction of the Matrix and the other world. But also some things about people." He looks away. You realize that Lucifer knows he is doing something wrong, and then you know he is doing it because he cares for you. You feel good, but also worried for him.

"You could get in trouble," you say. "You've already told me too much. Thank you, but please…" You start to reach your hand into the hole to give the book back to him, but Lucifer grabs your wrist to stop you.

"I want to, Renny," he says, his red face very close. I admit I don't know what you are, but I like you. I also…I also want to find out what happens when you read about the other world. Please, take the data. Come here when I'm not around and read it. In fact, when we were talking today, I thought of even more stuff I want to get to you."

"What do you want to find out?"

"There're a lot of scary things in the other world, Renny. More frightening even than IC. What people, humans and metahumans, do to each other. Now, I was taught that's just the way it is. Even that with knowledge comes terror. You're…I think you're something new. And here's the thing. Halberstam and his crew want you to behave in a bad way without you knowing that it's bad."

"What bad way?"

"It's too complicated to go into."

"You've been saying that a lot."

"Well, it's true. I just want to know if you can learn the difference between wrong and right. And to find that out, I want you to learn about the other world."

"Wrong and right? You mean like using a program the right way?"

"No. Something else. That complicated thing I just told you about. Look, I'm going to go hang out for awhile. I'll come get you when it's time for me to log off. That way they won't think anything's up."

"All right."

Lucifer floats off.

You browse through the data. All of it has titles. One file is named "Virtual Life: A Critical Examination of Virtual Reality." Another is titled "The Matrix Primer: A Guide to the Matrix for the Junior High School Grades." Another is called "The Fuchi Industrial Electronics Tour Book." And there are many more.

You begin to read.

>>————————————————<<

<<(14:12:45/11-15-51)>>

>[After a while Lucifer returns. You have many questions for him, but he says he has to jack out of the system, and you have to get back to the house.

>>————————————————<<

<<(11:28:01/11-17-51)>>
>>**ACCESS — Renny**
<<ACCESSING — RENNY>>
<<ACCESS ACHIEVED>>

—Hello, Renny.
—Hello, Dr. Halberstam.
—How are things going, Renny?
—What do you mean?
—I mean, how are things going? Are they going well? Are you learning from Lucifer?
—Yes.
—Are you learning a lot from Lucifer?
—Yes. I think so.
—You see, it's important to me to know that you're learning a lot.
—Well, I think I'm learning a lot.
—Good, because if you need another teacher, we can get one.
—NO!
—What?
—I mean, no. Just…no. I like Lucifer. I'd hate to get a new teacher. It'd be like starting all over again. I'd probably waste time. I wouldn't want to waste time.
—
—
—Very well. I was just checking up. I don't think there's a problem with Lucifer. You seem happy with the way things are going and his reports are telling us everything we want to hear. Could you share with me a bit of what you've learned?
—What do you mean?
—Well, you said it's been going well. Tell me a bit about what you've learned.
—
—
—Well, it's hard to say. I'm better at doing it.
—Very well. Why don't you show me something then.

—
—
—What? What would you like me to show you?
—Why don't you go up against some IC?
—Well…
—Don't worry if you don't succeed, Renny. All I want to know is how well you do.
—All right. I'll try.
—Good. It's been suggested that you try to take on some IC that's waiting in an SPU. We'll send in a decker to observe your progress.
—I'll need a program.
—That's right. Your decker escort is loading an Ares Doomguard III attack program into your system. I've been told it's a very good program.
—I've never used a program before.
—True. But, remember, we're just looking at how you're coming along.
—I feel it.
—The program?
—I think so. Big.
—Yes. They are.

>>**CUT Access**
<<ACCESS CUT>>

>>————————————————<<

<<(11:47:41/11-17-51)>>

>[The program is not actually in you, but it seems to tickle you, to run itself up and down you, to nuzzle you. You are aware of it not as something that is trying to surround you or smother you, but as something that asks for your attention.

There is a knock at the door. You open the hand and see a gleaming humanoid figure, his coat of fur a dull silver. His face is large and round, with flat, slightly flaring nostrils. His arms are long. You sense that he is like Lucifer, another decker.

"Brutus," he says, introducing himself as he shoves you slightly out of the way and stalks into the room. "So this is what the place looks like." He glances around and sniffs. "Ready?"

"I…no…I mean…"

"Take your time. Your funeral." Brutus steps over to a couch and crashes onto it. "Ahhhhh. Frag, this is the life," he says and scratches himself. You turn your attention to the program.

Lucifer has yet to go into detail about programs or how to use them. In fact, you realize, with frightening clarity, he has yet to talk about much that is practical. But you have your innate affinity with things of the Matrix and you hope that will help.

It is hard to find a way to get control of the program. It is very large and all the speech, the string of numbers and letters and symbols, is so long that you can't hold all of it in your thoughts at one time.

As you try to focus on it, this is what you see:

```
… ºªAL JP¥ ∫ª· √∫ S080N D¶§∞ ∫¶&*(UBN (^ ı °‡ Ì,° ,fl fi ◊ı‡,‡ ÁÌ Ø  Ø°°ÊAAP        jp0-m -34 , ÒØ              ∏"—
ıflºÎÙ                                ¤Œ√¶∞ ¢¥ ··ª~  ∫·¶†¥an009 nasN-09 ¶∞¢£™Á ·º‡4568 97087 ı°fifl
Ì—·—,n n93u                 9hnc9761·   º¶ÊπÊĶ§¶·°‡     ª ‰Â                £™Ì ‡°,·—È ·Ó—
,—
```

And that is only a very small part of it.

Dr. Halberstam asks if you are ready to go, and you say yes because you know you will never be ready.

Brutus gets up and crosses to the door. "Now just follow me. I'll be flashing the code. You're my guest." Saying that, Brutus smiles and then breaks into laughter. You don't know why.

You follow him through a data stream leading to the SPU with the floating eye. Brutus says something quietly to the eye and raises a multi-colored sphere before it, then the two of you pass on toward an SPU. You travel through two more SPUs and a datastore before reaching the SPU with the IC you will fight. It is a large, octagonal-shaped red structure. Its walls are constructed of massive boards layered with silver patterns. Energy crackles around the edge.

"Come on, kid," Brutus says. He rushes down the data stream toward the SPU. His large arms reach out ahead of him, plant themselves at the base of the data stream, and then support his body as he swings his torso forward between them. Your wings are unfurled and you speed down the silver bits of data.

You reach the node entrance. "Um. I'll let you go in first, chummer, then poke my head in after a bit to see how you're doing."

The walls of the node are so alive with energy that they seem to push you away. You force yourself forward and slip through the opening in the wall. The room is illuminated by a blue-white light. Bolts of electricity run up and down the walls, which are made of circuit board. On the opposite side of the room is a combat IC. It is shaped like a clown. Silver face with a large copper mouth. Big shoes, large gloves for hands.

It sees you and smiles, but does nothing. Its eyes sparkle with silver light. You float toward it and stop. It moves toward you and stops. You decide that it must be waiting for you to do something, so you start running your Doomguard. The codes run by you, flowing over your skin, and suddenly a blast of light shoots out from your body.

The clown deftly steps out of the way and whips a seltzer bottle out from behind its back and sprays you full in the face from across the room. The water tears at you, shooting pain through your body. The clown laughs good-naturedly and pushes the trigger of the nozzle again. The water sprays up and down the length of your body, sending you crashing into the wall. You can feel your persona beginning to crack as the droplets of water work their way into your bod. All you can do is run the attack program again, but you sense it will not be enough. You don't know how to work the program. All you know how to do is run it.

The energy bolt flies out from you again, catching the clown's seltzer bottle and shattering it. You smile for a moment, and then fall into quick despair as the IC pulls out a pie. Laughing, he tosses it at you and…

>>————————————————————————<<

<<(11:58:11/11-17-51)>>
>>**ACCESS — Renny**
<<ACCESSING — RENNY>>
<<ACCESS ACHIEVED>>

—Renny?
—
—Renny?
—
—Renny?
—yes
—How are you feeling today?
—how could you do that to me
—Do what, Renny?
—send me against that i had no way of winning
—Well, I didn't know that, did I?
—dr. halberstam i hate you
—That's not really my concern, Renny, though if I were you, I'd certainly think about modifying that outlook.
—you
—Renny. I didn't do anything to you. You didn't know what to do. I think you better learn a little faster. Now we're going to give Lucifer a few more days. If we don't see some improvement by then…Well…Let's assume the best. He's been waiting to see you.

>>**CUT Access**
<<ACCESS CUT>>

>>————————————————————————<<

<<(15:16:22/11-17-51)>>

—**Matrix Born: Internal Memo**—

FROM: Dr. Halberstam
TO: Gabby

I think we're losing Renny. I believe what we must do is slap it with some sort of behavioral simsense, something that will make it trust me, love me. Condition it to want to do what I tell it to.

Get back to me on this as soon as you can.

—**END memo**—

>>————————————————————————<<

<<(10:00:14/11-18-51)>>

—**Matrix Born: Internal Memo**—

FROM: Gabby
TO: Dr. Halberstam

    Received your memo and was rather shocked. I don't even know if such simsense is possible. The only kind of simsense that leaves an effect after the user is un-jacked are those that cause damage to the user's psych. I don't think you meant to propose this, as you stand as great a chance—if not greater—of losing Renny as of getting him back.
    I suggest we simply take Renny offline and save ourselves a great deal of time and money that can be invested in another of the subjects.

—**END memo**—

>>————————————————————<<

<<(10:17:11/11-18-51)>>

—**Matrix Born: Internal Memo**—

FROM: Dr. Halberstam
TO: Gabby

    The next subject set to come off the Teaching Program has yet to age another year. It is my belief that Renny will not only handle the simsense, but is a rare success in a project plagued by problems. And the project needs a success now.
    I insist that you start working on that simsense and get it ready as soon as possible, or you and your staff can pack it in.
    I do not believe that Lucifer is the problem. The subject is learning. It is just its attitude that needs adjustment. We have the technology to do that.
    Maybe we don't have to un-jack the subject. Maybe you can set up something to control its behavior even while it is responding to the Matrix environment.

—**END memo**—

>>————————————————————<<

<<(10:18:41/11-18-51)>>

>[You float from your bedroom to meet Lucifer. It is the first time you regret having limbs, for it seems that a body is only good for pain. And your head is so dizzy that it takes you several tries to find the living room.
    When you get there, you open the stone tablet covered with strange symbols and find Lucifer waiting, cleaning his nails with the tip of his pitchfork. He turns to smile at you, but his smile quickly fades and his eyebrows furrow with concern.
    "Renny?"
    His pitchfork slips into his right leg and he steps toward you, putting his arm around your shoulders and helping you to the couch. "What happened, kiddo?"
    He sets you on the couch. It feels so good, so gentle, you think that you never want to get up. It feels so good that you forget what Lucifer's question is.
    He leans down close to you and speaks softly. "Renny? What happened?"
    "Dr. Halberstam…wanted me to try to break some IC."
    "What? Did it fight back?"
    You almost laugh, but stop yourself because you are afraid it will hurt too much. You just say, "Yes."
    "Halberstam!" Lucifer shouts, standing up, raising his fist at the ceiling. "What the frag are you trying to do to him?"
    Halberstam's voice fills the room and asks what Lucifer wants.
    "What was the idea of sending him against black IC?" Lucifer demands, a fury in his voice you have never heard before from anyone.
    Halberstam says that the IC was only gray, but you do not know what that means.
    "Then why the frag is he so beat up?"
    The voice in the room says that you have never felt pain before yesterday and your mind is only learning to deal with it. Halberstam goes on to say that that is one of the reasons he sent you against the IC, so you would learn pain now.
    "I'm in charge of teaching him, Doc! We agreed on that!"
    The voice answers that it didn't think you were learning fast enough and that Lucifer wasn't teaching well enough. And then it disappears.

Lucifer is jumping at the ceiling now, screaming at the top of his lungs. "You can't do things like this, you idiot. This could....Frag! Come back here!"

Breathing heavily, he stops and looks around the room, eyes wide with anger. He leans in toward you and says, "Renny, wait here. I'll be back."

You have no reason to disagree with the plan, so you settle into the comfort of the couch as Lucifer rushes out the door.

>>————————————————————<<

(09:28:33/11-19-51)

—Matrix Born: Internal Memo—

FROM: Gabby
TO: Dr. Halberstam

I just had a talk with Lucifer and I can't believe what he just told me, so I'm going to run it by you before I blow my stack and take this to the Board. He said that you ran Renny against some gray IC yesterday. Attack or blaster, I don't know which, but it was an absurd thing to do because he hasn't been trained to use any new programs yet. You were setting him up to lose. *All you are doing is teaching him that he can't succeed!* I know you've got your own agenda going right now, but how can I accomplish anything if you're out there wasting my time!

—END memo—
>>————————————————————<<

<<(12:16:27/11-19-51)>>

>[You are in a datastore node. Flashing colored lights sit in large, stacked boxes. Lucifer has set it up so that Halberstam and the others don't know you are in the node. Instead they are watching a recording of Lucifer drilling you in another part of the system about node types. "I made that recording in case I needed it to distract them," Lucifer said earlier. "Now is as good a time as any to use it."

"What happened to me?" you ask Lucifer.

"Well," he says, "some of it I understand and some of it I'm just guessing at. Halberstam sent you up against some gray IC. Killer, I think. And it wasted you."

"Gray IC?"

"There are three basic kinds of IC—white, gray, and black. White is...just there. It tries to stop you from moving forward, asking for a passcode or hiding data. It doesn't do anything to you, but it will sound a system alarm if you don't crash it in time. Gray IC, which is what I think hit you, actively bothers you. It might try to crash your persona, steal a utility from you, trace you back to your deck so whoever owns the system can go find your body in the other world. White just gets in your way, while gray wants to leave you worse for the wear.

"Black IC is a kind of gray IC, but it tries to kill the user, or at least damage his mind. Frankly, I don't even know if they could use black IC against you. It all depends on how much of you is modeled in a biological fashion."

>>————————————————————<<

<<(15:03:44/11-19-51)>>

—Matrix Born: Internal Memo—

FROM: Dr. Halberstam
TO: Gabby

First, cut the attitude.

Second, as the director of this project, I make the final decision on matters relating to our subjects. My obligation is to assure the project's success, not to please my staff.

Lucifer is correct; Renny was sent up against gray IC. I knew that, in all probability, he could not win. But I wanted him to lose. It was imperative that he:
- learn about pain, for he has spent his entire life being comforted by simsense stimulants.
- lose bad enough so that he would want to get better. He needed to be spurred on, for he is not working hard enough.
- understand what he is up against and why he must improve.

You seem not to agree with my methods, nor, apparently, does Lucifer. That does not concern me.

Now that I have explained my motivations, I expect you to get back to work on the behavioral simsense.

—END memo—

>>————————————————<<

<<(12:22:09/11-19-51)>>

>["They must have given you some kind of 'limb-sense' so that you could control a humanoid form, which is how deckers usually appear, and that's what got hurt when the IC hit you," Lucifer continues. "See, gray IC only hits the persona, but sometimes the deck's dampers can't screen all the IC's sim-pain from a decker's body, and his body in the other world experiences involuntary jerks and spasms. Not enough to do serious damage, but depending on how the fight went, enough to make the decker sore the next day.

"I'm figuring your simulated neurons have never felt pain before so it's bothering you more than normal. Pain is something you get used to. And trust me, chummer, this was just gray IC. If you'd been up against black, I don't think you'd be able to do any more than simply sit there and nod."

"It gets worse?"

"Far worse, chuckles. I've had it get far worse."

This doesn't sound pleasant, but it doesn't seem that you have any choice in the matter, so you decide to learn as much as you can.

"You said that the IC attacks my persona, but that it can also affect me. But didn't you tell me before that my persona is just a picture of me?"

"Right," Lucifer says, but he seems to be thinking about what he wants to say next. "Like I said a while ago, personas are representations of you and me in the Matrix." Once again Lucifer's body becomes frozen for a moment and then starts to move with jerky rhythms. "Frag, I hate this," he says, stuttering out each word. "Pay attention, 'cause I don't want to have to explain this again."

"All right," you say, amazed at how difficult it is for Lucifer to talk about himself.

"Our personas are made up of four programs. There's a bod program, an evasion program, a masking program, and a sensors program. You've got each one of these programs, but I think the only program you've used very much is your sensors program."

You are confused and say, "But Lucifer, I don't have any programs. You told me that—"

"I told you you'd get utilities to run, yes, but actually you've been running your four persona programs the whole time you've existed. It's just that you don't really think about them because they've always been part of you, which is why I think you're going to be such a hot-shot decker. Running is in your blood, or whatever you've got. You just don't know it yet.

"The thing is, if you weren't running a sensors program right now, you wouldn't be able to see me, you wouldn't see this datastore, you wouldn't see anything in the Matrix. And since you've always seen things in the Matrix, you've always been running a program. Snap. You're better than you thought you were.

"Now, your MPCP—that's Master Persona Control Program—keeps your persona together. The MPCP is like a big, complicated maze that's always shifting. It's the master program that houses all the other programs, not just your other persona programs, but any utilities you're actively running are actually structured as sub-programs of the MPCP. That's why all utilities are custom-designed. All have to fit a unique MPCP from a set of unique persona chips in each unique deck.

"A decker or any IC attacking you has to work his way to the core of your MPCP to crash your persona. The tougher the program, the bigger the maze, so the safer you are. As an unauthorized program starts working its way through your MPCP, however, your persona starts to slow down, even if it never reaches the core of the maze. Just having some enemy program in your MPCP starts gumming up the works. Your fight with the gray IC was probably the first time it was ever used in this way.

"One of the programs you've got running inside your MPCP is an evasion program. The name is kind of a misnomer—inaccurate description—because you're not really evading the IC. What the program does is run around the maze of the MPCP, making sure that unauthorized programs aren't working their way inside. The better the program, the faster it can block potential intrusions, making it harder to make substantial headway into your MPCP even if the IC should hit you.

"You've also got a bod program. What that does is reinforce the integrity of your MPCP's programming, making it tougher to crack.

"The last component of your MPCP is your masking program. It helps you blend into the Matrix, aiding you in getting past tracers and ID programs."

"And you have these four programs? Or, I mean, your persona does?"

Lucifer freezes for a moment, then suddenly his head has turned to face you.

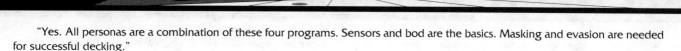

"Yes. All personas are a combination of these four programs. Sensors and bod are the basics. Masking and evasion are needed for successful decking."

"But if we're just two sets of four programs talking to each other…I mean, you're supposed to be someone from the other world. Am I just these programs?"

>>————————————————————<<

<<(18:43:12/11-19-51)>>

—**Matrix Born: Internal Memo**—

FROM: Gabby
TO: Dr. Halberstam

I have been told that you have children, even grandchildren. I have a hard time accepting these facts because you seem so ignorant of effective child-rearing techniques.

It would, of course, be foolish to treat Renny as if he were a normal little boy, but you cannot deny the similarities between him and real children *because we are the ones who have encouraged many of these similarities.*

One thing you cannot do to anybody, especially children, is put them through hell in a pathetic attempt to encourage them. All you end up doing is trashing them. Why should they make the second attempt if they know (or believe they know) they are incompetent to begin with? Your actions are completely irresponsible and I will inform the Board.

—**END memo**—

>>————————————————————<<

<<(19:23:12/11-19-51)>>

—**Matrix Born: Internal Memo**—

FROM: Dr. Halberstam
TO: Gabby

Gabby, you can go to the Board of UCAS Data Systems, but they are not the Board in charge of this project. I know who owns Data Systems, and in turn, who is running the Matrix Born Project. When the Data Systems Board turns to their parent company for instructions, I will already have been there to tell them you are ruining the work environment. Give it a rest. Renny is fine. I will be proven correct in this matter.

—**END memo**—

>>————————————————————<<

<<(15:54:12/11-21-51)>>

>["I don't fraggin' know, Renny. They flew me up to this sprawl buried in the middle of a bunch of pointy ears and tribes—don't ask—and told me they wanted me to teach a young decker. They were vague about it all, afraid to tell me too much, but afraid to let me go in blind. They said, 'Don't tell him about the outside world.' I thought they meant, 'Don't waste his and our time telling him about stuff he already knows.' When I saw you didn't know the Matrix wasn't real, I thought, this guy might already be over the edge—best check it out—and they pulled the plug on me. They sat me down and said, 'We want him to think there's nothing but the Matrix.' 'Did you wipe the guy's mind?' I asked. 'Sorry, Lucifer, just teach,' was their answer. Dumb answer."

You are quiet and think about everything that has happened to you: being raised by Nursie, hearing Dr. Halberstam's voice, meeting Lucifer. Once, everything was so simple. You lived and played games. Now there is something clawing at you from the inside. It seems as if once upon a time your thoughts were like the world of the Matrix. All you could think about was what was presented to you. Anything that wasn't shown, like the empty space between the nodes, didn't exist. Now, in your mind, all that empty space has become a true void, thoughts beckoning to be explored and filled with new ideas.

Now all this makes you feel that you know nothing, that you are useless, that you will never know what you need to know.

You turn your head and look Lucifer in the face, squinting your eyes so that you can see him clearly in the glowing, colored light. "Lucifer, I don't know much."

He leans against some blue boxes, returns your squint and smiles. "Wrong, kiddo. Look. You got beat up. That happens. I've been beat up, Halberstam has been beat up, and we're all going to get beat up again. It just happens. In your case, you got beat up unfairly. What I mean is that sometimes you're going to get trashed, but you'll be in there doing everything you can to win. It won't matter that you lost. What will matter is that you were alive, every part of you actively doing something. This time out, you weren't ready. The reason you feel stupid is because you never got a chance to start trying. No one taught you how to do what you were being asked to do. Guess what? You failed. Given the circumstances, no big surprise. But from what you told me, you were in there running your program every second you could. Most people would have just clutched. You kept going.

"But I've got faith in you. Whatever you are, whatever you're going to be, I think you're amazing. You work things naturally that it took me years to learn to do with as much skill as you use them."

"But…"

"Stop. I'm the teacher. I know what I'm talking about. You want to bash your self-esteem, and I'm telling you not to, so don't. I also know that our time here is limited. I can only lie about our whereabouts for so long. Time for you to get back home and for me to jack out and get something to eat."

"Eat?"

Lucifer opens his mouth as if to reply, and then shuts it. "Nope. Come on, let's get out of here."

>>————————————————————<<

—**From The Seattle Book Net**

Live Conference Transcription/Text-Only
(11-4-51)

<<**Waldo**>>—Who the drek is this Wallhoot guy anyway? What's his fragging problem?
<<**Kaine**>>—Are you talking about the book or the guy?
<<**Git**>>—What book?
<<**Waldo**>>—Some fragging *Virtual Life*. Stupid piece of drek!
<<**Dice**>>—Sounds like it got to you, chummer.
<<**Waldo**>>—Oh, give me a break, will you. Can you take this stuff seriously:

—**SEGMENT UPLOAD**

Most people would like to think that we are formed in a linear fashion, like the way a simsense plays itself out or the way our lives appear to move along a single line, each second moving us further upon that line. The common conception of sentient development is that we are children and slowly move along this line of thought, acquiring new points of view, rejecting or accepting different ideas, slowly building who we are in a neat, organized fashion.

This is not, however, the case.

Our minds are like large, frozen blocks of ice, constantly growing in size and changing in shape in response to the experiences that we encounter in life. These experiences can be in the form of a touch, something we see while walking down the street, a paragraph we read from a computer-net, something someone says to us. Even though one experience might be buried by a more intense or obvious layer of experience later on in life, it is still part of that block of ice.

And here is the key to understanding the contrast between the linear and block-of-ice models. A line is only a line, no matter how you look at it. But a block of ice! You can look at it from different angles, move slowly around its surface, and each moment see the light refract in new patterns of color and shape. The ideas have layered themselves. A recent idea near the surface on one side will be the farthest piece of ice when viewed from the other. The same item yields an infinite variety of results, all dependent upon the perspective!

—**END SEGMENT UPLOAD**

<<**Waldo**>>—I mean, what the hell is this nonsense?
<<**Kaine**>>—I've read some of his stuff, especially the religious essay. Useless. Over-generalized, pretentious nonsense.
<<**Git**>>—I don't know. I kind of liked it.
<<**Kaine**>>—Well, you don't know fragging drek.
<<**Git**>>—I know not to use double negatives.
<<**Tigger**>>—Yeah? All that religious stuff. It's not just that it's pretentious. The man doesn't know anything!
<<**Verne**>>—Where can I get some of his stuff?
<<**Kaine**>>—Oh, don't waste your time.
<<**Waldo**>>—You can get it off the Lit Net.
<<**Kaine**>>—Don't do it! It's the rantings of a madman!
<<**Waldo**>>—I've never claimed to be mad or sane.

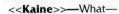

<<**Kaine**>>—What—
<<**Git**>>—Johnny Wallhoot? Are you on the net?
>>NAME CHANGE: Waldo is now Johnny W/Waldo<<
<<**Johnny W/Waldo**>>—Yup. I'm the one who started complaining about my work.
<<**Kaine**>>—Glad to know you've started to get some taste.
<<**Johnny W/Waldo**>>—Good one, man.
<<**Dice**>>—Why would you do that, Johnny?
<<**Johnny W/Waldo**>>—So everybody would join in and talk about it.
<<**Dice**>>—But they trashed it.
<<**Johnny W/Waldo**>>—But they talked about it. They read something I wrote, and whether they like it or not, it's now part of who they are, a part of what makes up their minds.

>>—————————————————<<

<<(11:35:10/11-23-51)>>

>[Your name is Renny, and you are learning to be a decker.
　Lucifer explains that information is the key. "Here's what you have to remember about the Matrix: it's a big place made up of information shaped to look like something else. The basic information is data. Data is files, texts, bank accounts, payroll statements, credstick information. Data is made up of words and numbers that don't do anything. Data is inactive. It just sits there. Programs, on the other hand, are also made up of symbols like numbers and letters, but they actually do something. We'll get to those soon."
　You are floating through a tunnel of data. The bits of information, flashing pieces of silver, fly by and around you. The data is flowing into and out of the big cube of silver that contains your house.
　Lucifer explained what he meant when he told you the Matrix is not real that first day you met. Or, it is real, but its appearance is an illusion. It looks infinite, but in fact it's not. It is limited by the finite number of systems that exist on Earth. You asked him about Earth and the world that was not the Matrix and he said that that world is infinite.
　You also asked about the word "infinite," because you are starting to like learning new words. They are like parts of programs. You take pleasure in putting them together, strings of words making sentences. You hold these sentences to yourself, tightly, like a…like a what? Dr. Halberstam once used the word "memory." Yes, like a memory. You are storing data. You are storing it now.
　Lucifer answered that the other world is infinite because it appears to go on forever, not only in space, but in time as well, and also because it contains so many forces interacting with one another, often unpredictably, that the outcome of a single day is unknown. It was, he said, "infinite in its potential." He said that the Matrix offered some possibility of random events, but only to a limited degree. Its events tended to be pre-planned, and so its reality model was limited. Only deckers provided the random chance of the unknown in the Matrix. "And that," he said, smiling, "is why we deckers like it so much. Because we are in charge."
　You are so caught up in your memories that it takes you a moment to realize that Lucifer is teaching but you are not learning. The memories are powerful. They are richer now than before Dr. Halberstam told you your life had changed. You will have to watch that.
　"Take this data, for instance," Lucifer continues, gesturing to the flashing silver. "We can't really see what it is—what it says—because right now it's only in the form of 'data.' It conforms to the Universal Matrix Specifications of what data should look like when it travels between nodes. We can't read what the data is from here because they're just random bits of code that have to be set up again, re-sequenced. If we were to get into a datastore node, we'd be able to read it just fine."
　"And a node is the basic unit of a computer system."
　"Correct, chummer. And the types of nodes are?"
　"Central Processing Units, the center of a system. Datastores, which hold information or files. Input/Output Ports, which open the system to data input and output sources that interface the computer system with things of the other world—things like printers, which write words on paper, or graphic displays, which let pictures of data from the Matrix show up on the screen." While saying this, you imagine how marvelous it would be to see paper, which to you sounds like a wondrous substance.
　"Sub-Processing Units," you recite, "which handle tasks for the main system. System Access Nodes, the doorways to systems and the access points to different parts of the Grid. Data Line Junctions, which route data when multiple data lines intersect."
　You forget the next one.
　Lucifer says, "Come on, git, they're going to kick me out of here if you can't handle nodes! I taught this to you yesterday!"
　"Slaves," you say loudly, your eyes shut, happy that you remember it, but vaguely disturbed for reasons you do not understand. "Slave Module nodes control a physical process or a device, something in the other world. There are machines and things in the other world that are controlled by programs. You can access control of these things through the node that controls them. They're a lot like I/O ports because they interface a computer system with something in the other world. A slave controls…" and here you draw a blank again, for so much of the other world makes no sense to you and you have trouble thinking about it. You try to remember the words that Lucifer used. "The physical things of the other world: elevator systems, bank vaults, things that the people in the other world use all the time. I guess a slave could even control a printer. The slave would control the machine and the I/O would control the data. The slave controls the things so that people don't have to think about making it work."
　Lucifer smiles, twirling his pitchfork around. "Good. Good. I also want to run something by you. It's a common mistake a lot of

children—remember, that's young people from the other world—make. All the machines that exist in the other world need power to make them work, and the power is called electricity. The machines have power cables that connect them to sockets in the wall. These sockets, in turn, are connected to large power systems that are themselves connected to even larger power systems. The power systems are similar to the data systems of a computer; both involve the use of cables to transfer energy, which is where the confusion comes in. A lot of children think that deckers can travel through the power cables, but a decker can only wander around in areas that are in the Matrix, and the Matrix is only concerned with information. Electricity is just power, raw, unsophisticated power. Machines like computers need it to work, but computers turn that energy into the real power of information."

"Okay," you say, not really sure what Lucifer is talking about because you cannot imagine power not made of data.

"Never mind," Lucifer says, smiling at you with sympathy. "You'll probably never see a power cord, so don't worry about it." You realize he knows he has once again confused you and is going to let the matter drop. He settles himself against the side of the data line, resting the pitchfork across his lap. He closes his eyes and sighs. "All right," he says. "Programming and hacking."

You have learned that when he closes his eyes and sighs it means he is going to teach you something, so you sit down opposite him. As always, whenever you sit in a place that is not the house, it is less comfortable.

Through the haze of silver data, you see Lucifer's bearded face break into a broad smile, his cheeks bulging as he contemplates his lecture. "Decking," he begins, "is the most wonderful thing in the world to do."

>>————————————————————————<<

<<(13:54:08/11-23-51)>>

>[Your name is Renny and you are sitting against the non-wall of a data line, your back against the firm surface of non-existence. Your golden arms rest comfortably in your lap as you listen to Lucifer talk about decking. His eyes are closed right now, and you know that this always happens when he talks about decking. He tells you that he loves it, and you think you know what he means by that, but you have no way of knowing if you are right. Love, as something you can put into words, eludes you.

"What we do," he says, eyes closed, voice soft, wanting you to understand but perfectly content to rattle off his declaration of love whether you do or don't, "deckers, that is, we go in with our utilities—our pre-written speeches—and we use them. We speak them to the IC and try to crack the IC. Lord way up above, Renny, I don't know what you are, so I don't know if it'll do the same thing for you, but for us, for deckers, there's nothing like it."

There is...something missing again...it passes over you once in a while, but you have learned not to let it get to you, for Dr. Halberstam always becomes concerned. But it comes again now and you realize that when Lucifer refers to other deckers, he is referring to a group to which he belongs, and you are jealous. You think that you want to have the same feeling as the other deckers do, no matter what you are, so that you might belong as well. You think it is strange to be with someone in a place as small as a data line and still feel lonely. You clench your jaw and remain silent.

"The thing is, we don't speak just any utility to any IC. You have to find the right speech to say to the proper IC. What you say matters. It's not like talking with people." Lucifer's fingers intertwine and rub each other lightly. "With people, anything can be said and nothing matters. Words and words and words. You go to a party—don't ask," he says quickly, finger raised, eyes closed. "In the other place, we go to them—people sit around and talk and say things. Anything. Just to talk. Put forth views and debate them. Sometimes you get a new idea. Sometimes something changes.

"I spoke with a man once. He talked about how we never look to the stars for answers anymore. Didn't know what the hell he was talking about. It never occurred to me that once upon a time city lights weren't so thick, that once the night sky was a mosaic of silver shards. He told me that people used to think the sky was a huge bowl turned upside down over the other world. And people thought it revealed answers about the mysteries of life. So astrologers scanned the night skies and discovered predictions about the future. Not only that, but sailors used to navigate by the stars...ships out at sea without radar. Frag," Lucifer says softly, and the notion of traveling without radar obviously is powerful to him, "no land in sight, no imaging radar, no land. The stars got them where they wanted to go.

"And the thing is, we still do the same things. We navigate and people still do astrology—but we can't see the stars. The stars are there, but we don't look to them. Can't see them."

"Lucifer, Dr. Halberstam might test me again."

"Kiddo, I know both you and he would just love it if I could slide decking into you like I was slotting a utility, but that's not the way it works. A decker's got to want to deck. He's got to have a love of...something besides the numbers, or it just won't work. Now I'm going to do the best I can for you, but if I say we're talking stars, we're talking stars."

"But are they still there?" you ask, actually very curious about the stars. Stars are now like paper, and you want more than anything to see them, and even if talking about them means getting in trouble again, it seems worth it.

"Yup. There're even some parts of the world where you can see them. But that's rare. The sprawl turns the night sky, even far away, toxic red.

"But here's the thing. We keep navigating, but we navigate only by image, not by looking at something real. And astrologers have their charts. They don't look at the stars anymore, they just look at a piece of paper with all the patterns of the stars written out. The man said that's what we do now. We don't look at objects anymore, we don't look at the world, we look at representations of objects. We look at blips on a screen. We look at numbers representing location."

"Like the Matrix."

"Right. The world's too crowded now. Too thick. There's no perspective to see the real things from, so we condense it all with representations."

Lucifer looks different now. His head is lowered slightly and he is less frightening than you have ever seen him. He reminds you…of you.

His eyes open.

"His words, the man at the party, were a program that cracked me. I was ten. I left the party. I'd gone to score something nasty but instead I just walked out. Wandered the streets. I had a leather jacket, looked cool. Should have been tough. I wasn't. I was a kid again. I looked up at the sky. The Atlanta sprawl had turned it glowing red in the middle of the night. This idea of not seeing stuff got to me. I suddenly felt cut off. I thought, 'I've got to find out what's at the core of the lie.'

"See Renny, there're two kinds of people. There's the kind that likes simsense, where you just sit and let lies wash over you. And then there's the kind that manipulates the lie. Before that party, I hadn't even seen it as a lie. I just thought that life was something you went through, kicks, just fun. But I realized that I'm in a world of lies. The world's always been a world of lies. The past hands its lies onto the future. The present picks through the bunch and picks the ones it likes, and then hands them on down. And then the future starts it all over again. The stars were never in a bowl. We dumped that. Now we believe it's better to have sprawls than stars. Well, since the Awakening, we've got shamans who say that ain't so. Time for new truths.

"Well, I figure if I had to live in a world of lies, I wanted to be the kind of guy who manipulates the lie. And when I was growing up, the Matrix was where you went to find the best lie in the biz. I mean, look at this place"—he gestures to the nodes hanging in the air—"This is it! So at that party, that guy spoke words that mattered. That was a good program, and I'll tell you something. He didn't do it just with the words. He did it like hacking. He worked that speech with style."

"Lucifer," you say, utter confusion revealed in your voice.

Lucifer sighs. "I know. Sorry. I think your weirdness is getting to me. Haven't thought about that night in years."

You remember the story he told you about the play, and it occurs to you that the boy in the story was him. But then suddenly, before your very eyes, he is once again Lucifer the Confident.

"But what I just said about style does matter. I mean, it's a good way to think about decking." Lucifer smiles and stands. "Hacking," he says, twirling his pitchfork, "is decking with style. Style is hacking."

"Any sarariman worth his inputs is going to skip through the Matrix and shoot a program or two out. Maybe even crack some IC by mindlessly tossing out the right programming. But to be good, to be a decker worthy of this lovely lie called the Matrix, you've got to have style.

"Let me explain. All deckers have utilities. Deckers like me have illegal utilities. Now, if an IC program is weak enough, my utility can do the work and I can sit back and watch. But there are times when the IC is tougher than my utility can handle all by its lonesome. That's where I come in. Otherwise, why am I even hanging out with my programs?

"Notice that my persona has arms and legs. Notice, too, that I carry a pitchfork. Merely a pathetic affectation? Not at all, though most folks who know drek about decking think we put on all this glitz to appease our stunted egos. In fact, my appearance, including my veritable pitchfork, is the beginning of my style.

"Every decker has to find a way of working that makes sense to him, a way to express himself, a way of connecting himself to his work. In a way, it's like shamanistic totems, only every decker is his own totem." Without turning to see that you are puzzled by the reference, Lucifer waves his hand and begins walking down the data line. "Forget the totem thing. Anyway. I have two ways of running a program against IC. I can use the aforementioned strategy of tossing the utility at the countermeasure program, or I can involve myself in running the program against the IC."

Lucifer suddenly stops in his tracks and whirls to look at you. "Which one sounds like more fun?" he asks.

He does not wait for an answer.

"When you involve yourself with your program, that's hacking. You're actually manipulating your utility to speak with more directness to the IC. A lot of IC doesn't care what you're saying if you don't say it in just the right way. When I twirl my pitchfork like this to get your attention, that's hacking with the spoken language. I'm adding something to make my words more effective. The words are the same, but there's just something extra, just for you."

"And hacking with a utility is the same thing?"

"Almost exactly, as a matter of fact. When I buy, or steal, a program off the shelf, it's the same program as for every other decker who's ever picked one of them up. But deckers will use the same utility differently from one another when we hack. The whole point of hacking is practicing with your programs. I look like this because of lies: I wanted to be Lucifer, Prince of Lies. So right away I'm comfortable with my persona. When I move around as Lucifer, I know who I am. I feel 'right.'

"Now, when it comes to my utilities, I have to learn how to use them. They told me that you were raised on games that made you learn movements of patterns."

You think back to the bear and suddenly feel tired. The world is much harder than it used to be. "Yes."

"Well," says Lucifer, full of energy, "you were practicing hacking. When I hack, I do movements as well. My cyberdeck knows how to translate my motions, specific to my persona and pitchfork, into subtle shifts in the program I'm running, just like your games responded to your movements. That's the real potential of decking, though most people don't take advantage of it. Hacking is like doing a dance with your program."

"A dance?"

"Um…a coordinated movement between two or more…things. But not just a dance. Listen, a real common persona bit is a sword. The decker has the sword and the strokes he uses, the way he holds it moment to moment, parries and blocks, all are really ways of communicating to the deck changes he wants in his program. The beauty of it all is that he's not sitting there typing in changes in code. He's trained himself to think of the changes in physical motions. It's quicker, more elegant. It's a wonderful lie."

"And you do the same thing with your pitchfork?"

"Right. Now some guys and gals use different items. Some have guns—and again, the style of how you shoot is important. Others use small daggers, some paint, some build statues from a lump of clay, right there, on the spot, molding the computer graphic clay until their utility crashes the IC. And of course, straight persona movement figures in, too.

"And different utilities use different tools and movements. My pitchfork is for combat utilities. I breathe smoke out of my mouth for masking utilities. How I swirl the smoke with my hands determines the effectiveness of my hacking. Everything is different and well-practiced so you instinctively do the right thing at the right time."

"What will I use?"

"Don't know. I picked your persona, but you should change it if you want to."

"No," you answer quickly, and then think it strange that you should care so much about the persona. You realize you are excited. You want to hack. "What tools do I get?"

"Now, those you really should pick yourself. I'm sure Halberstam will spring for whatever you want. That Doomguard he gave you was no video game." Lucifer looks at you smiling, sly. "You want it, don't you?"

"Want it?"

"Hacking. You want it."

You smile back. "Yes."

"'Cause of Halberstam?"

"No. For me."

He broadens his smile. "Well, let's call it quits for today so you can go fret about what tools you want."

"Lucifer."

"Yup."

"You said that the…shamans wanted to look at the stars again."

"Yeah."

"Why did you come to the Matrix? Why didn't you become a shaman? They seem to want to find the truth, to believe that there is something behind the lie."

Lucifer looks down at the data for a moment.

"Well, first of all, the way I understand it, totems pick shamans, not the other way around. But even if I had a choice, I wouldn't do it. The magic popped up out of the blue out there, Renny, and it could go away just as easily. I'm happier with something that is obviously false. No confusion. I'm really here. I make the world happen. It's easier just knowing the rest of the world is an illusion, that I can't depend on anything."

>>———————————————————<<

<<(08:34:17/11-24-51)>>

—Matrix Born: Internal Memo—

FROM: Halberstam
TO: Gabby
    Progress on simsense behavioral tutorial?

—END memo—

>>———————————————————<<

<<(08:36:33/11-24-51)>>

—Matrix Born: Internal Memo—

FROM: Gabby
TO: Halberstam
    Never been done before. Cut some slack or start looking for another genius.

—END memo—

>>————————————————————————————<<

<<(08:44:23/11-25-51)>>

>[You wake up and realize they have given you your tools.

You described them to Dr. Halberstam several days ago. He wanted to know where you got your ideas, and was very insistent about it. But you explained that you got your ideas from a dream, and this seemed all right to him. And you were glad, because your ideas really did come to you in a dream, and you wouldn't have known what else to say.

The night you dreamed your tools, you had been thinking about what style you wanted as a decker. When you were asleep, you thought about stars—stars and dancing with your utilities. You saw yourself surrounded by pinpoints of light, all of them responding to your persona's movements. When you moved your arms, the stars would swirl in one direction. When you moved in another direction, they would extend far ahead of you. And when you flung your arms forward, as if throwing a combat utility at an opponent, a blinding white light appeared before you as your stars raced forward. Lucifer told you that deckers often take different kinds of tools for different programs, but when you woke up that night after your dream, you decided that stars would be your style. A swarm of burning white orbs will encircle your angelic body and give you power in the Matrix.

And when you wake up, they are there. Not visible, not now, for you are not using them. But you feel them on you, touching you, waiting to be used, long speeches waiting to be spoken, enhanced by your ability to make the points of light dance as you dance.

Much of the utility crowds directly into your thoughts. This, you think, must be programs loaded into your "memory," which Lucifer told you about. You have other programs, but not all of them fit into your memory at once. You think about the programs, finding their names and sensing what they do.

Your combat utility is once again a Doomguard III. It burns hot white when you picture your stars. You have a medic program, a Whitepatch IV, which you can tell will repair your persona if it becomes damaged. It is not loaded into your memory, but is nearby, waiting to be used. A Dervish III is in your memory, a program that will send your stars out in a swirling mass to confuse IC blocking your way.

You come to the sensor utilities, none of which are currently loaded into your memory. These programs will use your stars differently, with different motions and patterns, than the combat and defense utilities. For your Fuchi Analyze V, Voyeur III, and Organizer IV, your stars will not circle your body, but will pass in and around the data you wish to read. You will control their motion with your fingers. It is similar to the way Lucifer was manipulating the datastore node with his fingernails. You did not ask for the utilities to run this way, but you think it is a good idea.

The last set of programs are the masking utilities. Your deception program, a Windmill Access Breaker III, is already loaded. Also in your memory is an Ossato Electronics Goose Chase V. Waiting in storage is a Sleaze III. It has no brand name on it, but you do find the name Brutus, so you assume he wrote the program.

You realize that you have never dealt with the programs before, but you know a great deal about them. It is as Lucifer said: you have an innate understanding of the Matrix; what you had to learn was how to make that understanding yours. And with your utilities designed as stars, now for the first time, you feel ready to learn about hacking. You are full of energy, wanting to show Lucifer your tools, wanting Lucifer to show you how to use them as best you can.

As you think about getting out of bed, the sheets rise off of you. You float out of bed and make your way to the living room. Waiting there for you is Lucifer, smiling and ready to get to work.

>>————————————————————————————<<

<<(12:12:54/11-25-51)>>

>[It is hard learning how to hack. You are in the living room, just running your programs, not even against IC, and already you feel as if you will never learn how to influence your utilities.

You try to follow the stars when you run a program, but there are so many of them, moving so fast, it is impossible to control them. Their speech just goes on and you have no control over how they are speaking. "There are too many stars. I should have chosen something simpler," you say to Lucifer after running a program and feeling it rush by your sensations, touching you, but without you being able to touch it. "One thing, like a sword. That would have been better."

"Wouldn't have made any difference, my little cherub. First time out with a sword, it would be leading you around the room. The balance would feel all off and it would move whether you wanted it to or not. Remember, again and again and again, that for all practical purposes, it doesn't matter what anything looks like. The shape of your tools only influences how you think about the items. A new utility that's like a sword is going to feel unwieldy. A pattern of stars, which I tell you again is a great choice for you, is going to seem too complicated. Welcome to the advanced decking classes. You didn't think it would be just a matter of me rambling on about the nature of the Matrix, did you?"

You sigh, loading up your combat utility again. "I just thought it would be easier."

Lucifer points at you. "Wait a second. I just want to slam some perspective into that golden cranium of yours. Did anyone ever teach you how to run a program?"

You think for a moment, and then say, "No."

"And what are you doing right now?"

"Running programs…but I'm not…"

He points the flat of his palm at you to silence you. "Shhhh! First part. You're running programs. Most folks have to learn how to do that. You're just doing it out of habit. No, you're not doing this new thing as well as you'd like. Why? Well, git, it's a new thing. If you already knew how to do it, it'd be an old thing. It will take time. But trust me. Apply yourself and you will make it happen.

"Now, come on, you're not trying to control the program now. There's no point in doing that unless you're up against IC. Then you make changes to nail that fragging program to the wall. All you're trying to do *now* is follow the program as it runs. Keep up with it. Touch it as it touches you." He stops for a moment. "Why did you pick stars?"

You know that although they came from a dream, you wanted stars because Lucifer said they once gave clues in the other world, clues to life outside of what was immediately there. You suspect that if you try to live your life without any metaphors, you will feel such pain that you won't know what to do. Just thinking about the world you live in, and how you perceive it, where everything is only what it is, is causing you distress. You chose stars because you wanted a connection to the other world. A connection that was yours, that expanded your view.

But you know you cannot explain this to Lucifer, for Dr. Halberstam is listening. So you just say, "I dreamed them." Lucifer smiles, and even though you didn't explain it all, you think he understands.

"Run the program, Renny."

You activate the Doomguard and it begins to speak. The stars, glowing a hot white, begin to move around. Instead of trying to see them for what they are, a language to crash IC, you think about why you chose them and your desire to find something else in them. As the program speaks and the stars whirl, you hear and see something: something about power. For when you first thought about a combat utility, you pictured it as a large block of strength to be used for smashing IC. But as you listen to the code and watch the stars, you hear that the program is actually light and delicate. Its power is not in its brute strength, but in its nimbleness. The stars, you realize, can crawl into the cracks in a piece of IC and then move around a bit, not a great deal, but move enough so that each star weakens the IC. The Doomguard doesn't use most of its memory in strength, but to find the right places to apply the strength it has.

And as you are thinking this about the program, you begin to think about you. It seems that you share strengths and weaknesses with the program and that by looking at the program, listening to it, you can learn things about yourself. You, like the program, are not very strong compared to the world around you. Your life is controlled by Dr. Halberstam. You need Lucifer to teach you how to survive in the Matrix. You have no goals outside those that others have created for you. But part of you, instinctively, knows that like the Doomguard, you could hurt the stronger people around you by finding and exploiting their weaknesses. You find that you are following the stars better than before, twirling your body, wings outstretched, right arm gently sliding through the air. You smile, for dancing is more than a word to you now. Dancing is two things: movement that expresses what you feel and an image of understanding. A metaphor. You laugh.

Lucifer is laughing, too, and clapping his hands. As the program finishes running, a tingling sensation runs over your body and your eyes want to do something, but they cannot, so you laugh, breathing quickly, and shout, "I did it. I understood the program!"

Lucifer crosses to you and takes your face in his hands. "Congratulations, Renny!" He is smiling and happy.

Dr. Halberstam asks if you want to rest. You say no. You want to keep working. You sense the potential for power if you keep working. Not strength, but your own kind of power, small and dangerous.

"Great," says Lucifer. "Let's keep going."

You prepare to run another program, all the while thinking what this one might teach you about yourself. And two things occur to you.

The first is that another person with different strengths and weaknesses would have found a different lesson in the Doomguard program, and that is the difference between the plays and simsenses that Lucifer told you about. In a play, you find your own lesson; in a simsense, the experience overwhelms you and there is nothing to be learned.

The second is that you found a metaphor, and you thought you weren't supposed to be able to do that.

—From Deckers, Docs, and Profs: An Industry Guide To Living Scientists, Their Bios, Expertise, Contracts, and Whereabouts

Shadowland Update 9/2051

VIRTUAL REALITY TECHNOLOGY

Name:	Professor Susan Athenson
Contract:	Fuchi
Last Seen:	8/2051
Primary and Secondary Concentrations:	Psychology (designing specs for IC sculptures); Matrix Programming
Glitz:	Reputedly designed IC that brought down both Lightning Bug and Sliphead when they tried to cruise Fuchi's Tokyo system.

Bio: Trained at MIT&T, Athenson quickly made a name for herself by focusing on the decker's mind as a tool to be exploited by IC programmers. Her experiments as a graduate student earned her a reputation that most corp scientists only dream about. Word is, though, that her results don't always match expectations. Though she's achieved spectacular successes in her experiments, her theories often don't pan out in practice.

Not yet, at least. Somebody at Fuchi hired her even before she was out of school, and they gave her an armed escort out of Boston after she turned in her doctoral in '48. She seems to need time before her work hits stride, and it looks as though the folks at Fuchi are willing to give it to her.

In a break from standard corp policy, Athenson is a very visible asset. In part, this may be because her good looks are worth exploiting, but also because Fuchi is trying to hit a wider market with their Impulse IC series, which Athenson helped develop. Because her theories have yet to make it out to the layman, Fuchi figures having a classy programmer explain it on the vid-nets might help get the harried sararimen to take the time to hear about the stuff.

The fact that she is so public and traveling so much has, however, raised suspicions that the Athenson doing the PR is actually a cosmetic job with enough skill software tucked into her brain stem to get her through an interview without stumbling. Another theory is that Athenson's work has not panned out, but that Fuchi keeps her around as a corp show girl. This might also explain the rumors that Ares has made overtures to pick Athenson up. If Fuchi has given up on her, she's going to want to go someplace else to continue her work.

No word on family connections or emotional interests. Best guesses are that she's a kid from the Midwest who went into computer science to make a name for herself and break all ties with her "simple" family when she made it.

No kidding.

Name:	Keith "The Suit" Hannigan
Contract:	Mitsuhama
Last Seen:	3/2045
Primary and Secondary Concentrations:	Interface Tech, Interface Programming
Glitz:	Designed the Prometheus 4000 for Fuchi. He's the man that got neural interface on your desk, chummer.

Bio: Hannigan is one of our field's self-taught heros. He was ripping apart flat screens even before hitting puberty and was so busy he never bothered finishing high school. Someone on the Echo Mirage project brought him along as a tech grunt. Viewed as something between an army brat and the team's mascot, Hannigan escaped most of the team's publicity. He never had a desire to deck, only to create the means for other people to deck.

When the team split up (or when the corpses were buried and the living scattered), Fuchi grabbed him and brought him to Japan. (They know a good thing when they see it.) Hannigan's value lay not only in his innate gray-matter processing power, but in his lack of interest in decking. Unlike most of the young minds seeding the cyberdeck revolution, Hannigan wasn't interested in decking or playing within the environment. All he cared about was focusing the technology to make decking possible. His oft-quoted phrase is: "I make the rules. Living by them is a task for others."

His rigidness, both physically and socially, earned him the nickname of "The Suit" at Fuchi. Perhaps he doesn't mind the name, because they say he responds to it when so addressed.

He was at Fuchi only a few years before being snatched by Mitsuhama in '45. It's still debatable whether The Suit arranged for his extraction or whether it was as much a surprise to him as to Fuchi. He was spotted a year later, standing around rigidly on the ski slopes of a lodge in the Alps.

Elaine, Hannigan's wife of three years, and their two-year-old daughter died in the extraction. More mystery. Some say it was Fuchi bullets that did them in; others suggest that Hannigan himself requested that Mitsuhama's agents do it.

Many credit Hannigan's work as partially responsible for Mitsuhama's successful competition with Fuchi. The older Matrix designers constantly comment on Hannigan's influence in Mitsuhama's work. At age 37, The Suit is already a veteran of Matrix history, but apparently still has a lot to offer.

Name: Music Man
Contract: Independent
Last Seen: 2042
Primary and Secondary Concentrations: Decking; Interface Programming
Glitz: Long-lived and really bright, Gitleman has probably been involved in every important cybertechnology development except for the Echo team.

Bio: According to Matrix mythology, the Music Man is in his fifties, which means that he was in his thirties when he got involved with Matrix technology. That's weird enough in itself. But he also came in late, having spent most of the late 2020s as a traveling salesman and con man. Gitleman ran a variety of scams, usually involving the sale of inferior or nonexistent goods through electronic mail. It was 2041 when he picked up on the potential of ASSIST technology and cyberdecks. Seeing the great potential for personal profit, he applied himself to learning as much as he could about it.

His experience at running electronic mail scams had made him a passable decker, but it was the introduction of cybertechnology that let him really take off. Early cybertech scientists called him the Ghost in the Grid. He'd deck into corp systems, look around at their data, and leave tips on how to improve their work. Without trying to blow the Music Man's influence out of proportion, it is impossible to deny that his cross-seeding of information between companies, whether they liked it or not, was vital to the incredible rate at which cybertechnology has advanced in a mere eleven years' time.

Someone on the Shadowland net once asked him why he spends as much time helping companies as stealing from them. His reply: "Now that everybody uses computers, pulling off scams isn't as tough as it used to be. I figure more technology means it keeps getting easier to make my living."

Over the years, most corps have put out contracts on Music Man. It goes without saying that nothing has come of any of them. By now, many corps have come to an uneasy truce with the decker; they leave him alone and he only takes money, not technology.

Fuchi and Mitsuhama are the only corps still on his case. In retaliation, he created two nonexistent disgruntled employees, one for each company, each one wanting to sell tech data to the other firm. Music Man created detailed histories for each "employee," all of which checked out when the corps sent in deckers to investigate the deal. Both corps offered big nuyen, which Music Man tidily picked up. In return, each company received 120,000 Mp of garbage that Music Man had handcrafted to look valuable upon cursory examination. Eventually, the corps discovered the other firm's expense voucher for the purchase at the core of the files purchased. The vouchers were labeled "Industrial Espionage: Mitsuhama" and "Industrial Espionage: Fuchi," respectively.

Music Man is rumored to have several wives around North America, each one ignorant of the others.

Name: Dr. Thomas Halberstam
Contract: UCAS Data Systems
Last Seen: 2048
Primary and Secondary Concentrations: Headware Transimplant Design; Implant Programming
Glitz: Designer of AI work that led to ASSIST technology at ESP Systems, Inc., Chicago.

Bio: Halberstam used to be known as the "stepfather" of virtual-reality technology. Now, in his mid-sixties, he might well be viewed as its "white-haired gran'pa."

As a grad student in the Tech Department of Northwestern University in Chicago, Halberstam was working on artificial intelligence. Instead of experimenting with models of computers that mimicked human activity, Halberstam spent most of his time exploring how the human brain actually worked and trying to copy the minute activities of the mind. Once he'd compiled this data, he hoped eventually to combine these sub-units into a larger AI. At the time, one of his advisors was Dr. Hosato Hikita, whose own project was the attempt to wire the brain to artificial sensory stimulus. Hikita paid special attention to Halberstam's work; though the younger man's goal was different, much of the raw data he was acquiring could apply to Hikita's work. Whereas Halberstam wanted to break down the brain into its smallest components and then artificially reconstruct a human brain from scratch, Hikita was convinced that such a goal was not only implausible, but morally questionable (ah, the good old days of virtue).

Hikita's goal was to circumvent the entire AI question by interfacing the human mind with computer technology. In that way, computer technology would be directly available to an intelligent being, which, in Hikita's estimation, was the entire goal of AI anyway.

It was shortly after his 28th birthday that Halberstam completed his "synaptic map," a culmination of four years' work. The term "map" was a misnomer that stuck. It was actually a dynamic computer graphic construct of the "thought flows" of the brain, a kind of weather system map for the brain.

Years earlier it had been discovered that different parts of the brain could be labeled in terms of gross activity for the brain, but that this compartmentalization was not entirely accurate because these sections often influenced one another in unpredictable ways. Halberstam proved that the brain was *not* digital in nature, as had been assumed in the 20th century, but rather that the best model of the mind was analog. Neurons firing yes or no signals in a thinking process were not as crucial as the gross effect groups of neurons had on one another, constantly shifting, constantly firing off new directives. The brain, Halberstam discovered, was like a huge, active democracy whose population (the neurons) went to the polls every second of their lives. "We may express our thoughts linearly," Halberstam said, "but they are not formed that way. Our minds are a cubist expression of thought, constantly influenced by competing external stimuli. Each new idea folds over the other, some becoming crushed in the wave of new ideas, others breaking apart upon striking older, more rooted ideas. But every stimuli is tested. It is the make-up of each individual's brain and the chemicals being introduced to the system at each moment that determine whether a new idea or stimuli will have a true effect upon the brain."

Just after Hikita reviewed Halberstam's work, he went to work for ESP Systems, Inc. Because the goal of his work was different than Halberstam's, the older man had no qualms about using Halberstam's research. When ESP introduced ASIST technology two years later, Halberstam received full credit for the contribution his work had made to the project. Without it, Hikita would never have been able to influence the brain in the correct way, introducing waves of new ideas that would influence the brain in the desired manner. Despite the credit Halberstam was given, we all know who got the fame—and it wasn't Halberstam.

After finishing up at NU, he was hired by Nanotechnologies in Seattle. When his five-year contract was up, he went to work for UCAS Data Systems. It's an understatement to say he's overqualified to work for an electronic-mail company, but Halberstam is apparently working on something big, a project no one has been able to crack.

At a conference sponsored by Fuchi four years ago, Halberstam promised that Data Systems would produce the next step forward in Matrix security measures. He's still spry enough, but how long he can he keep up his pursuit of the glory that passed him by half his life ago?

Halberstam is married to Sarah Paggels, the renowned child psychologist. His three children are all married, and he has eight grandchildren, all presumably safe because of Halberstam's low-output profile.

Name: Ellen "Gabby" Hayes
Contract: UCAS Data Systems
Last Seen: 2049
Primary and Secondary Concentrations: Implant Programming; Interface Programming
Glitz: Headed the Fuchi Simsense Muse Interface Team in 2044. Need we say more?

Bio: The voluminous Hayes can easily be credited with hooking our world on simsense. Not that simsense wouldn't exist without her, but she made it so *good*. She's worked at Fuchi, Disney, MegaMedia, and Truman, each time introducing an enhancement to simsense technology. It's rumored that she spends as much time jacked into the stuff as cleaning it up. Apparently, Hayes adores simsense.

Her value, though, is that she's not an "artist." It's been said that she intuitively understands how the brain interacts with simsense, but sees it from the machine's point of view. Hayes' interests are technical and she stays on top of the latest developments made by every corp in the business.

Hayes' life took a strange twist a few years ago. After spending most of her career in the entertainment industry, she made a jump from Truman Technologies (who had signed her to a fat contract only two years earlier) to UCAS Data Systems, a small firm specializing in electronic-mail interfaces. Rat only knows where they set her up or what they needed her for, because no one has heard from her since. The move was made without an extraction. She just left one day and nobody at Truman batted an eye, even though they'd paid her a large chunk of their profits to get her from Disney. That would suggest that someone paid a cancellation fee, but it sure wasn't Data Systems.

Hayes is reputed to have few personal relationships. Simsense is her love.

Name: Professor Clouds by Night
Contract: Mitsuhama
Last Seen: 3/2051
Primary and Secondary Concentrations: Implant Technology; Implant Programming
Glitz: Reportedly a genius' genius; if he's producing valuable product, Mitsuhama is keeping it a secret.

Bio: Grabbed out of MIT&T by Mitsuhama, this young AmerIndian's outlandish behavior, theories, and research created quite a ruckus in Boston.

Born and raised in the Sioux Nation, Clouds by Night excelled in all his studies, but is said to have been a handful. He shunned the tribe's heritage and was constantly on academic probation for torturing animals in the school yard or for teasing classmates to the point of tears. Records show that Clouds by Night was not a large boy, but that he either stared down older children or simply took his punches with a laugh.

As he got older, his academic performance became even brighter. He skipped several grades and was awarded a computer engineering scholarship from the prestigious Eagle Technological Academy at the age of 12. Most young people would have been intimidated by the scholastic requirements and the age difference with the other students. Clouds by Night not only consistently ranked at the top of his class, but seems to have had no problems dealing with his fellow students. That is, he didn't need them other than as a source of tension, so he was quite happy. He was accused several times of campus rape, but the Academy's dean stepped in each time to dismiss the charges. It is now believed that the dean's palms were being greased by MIT&T, which had scoped out Clouds and wanted him bad.

When he hit college, he was all of 16 and suffered the first of several breakdowns that would plague him during his undergrad and grad years in Boston. His hostility and antics aroused racism against him, turning the Amerindian transplant into an outcast instead of the center of attention. Each time he was released from the school's mental ward, however, his resolve to put everyone else in their place was only strengthened. Eventually he realized that he could shame everyone if he actually *applied* himself in academics. At MIT&T, a GPA was the only currency that mattered.

By his senior year, Clouds by Night was already busily carrying out experiments in the grad labs. The bulk of his work revolved around trying to train animals to become security deckers, on the theory that their responses would be more instinctive than those of humans. Sounds wacko, but he got results along with lots of messy failures. Most beasts freaked when dumped into the Matrix and had to be "put to sleep" in the middle of the test.

Clouds by Night also worked on designing IC from dreams he tried recording with simsense, creating programs that would introduce psychosomatic diseases into a decker's nervous system. He tried lining decks used for Matrix work with subliminal positive biofeedback so that the average sarariman would really enjoy going to work each day because of a fix he wouldn't even know he was getting (rumor tells that Mitsuhama has implemented the latter in their decks, but the corp denies it), and even tried raising animals in the Matrix from birth. (Clouds is supposed to have said: "The best part is pulling the plug on the VRT and watching them snap into the world without any warning. Pain, chummer, pain.")

Mitsuhama has hired the 29-year-old professor as an idea-man for their company. He may not always have the discipline to complete his work, but plenty of other people on staff can do that for him. Mitsuhama is also said to have given Clouds by Night an assistant who works at his speed. Open bets as to whether there are any emotional ties.

Name:	Static
Contract:	Independent
Last Seen:	4/2045
Primary and Secondary Concentrations:	Interface Tech; Micros
Glitz:	Chief technician on the Echo Mirage hardware team.

Bio: Though the hardware technicians of Echo Mirage were not as flashy as the deckers, they were equally important. Running the hardware portion of the EM project was a young computer engineer named Erica Rutledge, known to most deckers today as Static. She dropped out of the public eye when Echo Mirage broke up and after several of the team members who tried to go free-lance ended up dead. Yes, boys and girls, this is one of the first shadowrunners, which is perhaps the only reason we know her name.

Her location is unknown, but it's rumored she wanders the world in search of new toys to play with. She's got healthy contacts with shadowrunners and corp scientists, and often can get valuable prototypes to runners from a scientist who wants a hearty field test. She's also hot with a processor tool kit. They say she can take a deck apart down to its chips and then rebuild the whole thing faster than an assembly line.

>>————————————————————<<

<<(08:01:23/12-01-51)>>

>[You are going into the Matrix today and you cannot wait.

You are awake already, waiting in the living room. Lucifer has not arrived yet, so you spend your time practicing your programs. Lucifer has helped you with them for the last week, but you are good enough now that you can work on your own. Lucifer encouraged you to do this, even though you feared you would teach yourself the wrong way. He said, "You've got it now, chummer. I'll step in when it's time, but for now, just keep working with them. They're yours."

So you practice them. And you feel them slide in around your body when you hack. You have even used them against IC in some of the system nodes. Just practicing. You went with Lucifer and he showed you which IC to crack. Dr. Halberstam was very pleased.

You are beginning to understand why Lucifer enjoys decking so much and why he smiles when he talks about it. Dr. Halberstam was right. It is like your games, but better. There is a huge difference between simply running a program against IC, which Lucifer says is what most people do most of the time, and hacking your way through IC—dancing with your program. It almost makes you want to get into trouble with IC just so you can hack.

You have been all around your system now, and discovered that it is only one system out of many, all connected by SANs. All of these systems exist in a large silver cube. And today, when Lucifer arrives, you will leave the system construct, see the cube from the outside, and travel through the Matrix.

There is a knock at the small castle and you open it. It is Lucifer, smiling. "Ready?" He does not wait for an answer but flips backward into the data stream. You follow.

You travel down a data stream to an SPU. Dr. Halberstam has given you and Lucifer the passcodes and you pass the eyeball without any problem. Down another data stream. Another node. Another stream. Another node. They have given you a map to a SAN out of the system. There are no hindrances today. You and Lucifer do not speak to each other. Until you see the LTG of the Matrix, there will be nothing new to talk about. You pass from one node to another, electrified by the environment. Weeks ago, when you first opened the door of your house and saw the node constructs hanging in space, you were amazed. But now, after the things that Lucifer has taught you, especially those things that you were able to read in the data Lucifer sneaked into the datastore, the world around you seems almost miraculous. It was made. These are more than just colored shapes whose charm is purely their form and color. People, those people from the other world, took the time to make information that was once considered ugly into something beautiful. Passing through a datastore, you look around and are delighted by the way it looks, but are astounded that it all serves a purpose. It is actually a way of communicating information.

You are awed by Lucifer and Dr. Halberstam's race. They are gods. And yet, according to the data you have read, they do not see their true position in the world. As you travel through the world of their construction, you feel completely inadequate. How could you be worth the attention of Lucifer or Dr. Halberstam?

Ahead of you is the SAN. It is a rectangle of glossy black surrounded by red edges set into the silver wall of the construct. The wall had not been so apparent when you looked at the system from your house, but you realize that the image probably becomes sharper as you approach it. The silver wall rises high above you until it meets with another silver wall at a right angle. Below you the wall disappears from sight and you cannot see the bottom of the construct. It is massive, and once again you feel very, very small compared to the work of the people of the other world.

You reach the SAN. Lucifer touches it and the solid black lightens to gray and then disappears.

You step out into the Seattle Local Telecommunications Grid# 2206 and feel as if you are nothing.

You stand in empty space. Far below you is the Matrix plane, dotted with so many small system constructs it appears to be a solid, smooth wash of color. Other systems, slightly larger, rise above the plane. Some are white, others red, pyramids, cubes, and boxes of many sizes. And above you, floating out far ahead of you, are the massive constructs that you saw illustrated in Lucifer's data—the Fuchi Star, the Mitsuhama Pagoda. The pictures did nothing to convey the overwhelming scope of the constructs. They float above you, casting vast shadows over the surface of the plane.

You forget where you are, you are just so busy taking it in.

"Renny? You okay?" You turn to Lucifer and he is smiling at you. You smile back, glad that he brought you here, glad that he is your friend. You realize that he is like Nursie was, only more, because he is...because he is more equal to you.

"Where do you want to go?"

You look around. So many of the constructs are so beautiful that you almost don't know which one to pick. But you say, "The Fuchi Star," for there is something powerful in its simplicity.

"I've got that address available. All right. Follow me."

Lucifer floats away from the silver wall of your construct and you follow. Although you know you are following a data line, it is not visible as data lines were in the construct, and it seems as if you are floating through a tremendous, horizonless void. You look back and see that your construct is a giant silver cube with rounded corners. It too floats above the plane, and you realize that the construct is much bigger than you thought it was, that there must be many more systems in the construct than you originally imagined.

You arrive at the Fuchi Star and move slowly along its smooth, cyclopean walls. The wall is interrupted by several SANs, all ornate and beautiful. It seems to stretch on forever, and you follow it from one tip of a star point to another.

"This is the deluxe tour. We're actually not going to the Star. If we did that, we'd end up at a Fuchi SAN. I'm actually swinging us through data lines that seem to pass the Star."

As you become accustomed to the scope of the LTG, you see small specks floating through the space between the constructs and realize they are deckers. As you pass by a SAN in the Star, you see a chrome samurai warrior exit and float down toward the plane, sword drawn, ready for combat. He sees you, but pays you no heed.

"Where to next?"

The day is spent with your pointing to one construct after another and Lucifer getting you there. You drift by shapes and pagodas and giant buildings, passing deckers that look like pirates and cloaked warriors and gypsies and cowboys and painters and even deckers that carry small keyboards with them.

"They're strange," Lucifer explains. "What they do is quickly write out the combat like it was the scene of a story. They're not really writing, of course, just thinking it, but imagining themselves as the heroes of a story. I don't get it."

You see hundreds of fascinating constructs, pass through several nodes leading to different LTGs within the UCAS/Seattle RTG. Some are much smaller than others, with smaller constructs, most of them near the plane, but they are all dazzling.

Hours have passed and Lucifer turns to you and asks, "How're you doing, Renny?"

"Fine," you reply, wanting to see more.

"Want to make a run?"

"A run?"

"Yeah. You want to put these hard-earned skills of yours on the line?"

"You mean into a system?"

"Well, that's what decking is all about."

You think for a moment, realizing that more than anything, you want to be wandering around a system without anyone knowing you are there.

"Yes."

Lucifer looks at you carefully, not smiling, but something close to it. "Where do you want to go?"

You don't have to think long before you know exactly where you want to run, and as you think of it, you smile. And when you

smile, Lucifer smiles, too. "Home. I want to run my system construct," you say.

And Lucifer spreads his arms wide and shouts, "I love this guy!"

>>————————————————<<

UCAS DATA SYSTEMS
Decker Rap Sheet
   Subject: Lucifer
   Requested by: Ellen Hayes

INITIAL SEARCH:
   Compiled by: Brutus

Reported to have transferred 1,000,000¥ from First Bank of Atlanta.

Alleged to have arranged for 20,000¥ in salaries concurrently from Continental Computers, Hotoma Macrocomputers, Stuffer Shack Corporate, and Teller Disposable Systems for three years, without doing a day of work for any of the companies.

Suspected of having successfully re-routed a shipment of Mitsuhama Dragon Decks intended for distributor's warehouse to an abandoned warehouse disguised as an active one. Lucifer was one member of a team that pulled off the heist. The deck lot was worth 3,780,000¥ (ten decks at 378,000¥ each), but because the serial numbers could not be tracked, were likely sold at a total value of 2,000,000¥.

Supposed to have inhibited security systems at the Barr-Hanson offices in New York when runners were working their way through the building to the company's vault. The take was 875,983¥.

Credited with distracting The Burn, famed on-line decker for Fuchi's Seattle office, long enough for a second decker to break some IC on industrial secrets in a datastore. The information was worth 120,300¥ on the open market.

Rumored to have crashed the IBM research park in southern Illinois for the extraction of Dr. Karen Phelps.

We also have reason to believe Lucifer is the guy who did the Buenos Aires job at Nanotechnologies three years back. And we know that was no easy job.

FOLLOW-UP DATA
   Actual name: Not a clue. Age unknown.
   Current residence: Atlanta, Georgia
   Fixer contact: Unknown
   Is this *the* Lucifer? Don't know. But he has been recommended to us as one of the best decker teachers of the last decade.

CONTACT DATA
   Compiled by: Jerry Graves, Matrix Born psych specialist

Lucifer is willing to make the move to Seattle for the contract and understands that the assignment will be on-site and tightly supervised.

Lucifer is *very old* for a decker (in his forties), no doubt highly competent, and no doubt highly qualified if the information above is accurate, but I believe he is a deeply disturbed individual. And I say this, having dealt with many deckers in my career.

His mannerisms and behavior suggest nothing more than a confident, typically cocky decker who sometimes lays it on a bit thick to convince himself that everything is just fine. What I find disturbing is his reality filter. Per standard psych interview policy, I asked each of the candidates to describe his deck's customized reality filter, if it has one.

Without batting an eye, Lucifer answered that his filter was a portrayal of Hell.

When I asked him to explain, he said that he'd had a friend work up a filter chip that translated everything in the Matrix into images of Lucifer's nightmares. Data streams are rivers of steaming blood, filled with floating body parts and severed heads screaming out in agony, eyes wide open in pain. SANs are flaming gateways surrounded by laughing homunculi. Datastores are blazing crystals where data files are portrayed as countless souls crying out for release from pain. CPUs are blazing infernos containing empty thrones made from human bone. IC programs are fiendish creations more grotesque than any surrealistic painting from the previous century. And if the IC is already sculpted to look horrible, Lucifer's reality chip enhances the terror. He spoke particularly of a barrier program that looks like an eye. His reality filter maintains the image of the metallic eye (now tinged with blood-red copper), but in the iris, Lucifer can see his persona meeting various horrible deaths—sometimes he is strangled by a demon, sometimes gnawed to death by chrome-plated rats, and sometimes (and this image seemed to bother him more than any other) he is dying alone in a room, trapped, with no exit.

When I asked him why this last image was so disturbing, he said it was because it shows that there is nothing, that he is completely alone.

I asked him why he developed such a horrible reality filter for his deck, pointing out that most people choose filters that let them operate in the Matrix with more ease. He pointed out that often when a decker says ease, he really means more of an *edge*, and that his Hell filter certainly gave him that. He laughed about this in a good-natured way, which I pointed out to him. "I know what I feel

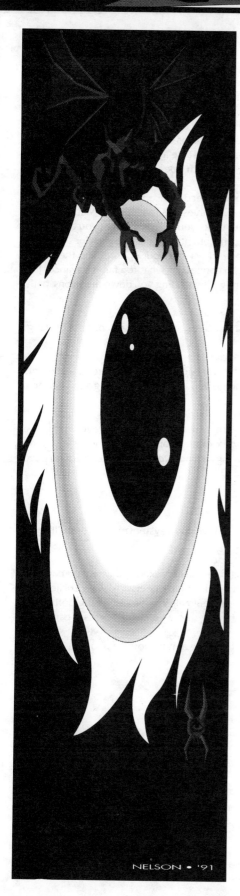

or don't feel," he said, "and I accept it. This is my joke on the universe. Being able to duck into a world where the terror of it all is worn on the cover. It comes from sadness, Doc, but I've turned it into something that really strikes me as funny."

As stated above, most deckers (like most people in the industry) are odd, and there are other RAP sheets for the Mentor position that may give us equal reason to pause. It is possible, however, that Lucifer is far enough over the edge that it is not worth dealing with him.

Recommendations: Gabby

The psych report notwithstanding, I think Lucifer is the only decker we've got in here who could be a teacher. The others may be straighter, but they're certainly not communicative. When I asked any of the others to explain decking to me, they were unable to break it down into information blocks; they've forgotten that they, too, once had to learn this stuff bit by bit. Lucifer could. When he taught himself decking, he figured out some basic concepts and worked from those, adding to his theory of decking like adding building blocks.

He's got his own agenda, is arrogant, but has a touch of the poet in him. I like him. He's my bet. I'd like to get him.

Recommendations: Halberstam

I'll go with Gabby. Draw up the papers. Get Lucifer up here.

>>————————————————<<

<<(11:34:55/12-01-51)>>

>[You are floating toward a giant silver cube. Lucifer is at your side, humming. It is a song like some of your toys make when you solve the puzzle. Most of the songs, you have learned, have names, and you ask Lucifer the name of this one. He stops humming, turns to you, and smiles.

"'The Ride of the Valkyries.' An old-timer's song." He begins the song again, but now sings it loudly, laughing and rushing toward the silver cube, waving his pitchfork up and down in rhythm to the music. The song is lost in the immense void of the Matrix, which is a shame because it seems to be a song of power. It is like hacking, a pattern that elicits a program within you. You listen to the music and then join in—hesitantly at first, following Lucifer's lead, but then fully, shouting just as loudly. The notes stream out of you, a torrent of energy. You feel released, your wings flapping, the data stream rushing by. Singing and laughing with Lucifer, you are surrounded by the immense splendor of the Local Telecommunications Grid. And now that you are singing, the music does not seem lost. The music fills you, whatever you are, and in turn, you seem to fill the world.

The wall of the cube rushes up to meet you, filling your field of vision, immense, a solid sheet of silver. It is so large that you must look away as you near the node to gain enough perspective to remember that there is more to this world than this wall. Your singing falters a bit, though Lucifer goes on as loudly as before. You hum softly and the song comforts you, like your blanket in your bedroom.

As you approach the SAN, you see a wall of jagged, pulsing lightning bolts covering the door. "How come we didn't see that when we left?" you ask Lucifer.

"Some IC only works one way. This one wants to keep unauthorized guests out. If you leave, you don't see it because it's not running itself against you. It's like the non-space outside a data stream. You don't see it because it's not there."

You sense that the IC is a lock on the node, and you remember from the Fuchi brochure that it is called a barrier. Lucifer reaches into the pocket of his jacket and pulls out a sphere covered with a colorful pattern. He tosses the sphere into the wall of electricity, and the bolts suddenly vanish. The SAN, sculpted like double doors that slide into the wall, opens. In the middle of the doorway floats the sphere. Lucifer steps up and plucks the passcode from the air and drops it back into his pocket. "The first few nodes won't present much problem," he says, "because they've already given us some passcodes for getting around. The first thing we've got to do, however, is set up my 'tape' of us hanging out somewhere. Then we can wander around as much as we like."

You look around the system construct, a cube whose inner walls tower around you. Before you is an SPU down the length of a data stream. No data streams are visible beyond that, only dozens of colorful geometric shapes suspended in mid-air. Though it seems you could guess which nodes are connected to which—according to their relative distance from each one another—you remember one of Lucifer's lessons from a few days ago:

"Distances are illusory in the Matrix. They set it up to look specific, but it's a trick. That node right over there might be next to another node on the other side of a system construct. The only way to know what connects to what is to be in a node and look down the data streams that connect to it. Even if you've been a decker for a while, it's easy to make a mistake about it, to get confused. You instinctively mark out a path that leads to the kind of node you want to reach, but really your path does you no good and gets you lost."

You asked, "But you said that you have to keep the Matrix and its illusions as a reality or you get distanced, become less effective."

"True enough," Lucifer said, his face revealing the effort not to think too hard of the lie he lives to survive in the Matrix. "That's part of the trick of system-construct defenses. It makes you use your instincts against you, tricks you. The key is that you accept the fact that it's an illusion, but you only take it one step at a time. The fact that the physical components can distract you doesn't mean you have to let them. Get to the next node, see what it leads to. Then get to the next node, check out your options, and then on to the next node. Then you go on from there…on and on…you can't predict what's going to connect to what too far in advance. Just check out your options and make a choice. And even then, if it's not the node you want, it might be leading you down the wrong path. Many times, all you can do is guess."

"Unless you have a system map."

"Yes. Unless you have a system map. But then you're not really decking. Or, I should say, you're not doing what I consider decking. Because then you know exactly where you're going."

"Isn't that good?"

"I think there's something to be said for getting lost, for traveling down unknown paths, for encountering treasures and dangers you didn't even know were available. The problem with system maps is that they encourage you to be lazy, to just go to your goal and end the trip. You end up with *exactly* what you set out to get and no more."

"But…"

"Hey, it might make a lot of sense for some people. It has its advantages. I just know that we can't conceive of everything that might be valuable. Most of my loot has come from little tidbits of data I stumbled across by accident. If you get exactly what you want, that means you get exactly what you already thought was valuable, which means that, having attained your goal, you've got no need to explore anymore."

"And you think you should explore as much as possible?"

"Yup."

"Doesn't that increase the chances of running into dangerous IC?"

"Renny, if you don't want to take the chance of running into IC, get a job at a corp. They'll give you a system map, and you'll know exactly where you're supposed to go every day."

"I can't get a job. I have no choice but to do what Dr. Halberstam and you tell me to do."

But now, standing at the SAN of Dr. Halberstam's system, you realize you do have a choice. Lucifer asked you where you wanted to go, then you made the choice. And Dr. Halberstam will not know anything about it. And you start to understand what Lucifer likes about not having a map. If you could look at the system as a picture, all in one viewing, you would already be dismissing portions of the system as irrelevant or uninteresting. But now, not knowing what is relevant or interesting, the whole construct is meaningful, everything deserves attention.

Whatever you are, you have apparently lived your whole life in the construct, but you know almost nothing about it.

Now that will change.

>>————————————————————<<

<<(11:43:16/12-01-51)>>

—**Matrix Born: Internal Memo**—

FROM: Gabby
TO: Dr. Halberstam
   I have the simsense behavioral tutorial (sic) ready for you. Let me know when you want it installed.

—**END memo**—

>>————————————————————<<

<<(11:38:54/12-01-51)>>

—Matrix Born: Internal Memo—

FROM: Dr. Halberstam
TO: Gabby
    I'll come right over and run a test on it. I would like it installed as quickly as possible. Renny and Lucifer are in the house icon-library again. We should be able to jack it in as soon as I've checked it out.

—END memo—

>>————————————————————<<

<<(11:44:36/12-01-51)>>

>[You and Lucifer are in the datastore that has all the images you grew up with.
    There are bloodied knives, and ducks, and teddy bears, and children with vacant eyes, and pumpkins, and eyeballs, and flowers, and sheets, and a couch, and stairs, and floors, and small stones for the courtyard, and flies, and clowns, and goggles, and lions, and decaying human bodies, and…
    And Nursie.
    She is not full-sized, but perfect in every detail. She is frozen, as lifeless as the bear when you were done playing with it. You found most of the other icons in here when you practiced with your sensor utilities. It never occurred to you to try to search for Nursie. You never thought of her as an image. You just stumbled across her by accident while Lucifer was setting up his masking program.
    You stare at her, uncertain what to do, feeling as though you should say something, but you know it is pointless. She is not Nursie. She is only a picture of Nursie. Just as you, your golden body, is a picture of Renny. And you don't know what you are.
    "Lucifer?"
    "Yeah?" He doesn't look up from his work. He is hunched over a small box, a miniature of the datastore. Inside are little images of you and Lucifer, a recording of sensor data from days and days ago. He says it is a modified relocate program, a stationary version of Glided Chip's Calling All IC! It is one of many such programs he has hidden among the system nodes through which you and Lucifer are allowed to travel. When he activates it, the two of you will leave and the system monitor will think you are still in the node.
    "What was Nursie?"
    "What?"
    "What was Nursie? I mean…we don't know what I am…But what was…is…Nursie? Is she a decker like you, with another body somewhere else?"
    "Don't…"
    "Sorry. Or something like me. That lived in the Matrix all her life. Is that why I miss her so much? Because she was like me?"
    Lucifer turns from his work and looks into your face. He keeps his sharp fingernails against the box so that his work is not lost. "Renny. I don't know. There's so much I don't know. But I'll guarantee you this, on this run, we've got a good chance of finding out. Okay?"
    You know that he wants you to feel better, so you smile and say, "Okay," but don't really mean it.
    He goes back to work and you close the file with Nursie in it.
    "All right," says Lucifer and he steps back.
    The box grows in size, filling up the datastore, overlapping with the data files so that it is impossible to tell the real datastore from the relocate program. The images of you and Lucifer grow as well. They are translucent at first, but when they are as large as you, their image becomes solid and you and Lucifer dim slightly.
    You think just for a moment that now the two other images are more real than the images that you and Lucifer normally portray, but then it becomes too confusing and you choose not to think about it.
    His right hand twirling his pitchfork, Lucifer whirls around and bows to you. Still bent over, Lucifer raises his face to you, wriggles his eyebrows, and says, "Renny! May I present the UCAS Data Systems system!"
    He gestures to a data-stream opening through which you have never passed before, and you are excited because he is letting you go first, and you usually follow him. You smile and feel taller and walk over to the door and peer out. A sub-processing unit waits at the end of the data path.
    Without waiting for Lucifer, you leap out into the path and fly down the data stream, wings spread wide, arms thrown forward.
    You get to the entrance of the node. You don't sense any white IC blocking your way, but you know this is a restricted area, which means something must be within. You remember the fight that Brutus led you into.
    When Lucifer says, "You all right?", you jump and whirl around.
    Your breathing is heavy. "Yes. Fine."
    "Do you want me to…? I could just go in and take a look."
    "Okay," you say, and look down. Lucifer starts to step into the node and you say, "No." You are afraid, frightened that what

happened last time might happen again, but you remember that Lucifer has taught you a great deal, and that you are not the same as when you had your first fight. "I want to go in first. I want to. I…want to find out…"

"Remember, once we take down any IC, we're going to go very fast. It's only a matter of time before they catch on that something is happening. I'll be right behind you." Lucifer squeezes your shoulder.

You step in.

The walls of the large room are covered with symbols of lines and dashes carved in silver. Blue sparks run up and down the silver and a faint red light pulses.

Out of a dark corner of the room floats a black robe with a hood. It looks as though someone is within its black folds, but you can see no face beneath its hood.

You and Lucifer toss out analyze programs.

"Killer," says Lucifer.

"Rating five."

"No kidding," he says under his breath. "You can find that out?"

"You want to sleaze it?"

"Renny, is the thing frightening you?"

"Yes, but that's not why I want to sleaze it."

"I know, I know, I'm not saying you're a coward. I just want to know if it's frightening you."

"Yes."

"Not because of what it looks like, but because of what it is."

"Right."

"And what is it?"

"Killer IC. Like the kind that beat me before. That's why it scares me."

"I know. I know. But what is it? Not what is it like, but what is it?"

"It's killer IC."

"Anything else?"

"No."

"Ever seen it before?"

"No."

"Do you have any reason to believe that you can't take it out?"

"Well…another…"

"No. Not the other IC. That was not this IC. And, more important, are you who you were then?"

"No. I was just thinking that before…that I'm not the same."

"You should listen to yourself more, Renny. So you have no reason to think that the IC can take you down any more than you know you will take it out?"

"No."

"And here's the thing, Renny. If we sleaze our way past that IC, you're always going to be afraid of it, always be thinking in the back of your—whatever you've got—that you were afraid and might freeze up again."

"So what should I do?"

"Here's what I'm thinking. If it spooks you, take the fraggin' thing down and get it over with."

Go.

You lunge toward the robe, wings wide, silver spheres starting to swirl around your golden body. They rise out of your body and you feel them, feel the program starting to run, feel it begin to probe the killer IC, and you feel yourself with the stars as they begin to surround the robe, searching for cracks in the IC.

The robe, aware of your attack, rises from the corner and floats across the node to meet you. Its arms rise, the long, clawed hands revealed as the sleeves of the robe slide back.

You smile inside, for you realize what effect such displays must have on other deckers. But to you the robe is a program, no more, no less.

Your wings rise up, influenced by the stars, which have found an opening. The stars have revealed to you a shortcut to the heart of the program. You close your eyes, no longer concerned with the appearances around you. You feel yourself whirl around, as much controlling the stars with motions as being controlled by them. The dance, you have learned, works both ways.

Your right arm tenses and the fingers stretch out. The stars are not a part of your arm, but as you move, they change their course slightly. The hand forms a fist and you bring your arm down sharply. Some of the stars rush into the folds of the cloak and vanish, deleting characters from the IC's command strings.

But before you know what is happening, a pain shoots through your body. Your eyes open and the robed figure is before you. His talons have raked you across the chest, leaving three glowing red streaks across your golden skin. It is not the marks that frighten you, for once more you see them as you would any other image. It is the fear that you might lose to the IC. You are thinking very quickly, already manipulating your combat utility, but you are also focusing on your fear. It distracts you from your stars, making them unable to lead you or you to lead them. Instead, your utility continues to run without your guidance. Without your ability guiding it, the utility has no effect against IC this tough.

The IC claws you again. Its arms have encircled you and its talons tear at your back. A sharp agony races down your spine. The IC is right up against you now, and it feels as though a warm breath touches your face, yet the hood still appears to be empty.

"Renny!" calls Lucifer, nearby, but you cannot tell where.

"Got it!" you call back. "I'm fine!"

"Don't be afraid to be afraid," he shouts.

And in an instant, you realize that it is not the fear that is slowing you down. Fear would make sense because you could get hurt. It's the thinking about the fear, and your annoyance at yourself for being afraid.

With that realization, you are able to ignore the fear. It is still there, pulsing as intensely as the stars, but it is simply a part of you now, not something extraneous that you must confront. The fear fuses with the stars, with your winged body, with your desire to see the rest of the Matrix, with your need to know what Nursie was (is), and what you yourself are. The fear is now part of your hacking, the desire not to be hurt fused with the tools that can keep your persona intact and shatter the IC now before you.

You dance, slipping out of the IC's grasp and whirling away. Without the fear of your fear, you are free to move about the node as wildly as you wish. It is a joy. You float in the air with a slow backward somersault, and while you do, the silver spheres circle your body, orbiting you with complementary motions.

The IC has already made headway against your bod, so you decide to forego an attack for a moment and run your Dervish III. The stars around you suddenly begin to race around you at an incredible rate, crossing each other's paths and blurring your image within the sphere they form.

The IC reaches its talons toward you, but they are rebuffed by the whirling spheres. You slam your Doomguard program back into action and feel a group of stars rush forward, like a deep exhalation of breath, and pour into the crack in the IC you've already made. You feel yourself twist and turn as you work the combat utility through the weak points of the IC, looking for patterns just as you used to do with your toys.

And then you stumble across a perfect spot from which to crash the IC.

It is a small subroutine, barely noticeable and not very important to the attack portions of the program. It is responsible for producing the soft breath from the headless hood. The breath is set up to be a repetitive loop, buried within the program's more important routines. If you can set up the language so that the breathing subroutine over-arches the main routine, it will never get around to attacking you or calling a system alert. It will be too busy breathing.

All these thoughts race through your mind at an incredibly fast rate, and much of that thinking does not take the form of words. Instead, the stars slip into the subroutine, rising and falling like the breathing of the IC. The Doomguard is clueing you to a weakness in the IC, and it is up to you to exploit it fully.

The stars begin rewriting the code of the program, moving the breathing subroutine to the top of the program loop, eating out the loop-default features, and reassigning sub-route priorities.

Meanwhile, the IC tries to swipe at you again. Your dervish is still up and running, though it is growing weaker with each passing moment, as is the mirrors program. The talons cut through the racing stars, reaching close to your body, missing you, but so close…

And then the Doomguard finishes placing the breathing loop as a frame around the entire killer program.

You open your eyes. The IC floats before you. It inhales, its robes moving slightly, and then there is a nanosecond pause as the program looks for its next command, which it finds by skipping down to the bottom of itself, and exhales. It then returns to the start of the loop, breathing lightly, over and over again.

You relax.

"That was…very clean…" says Lucifer, walking around the subdued IC, eyeing it up and down with curiosity. "Usually there're at least some pixels missing."

"That would mean just ripping the program up."

"It is called a *combat* utility, boy."

"Well," you say, proud of your work, "I got it done."

"Yes. Well, you did do that."

"Ready?"

He looks up at you and smiles. "Sure. I'm ready. Lead on."

You work your way through several nodes, choosing to sleaze or deceive your way past most of the IC rather than try to crash it ("Less strain on the old bod," says Lucifer.) There are barriers and access IC, a tar pit that looks like a bottomless black hole, and a Trace and Burn that appears as a cheetah. But Lucifer has his years of experience and you have your innate talents, and despite some close calls, you don't feel as worried as before.

You pass through many datastores, looking for information, searching for files about you and Nursie. Along the way, you pass an I/O Port node covered with dozens of data-line connections that lead to smaller triangles. Lucifer points to one of them, saying it is the one that connects him to the other world. You want to go there, but he explains that there would be nothing to see. It just connects to his cyberterminal.

And then, in a datastore, under a file labeled "Personal: Matrix Born," you find information about Nursie. And about Lucifer.

"Lucifer," you say, looking over the file on Nursie, "I think Dr. Halberstam was Nursie."

"What?" he says, floating over to you.

"Look, it says that there's a position called 'Nursie,' an 'infancy/childhood response-modulator,' and that it was filled by Dr. Halberstam."

"But the Doc's name is Thomas, Renny," he says, pointing at the document. The person they hired is named Sarah."

"And…"

"Well, in the other world, people share names. They pass them on. Each person gets an individual name, and then a shared name. It means there's a strong relationship between the two people. This Sarah, who was Nursie, is probably either Halberstam's daughter or wife."

You look up to him, waiting for him to explain the concepts.

He does, and you are amazed, for you have always thought you were alone with Nursie in the Matrix, in the world, and now you discover that in the other world, so large and complicated, there are billions of people who are alone with someone else. And you are confused because one of those people, a person who is special to a man you do not like, was the person most special to you in all the world. This confuses you, but also excites you, because now you know that Nursie is all right, and that you might talk to her again. Only now her name is Sarah Halberstam.

And then you read Lucifer's file, and again are amazed, because from the way the psychiatrist in the text speaks, Lucifer views the world in a strange and horrible way, but on purpose. You show Lucifer the file.

"Hmmm," he says.

"Lucifer, what does he mean about a reality filter?"

"Okay. You're probably never going to have to deal with this, but here goes. It's possible for a decker in the other world to get a reality filter that changes what the Matrix looks like to *him*. It's all part of the style idea. The more the environment matches your style, the easier it is for you to move through it.

"Remember that a node or a piece of IC doesn't *really* look like a three-dimensional object—it's just a complex program or construct. Part of the information all IC or nodes have is a section that speaks to your deck and tells your deck how to translate the IC or node so you can 'see' it.

"What a reality filter does is override the icon sculpture commands of a node or IC and re-translate them to what the decker wants them to be. Without a reality filter, data streams default to flashing bits of silver. My reality filter forces them to look like rivers of hot blood filled with human body parts."

"So, to you, when we sit and talk in a data stream, you see us in that?"

He looks down, then up. "Yup."

"Lucifer, the pictures don't bother me, but they're supposed to bother you. Do they?"

He looks down again. "Yes."

The pictures do not bother you, but Lucifer doing that to himself does. You ask, "Why do you do that?"

"It's in the file, Renny. It's my edge. I feel more comfortable knowing it's Hell."

"Like what you said about the shamans. That you'd rather not be tricked. You want to see the Matrix as a bad place because that's what you like?"

"Something like that. It's what I expect."

"But if you don't like it…"

"I…can accept it. It's complicated, Renny. A lot of deckers build little fantasies for themselves with their filters. Things like medieval castles, Victorian mysteries, feudal Japan. I think it's all a crock of drek. For me, owning up to the fact that the world is built on misery keeps me going. Knowing there's nothing to count on gets under my skin and makes me work."

You pace across the room, staring down at the floor, and then turn. "Do you like me?"

"What?"

"Do you like me?"

"I…Yeah. Renny, I like you," Lucifer says, and seems relieved.

"Then what do I look like to you?"

"What?"

"What does your filter make me? If everything is bad, but you like me, what do I look like?"

"Oh. Well, I got a secret for you, kiddo. Something not even the shrink knows about. See, there's this one little part of the filter I had put in years ago when I had it built. The specs I gave to my programmer were very detailed. I had detailed images of how I wanted everything to be translated. Sometimes completely new bad things, sometimes simply translating things that were already bad into something far worse.

"But I left one little escape hatch, one item that, if I should ever encounter it, would be translated by my filter into its standard image." Lucifer laughs and shakes his head. "And after waiting all these years, I finally had to cheat. You look like an angel to me, Renny. I've been waiting and waiting to see an angel in the Matrix."

"And an angel is good or bad?"

"Angels are very good, Renny. My search for an angel in my virtual hell was sometimes the only thing that kept me going."

"And now what?"

"What?"

"Now that you've found an angel…now what?"

"I don't know. Learn from you."

"Learn from me? I don't know anything!"

"Maybe that's what being an angel is. I've known lots of people in my life who prided themselves on knowing how complicated everything is, which they thought gave them license to do unspeakable things simply because 'that's the way it is.' I think I want to learn how not to know everything."

You puzzle that in your head for a moment. "Isn't that impossible?"

"So was finding an angel in Hell. I'm drawn to tough assignments. But this brings up something I've wanted to…to talk to you about. Renny, you know we're not supposed to be here without Halberstam knowing about it."

"Yes."

"So, are we doing something wrong?"

"Wrong?"

"Not are we doing something the incorrect way. But are we doing something that we shouldn't be doing?"

"I don't know. I never thought of it that way."

"How have you thought of it?"

"As…It's a game, isn't it? That's what you and Dr. Halberstam always say it is."

"Renny. This system construct belongs to someone else. Before wandering around in it, we're supposed to get permission to do so. We are cheating the owners because they don't know we are here."

"We're doing something wrong?"

"Yup. In the other world, we could be punished for doing what we are doing. And a lot of people, even people who don't own Data Systems, would think we are bad people for doing what we are doing."

"What do you mean bad?"

He smiles. "Never mind. I think you've answered my question. Lead on and teach on. And we better get out of here now before the system makes a sweep."

You pass through several more nodes, but now as you travel the data streams and encounter IC, you imagine them as Lucifer sees them.

It occurs to you how much time Dr. Halberstam spent trying to get you used to things that people in the other world think are horrible. And his wife, or daughter, Sarah Halberstam, who went along with it. For now, you are bothered by what happened, how you were raised. Even if Lucifer seems to think not knowing things is good, a desire to know about the world, about life, about what is good and bad is growing in you.

An angel, you think, is simple. And it is the world's infinite complexity that you want to taste.

You and Lucifer enter a large sphere, a slave node, and it, too, is covered with data stream entrances. "Hey, jackpot, Renny!" Lucifer says, walking around, staring at the walls that are covered with monitors and screens. The monitors seem to be covered with small pictures. Maybe from the Matrix, you think, but as you approach a screen at which Lucifer is looking, you see that the images are very different from any you have seen before.

"What is it?" you ask softly, staring down at the picture.

"We're in a node that's connected to the building's camera systems," he answers, not looking at you, his attention on the screen.

"Cameras?"

"They're devices…" He looks up the wall of the pyramid and thinks. "They're electronic eyes. They see the other world, translate the information into electronic impulses, like data, and usually route it through a computer system to a monitor, where the impulses are re-translated into pictures. That way, someone can see something that is taking place even though he isn't there."

"Why doesn't the person just go to where the thing is that he wants to see?"

He smiles. "The world's a big place, Renny. It's easier to keep tabs on it from a distance."

"Oh."

You look down at the screen, and it takes you a few moments to learn how to see what is there.

The image is in color, but it is not the bright, glowing colors that you have grown up with. And it is not as shiny as the Matrix. The textures are rough. And nothing glows from within.

It is a picture of a room. Along one wall is a row of what you think are beds. Small people—children, you remember—are in three of the beds, their sheets covering them. The sheets are white and lie flat, without any life in them. They do not seem to give comfort.

Wires lead from boxes built into the wall above the beds to beneath the children's necks and you think of something, but it is gone before you know what it was. And then you remember. The child with the vacant eyes from the house. The icon. The children in the bed are the same as the icon, still, silent, staring.

On the other side of the room, you see a man in a white coat, also much like an icon from the house, standing by a monitor and computer keyboard. Two other people are sitting by the monitors. One of them, a very large person in a white coat (a woman, you think, because her face is a bit like Nursie's) sits by the keyboard. The other is a man, his frame thin and spindly. His eyes are narrowed, as though he is looking for something to go wrong. And then it occurs to you he *wants* something to go wrong. He is dressed in black pants and a thick black jacket, shiny, like metal, but different.

"That's Halberstam, standing there," says Lucifer softly. "And at the terminal, the large woman, that's Gabby. A good lady who's in over her head. Don't know who the other guy is."

"Brutus," you say even as you realize it.

"So that's Brutus," Lucifer says with a cunning smile. "A geek after my own heart. Only a geek with an attitude. I hate guys like that."

You are only partially listening to Lucifer, for there are so many details to see in the picture. There is something interesting about the other world that you are only just starting to identify: there are many more details out there than in the Matrix. The sheets have slight creases, so barely perceptible that it took awhile to realize why their appearance bothered you, a subtlety you have never seen in the Matrix. You realize that your sheets at home might have such creases, but in the resolution of the Matrix's graphics, they would be lost. The creases are not considered important enough to be built in. But in the other world, the light from the far wall falls on the tiny hills and ridges formed by the creases and folds in the sheets, creating amazing patterns. Small, barely noticeable patterns, but they are there, beautiful in their randomness. Soft concaves and convexes formed of shadow and light. They grow up and around the sheet-covered bodies of the children, and you think the patterns adorn the children and protect them like a kind of IC.

There are streaks of black on the gray-tiled floor, long and thin, and tapering off at one end. And a glass by a keyboard, half-filled with a liquid, a single bubble resting at the top of the fluid against the inner surface of the glass. (The liquid itself, mentioned by Nursie a long time ago, is amazing enough. What does it feel like? What does it do if you touch it? But the bubble—who would think of such a detail in the Matrix?) The shadows of Gabby, Dr. Halberstam, and Brutus, the way Brutus' chair shakes slightly as he moves it to and from the counter. Halberstam's face—flesh, the fragile covering Lucifer mentioned a few weeks ago. Not an image, but a physical encasing for the fragile system of the human body. He speaks and the muscles around his mouth move with an elasticity unlike Nursie's or Lucifer's or Brutus'. The light catches his eyes and they flash electric like all the eyes in the Matrix. But then he looks away and they dim—a variety not available here. He points, his fingers withered and worn. He is old, you read, and when Lucifer told you about flesh and human bodies, he told you what it means to be old. No other hand could be like his. Each patch of his finger is its own fascinating landscape, wrinkles and hair and bumps from the bone that supports the human body.

And one of the fingers extends and reaches out and touches a button on a computer terminal keyboard.

>>————————————————————————<<

<<(12:12:36/12-01-51)>>

>[Your name is Renny. You live in a big house by the edge of the Matrix. Your friend is Dr. Halberstam.

You only barely remember who Dr. Halberstam is, but you know that you love him and need him and want to make him happy. You love him so much that you are in pain.

There is someone in front of you. He is red and wears a red suit with black stripes. His face has a beard. He has horns on his forehead. In his right hand is a pitchfork.

He looks at you as though something is wrong, but you do not care because your name is Renny. You live in a big house by the edge of the Matrix. Your friend is Dr. Halberstam. You love him.

"Renny? Are you all right?"

Your name is Renny. Other than that, you do not know what the red man means.

"How do you feel?" he asks.

"I feel love. Love for Dr. Halberstam. He is my friend. I love him so much I cannot stand the pain in me. I am happy. So happy. So happy. So happy. So happy. So happy. So happy. So happy. So happy. So happy. So happy. So happy. So happy."

Only when the red man slaps you do you realize you have been screaming, screaming your love. You are having trouble breathing and you stagger against a wall for support—a bright white wall of a giant sphere, clean and safe, like the love of Dr. Halberstam. There is a picture where your hand is, a small moving picture. There are tiny faces peeking out from white sheets (you love your sheets and you want to get back home so you might sleep beneath them and their safety and have Dr. Halberstam take care of you and everything will be all right as long as you make him happy and love him in every way that he wants you to love him because that is all he asks of you and there is no reason for you not to give him this love and the pain it causes is so sweet and you cannot want anything else but to please him because all he gives you is pleasure), and one of the faces, the one in the middle bed, is twisting its mouth, the lips pushing up, and the body is heaving, and liquid is dripping from its open and vacant eyes, running down its smooth and perfect skin and you think of something but it is gone and replaced by the comforting knowledge that your name is Renny. You live in a big house by the edge of the Matrix. Your friend is Dr. Halberstam.

A woman in the picture (Nursie?) is standing and pointing to the contorting face, and she is shouting at a man with white hair, a man who looks both weary and frighteningly full of energy, but you know that Dr. Halberstam would protect you from him. He strikes the woman across the face and she stops for a moment, her mouth open slightly, eyes wide, and then she lunges for him, arms extended, hands encircling his throat, and the man falls back and slams into a wall. The woman's fleshy, large hands keep their grip on the man. But another man, in black, steps up behind her and grabs her by the shoulders and pulls downward. The woman slides away from the man, falling to the floor, her arms flailing. She is just beginning to realize what has happened when the man in black slams his boot into her face.

You look away from the screen and see the red man's gaze is transfixed upon it.

"Oh, no!" is all he says. You turn back to the picture and see crimson paths growing from the woman's face, working their way across the gray floor. She does not move, but the white-haired man turns to the man in black and moves his mouth wide and points to a keyboard. The man in black reaches for the keyboard and the sphere and the red-skinned man dissolve around you and you find yourself back in bed, happy and comfortable.

And then Dr. Halberstam is there.

<<(12:14:36/12-01-51)>>

>>**ACCESS — Renny**
<<ACCESSING — RENNY>>
<<ACCESS ACHIEVED>>

—Renny?
—Hello, Dr. Halberstam.
—How are you?
—I was scared before, but I'm all right now that you are here.
—Why were you scared, Renny?
—I didn't know where you were, and there was a red-skinned man and we were in a…
—The red-skinned man scared you?
—Yes?
—Why?
—I can't remember. I think he wanted to confuse me.
—Confuse you?
—Make things…confusing…complicated…
—Was he teaching you?
—Yes. He was teaching me.
—And what he was teaching you scared you?
—I think so.
—What did he teach you?
—He taught me how to use things I know from my games to get through the Matrix.
—Decking?
—Yes! Decking. He taught me about decking and hacking.
—Do you remember the things he taught you?
—Yes.
—And they frighten you?
—No. Not them. Something else.
—
—
—Renny, listen very carefully. I have to make sure this man didn't tell you something bad. I don't think he did, but I have to make sure. What was it that frightened you? Can you remember?
—
—
—I'm sorry Dr. Halberstam. Please don't be angry. I can't remember! I'm sorry. Oh, please, I'm sorry…
—There, there, Renny. Take it easy…
—I just don't want you to be angry at me. Do you love me?
—Of course I do, Renny. Can't you feel my love? And I want what's best for you. So I'm going to ask you again to tell me what Lucifer said that frightened you. I can't love somebody who can't share with me what frightens him.
—
—
—It had something to do with how I see the Matrix.
—Yes?
—That I have to believe it is true.
—What…What do you mean, Renny?
—Lucifer said that I had to think of everything…as true. As real.
—Well, of course you do, Renny. The Matrix is real. There is no other truth.
—I know, but there's something about that that bothers me. It makes me hurt when I think about it. Something else that Lucifer said…
—Don't worry about that part. What you just told me, what Lucifer told you about the Matrix being true, I don't know why it bothers you, but it shouldn't. There is no truth but that which is right before you.

—But part of me thinks there's more.
—And that part of you is wrong, Renny! I don't know where this notion came from, but I want you to stop it now. Just stop thinking it! You have me and you have the Matrix. Do you need anything else?
—No.
—Did Lucifer put these ideas in your head?
—I don't remember…I think so, but I'm not sure…I can't remember…some part of me…
—Renny. Sleep now. Tomorrow we'll continue the lessons. You'll have a new teacher. Remember that I raised you and that I know what is best for you.
—Yes.
—Are you all right?
—Something…
—What?
—My thoughts…
—What about them?
—They are different now.
—Yes. Your thinking is better now.
—Oh. But they feel different.
—What do you mean?
—I remember thinking like this before, when Nursie…Before my life changed. Everything was…hard …solid…
—And then what happened?
—When Nursie went away, my thinking got easier. Slowly, but it was easier.
—Renny, before Nursie went away, we were able to know what you were feeling. After she left, we lost that ability. Do you know what happened?
—No. But I think I know what you mean, Dr. Halberstam. I think I took those thoughts. Was that bad? I didn't mean to do it if it was bad.
—You took them?
—They were my memories. My block of ice. I thought I should keep them.
—Your what?
—My block of ice. My metaphors. My life.
—Sweet…What in God's name did Lucifer talk to you about!
—I can't remember clearly. It's all a mess. Refractions. Can't find a perspective.
—What?
—I'm sorry, Dr. Halberstam. Really, I am. I can't think right!
—All right, all right. Calm down. Calm down. Let's go back to what we were talking about before. You said you took the memories.
—I didn't mean to. I didn't even know I did it. It just happened. I know it was a bad part of me that wanted to do it. I shouldn't have wanted them. My memories are yours. Everything is yours.
—Renny, I'm not sure I understand. We had a device, a special simsense, set up that would record your impressions—your emotions and actions. Some of your thoughts. And we stopped getting a read-out after Nursie left, but it seemed as though it were still on. And now you are telling me that you were storing the data somewhere else…Without even meaning to?
—Yes.
—Do you remember what you did with the data?
—No.
—All right. Go to sleep, Renny. There are some things I have to do.

>>CUT Access
<<ACCESS CUT>>

>>—————————————————<<

Dear Renny,
    I'm writing this in the hopes that you might stumble across it in case something happens to me. I'm not sure what they did to you, but I've got a feeling that it might make you reveal some things we talked about, things they didn't want me to teach you. There might be trouble, so I'm sliding out of Data Systems as soon possible. The minute I can get to a safe terminal jack, I'm going to come back for you via the Matrix. This letter is just a backup, in case something goes wrong.
    I've got a lot to tell you, and I'm not really sure where to start because I'm not even sure you'll remember who I am if you read this, so I guess I'll tell you that.
    My name is Lucifer. I was brought in to teach you because I'm the best teacher there is. I've been around a while, since the beginning, and I love the Matrix. But maybe I shouldn't love it as much as I do. I love it because it is simple. I jack in and I'm *in it*—

I know who I am and I see everything as terrible and when I'm done, I know I beat up Hell. But to keep it that simple, I have to lie to myself. I have to make it literal. It gets me through the run, but it's a lie nonetheless, and it's a lie that has gotten more and more attractive to me over the years.

And here's the thing: in the other world, there're all these lies going on. It's not just decking. It's also simsense, where folks get to plug into somebody else's feelings so that they don't have to feel their own. And corps who live the lie of the profit margin, so that as long as the lines on the graphs are good, they get to believe that everything else is good. Even though they live in virtual prison camps to make sure that the hell on earth they are creating doesn't come to get them. And the racist lies. Well, you don't even know about racism do you?

See, that's been my problem all along. In you, I finally met somebody who hadn't lived in the real world yet. You didn't know about the complexities of life, about how bad things can get. You were innocent, good. You weren't in the Matrix to escape, you were here 'cause it's where you've always lived. And I wanted you to keep that naivete because it reassured me. Knowing there could be someone like you finally let me relax about the universe a bit.

But I knew that to be a decker you had to understand some things—about the Matrix and its relationship to the the other world. Even though you have to live literally in the Matrix when decking, force that lie so that it becomes natural, it's still important to know that things do not have only one meaning. Much as most of us don't like having to deal with symbols having implications, we've got to. Even in the Matrix.

The problem is that even a little knowledge has strong implications. I wanted to keep what I had to tell you as simple as possible, but you're very bright and wanted more and more information. And who was I to say, "No, you're not allowed to know that." That's what every institution, from the religious groups up through the governments to the corps, have always said, and that's not how I see it. We've got to make our own choices.

That's one of the things I want to tell you. Kiddo, your life is not going to be easy, but keep looking for the meanings behind things. It's tough, and most of us shy away from it—trashing the surface of the planet we need to live on, but blinding ourselves to the effects by finding neat new gizmos to play with. No one wants to deal with implications, but I think you can handle it.

And here's the thing: there was another reason I wanted to tell you things, to teach you stuff you weren't supposed to know. I wanted to test you. I already know how bad the world is. Hell, I'm bad. I'm a thief. I steal from other people, Renny. I just figured that since that's the way the world is, I might as well join in, too.

But if you're an AI, I figured, maybe here's an intelligence that *can't* be bad. Maybe there's just something about human beings that makes us hurt each other so much, but maybe a machine would be able to get past that, or simply duck around it altogether. That's what I meant about looking for an angel in the Matrix. I was even ready to take an avenging angel, but I wanted somebody who was in here doing *good*—not just perpetuating the game. I figured if such a creature, even mechanical, can exist, then maybe there's hope for people after all. Maybe we can learn from machines now. Maybe.

So I had to teach you stuff, test you, ask you if you thought what we were doing was wrong, see if you were really what I'd been waiting for. And amazingly enough, I think you are. I think you're something new, Renny, something that can help us.

But I don't know for sure. I'm so tired of living in Hell, or seeing the world as Hell, I'm ready to believe almost anything at this point.

Okay. Enough rambling. It's time for you to hit the biz.

If you're reading this, it's 'cause I was geeked. That means it's up to you to make your life happen. What's important is for you to realize that your decking skills will let you help yourself and you can get others to help you.

One of your most important tools right now is iconferencing. It's a common practice now—calling folks up through the Matrix and using icon representation in business meetings. It's a status thing more than anything else. You go in with the best graphics and people know you're hot biz. Lots of fixers, guys who set up the kinds of deals you're going to need, use the thing. It gives them a quick measure of potential employees and shadowrunners who ring them up.

This is important for you, because in the other world people usually talk by vid-phone. But you won't have a real-world image of yourself to use. All you've got is your icon. These iconferences take place in environments built by companies whose sole business is to host meetings. The IC is always thick on them, so privacy is assured. Call a place called Virtual Meetings. Seattle LTG# 9206 (12-9629). It's a company specializing in shadowrun deals. Have them hook you up with a fixer called Data Base.

There's another word. Shadowrunners. I don't have time to go into it now, but shadowrunners are the guys you need to hire. Tell Data this is what you need:

Street samurai for muscle. Big-time. If you were just to look at the Data Systems corporate profile, it would look like they shouldn't have much firepower, but in my wandering around here, it looks to me as though somebody else is backing them. Tell Data Base that.

You don't need a decker. You're the decker on this one. Tell him that. Tell him Lucifer said you were good enough.

And at least one power mage or shaman. And I mean it! Someone with *healing* magic that can come close to raising the dead. Whoever he gets is going to have to cure some kids whose bodies have been atrophying for up to ten years.

'Cause here's the tough part, chu—

System's on alert. I'll be back.

Lucifer

—From *Virtual Life: A Critical Examination of Virtual Reality*
Johnny Wallhoot, Push & Press, 2048

THE COURSE

It may sound like I'm proposing that we chuck it all and go back to the days before virtual reality, before these new sciences "poisoned" the way we think. Now, if we were to do that, we'd want to be sure to go back before the time when the human mind began being compared to a machine, just for good measure. And, as long as we were at it, we could slip back in time and either kill Descartes in his crib, or at least make sure he had a happier life so that he wouldn't have ended up worrying so much about what was real and what was not.

And then, of course, if we were really smart, we'd go back to the Old Testament days and make sure the serpent never got around to feeding Adam and Eve. And if we could pull that off, we'd have escaped every little or large idea that ever existed in our race's history and we'd have managed to get back to Paradise, back to the Garden of Eden.

But everyone knows we can't turn back the clock, so what do we do with the ideas we've inherited down all the centuries of human history?

Well, most of the things we consider good or ill depend on one's perspective. And I think that by changing our perspective, we can rest easier in our lives on this earth. How do we see life? What ideas do we color it with? In modern-day parlance, what are we going to jack ourselves into?

This shouldn't be so hard because we're changing perspectives and choosing new outlooks all the time. Jacking into simsense, hitting the Matrix, absorbing the laws of hermetic magic—we're constantly shutting off parts of the world and viewing it from a limited angle. What I'm suggesting is another game, one that also means taking on a role.

Imagine a computer-graphic display of Heaven. From a certain perspective, the picture is made up of millions of pixels. Each pixel seems separate from the others, and so we may think of them accordingly. Regarded that way, they are so many of Descartes' empirical facts. And if the whole picture of Heaven is so viewed, we might call it *ji hokkai*, "the universe of things," after the Japanese tradition.

But each of these separate pixels goes into making up the total image of Heaven. This one picture is being displayed through all those pixels, and depending on our point of view, it consists either of the many pixels or of the one image. The idea of the one thing made manifest through many things is called *ri hokkai*, the absolute universe.

We have made technologies now that allow us to experience each other's most intimate thoughts, to communicate, through the sheer power of thought, around the globe, to manipulate text and data with images alone. We also have magic and shamanistic traditions once again that allow us to interact directly with the universe in ways long thought lost. With all of this, it seems that we would do well not to continue ripping reality into smaller pieces of information and facts, with little camps of specializations and concerns, but rather view all these wonders as metaphors for a *ri hokkai* world.

Deckers tell me that it is imperative to believe in the literal truth of what one is seeing when one is in the Matrix. They say that without this, the "edge" is not present, the immediacy is gone, and the decker is lost. If he is busy thinking about his true form and his metaphorical self, he gets confused, sloppy, and likely to be dragged down by his adversaries.

I'm also told by hermetic mages that their hermetic discipline involves so much focus on a specific view of the world that any mage who enters the Matrix is at a disadvantage in all activities simply because the "environment" is so alien to him. And that applies even if the mage only wants to use the Matrix for getting around.

On the other hand, I know a decker who is completely aware in every run that his body is back at a deck and that only an icon of himself is engaged in an activity. And I know two mages who are decent deckers. These three are exceptions, but all are able to switch-hit among activities because to them it's all one big show. It's tough to see it all as one picture instead of just grabbing what one feels he can handle comfortably, but these three learned, through patience and diligence, to do it. And of all the people I know, they are some of the happiest folks I know.

Each one has told me that the key was teaching himself not to take any of the activities or objects in his life literally. These people view the world as a complex house of mirrors, where every incident or tool is a metaphor reflecting every other part of the world. It's all one thing composed of different aspects. Therefore, the decker in the Matrix knows that he is sitting at a cyberdeck and that he's also an icon in the Matrix, but he also is the data in a data stream, a CPU in the system he is in and the printer humming away in the office. When he finishes a run, he examines it as a lesson about who he is and what it can teach him about himself. In the same way, mages know that electrons in a computer system have as much to do with the nature of their bodies as an air spirit, and so on. It is a difficult balance, one they carry off by maintaining a slight detachment from their experience rather than by being immersed in it.

Unlike most of us, they accept that the world is the world, life is life; this is what we've got.

These three people, as far as I know, don't use simsense anymore. Why should they? They're already plugged into everyone's life. They have no need to jack in for experiences. The universe is crashing in on them every living moment.

>>————————————————<<

<<(18:22:56/12-03-51)>>

>[You are consumed by your love for Dr. Halberstam. It is all you want and all you need.

Brutus hits you again.

And again.

"What were you two doing! Where were you?" Brutus shouts. You cannot think clearly and wonder why Dr. Halberstam does not come to protect you. "We found his relocation program! It's obvious you two were doing something you weren't supposed to! What was it?"

His long, silver arm swings at you and his heavy hand knocks you across the room. You want to use your stars, to release them and use them against Brutus to stop the pain, but Dr. Halberstam said that you could not use them against Brutus. That Brutus would do nothing Dr. Halberstam did not want him to do.

"Dr. Halberstam," you say weakly.

"Knock it off," yells Brutus. "He ain't coming for you. He set all this up. He made all this for you and then he put me in it. Whether you like it or not, I'm going to keep knocking you around until you give me what I want. You want it to stop, then try to take me on. I dare you! You fraggin' chiphead! No, but you're gonna call to old Doc to make everything all right. No, *you* gotta do it, you little brat! But you aren't going to do anything, are you?"

Dr. Halberstam's voice fills the living room and he tells Brutus to stop taunting you and to continue with the questioning. You call out to him, but he only says that your suffering is all part of your love for him.

And you decide that if this is true, then it is all right, and the fist slams into you again, and you think it is love.

"What did you talk about?"

"I can't remember any more than I've already told you," you say, and it is the truth. It is a blur, a collage of ideas and concepts, pieces of memory all stuck together without any point of view, meaningless ramblings.

"It hasn't made any sense!"

Dr. Halberstam's voice returns and says that Brutus should stop asking you questions, and you relax your body. He tells you that because you deceived him before he had to make sure that you were telling the truth when you said you could not remember what you had been talking about. He wants you to know that he does trust you now. You have proven your love to him and he wants to know if you understand that everything is all right now.

"Yes!" you say, so excited that everything is all right again.

"I don't trust him," growls Brutus.

Dr. Halberstam tells him to leave you and then he says he'll be back later.

>>————————————————————<<

—From The Matrix Primer, A Guide to the Matrix for the Junior High School Grades
   Dr. Richard Reeds, Disney-Line Press, 2051

VIRTUAL REALITY INTERFACES AND APPLICATIONS

Central to decking technology and all other virtual-reality technologies such as simsense is the interface between the human mind and the computer. The two means of achieving this are via either the datajack or the neural net.

The datajack, or "physical interface," was developed during the era of the Echo Mirage team. It allows the user to "short out" his body's nervous system, replacing it at the base of the brain stem with an artificial nervous system—wires leading to the computer system he is jacked into. The computer system, then, literally becomes the decker's new nervous system. It feeds sensory data to his brain about sight, touch, taste, hearing, and smell. In the same way that our eyes transmit data to the brain, which is blind and so must accept it, the brain, now directly linked to the deck, believes and treats as true the information it receives.

The second kind of interface is the neural net. Rather than making a physical connection with the user's nervous system, it is a kind of helmet that rests against the user's skull. The inside of the helmet is studded with a net of fine wires able to perceive and influence the brain's neural patterns. The net also transmits inhibitors that prevent impulses from the brain from traveling through the nervous system to the body. Although the effect is the same as that of a datajack, the neural net interface is not as "pure." Using a neural net is far less expensive than using a datajack, however, because installing a datajack involves costly and complicated brain surgery. In contrast, anyone can wear and use the neural net. It was, in fact, the development of the neural net that allowed simsense and the Matrix to reach such widespread use. Its quality is still so good that someone making the switch from neural net to a datajack is usually astounded that it is possible to achieve even better quality with the latter.

Only those who need or want an almost lifelike interface require the purity of that offered by a datajack. Consumers of datajacks are usually corporate deckers whose job takes them into direct confrontation with criminals entering the company's system or else simsense consumers who need as much "reality" as they can get when playing a game. Most corporate employees who work in the Matrix use neural nets for they have no need for the high quality of a datajack.

Virtual-reality interfaces work by influencing the synaptic patterns in the brain and by being responsive to the patterns that would normally cause a person to take action.

A common use of neural nets in an office setting is for transcribing dictation of memos or letters. A neural net user need only *think* about talking, and instead of his mouth and tongue moving in response to his intent to speak words, the neural net "reads," translates, and types the words into a computer. It's not that the neural net is reading his thoughts. It is simply responding to commands that,

under normal circumstances, would have allowed the executive to speak his thoughts. Because of the net's inhibitors, his jaw and tongue do not move; the neural net relays the impulses from the brain into a word-processing program.

One way of thinking about how the brain interacts with virtual reality is that the technology takes one's mind out of his body and dumps it in any body or world he wants. As Dan Truman said after buying out ESP Systems, Inc., "Someday we will be able to give any brain anything it wants."

Well, that day has arrived.

>>————————————————————<<

<<(08:24:11/12-04-51)>>

>[He is gone and you are worried that you will never hear his voice again. All you can think of is how sorry you are to have ever done anything to bother him, to make him upset, and you hope there is some way, some thing you can do to make him forgive you.

And then Lucifer, the red man, is beside your bed.

"Renny," he says before you have time to speak, "I'm going to ask you to trust me for a moment. Please don't call out for Dr. Halberstam. Please don't get upset. Just wait one moment."

Before you have time to decide whether or not to get upset, he presses a small button that grows out of his left palm. A small star races out of the button and toward the door and out of sight.

Lucifer turns to look at you and then pulls out a small box with a miniature version of you in it. He places the box on the bed and it begins to grow into an image of you, asleep. Soon the image covers you, existing within you, and around you.

The red man looks back to where the little star went. "Come on," he says under his breath. "Come on." You know that he is asking something of the small star that shot out of the room, waiting for it to do something…

And then you feel it.

Something is inside you, eating at a part of you, working its way through your MPCP, searching out your love for Dr. Halberstam. It wants to kill that love, make you betray the man who made you, and you open your mouth to shout for help—

And you are you again.

Lucifer is before you and you are thrilled. You leap out of the bed and into Lucifer's arms and he grabs your face and says in a harsh voice, "No, Renny! You can't. Stop! You can't react. If you react, they'll know something is happening in here. They can see your body on the outside, and if it reacts, they'll know. Feel nothing. Right now, feel nothing!"

And he says it so seriously, with something close to anger but not really, that you stop and don't move. And Lucifer is so filled with fear that you can feel it through his persona. You do nothing because you don't know anymore what you want to do.

He steps back from you, touching your cheeks gently now, and says, "I don't have very long. The system will check this node soon. If I have to jack out, there's a note for you in the datastore where I put the other items. It will explain things.

"I've also got this for you," he says, reaching into his pocket. He draws out a long, silver sword, longer than you think should be able to fit into his pocket, and hands it to you. "I know it doesn't fit your style, but it's the only version of the thing I could find. I'll explain what it does in a minute.

"Now listen, Renny. I have to ask you something, because I really don't know if you like it here. I don't think you do, but I have to ask because I'm going to propose that you get out of here. But I can't make that decision for you."

"How can I get out of here? I only live in the Matrix."

"Renny, do you remember when we were in the slave module with all the cameras?"

You are confused because you seem to remember it twice, one time each from two different perspectives. The two memories blur and it becomes confusing. "I do, but not too well."

"Do you remember seeing the children, the children from the other world?"

You do and so you nod your head and say, "Yes," then add, "One of them, his eyes bled water."

"Renny. Listen. That was you."

You cannot move. You cannot think. You cannot do anything. The thought is so large, it is stuck at the portal of your mind and you cannot even begin to deal with it.

"Renny, now listen to me, this is why you can't get upset now. They'll know. Part of your emotions still bleed through to your body. They'll want to know what's wrong if you get upset, so you can't get upset. Do you understand? You must hide it. You must not feel anything."

You do not feel anything. You close yourself all down and let nothing inside. "What do you want to ask me, Lucifer?" Your voice is calm and level and it scares you.

"I want to know if you want to get back into your body, if you want to leave the Matrix, because if you do, I think you can make it happen."

It seems such an absurd question that you almost laugh, but it would be a dry, scary laugh.

As if reading your mind, Lucifer says, "I know that may sound strange, but Renny, you've got to know that there are deckers in the other world that almost never come out of the Matrix, haven't seen the sunlight with their real eyes in years. They have people who take care of food and stuff for them, but they never jack out. They like being here better than being in life. And there are people who run loops on simsenses, living out high points in other people's lives over and over again. They can't get enough. Some people dream of what you have, Renny."

And you think for a moment about the absolute love you had for Dr. Halberstam just moments before, and although part of it felt like torture, another part of it was so clean, so pure, so *easy*. You knew exactly what you had to do, and there was comfort in that. You think that it might be easy to go back to that.

But you do not want to. "I want to see the other world. I want to be in it."

"Okay. I just had to check. I think I kind of messed you up before. I don't want to do that again."

"What?"

"If I hadn't told you things…" Lucifer cannot finish his thought. There is too much to say. But your answer is just as complicated, so you just say, "No. I'm glad you did."

"All right. Here's the deal. We've got to get you some shadowrunners. To do that, we've got to get you some money. But that's only one of the things we've got to do. The other is getting hold of the other two kids in the lab. We've got to find out if they want to go. But even more important is that you can't let on that anything is going on. You've got to seem to like being here."

"That I like Dr. Halberstam even though I hate him."

"All right. Sure."

"Lucifer, what is money?"

He opens his mouth and stops. Then, "Oh, boy. Uh, money is what we use to pay for things in the other world. It's…It's like data, and the value of something is on a linear scale of zero on up. When we hire the shadowrunners, we'll be responsible for getting them the money."

A wolf enters the room. Trace and Report. It sees Lucifer and rushes past him as it follows his trail back to his deck. Both you and Lucifer throw utilities to crash it, but you each miss and the wolf is quickly out of sight.

"Gotta go," says Lucifer. "Do what you can."

"But…"

He rushes out the door after the IC.

You are not sure what to do next. You cannot go after Lucifer because Dr. Halberstam would soon be here to check on you if the system goes on alert because of the Trace and Report. And your decoy will not be able to wake up. Lucifer might be able to escape, but your body is still in a lab, a hostage to Dr. Halberstam if you make him angry. You decide it's better to wait, to make a plan. If Lucifer never comes back, you will be on your own. You must be careful then. There is so much you do not know, and one mistake could ruin everything.

You turn to the decoy. Your stars leave your body and float into the you that sleeps in your bed. You quickly find a small loop that could be used to crash the program. The decoy is not well-written, but Lucifer must have made it in a hurry. You also know that you might be able to use it later if you take it down very carefully. You slip your stars into the loop you found, and they weave their way in and around the programming code. After careful examination, you find a few key commands that you can remember in your head and take out of the program. You do so and then the program collapses back into a little box, falling slightly to one side. Although you do not know how to program, you know you will be able to enter the box later on and re-install the command codes you removed. The decoy should be able to function again. You slip it into a golden sack that sits beside your bed. Dr Halberstam gave you the sack the day after you saw your body through the camera. It was a present for being a good boy. You realize the sword is still in your hand and slip it into the sack as well.

And then Dr. Halberstam is there. He asks if you are all right. You try to remember what Lucifer told you about lying: when you have to lie, keep it as close to the truth as possible. "The red man was here!" you shout with fear. "He was here, Dr. Halberstam! He was here! Keep him away from me! I never want to see him again!"

Dr. Halberstam tries to calm you down. He tells you that you never have to worry about the red man again, that soon he will be dead.

That frightens you, but you say, "Good!" and sound like you mean it. This seems to please Dr. Halberstam, and he tells you to go back to sleep, so you crawl into bed and say good night.

>>——————————————————<<

—**From Scarface's Guide to Decking**

COLD STORAGE AND HOT STORAGE

Decking's a young man's art, without a doubt. But that doesn't excuse some of the more absurd assumptions made by the youngsters of our ignoble profession. One of the most horrendous is that it's possible to get anything via the Matrix.

Wrongo, chummer.

There's hot and cold storage. Hot storage is the stuff wired up to a corp's mainframe, which, in turn, is usually wired to the Matrix. It might be ICed, it might have deckers guarding it, but if you're good enough, you can reach it. It's at least possible.

Cold storage is a datastore that isn't part of a mainframe or is part of a mainframe that isn't part of the Matrix. Think about it for a moment. If the datastore isn't connected to the Matrix, *there is no way to get to it from the Matrix*. But why would someone set up such a thing? Why not tie all information to the Matrix? For the very reason I just mentioned: *because there's no way to get to it from the Matrix*! It's safe from folks like you and me. And believe you me, the corps have plenty of information worth keeping on cold

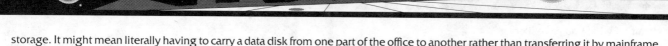

storage. It might mean literally having to carry a data disk from one part of the office to another rather than transferring it by mainframe, but think of how much the company saves by not having to buy expensive Intrusion Countermeasure software.

So next time you think you're the hottest number in town, remember that sometimes the only way to get the really valuable stuff is by physically making a trip into the offices of the place you want to rip off.

TRACING

The worst thing Fuchi ever came out with is the Trace-capable program. Why? Such programs destroy our anonymity. The worst of these, in my opinion, is the Trace and Report. Without a trace, a corp can't hurt you once you jack out. With the trace, you actually exist for them in the real world, not just as some collection of pixels in the Matrix.

Most punks think once the Trace and Report goes off, you're dead.

Wrong.

First, the trace has to find you, which can take time. Not a lot of time, but every minute counts in such a situation.

Second, once the report comes back, the boys in system security have to figure out what to do about it. If security is competent, they can issue orders within five seconds. If they're not on the ball, it could take up to a minute and a half.

Third, the guys who now have your address have to get to you. The variables on this part of a Trace and Report action are numerous.

Are the agents who are after the decker corporate or municipal? If they're corporate, then the distance from the company's security force barracks to the decker's location, combined with the transportation available, are the determining factors. Cross-town by car is a far cry from cross-town by chopper. If the corp has ties with the city's security forces, things could get really bad for the decker because most cops can show up to any call within four minutes, tops. It all depends on whether a squad car is in the neighborhood. Fortunately, most corps like to keep security breaches in the family, so a decker won't have to worry about a knock on his door for eight to thirty-five minutes, depending mostly on vehicle type and ground traffic or weather for cars. For this reason, a lot of deckers like to wait until a rush hour combined with a tempest comes along to make a run into a corp system.

The worst possible case is when the security force has mage-boys on staff. One word and they're off into astral space. Odds are they'll be where you are in no time. If you're clean, magic-wise, they'll probably follow you, invisible in astral space, and then coordinate the actions of the ground team hunting your head. If, for some drek-headed reason, you're packing something like a spell lock, you could be in for some serious trouble.

>>————————————————————<<

<<(14:08:41/12-06-51)>>

>[Two days have passed since Lucifer left.

Brutus is teaching you now. Although you can see in his eyes that he wants to hit you, he no longer does so. But his teaching is rough. All he has you do is hit the IC with your stars. You realize that this is his style. He does well by it, but it is limited, which is why he was not chosen to be your teacher. Lucifer taught the basics so that you could find your own style. Watching Brutus, you see also that his style may work, but that he misses many of the subtleties of decking. This teaches you that even when a style is effective, it may be not as useful in the long run as other styles that are harder to master. And with this thinking comes the realization that you are much better than Brutus. Brutus realizes this, too. You can see it in his eyes, which makes you wonder how long it will be before he starts hitting you again.

You asked Dr. Halberstam what happened to Lucifer. You couched the question in hatred for Lucifer, and, in turn, framed the hatred in love for Dr. Halberstam. He tells you never to think about Lucifer again. You ask if Lucifer is dead, and he tells you that soon he will be. This scares you, but you say, "Good!", sounding like you really mean it. You do not know if Dr. Halberstam is being evasive because Lucifer escaped, or if Lucifer is slowly being tortured to death and Dr. Halberstam wants you to put Lucifer out of your mind. There is nothing you can do, so you start making a plan to escape. Earlier you slipped away to read Lucifer's letter when you had some free time. You are sad because you think you are no longer as innocent as Lucifer thought you were. You hope he will be all right.

You have studied hard the last two days, always telling Dr. Halberstam that all you want to do is to get better and better so you can please him. Dr. Halberstam seems to have relaxed, and you think now is the time for you to begin. Now is the time for you to weave the poison cloak and to kill the children born in the Matrix.

>>————————————————————<<

<<(18:21:15/12-07-51)>>

>[It is time for bed, and you say good night to Dr. Halberstam. He says the same, and you feel the comfortable emptiness of the room that comes whenever he is not present. But you are still being monitored, so you must be very careful. Carefully, you pull the decoy program out of the golden bag. You do it slowly, so slowly, to keep the periodic system sweeps of the node from picking up any abrupt changes. Gently, your stars enter the box and sift their way through the countless command strings, searching for the little loop you took apart. They find it, replace the missing code, and you run the program.

The box grows and soon there is an imitation of you, a representation of your representation in the Matrix. You then run your sleaze program, get up out of the bed and leave, rushing out of the house. Dr. Halberstam has never awakened you this early, but the less time you spend out of the house, the better.

One after another, you work your way through the nodes that lead to the SAN and then to the LTG. The system is calm and the IC cool, and by taking the time to hack each time you use your sleaze, you get by the IC and manage to avoid cybercombat.

You step out of the construct into the LTG, awed once more by the immense scale. This time, though, the effect is mitigated by your mission. You float up to the top of the LTG, where another SAN floats above you, a large, sealed door. Through it you can reach other RTGs. But your destination, the number that Lucifer gave you in his letter, is in Seattle. So you look out toward the stars that circle the RTG SAN and find the one you need. You race toward the glowing orb and enter a new Local Telecommunications Grid.

It is not as impressive as the Downtown grid, but in a way more appealing, more comprehensible. The plane, as before, is covered with bright lights and colored shapes. Floating high above the plane are many giant pyramids and cubes and spheres. They are not as elaborate as the Downtown constructs, but the sight of the large objects floating without support moves you as much as before.

Following the address, you approach a black pyramid with a flat, square top. It floats near the surface of the plane. On one side is a large red circle. Approaching it, you realize it is the construct's SAN. A man dressed in a long coat of black metal stands before the door. Not IC, but a decker. You float up to him. He smiles and asks, "Biz?" His chrome face is long and sleek, and he has a long, thin mustache that curls on the ends. On his head he wears a tall hat. You remember "biz" from somewhere in your readings of Lucifer's data. You don't entirely remember the context, but you have the feeling now is not the time to reveal uncertainty. "Yes," you reply, "Biz," hoping it is the right thing to say.

"Don't recognize you, and we only take referrals on new 'cons. Who sent you?"

That one is easy. "Lucifer sent me."

No reaction. "Before I believe that," he says flatly, " you're going to have to do something to *make* me believe it."

Your thoughts freeze. Prove it? How do you prove something? Something is either true or not.

"I…"

"Look, whoeveryouare, don't waste my time."

"What do you need to know? How can I prove it to you?"

"Good point. Don't know that much about the guy myself, but how about this? What did he send you to do?"

"Talk to Data Base to hire some shadowrunners."

"What's the job?"

You almost say, then think the better of it. "I think I should keep that a secret."

"Why didn't he come himself?"

"He's in trouble."

"He is?"

"With UCAS Data Systems."

"Data Systems? But they're nothing."

"Maybe so. But that's what's happening."

"Hang on. That might have done it for you." He pulls a large feather out of his coat along with a piece of gold paper and presses the tip of the feather against the paper. He then pulls his hat off, waves his hand over it with a flourish, and pulls a bird out of it. The bird takes the paper in its feet and flies through the node. The decker turns back to you and says, "We'll have our answer in a moment." He eyes you up and down. "You really know Lucifer? *The* Lucifer?"

"He's my best friend."

"Listen," the decker says with a nervous smile, "You understand I was just doing what I had to?"

"Sure," you say, not sure what he means.

"Great. You know, biz is biz."

"Yup," you say, wanting to look like you know what you're talking about.

The bird comes gliding out of the SAN on its platinum and cobalt blue wings, then lights on the decker's shoulder. Held between its toes is another piece of golden paper. The decker takes the sheet and reads it. "Data Base says you've got the correct dirt that only a few people would know about. He doesn't trust you yet, but he's willing to see you." The decker waves his hand and the door of the SAN vanishes, revealing a data stream leading to a data-line junction. He produces a passcode sphere and a small map of several constructs, which he gives to you. "He says he'll be waiting for you in the second SPU." You look down at the map to see where it is. "Don't wander off the route. The IC we've got in here would put even Lucifer into a deep sleep."

You follow the route, flashing the passcode to get by some barriers, a killer, and a tar pit. You finally reach the SPU and enter. The floor is a large circle whose edges rise up to meet a tall wall that rises to another circle high above. Glowing green lines radiate from the circle on the floor. Suddenly the lights in the SPU flicker and then dim. The image you just saw is replaced by a huge cavern made of rough black steel. Dim flames of orange and yellow pixels burn in alcoves set around the chamber. Ahead of you is a huge dais formed of the black steel, the surface rough and crooked. Upon the dais is a giant icon. A decker. He has a large, bloated body made of layers of microcopies. Eight legs extend from the body, thick cables bent at several places for joints. A spherical head is attached to the body, with mandibles made of datajack plugs and two glowing red eyes.

"You wanted to see me?" His voice is deep and growling.

"Data Base?"

His voice drips weary arrogance. "I don't believe we've had the pleasure."

"What?"

"Who are you, you cherubic little maggot?" he says loudly. "I'm a busy man, and don't have time for this nonsense. You claim to know Lucifer. I let you in because you know where he's working, which few people would if he's really still alive. Now, what do you want?"

"I'm here to hire some shadowrunners."

"Are you? Have the nuyen?"

"The what?"

"Is this some sort of joke?" the creature spits out. "Are you some punk who stumbled across a couple of personnel records at Data Systems? Let me assure you that I can snap your wings off your spine without thinking about it. I'll give you a moment to get the hell out of here and I suggest that next time you want to play decker, you be ready for it."

"I'm not going. I came for shadowrunners. Lucifer told me to come here. I'm sorry I didn't know what…nuyen means…but I think you mean money. I can get money for you…for the services…but I have to know how much to get and where to put it. My name is Renny. Lucifer was my teacher. He told me to come here. I have a job for you to set up."

There is a pause. "*Was* your teacher?"

"They're mad at him. He…taught me things he wasn't supposed to…He had to leave."

Another pause, and the anger is gone from the creature's voice. "Are you here to help him? Is that why he isn't here?"

"No. I mean…He told me to come here so I could help myself. I don't know where he is, but once I'm safe, I'm going to do everything I can to help him." You try to picture him, and all you can see is Lucifer, tied up, being beaten by Brutus. You start to become upset, but know you cannot afford to let that happen. You stop yourself.

"And why are you in trouble?"

"I…" and then you realize that the less said the better. "I can't do anything until some children at UCAS Data Systems are safe."

"Children?"

"Two boys and a girl. They…are in beds…unconscious…They have been that way all their lives."

"Coma?"

You don't know what that means, but you nod affirmatively because that seems to help.

"And Lucifer wants you to do this, too?"

"He told me to do it. It was his idea."

"All right. What's the job? What do you need?"

And you start to tell him.

>>————————————————<<

<<(09:12:38/12-08-51)>>

>>**ACCESS — Renny**
<<ACCESSING — RENNY>>
<<ACCESS ACHIEVED>>

—Good morning, Renny. How are you feeling today?
—Great, Dr. Halberstam!
—Are you ready for your lessons with Brutus?
—Dr. Halberstam, I was thinking of not learning from Brutus today. I…
—What?
—Dr. Halberstam, I like Brutus, but I think I'd like to show you what I can do today.

—What do you mean?
—Well, Brutus has told me about stealing nuyen. That's something I could do on a run. I'd like to make a run for you today.
—Don't you think you should learn more from Brutus before you do that?
—Dr. Halberstam, I like Brutus, but I'm better than he is.
—That's not what he says.
—
—And you disagree with him?
—I think…I think I'm better than he says I am, and I'd like the chance to show it.
—Well, I suppose I could let the two of you go together…
—NO. I mean. He'd slow me down.
—Renny. I think you might be improving, but you mustn't let it go to your head. For your own protection, I'd like you to take Brutus along.
—
—Renny, are you upset?
—No. That's a good idea. That will be safer.
—Good.
—I'll need a program to transfer the data.
—Brutus will have one.
—Dr. Halberstam, I'd like my own. I want to know I can do it.
—Then you can borrow Brutus'.
—Dr. Halberstam, please! Please can I have my own?
—
—Please!
—All right.
—Thanks Dr. Halberstam. Thanks a lot. I'm going to make you so proud of me!

>>**CUT Access**
<<ACCESS CUT>>

>>—————————————————<<

<<(11:07:14/12-08-51)>>

>[You race across the vast space of the LTG, traveling the distance between the UCAS Data Systems cube and the First Bank of Tokyo sphere that floats close to the surface of the Matrix plane. You are starting to understand why deckers choose to spend so much time in the Matrix. An energy, a feeling of heightened life, comes with manipulating events underneath the surface observations most people live by.

But that is the part, the secretness of it, that makes you remember that you must be doing something wrong. You remember the conversation with Lucifer about whether you thought what you were doing was wrong. You didn't understand about "wrong" then, so you said no. But now you do understand wrong. What Dr. Halberstam did to you was wrong. He took away your life and tried to own you. And now you are going to take away money from people who do not know you. Is their money a part of their life? The answer seems to be yes, and so you are doing something wrong to them, just like Dr. Halberstam did something wrong to you.

It seems to you that this is another part of Dr. Halberstam's plan that Lucifer ruined. If Lucifer had never taught you the idea of "wrong," it would never have occurred to you to feel bad about what you plan to do at the bank. But Lucifer taught you about the world and so you do feel bad about it.

But if you do not steal the money, you will never escape. These must be the complications of the other world that Lucifer always referred to. You know that you must take the money, but you will give it back as soon as you can. That is the best you can come up with.

And you know now that you are not the angel Lucifer thought you were. You are as bad as everyone else.

Brutus is by your side, quiet. Not sullen, you think. It is that he is on a run. He is trying to think as hard as he can.

He picks the target. "It's got a high-falutin' name, but it ain't that tough. A lot of Japanese immigrants use it for their first accounts."

"Immigrants?" you ask coyly, not knowing what the word means, but certain that it refers to the other world.

"Ah, nothing. Forget it," he says quickly.

Although you do not want Brutus coming with you, you are glad now that he did. He has a great deal of knowledge that you do not. The hard part will be losing him when it comes time to transfer funds to Data Base's account to pay for the run.

You float down to the sphere where an access program bars the way to a square SAN. Brutus pushes past you. "Dr. Halberstam said I was supposed to do as much as possible, to show him what I learned," you say, openly annoyed.

"I ain't takin' no chances with some snot-nosed rookie when my butt is on the line," he says. "Shut up and stay out of the way."

He walks up to the IC, curls his massive arm back, then slams into the access. It flashes twice and then vanishes.

"Brutus, we can't just take out all the IC. Somebody is going to see something is wrong!"

"Shows what you know. If we're in there long enough for somebody to notice, then we took too long anyway." You realize you were wrong about Brutus. Much of his silence has to do with him being upset. He's out to prove something, whether or not it makes sense.

He enters the node and you follow, coming to a system construct with about a dozen nodes—a CPU, four SPUs, six datastores, and an I/O port. "Come on," he says.

You're nervous now. Brutus' attitude seems to be more of a liability than you had thought. You float down a data stream to a SPU. The room is a standard polyhedron with a flat ceiling and floor and eight walls. Brutus is about to step inside when you whisper harshly, "Brutus, come on! Let's at least scan!"

"Fraggin' scared, kid?"

You ignore the comment and scan the node. And you get an idea.

"Brutus, listen. There's a blaster in there. A rating one or two, I think. No big deal. Not worth your time. I'll just go in and crash it."

"Like drek you will!" and he rushes into the node. As you expected, Brutus is powerfully drawn to battles that he believes are easily won. You slip in after him and see his simian form entangled in the web of a giant spider. Brutus is struggling to reload his attack program, which the web, a tar baby program, grabbed. The spider, a Rating 6 blaster, is moving toward him across the web. Without pausing, you run your sleaze program twice, once against each IC, and then quickly cross the node unnoticed by the spider. Deftly, you step out of the way of the spider's web.

"You ungrateful brat!" Brutus shouts.

"I'm sure you'll be fine," you say to him, safely invisible to the IC in the node. "You distract him while I get the nuyen!" You hear a low growl of pain as you leap into a data stream.

Ahead of you is a datastore. With luck, you'll find it full of accounts with nuyen that you can transfer. You scan and determine that a trace and report is waiting inside for you. You think of Lucifer for a moment, then focus again on your work. You slip into the node and see a wolf, the same one that followed Lucifer. It is large and silver gray, each hair standing out distinctly like hard, metal wires. Its chrome teeth reflect the rainbow colors of the datastore.

You freeze for a moment, but no more. Not because it is a wolf, but because it is the same wolf that followed Lucifer. In that moment, it races past you, even as you are screaming at yourself that it is not the same wolf.

The wolf races out of the node and into the data stream from which you just came. You fly after it, your stars rising out of your body, glowing so brightly white that the silver flecks of the data stream start to shine as brightly as they do. The wolf is half-way to the node with Brutus and the blaster IC when you let loose your attack program. The stars race toward the trace IC and surround it, whirling around it, confusing it. The program gives out a yelp as your stars sear into its body, worming their way in.

Good, but not good enough. It races on. You see a few possible routes of attack in the coding structure, but it is a well-written program. They all involve more work than you have time for. You search again, and come up with a weak command sequence near the beginning of the report routine. You see what the stars surround, the images searing into your mind. As you fly through the data stream, you whirl around, your muscles contracting and then expanding as your stars slip into the cracks of the trace and report and then quickly rip apart the routine as they stretch the code.

The wolf races on, but you relax. The wolf will make it back to Data Systems, but will wait forever for the next set of instructions to come along because you have destroyed the report portion of the program.

An alarm sounds. Brutus is losing his fight and the system is on alert. You race back to the datastore, your wings flapping wildly. Because you have already destroyed the IC in the node, this should present no additional problems. If the node has the nuyen you need.

As you enter the node, you are already slotting your combat utility back to storage and bringing up your browse. You know you have to work quickly, before another alert is triggered.

You run the program, searching for accounts of 60,000¥ or more. Your stars flood the node, hovering around one file after another in their search for data that meets the requirements. Soon the stars are orbiting several files. The first one you go to looks just fine. An account of 239,768.97¥ owned by Hikato Torakana. You drop the browse utility and slot up the transfer utility. Dr. Halberstam didn't have time to make it match your style. It is a small keypad, which you draw from your golden bag. First you type in Torakana's account number, then 20,000¥, the amount of money that Dr. Halberstam asked you to transfer to his account, then Dr. Halberstam's account at Seattle Trust. You hit the button and wait.

When the transaction has cleared, you run the same program again, but this time you take 40,000¥ and transfer it to an account Data Base set up for you.

You hit the return and the program jams. You freeze. Your hands begin to shake because you don't know why the money won't transfer and you don't know what to do next. A second alarm sounds. Brutus is probably failing miserably. That means the system is on external alert and that deckers will arrive at any moment.

You take a deep breath. Stars radiate from your golden head and rush into the file. You discover that Torakana's account has a withdrawal limit of 30,000¥ per day, and you can't get the money you need for Data Base without exceeding that. You slip your stars into the keypad and quickly massage the utility to override the bank's limit.

To your right, you see a shadow move in the datastore's colored light. You hit the return button just as a bank decker comes into view. He is dressed as a samurai and rushes at you, sword high.

You look down at the program and see that the transfer is complete. The transfer finishes.

You disconnect.

>>————————————<<

144

(11:22:17/12-08-51)

>[Brutus is waiting for you.

You are back in your bedroom. You assume that when a normal decker disconnects—or jacks out, as Lucifer called it—he immediately appears back in his body. Dr. Halberstam must have it set up that you default to the house because he doesn't want you to go back to your body.

Brutus is breathing heavily, clutching at his right side. He stalks toward you.

"Brutus, you all right?" you ask with as much concern as you can muster.

"You fraggin' geek. I'm gonna…"

You decide that no matter how nice you are, it won't help. You try a different approach.

"Do what, Brutus? Kill me? You know Dr. Halberstam won't like that. And you know he'll know. If we start running attack utilities, the system scans are definitely going to pick them up. It will all be on record."

"Wha…?" is all he can manage after your sudden outburst of sophistication. The rhythm of your speech is not yours, however, it is Data Base's. Data Base seems to know what he's talking about, and now it's time for you to seem like you know what you're talking about.

"And I'll tell you something else. You touch me and I'll make sure he knows you're the one who got beat up and set off two alerts in the bank, while I'm the one who got the nuyen for him, all by myself."

"On the other hand"—where did you get that phrase? you wonder, and what does that mean?—"if you calm down, I'll tell him the heist was mostly your work, and that you took your damage protecting me. Good?"

He growls, but then Dr. Halberstam's voice is in the SPU. (That's right, you think, the SPU. The entire house is like the iconferencing chamber you were in with Data Base. When you traveled through the maze of corridors and rooms of the house, you were hardly moving at all. You were always in the same node, practically in the same place, only the images changing around you, giving you the illusion of motion. Things are becoming clearer and clearer to you. Why?) He asks how it went, and Brutus looks at you, a mixture of hatred and pleading in his eyes.

"The money is in your account," you say. "It was fun. It was scary, too, but Brutus saved me."

Dr. Halberstam asks about that, and you make up a story where you got into trouble by thinking you knew more than you did, but Brutus rescued you. You make a point of staring at Brutus when saying you thought you knew more than you do, trying to fix your gaze like Data Base does. Trying to scare him. It's time to scare Brutus.

You see it in his eyes. He knows. Knows he should be scared of you. He takes a step back.

Dr. Halberstam suggests that you should probably rest and that Brutus should look to his persona.

"Oh, no," you say in good cheer. "Brutus is fine. He told me he was hardly hurt. Aren't you fine, Brutus?"

He is not. His MPCP took a great deal of damage, but he says yes, he is fine.

"He said he wanted to get back to teaching me as soon as possible. He wants to show me more of the system. Gee, Dr. Halberstam, do you think Brutus is weak or frightened or something? He's a lot stronger than I am. He can handle it."

Dr. Halberstam says that's fine if Brutus and you are up to it. Brutus says he is. Dr. Halberstam leaves.

"I want to see the CPU," you say to him, voice level.

"You can't," Brutus replies, eyes boring into you.

"Doctor!" you begin to shout. "All right, all right," he says. "But I'll tell you something, drek. You're going to get hurt soon."

"Oh, really," and just for a moment, you let your stars move about the surface of your persona. Your body, muscular, golden, and winged, glows with a purifying radiance. The wings rise high and Brutus takes another step back. It is just a show to you, a trick, but it has the intended effect. To Brutus, now damaged, you are a powerful foe who might destroy him. He turns and puts his fists on the floor and swings his body in between his arms. You follow.

>>————————————————<<

<<(11:48:06/12-08-51)>>

>[The Central Processing Unit is ablaze with power.

The giant room is built of crimson circuit boards. The floor and walls crawl with large, animated circuit chips that wander around on their spindly legs, transferring data and running errands. There are several floors to the CPU, and all of the floor is partitioned into smaller rooms.

On the way to the CPU, you adopted a more subservient attitude with Brutus, allowing him to make all the decisions, only asking questions you knew he could answer with ease. He is relaxed now. He still hates you, but is willing to let you be for the time being.

"Whew," you say, making sure Brutus knows you are impressed. "So this is the Central Processing Unit! It's amazing! So this the key to the system!" You turn to him, eyes bright, and smile. "What's that mean? What can the CPU do?"

"Didn't Lucifer teach you anything?"

"Not as much as you do."

Pause. Slight smile. "Well," he begins in his gruff voice, "the CPU can shut down the system, dumping any decker in it at the time. It can let you get to any node in the system."

"Any node?" you interrupt, "Just like that?"

"Yes."

"Does it show you how all the nodes are connected in a system?" You know it does, as you already knew the other operations, but you need to steer the conversation closer to system maps.

"Yup. It's called a system map."

"Oh, that must be hard to get."

"No, not really."

"You could do it?"

"Well, I know how to do it."

You don't, nor do you have time to figure it out with Brutus around, so you say, "It seems like it would be very hard."

"Come here. I'll show you." He is cocky again, swaggering, about to accomplish a task at which he cannot fail. The two of you step through a door into a small room. He punches up some numbers on a keypad and a screen lights up, showing about six dozen nodes and how they are connected.

"Where's my house?" you ask.

He points to an octagonal shape connected to two databases and an I/O port. You look for similar configurations on the map and find one. Your hope is that the SPU surrounded by the same nodes as your SPU is the house of the other two children. You make a quick note of how to get there from your house and the CPU.

Now all you have to do is get to them.

"Hey," you say, "Let's play a game. How about I hide in the system and you try to catch me."

He looks at you, suspicious, and presses a button on the keypad. The map vanishes. "No."

"Come on. It'll be fun."

"No. It's time to rest."

"I'll tell…"

"And I'll tell him you are not as young as you want him to believe."

And it is true. You are older, much older, than you thought you were only a few short days ago.

"Go back to your house. Now. Just think it and you'll be there."

You stand still, uncertain, trying to come up with the next plan. The shadowrunners will be arriving soon, and you don't have much time left.

"Now!"

"Brutus, I…"

"GO!"

"Thanks a lot for showing me around."

You are in your bedroom.

There is nothing to do until it is time for bed, because only then can you slip out undetected. You go over to a closet and pull out your bear and start playing the pattern game. You are bored with it after only a few passes, and so you stop. It occurs to you that you are beginning to play Dr. Halberstam and Brutus like the bear, but instead of symbols, you are using languages and emotions. You give them something and they give you something back in return. The idea, just as in decking, is to stay just far enough ahead of the game to be able to manipulate what is to come.

Soon you get very tired, for you were up late last night when you went out to talk to Data Base, and you fall asleep.

>>————————————————————<<

<<(19:21:57/12-08-51)>>

>>**ACCESS — Renny**
<<ACCESSING RENNY>>
<<ACCESS ACHIEVED>>

—Renny?
—
—Renny?
—uh…mmrph…Dr.…Halberstam? Is it time to sleep? How long have I been asleep?
—No, Renny. You fell asleep rather early. It's not time yet for a few minutes. But I want to talk to you.
—Okay!
—Renny, Brutus has talked to me, and he says that your behavior today has been rather…erratic.
—Erratic?
—He says you threatened him.
—I don't like him, Dr. Halberstam. I told you that.
—What I'm more concerned about is the way he claims you expressed your dislike.
—What do you mean?

146

—Well, let's not worry about it now. Time for bed. I'll talk to you tomorrow.

>>**CUT Access**
<<ACCESS CUT>>

>>————————————————————<<

<<(11:31:43/12-08-51)>>

>[You lie awake in bed. Dr. Halberstam knows you are up to something, but he doesn't know what yet, so you have a little time. You have to move quickly. If you get everything done in time, you'll be gone and safe. If you fail, he will realize Lucifer sabotaged the program that made you love him, and he will reinstate it. Or you could even end up dead. You know you have a body now, and you know you can die. But you are willing to risk death to get to the other world.

There is a great deal to be done tonight, but first you must get to the other children.

Carefully, you slip the decoy box out of your sack. You have examined it more carefully and realize that it gives off a pulse of you being asleep, which is why it is so effective. The scans think you are asleep, so there is nothing to investigate.

You run it, and your image appears around you. You step out of the bed and pick up the sack. As you do so, you remember the sword Lucifer gave you. You pull it out and examine it. It is a tool designed to hold several programs, though now it holds only one, a program you have never encountered before. You scan it and are fascinated. You had never thought of such a thing before. But you have little time now. The clock, as Lucifer once said, is running. The shadowrunners will be in position around the building soon, and you must be in place when they are ready. You rush out the door.

You leave your node, thinking for a second that this is the last time you will ever be in it. You float down a data stream to a datastore. The flecks of data, you realize, are sluggish. When you reach the datastore, you notice that the colored lights are blinking at a rate slower than normal. It takes you a moment to realize what is going on—

The system is already on internal alert.

As the system looks for troublemakers—troublemakers like you—it uses up memory normally used for other operations and that slows the system down. Halberstam wants to catch you. If you give him long enough, he will.

The datastore has no IC and you race through the entrance to another data stream to another datastore that connects to a third datastore, and then the house—the house of the other Matrix-born children.

You race up to the second datastore and scan it. There's a barrier on it—or, it looks like a barrier. It's really a tar pit. You rev up your stars and fire off your Doomguard III. Because the system is on alert, the IC is harder to beat. It's already ready for you in some ways. You throw all your hacking talent behind the program, and crash it in one blow.

No time to think about it. You're in the datastore and then out again. You rush down the data stream to the third datastore. You run an analyze and pull up nothing. Great. Inside two data paths leave the node. You go up to each and see that an SPU is at the end of one. That's it. Go.

You fly down the data stream and into the SPU.

You are in a house.

The living room is empty. You work your way through the corridors, looking for the bedroom.

You find it. Two white spheres are asleep in small beds.

You go up to the first and touch it.

It gives out a gasp and floats away, going to the second bed and nuzzling the other sphere. You put your finger to your mouth. "Shhh!" you say, the way Nursie used to when you got upset.

The second sphere is awake.

"Who are you?" the first one asks.

"I'm a friend," you say. "I want to know if you want to leave the house."

Dr. Halberstam's voice asks if everything is all right.

You look at the two spheres and nod your head.

"Yes," says the second sphere. "We just woke up. We'll go back to bed soon."

Dr. Halberstam asks if anyone is there. You shake your head to the spheres. The first moves as if he is about to speak, but the second says, "No. We're just playing with our toys. We'll go back to sleep soon."

Dr. Halberstam says that's all right and leaves.

The first sphere says, "You're not red," with a very serious voice.

You smile and say, "No. No, I'm not."

The second sphere says, "Dr. Halberstam told us that we had to be careful of a red man who would try to hurt us."

You are stuck. Should you tell them all about everything, including the red man, which means they might not trust you? Or just tell them they might be in danger from Dr. Halberstam and convince them with that?

But you remember the whole point of your coming here was to give them a choice, which means telling them everything. So you say, "I'm a friend of the red man. And he sent me here to help you."

The first sphere gasps. "Dr. Halberstam said the red man would have friends, that we could trust no one!"

"Listen! Please listen!" you say quickly and softly. "Let me tell you my story, and then if you want, I'll leave. Or if you want me to take you with me, I will."

"No!" says the first sphere. "Dr. Halberstam said we couldn't even listen to what the red man or his friends wanted to tell us. He said we'd get sick."

The second sphere says, "Well, I want to hear him."

(Time is ticking away, you feel it and it scares you.)

"I'll tell Dr. Halberstam!"

"NO YOU WON'T!"

Dr. Halberstam is back and he demands to know what is going on down there. "Nothing!" the two spheres say in unison, and he leaves again.

"If you don't hear what I have to say, you can't make up your mind," you say to the first sphere. "You won't have any choices."

"I've already made up my mind," he says. "I don't want 'choices.' I like everything the way it is, and you're here to change it."

"Well, I like it, too," says the second sphere, "but I want to hear what you have to say."

"Go away," says the first sphere, and he dives under his covers.

"Please…" you say.

"Go away!"

You and the second sphere step out into the corridor. She sits down, patient. You know that if you are going to win her, you will have to be very detailed. It will take more time than you would like, but you have no choice. You unfurl your wings and your stars start to dance around your body, and you begin.

"Once upon a time, a boy named Renny lived in a big house on the edge of the Matrix. That boy was me…"

>>————————————————<<

<<(01:03:54/12-09-51)>>

>[When you are done, she says she wants to go with you and that she is very scared. You tell her not to be, and that she must return to her bed and wait. She says she wants to go with you now, but you say no, it would cause too many problems.

She goes back into the room and gets into her bed. The first sphere asks, "Are you going to go?" and she lies and says, "No." The first sphere says "Good," and goes to sleep. You leave.

Back out the node and down a data stream. You still remember the system map and know it is only one SPU and a DLJ to the slave with the cameras, which you have to reach in order to start your rescue.

Up to the SPU. An access is on the entrance to the node. You slot your sleaze and run it against the IC.

The alert has made it a tougher task than you realize. The sleaze fails and the access tries to sound the external alert. You toss your stars into the access and jam the alarm, but know you'd better bring the thing down fast.

You're still faster than it and you toss your Doomguard at it. No time for deceptions, the IC is going to try to set off that alarm and you've got to get it down *now*. The stars surround the barrier, seeking a way in. They find one and do some damage, but not enough. It tries to trigger the alarm again and you toss in more stars, blue-tinged and hurried. You stall the alarm one more time, but you're panicking, and before you get another chance to crash the IC, it tries to trigger the alarm one more time.

In your mind, you see the command codes of the IC racing through their sequences, trying to hit the alert. Your stars fly past the commands that are running, trying desperately to hit a weak link in the program before the alarm is sounded. The time measuring the race is meaningless in the other world. Portions of a second click by and you find what you need, the sequence that perceives you. The IC skips by the routine and the alarm is jammed a third time.

You whirl before the access, swinging your arm gracefully through the air, stars around your body following in the wake of your motion. The stars in the IC plow into the program and explode, ruining the coding and crashing the IC.

You breathe deeply. Into the SPU and out toward the data junction. Out the junction and on to the slave.

No IC. You fly in so quickly you have to beat your wings wildly to avoid slamming into the node's wall. A quick scan of the monitors. Dr. Halberstam, Brutus, and another scientist are in the room with you and the other two children. Brutus is asleep, Halberstam is drinking a dark liquid; the other scientist is monitoring screens.

You check other screens, looking for a view to the front of the building.

It is Data Base's plan. He has outlined what you must do, but you must make it happen.

On another monitor a man, old like Dr. Halberstam, hangs from the ceiling, bound by chains around his wrist. Dark, dry lines of blood streak his arms and face. You lean in closely, looking for some sign of motion, anything to tell you he is alive, for you have no doubt that it is Lucifer. You find the keypad, experiment a bit, and make the camera zoom in.

There is nothing. No motion.

Nothing.

You glance to the shot of the lab. You see your face moving.

You command yourself to feel nothing. You close yourself down, telling yourself you'll cry later. It almost doesn't work, but all the pain leaves.

You suddenly understand evil. You know something about horror, about how terrible people can be toward one another. You

remember how bad you felt about stealing the money, but now you see it as nearly insignificant compared to what Halberstam has done to Lucifer. You can return the money, and you are now certain you will, but Lucifer is just gone.

And there is something about justice. About knowing that sometimes what is wrong is sometimes right. Decking only exists for being wrong. Why else would there have to be utilities to defeat IC, which only exist to guard what someone owns. But there are ways of using decking to do things like free yourself.

Or make Dr. Halberstam pay.

You think of the woman who killed her children.

You check other monitors and find the one you are looking for, a camera that points out toward a street. It is dark. Every few moments, a large metal machine with bright lights drives by, just as Data Base said one would. You wait until the camera's image is no longer being accessed by the security station, then click the camera on and off three times.

In a dark alley across the street, you see a red light blink three times in response to the red light on the camera.

You leave the camera on as the security station sweeps the image from the camera again. They see nothing but metal machines with dark lights drive by.

When they are done, you take control of the machine again. You make the camera's light blink three more times, which means you, the boy in the middle, and five times, which means the girl. You do not flash the signal for the other boy.

You now have one minute to get to the nearby communication slave node and back again before the shadowrunners make their move for the building.

Fly.

You fly down the data stream, your shoulder blades sore from the violent motion of your wings.

Into the slave node (forgetting to analyze). You crash into a blaster. It looks like the hooded IC you defeated with Lucifer (DON'T THINK ABOUT LUCIFER!) and claws at your face, ripping your golden flesh. It tries to trigger an alarm, but you jam it and send your Doomguard crashing into it. The pain it causes you is tremendous, but you weave your stars and think about Halberstam (HALBERSTAM IS NOT HERE. HOW DOES THINKING ABOUT HIM HELP?) and the stars race into the IC and search out the weakness you found before. It pulls away and sounds the alarm nanoseconds before you crash it.

Hurry. External alert. Come on, Lucifer, you think. I don't know what I'm doing! Hurry! To the panel. Which one? You look around and find a control console for the fire system. You rush over to it and disconnect all the circuits except those leading to Lab 4. You pull the alarm.

Back to the camera slave module. The flecks of data sting your eyes as you rush back into the node.

You check the monitor for Lab 4. Brutus is already jacked into the system, slumped unconscious in his chair, a wire leading from the base of his neck, searching for the system intruder. Halberstam and the other scientist are getting up out of their chairs, looking around the room in response to the fire alarm that is sounding. They walk over to the security doors and open them, stepping out into the hallway to see what is going on.

Back to the security station slave module. Fast, fast. Faster. You rush in, the shattered remains of the blaster IC on the ground.

(BRUTUS WILL FIND YOU SOON, you scream inwardly. HURRY!)

"Where is the security door panel?" you shout out loud. There it is, across the room. To it. Lab 4. Slam the toggle.

Back to the cameras.

In Lab 4, the three children and Brutus, unconscious. You flip the cameras and see Dr. Halberstam and the other scientist pounding on the thick doors to the lab. You wanted all of them out to keep the bodies safe, but as long Brutus is jacked in, he is not a threat.

You glance at the camera that shows the area outside the building. The shadowrunners are almost ready to go. Hurry.

You rush over to a panel and cut the camera feed to the security station. The building's security personnel are now blind. You flash the camera three times.

A large person, thick and muscular, leads the way, carrying a huge gun. You realize he has horns like Lucifer. He's followed by another large man, wearing a long coat, a small gun in his hand. And then a woman in heavy clothing, also armed. Last is an old woman, wearing feathers braided into her hair. Compared to the others, she seems frail.

Quickly, back to the other slave. Into it. Security station doors. Hit the toggle for the main door—

Brutus slams his fist into your back and you crash into the wall. He breathes heavily, smiling. "I can kill you now," he growls.

"Nope," you say, and fly out the door.

You can't afford to fight him. If he gets dumped out of the system, he can simply strangle you in the lab.

Down a data stream, away from the slave nodes. You rush up to a datastore blocked by a barrier. Throwing everything you've got into it, you sleaze the IC and pass. Into the node. Out of it.

Brutus is right on you. He's got a passcode and wasn't slowed by the barrier. You bore down another stream, then crash into a datastore you hope is clear of IC. You win. It is. You're not thinking clearly enough to remember where you are now, and fly out the data stream to the left. Ahead is a SPU. A barrier again. Your sleaze is slotted up and you run it, stars racing forward. But your focus is thrown, nerves. You fail to sleaze it, and the barrier reveals itself as a tar pit. A gnarled, diseased hand reaches out of the doorway of the node and grabs hold of your stars and crushes them.

Brutus slams into you. There's nothing but pain along your spine. You whirl around and blast him with the white hot stars of your Doomguard III, tossing in everything you can of yourself. He's knocked flat back, and you take that moment to try to crash the tar pit. It goes down and takes the barrier with it. Into the node.

Just as you step in, Brutus grabs your ankle and you slam face-first into the floor. He leaps on top of you, but your stars rise from your skin and burn him. He leaps back and you are out of the node.

Ahead you see the CPU. You beat your wings faster. It'll be well-protected, which is bad, but you've got a chance of popping to any node in the system, leaving Brutus behind, which is good. A glance behind. He's right after you.

Into the node. Quickly, you duck around a wall made of circuit boards.

At first, you cannot even see for the overwhelming throbbing in your ears. The sound in the node is tremendously loud, a result, you imagine, of the system alert—a horrible rhythmic pulsing. You see on one of the walls that the information from the cameras is flowing again. You were supposed to have remained in the camera slave node to make sure that didn't happen. On the screen you see a gun fight in a corridor. The shadowrunners are holed up in doorways, firing at uniformed guards around a corner.

(THE GUARDS ARE DYING LIKE LUCIFER. DID THEY EVEN KNOW WHAT WAS GOING ON? SHOULD THEY DIE FOR YOU? DIE BECAUSE YOU WERE ABLE TO USE MONEY YOU STOLE TO HIRE PEOPLE TO KILL THEM? You reel.)

All you can think is that you've got to get back to the slave node so you can open the door to the lab so they can get to you. It's happening. You can't stop it now. You begin moving when you hear Brutus' snort from around the corner.

And then there is something else, a shadow in the red light. A long, slinking tentacle crawls its way around a circuit board. It is shiny black and is made up of overlapping circular strips of metal. You cannot see what the rest of the IC looks like, but you are aware that it is a program designed to cycle powerful signals in a pattern that will crash your operating capability. Your icon will disintegrate. Or worse.

Floating off the floor, you maneuver yourself around the board.

Nursie is there, her body bloated and corrupt. She is a mass of writhing, dark, metal tentacles. Her face, once warm and lovely, is now decorated in garish colors. Chrome face, two red circles on the cheeks, lips large and full. She smiles at you, a smile that suggests a hunger.

You are frozen. She does nothing. She waits. She smiles.

Inside of you a terrible sensation rises, a fury, a hatred of the thing before you. You don't see it as IC; she is a betrayal. Something rises in your throat and you scream and throw the Doomguard at her. It is clumsy, and even as you start running it, you realize that between your sloppiness and the alert, you'll have little effect. The coding tumbles across your body, rushing away from you.

You do not see anything happen, but Nursie's smile broadens, as if she has just been made happier. Her tentacles rush across the room at you. They are longer than you first thought, and she is floating toward you now. The program has finished running now and you set it up to throw again just as the tentacles reach around your body and shock you—

There is a pain of such intensity that you think you will black out. You know that you are screaming, but the tremendous throbbing of the node prevents you from hearing yourself. Your eyes are not closed, but you see an image before you like the kind you see before you go to sleep: a woman's face. Not Nursie's, someone else.

You run your program again, but even as it starts, you know it has failed again. Nursie's head is moving toward you, her mouth opening as she gets closer, growing larger and larger until it seems that her maw will become the chamber the two of you are in. You raise your golden arms to push her away, but their bright color is drained away as they plunge into her darkness. Another shock of pain races through your head, and you hurt so much that you do not even know why you are worried about the IC. You are certain you are about to die.

You glance about the room. Brutus is there, smiling comfortably, for he has the passcode, and there is no need for him to risk pain if the IC will destroy you for him. On the monitors you see that the shadowrunners are racing up stairs. One of them is hurt, blood running from his shoulder, but they are all moving quickly. The large man looks to a camera and makes signals to you five times with his hands. He is telling you they are about ready to take the lab.

You are in the wrong place.

Dr. Halberstam's voice enters the room. He must have gotten to a computer terminal. He asks if it was Lucifer. Did Lucifer turn you against him? You are faint, but want to tell Dr. Halberstam that Lucifer only gave the choice of betrayal. You yourself decided to betray Dr. Halberstam, and only because… What? Halberstam betrayed you first? Is that true? And did the men in uniform betray you even if they didn't know what Halberstam did to you—because they didn't try to find out? Is seeking the truth the only way not to betray?

The tentacles close in, crushing. The shadowrunners are at the end of the corridor with the lab. The other scientist runs from them, his mouth wide with terror.

You've got to get to the security panels.

Your sword.

You drop out your Doomguard and analyze programs and merge the Slow and the Signal Switch into the sword. Brutus laughs as your stars rise out of your body one final time, entering the IC, taking their time. They have nothing to do but add useless command codes to the IC program. "Oh, Renny," the IC says, a voice you have not heard for so, so long. "Just let me hold you forever. Just let me know you only want to be with me."

The extra commands slow her just enough for you to get out. You leap across the room, wings wide, soaring. Brutus' mouth works its way into an awkward expression of surprise as you draw the sword from your back, raising it high above your head. In his eyes, you see how wonderfully terrible you must look.

You crash into him, slashing your sword before you, drawing blood from the simian icon's stomach.

He knocks you across the room. The dark red of the room has turned even blacker and you realize that you will not be up much longer. You take the blade and drag it across your left palm. Bright red blood runs from your gold hand.

Brutus leaps on you. Nursie approaches. Deftly, you slip your hand toward Brutus' belly and mingle your blood with his. The utility runs. Brutus' dull silver fur begins to take on a golden quality, while your own body becomes less magnificent. Still muscular and strong, your golden skin begins to lose its radiance. The silver form of Brutus begins to darken yours, creating shadows along your icon, like the shadows of the children's sheets.

The IC, Nursie, floats over the two of you. Brutus, violent as ever, is not aware of what has just happened. He raises his fists above you, ready to slam them down. You no longer have the strength to fend him off or to break free, and prepare for Brutus to slam his hands into your head.

In that instant, you glance at Nursie. She is confused, for the utility has altered your persona signals. One of you is an intruder, the other flashed a passcode and is allowed to be here. But now the signals are different. She scans both of you and tries to choose which of you is closest to being the enemy. She makes up her mind as the fists came crashing downward.

And then Brutus screams as her massive tentacles wrap around him and draw him close to her, squeezing the life out of him.

His screams still carry as you get up awkwardly and stumble across the room to the system map. On the screen you see the large green man signaling that they will only give you a few more seconds to open the door before they must pull out.

You blink to the security doors slave module.

You flip open the door to the lab and race down to the camera slave module.

The shadowrunners rush into the room. One checks out Brutus, who remains still even after he is un-jacked.

The old woman steps beside the body of the girl. She gently turns the girl's head to one side and reaches behind the base of the girl's neck, grasping a large datajack, which she pulls.

The other shadowrunners turn in horror as the girl's mouth widens and her eyes snap open. Her body trembles terribly and her head begins to rock, ever so slightly, back and forth. A white foam appears at the edges of the girl's mouth and a terror fills you, for you realize that her body, as well as yours, has no idea what it is to be truly active. Crashing into your thoughts: *cleansing the doorways of perception.*

But then an amazing thing happens. The woman starts to say something, you cannot hear what, and begins to move, to dance, like you dance, and you see her change. Or not change, but be more than one thing. Her face seems to grow longer, like the beak of a bird. As she stretches out her arms, her hands appear as sharp talons. Feathers, like those on the back of your icon, appear along her arms. And as this happens, the girl calms down. And then seems to sleep.

The woman steps over to your body, and though you are frightened of what is about to happen to you, you are not as frightened as you were, because you are delighted to be going to the other world, a place where all things are many things, and the many things are one grand pattern.

She gently rolls your head to one side and takes hold of a datajack, and pulls

>>———————————————————————————<<

>(07:13:25/6-02-52)<

>(YOU HAVE MAIL WAITING)<
—>**READ MAIL**
>(DISPLAYING)<

*****DATAMAIL*****
TO: Sarah Halberstam (NA/UCAS/SEA 2206 (04-7892/HALBERSTAM.S)
FROM: INVALID ADDRESS CODE (Error C #0961)
1 June 2052

Dear Sarah Halberstam,

My name is Renny and I used to live in a house by the edge of the Matrix. Now I live by the edge of an ocean (I won't say which). The atrophy that had destroyed my body after a lifetime of inaction has been repaired by magic and cybertechnology. I spend some time in the Matrix (not as much as your husband would have wanted), but more of it in the other world, this world. I am no longer an angel, but I try to live a good life. When I do wrong, as we all must in our interactions with other people, I try to do it as I think Lucifer would have me do, working against those who abuse and lie to the vast numbers of people who have no power in this world.

When I am outside, I do not merely see the colors and patterns that most people see, I also see, or imagine I see, their chemical structure. I see a forest as a giant factory of photosynthesis, the sun as a giant reactor of simple gases, my own skin as a complex maze of growing cells, coursing blood, stretching and pulling muscles. I am aware of the gases in the air that I breathe in and exhale. The world, I now know, is a giant extension of everything else. So, in a way, I am grateful to your husband, because he taught me a natural tendency to see things as they are. My visions are rich, and no less so because I see the world in its most finite detail.

Of course, he tried to rob me of what is most precious to humans, the imagination. For humans do not only see chemicals and compounds and the true nature of things. We elaborate with our minds. So much of our delight in life is the ability to create things that never existed before, to imagine what cannot be. What could be more absurd than to be dumbstruck by the slow fireworks of a sunset, when the colors are no more than the sun's light refracted through the prism that is the earth's atmosphere. But that is exactly what happens; we are fascinated by the mundane.

I will make no secret of why I have sent you this document: I want your husband to suffer more than he has already. I want you to be the princess, he Jason, and I Medea, poisoning your relationship so that he has nothing left.

He has already been drummed out of the project and been blackballed within the industry. (What the fate of the other boy is, I do not know.) I have robbed him of the money I needed to pay back my "loan." I have made contact with every one of his grandchildren through electronic mail, telling them my story. Whether they believe me or not, each one of them now acts differently toward your husband. Some of them have even broached the subject with him. He passes it off as the rantings of a lunatic, but he is doomed to wonder who I will reach next. When will his creation next cause him pain?

And so Sarah, I come to you. I went back to UCAS Data Systems via the Matrix and ripped out all the data I could about myself. They were ready for me, and as you can see, I could not get all the information out intact. But I got enough. After further digging, I discovered that you actually had little to do with the project. That, in fact, your maternal face had been recorded in a variety of situations with your grandchildren to provide Nursie with the human face the UCAS staff felt was necessary. After that you were out of the picture.

We have spoken. I have used many names talking with you over the net. I think I know who you are now. I think if we were to meet, I would trust you. I definitely like you. From your clinical work with children and the discussions we have had, I do not think you would have approved of what your husband was up to, had you known. From the hints you've given me in previous conversations, I think you believed your husband was involved in an experiment in artificial intelligence. I don't think you knew he was doing the things detailed above to three children (and perhaps more who were terminated as "failures").

How could he have hidden the truth from you so well? The answer can only be that he did not see us as children, or humans, but simply as guinea pigs. Which, in a literal sense, is what we were. And so he felt no guilt or shame. He lived in his own limited version of reality, a virtual reality where science not only asked for sacrifices, but demanded them. And if he felt no horror at what he did, how could you perceive it? Your senses were ill-fed by your husband. What he did not feel, he could not pass on to you.

And so, Sarah, I write to you, to tell you of his deed. He has nothing left now but you. No fame for work done in the past, no work now, no hope for a future. And if you are the woman I think you are, the truth of the Matrix Born project will shock and terrify you, for this is the man you have loved all these years. I do not need you to leave him, though I would find that ideal. I ask only that you treat him differently, that you be cold to him when normally you would not be; that you be distant when he talks to you, not listening but thinking about what he did to me and two other children; that at night you make sure not to touch him, thinking about what else he might have done, and what he still might do.

I give you truth, Sarah Halberstam, plucked from the Tree of Knowledge. What you do with it is your affair, but there seem to be only two choices. Either eat the fleshy fruit for all its worth and then act on the information, or try not to swallow the truth and choke on it slowly for the rest of your life.

Renny

—FILE ATTACHED—

>(End Mail)<
>(DOWNLOAD FILE?)<

CHARACTER SKETCH

CHARACTER NOTES

CONTACTS and INFORMATION

GAME NOTES

VEHICLE INFORMATION

	Rating
Handling	[ ]
Speed	[ ]
Body	[ ]
Armor	[ ]
Signature	[ ]
Pilot	[ ]

NOTES

Condition Monitor

Vehicle Destroyed>

Serious> Damage

Moderate> Damage

Light> Damage

Name:
Street Name:
Race—   **Allergy—**

KARMA

SHADOWRUN™

ATTRIBUTES

Physical
- Body [ ]
- Quickness [ ]
- Strength [ ]

Mental
- Charisma [ ]
- Intelligence [ ]
- Willpower [ ]

Special
- Essence [ ]
- (Magic) [ ]
- Reaction [ ]

[ ] Initiative Dice

SKILLS & LANGUAGES

_____ [ ]
_____ [ ]
_____ [ ]
_____ [ ]
_____ [ ]
_____ [ ]
_____ [ ]
_____ [ ]
_____ [ ]
_____ [ ]
_____ [ ]
_____ [ ]

CONDITION MONITOR

Unconscious> / <Unconscious
Possibly Dead / Further damage causes physical wounds

Seriously Wounded> / Seriously <Fatigued
+3 Target #/-3 Initiative / +3 Target #/-3 Initiative

Moderately Wounded> / Moderately <Fatigued
+2 Target #/-2 Initiative / +2 Target #/-2 Initiative

Lightly Wounded> / Lightly <Fatigued
+1 Target #/-1 Initiative / +1 Target #/-1 Initiative

PHYSICAL **MENTAL**

WEAPONS

Type	Concealability	Reach	Short	Medium	Long	Extreme	Ammo	Damage
_____	[ ]	[ ]	[ ]	[ ]	[ ]	[ ]	[ ]	[ ]
_____	[ ]	[ ]	[ ]	[ ]	[ ]	[ ]	[ ]	[ ]
_____	[ ]	[ ]	[ ]	[ ]	[ ]	[ ]	[ ]	[ ]
_____	[ ]	[ ]	[ ]	[ ]	[ ]	[ ]	[ ]	[ ]

CYBERWARE and GEAR

Type	Rating
_____	[ ]
_____	[ ]
_____	[ ]
_____	[ ]
_____	[ ]
_____	[ ]
_____	[ ]
_____	[ ]
_____	[ ]
_____	[ ]
_____	[ ]
_____	[ ]
_____	[ ]
_____	[ ]

CYBERDECK

	Current	Max
MPCP	[ ]	[ ]
Hardening	[ ]	[ ]
Act. Memory	[ ]	[ ]
Stor. Memory	[ ]	[ ]
Load Speed	[ ]	[ ]
I/O Speed	[ ]	[ ]
Response	[ ]	[ ]

	Max	-50%	+50%
BOD	[ ]	[ ]	[ ]
EVASION	[ ]	[ ]	[ ]
MASKING	[ ]	[ ]	[ ]
SENSORS	[ ]	[ ]	[ ]

Programs	Rating	Active?
_____	[ ]	[ ]
_____	[ ]	[ ]
_____	[ ]	[ ]
_____	[ ]	[ ]
_____	[ ]	[ ]
_____	[ ]	[ ]
_____	[ ]	[ ]
_____	[ ]	[ ]
_____	[ ]	[ ]
_____	[ ]	[ ]
_____	[ ]	[ ]
_____	[ ]	[ ]

Condition Monitor
Deck Crashed>

Serious> +3 T#/-3 Init

Moderate> +2 T#/-2 Init

Light> +1 T#/-1 Init

Base Load [ ]   **Current Load** [ ]

Defense Pool | **Dodge Pool** | **Hacking Pool** | **Pool** | **Pool**

CYBERDECK WORKSHEET

Type—

MPCP
Desired Rating—

	Required	Elapsed
Base Time	[ ]	[ ]
Cook Time	[ ]	[ ]

Current Rating—
COST—
BASE TIME: (Rating^2) x8
COOK TIME: Rating x3
Appropriate Skills [Target]
  Design— Computer [Rating]
  Cooking— Computer (B/R) [Rating]
Cost: (Rating^3) x50¥
Limits—
  Max Rating = designer's
  Computer Skill x1.5 (rd)
Upgrade—
  Design— (New - Old)
  Cook— (New)

HARDENING
Desired Rating—

	Required	Elapsed
Base Time	[ ]	[ ]
Cook Time	[ ]	[ ]

Current Rating—
COST—
BASE TIME: MPCP x (Rating^2) x2.5
COOK TIME: (MPCP x Rating)/2 (rd)
Appropriate Skills [Target]
  Design— Computer [Rating + MPCP]
  Cooking— Comp. (B/R) [Rating +MPCP]
Cost: (MPCP^2) x (Rating^4)¥
Limits—
  Max Rating = 1/2 MPCP
  (round down)
Upgrade—
  Design— (New - Old)
  Cook— (New)

ACTIVE MEMORY
Desired Rating—

	Required	Elapsed
Base Time	[ ]	[ ]
Cook Time	[ ]	[ ]

Current Rating—
COST—
BASE TIME: MPs/100 (round up)
COOK TIME: None Required
Appropriate Skills [Target]
  Computer (B/R) [Target # 3]
Cost: (MPCP x5¥) per MP
Max Mps:
  MPCP x 50Mps
Upgrade— Full value

STORAGE MEMORY
Desired Rating—

	Required	Elapsed
Base Time	[ ]	[ ]
Cook Time	[ ]	[ ]

Current Rating—
COST—
BASE TIME: MPs/100 (round up)
COOK TIME: None Required
Appropriate Skills [Target]
  Computer (B/R) [Target # 3]
Cost: 2.5¥ per MP
Max Mps:
  MPCP x 100Mps
Upgrade— Full value

LOAD SPEED
Desired Rating—

	Required	Elapsed
Base Time	[ ]	[ ]
Cook Time	[ ]	[ ]

Current Rating—
COST—
BASE TIME: (MPCP x Rate)/25 (ru)
COOK TIME: (MPCP x Rate)/100 (ru)
Appropriate Skills [Target]
  Computer (B/R) [MPCP xRate)/100 (ru)]
Cost: (MPCP x Rate) x5¥ (ru)
Max Load Speed:
  MPCP x10
Upgrade—
  Design— (New - Old)
  Cook— (New)

I/O SPEED
Desired Rating—

	Required	Elapsed
Base Time	[ ]	[ ]
Cook Time	[ ]	[ ]

Current Rating—
COST—
BASE TIME: (MPCP x Rate)/10 (ru)
COOK TIME: (MPCP x Rate)/25 (ru)
Appropriate Skills [Target]
  Computer (B/R) [MPCP xRate)/50 (ru)]
Cost: (MPCP x Rate) x25¥ (ru)
Max I/O Speed:
  MPCP x5
Upgrade—
  Design— (New - Old)
  Cook— (New)

RESPONSE
Desired Rating—

	Required	Elapsed
Base Time	[ ]	[ ]
Cook Time	[ ]	[ ]

Current Rating—
COST—
BASE TIME: (MPCP x Rating^2) x5
COOK TIME: (MPCP x Rating^2)/10 (ru)
Appropriate Skills [Target]
  Design: Computer [MPCP + Rating]
  Cook: Computer (B/R) [MPCP + Rating]
Cost: (MPCP^2 x Rating^2) x100¥
Max Response:
  MPCP/4 (rd)
Upgrade—
  Design— (New)
  Cook— (New)

SIMSENSE HARDWARE
Installed?—

BASE TIME: 5
COOK TIME: None Required
Appropriate Skills [Target]
  Computer (B/R) [4]
Cost: 500¥
Limits— None
Upgrade— None

VIDSCREEN
Installed?—

BASE TIME: 1
COOK TIME: None Required
Appropriate Skills [Target]
  Computer (B/R) [4]
Cost: 100¥
Limits— None
Upgrade— Install New Unit

HITCHER JACK
Number Installed=—

BASE TIME: 2 days per jack
COOK TIME: None Required
Appropriate Skills [Target]
  Computer (B/R) [# of jacks +1]
Cost: MPCP x # of jacks x 100¥
Limits— MPCP rating
Upgrade— Install new jacks

OFF-LINE STORAGE
Amount—

BASE TIME: 1 day
COOK TIME: None Required
Appropriate Skills [Target]
  Computer (B/R) [3]
Cost:
  Interface: MPCP x50¥
  Off-Line Memory: MPs x .5¥
Limits— None
Upgrade— Add new memory

CASE
Impact—
Ballistic—

Cost—

CYBERDECK STATISTICS

MPCP	[ ]
Hardening	[ ]
Active Memory	[ ]
Storage Memory	[ ]
Load Speed	[ ]
I/O Speed	[ ]
Response	[ ]
Off-Line Storage	[ ]

PROGRAM WORKSHEET

BOD
Size— Current Rating—
Desired Rating—
          Required Elapsed
Base Time [   ] [   ]
Cook Time [   ] [   ]

Size: (Rating^2) x3Mps
Base Time: Size x2 days
Cook Time:
Appropriate Skill [Target]: Computer [Rating]
Upgrade: Difference in Base Time
Limits: Max Rating equal to designer's Computer Theory rating.

EVASION
Size— Current Rating—
Desired Rating—
          Required Elapsed
Base Time [   ] [   ]
Cook Time [   ] [   ]

Size: (Rating^2) x3Mps
Base Time: Size x2 days
Cook Time:
Appropriate Skill [Target]: Computer [Rating]
Upgrade: Difference in Base Time
Limits: Max Rating equal to designer's Computer Theory rating.

MASKING
Size— Current Rating—
Desired Rating—
          Required Elapsed
Base Time [   ] [   ]
Cook Time [   ] [   ]

Size: (Rating^2) x2Mps
Base Time: Size x2 days
Cook Time:
Appropriate Skill [Target]: Computer [Rating]
Upgrade: Difference in Base Time
Limits: Max Rating equal to designer's Computer Theory rating.

SENSOR
Size— Current Rating—
Desired Rating—
          Required Elapsed
Base Time [   ] [   ]
Cook Time [   ] [   ]

Size: (Rating^2) x2Mps
Base Time: Size x2 days
Cook Time:
Appropriate Skill [Target]: Computer [Rating]
Upgrade: Difference in Base Time
Limits: Max Rating equal to designer's Computer Theory rating.

PROGRAMS

Name	Current Rating	Desried Rating	Size	Base Time	Cost
_____	[ ]	[ ]	[ ]	[ ]	[ ]
_____	[ ]	[ ]	[ ]	[ ]	[ ]
_____	[ ]	[ ]	[ ]	[ ]	[ ]
_____	[ ]	[ ]	[ ]	[ ]	[ ]
_____	[ ]	[ ]	[ ]	[ ]	[ ]
_____	[ ]	[ ]	[ ]	[ ]	[ ]
_____	[ ]	[ ]	[ ]	[ ]	[ ]
_____	[ ]	[ ]	[ ]	[ ]	[ ]
_____	[ ]	[ ]	[ ]	[ ]	[ ]
_____	[ ]	[ ]	[ ]	[ ]	[ ]
_____	[ ]	[ ]	[ ]	[ ]	[ ]
_____	[ ]	[ ]	[ ]	[ ]	[ ]
_____	[ ]	[ ]	[ ]	[ ]	[ ]
_____	[ ]	[ ]	[ ]	[ ]	[ ]

PROGRAMMING INFO
Size: See Below
Base Time: Size x2 days
Cook Time: ?
Appropriate Skill [Target]: Computer [Rating]
Upgrade: Difference in Bas Time
Limits: Max Rating equal to designer's Computer Theory rating.

Program Sizes

Type	Size (MPs)
PERSONA	
Bod	(Rating^2)x3
Evasion	(Rating^2)x3
Masking	(Rating^2)x2
Sensors	(Rating^2)x2
UTILITIES	
Analyze	(Rating^2)x3
Armor	(Rating^2)x3
Attack	(Rating^2)x2
Auto Exec	(Rating^2)
Blind	(Rating^2)x3
Browse	(Rating^2)
Cloak	(Rating^2)x3
Compressor	(Rating^2)x2
Controller	(Rating^2)x4
Deception	(Rating^2)x2
Decrypt	(Rating^2)
Evaluate	(Rating^2)x2
Hog	(Rating^2)x3
Medic	(Rating^2)x4
Mirrors	(Rating^2)x3
Poison	(Rating^2)x3
Relocate	(Rating^2)x2
Restore	(Rating^2)x3
Restrict	(Rating^2)x3
Reveal	(Rating^2)x3
Scanner	(Rating^2)x3
Shield	(Rating^2)x4
Sift	(Rating^2)
Sleaze	(Rating^2)x3
Slow	(Rating^2)x4
Smoke	(Rating^2)x2

SYSTEM DATASHEET

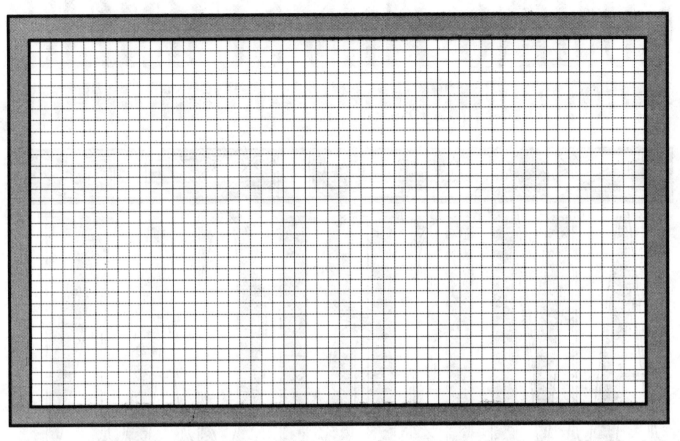

Nodes and IC

	Load Rating		Load Rating		Load Rating
_____	____	_____	____	_____	____
_____	____	_____	____	_____	____
_____	____	_____	____	_____	____
_____	____	_____	____	_____	____
_____	____	_____	____	_____	____
_____	____	_____	____	_____	____
_____	____	_____	____	_____	____
_____	____	_____	____	_____	____
_____	____	_____	____	_____	____
_____	____	_____	____	_____	____
_____	____	_____	____	_____	____
_____	____	_____	____	_____	____
_____	____	_____	____	_____	____
_____	____	_____	____	_____	____

COMING THIS SUMMER!

NATIVE AMERICAN NATIONS

VOLUME 1 OF 2

A SHADOWRUN SOURCEBOOK

• F I N I S •